MW01206278

THE IMPRISONED

Name: Brian Marotto, author/editor/illustrator

Title: The Imprisoned

Description: First Edition

Series: The Creature Within; Book Three

Identifiers: ISBN 979-8-9855207-8-1 (ebook) | ISBN 979-8-9855207-7-4 (paperback) | ISBN 979-8-9855207-6-7 (hardback)

Printed in the United States of America

First Printing Edition - 2024

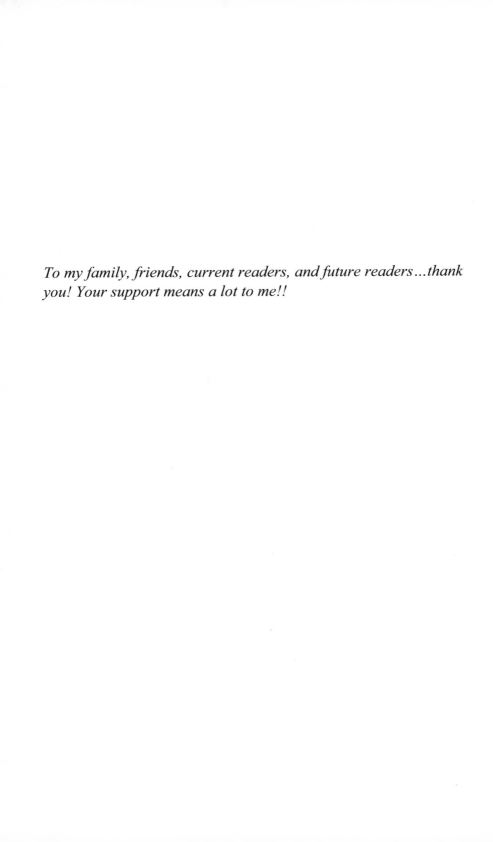

To my family, friends, current readers, and future readers…thank you! Your support means a lot to me!!

THE CREATURE WITHIN
BOOK THREE

THE
IMPRISONED

BRIAN MAROTTO

CHAPTER 1

Owen slowly released his grip on Isaac and took a couple of steps backward. He stood in front of Isaac, dumbfounded, with his brow crinkled and his mouth slightly open…speechless. He quickly glanced around at his friends and they also shared his reaction. "She's your what?" Owen loudly whispered after a few moments of silence.

"Astrid is my daughter," Isaac calmly repeated.

"I know. I heard you the first time. I'm just trying to process what you just said," Owen responded. His mind raced with all the implications of what Isaac's response could mean.

"I have so many questions," Avery muttered.

"Me too. For starters, how long have you known that Olivia, I mean…Astrid, was involved?" Bailey sternly asked while she took a few steps toward him.

"I'm sure Isaac would have informed us if he knew," Hailey politely interjected while she gently put her hand on Bailey's shoulder.

"Unless he was working with her," Cedric countered as he crossed his arms.

"Or he knew but was conflicted because of their relationship," Selena sympathetically added.

"Regardless, I would like to hear it from Isaac's mouth," Abigail commented.

All eyes were now on Isaac, who let out a long exhale while he laid his head against the beam that he still had his back against. His eyes drifted up toward the hole in the ceiling where Astrid flew through to escape. During this moment of silence, which felt like an eternity to Owen, his mind began to wander. This led to fear as he hoped that the man he held in such high regard, a person that he viewed as a grandfather figure, was not a fraud. Finally, Isaac's attention shifted back toward the group.

"I didn't know it was her until I saw Hailey and Astrid fighting. That is why there was a delay between my arrival and Hailey's. I was conflicted as a wave of emotions swallowed me whole. You'd think after being alive for thousands of years that one would be prepared for any situation, but apparently not." Isaac's tone became solemn with the last few words he spoke.

"So, you had no idea until you arrived here?" Avery inquired as her brow arched.

"I will admit, I had my suspicions. Each time that additional information was communicated, more pieces of the puzzle started to come together. However, some of the information caused some confusion. For example, I knew my daughter was a powerful psychic who also had a vampire within her, but the green dragon aspect threw me off," Isaac responded.

"Being a psychic is hereditary," Selena commented.

Isaac grinned, "Her mother was a psychic." He then paused for a moment before he scoffed.

"What is it?" Hailey inquired.

"Her mother…Olivia," Isaac replied. He slowly shook his head as a slight smirk appeared from disbelief.

"Really! That clue didn't smack you right in the face?" Abigail asked as she raised her hands.

"You know what they say about hindsight," Isaac rebutted. "Besides, it was hard for me to fully concentrate when I was preoccupied with defending the facility from waves of attacks, all while assisting in dealing with an Amarok."

"It was pretty crazy out there," Hailey added.

"Why did you let her go?" Owen finally broke his silence.

"Because…she is my daughter. I thought I could push past the shock of the discovery and the fact that she was my daughter, but as I looked into her eyes, all I could see was the little girl who looked up to me and loved me. At least, until her mother's death," Isaac responded as his eyes became glassy. With Isaac obviously not a threat, whoever wasn't fully out of transition, did it then, regardless of the pain they were feeling.

Abigail scoffed. "She was actually truthful about that."

"Did she say anything else regarding that subject?" Isaac asked.

"Not much. Basically, things were great until her mom died," Owen responded.

"I'm surprised she didn't mention how she felt it was my fault that her mother died," Isaac added as he wiped the tears from his eyes.

"Why does she blame you for Olivia's death?" Owen asked.

"I am more than happy to keep discussing this but first, I have a question," Isaac countered.

"What's your question?" Bailey asked as her brow furrowed.

"Why is there a vampire lying on the floor over there pretending to be dead?" Isaac inquired as he nodded in Caine's direction. Owen's eyes widened and he began to stammer while he tried to find a response. He first looked at Abigail, but she mirrored his reaction so he then turned to the rest of his friends to seek the answer. Cedric and Avery both looked away while Selena appeared protective as her eyes narrowed while she slowly placed herself between Caine and

Isaac. Hailey and Bailey's eyes grew larger as they both quickly distanced themselves from Caine. Owen's eyes darted back to Caine and that is when he saw his eyes open.

"To avoid the conversation that we are apparently going to have," Caine said in a stern voice as he stared at the ceiling. His eyes then turned to Isaac as he slowly sat up. Owen noticed Caine winced in pain as he held his chest. Regardless of Caine's condition, Owen felt nervous. He knew how brutal Caine could be and between his rage and ego, Owen feared that he might attack Isaac.

Caine winced again as he firmly pressed his lips together to mask the pain he was in as he stood up. Isaac only had a short timeframe before Caine's wound would fully heal, so the situation needed to be defused as soon as possible. Caine even waved off Selena's help as he stood up, keeping his scornful eyes solely on Isaac. When he was finally up and stable, he slowly began to approach Isaac. At that point, Owen walked between them to help calm everyone down.

Isaac turned to face Caine, who only stopped when he felt Selena's hand on his shoulder. As Caine glanced over his shoulder, he saw Selena's gentle smile as she leaned toward him. "Please," was the only word that she whispered to him. Caine grinned and nodded his head. At that point, Owen let out a sigh of relief since Selena was able to help defuse the situation.

Isaac's brow lowered as his head tilted while he glanced around at the group. "Wait, he's on your team? How many of you knew what his true nature was?"

"That's irrelevant," Owen blurted out.

"I disagree. It's quite relevant," Isaac quickly countered. "Any monster who doesn't reside within its host is deemed a threat to our world, especially one as evil as a vampire." Owen cringed with Isaac's matter-of-fact tone. He knew Caine wouldn't take Isaac's comments well and as Owen looked over his shoulder, he could see he was right. Caine gently moved Selena's hand from his shoulder and his face hardened as he intensely glared at Isaac.

"Not all vampires are monsters," Selena loudly defended.

"True, but unfortunately their nature is to kill humans to survive. No matter how good their intentions are or how hard they try to find other sources of blood, eventually, their nature will take over," Isaac calmly replied.

"It's about to take over now," Caine said through his teeth as his eyes turned blood-red. Owen took a deep breath as his fear was slowly becoming a reality. He briskly put himself back in the middle of the two as he raised his arms out, motioning them to stand down.

"My point exactly. Besides, what are you going to do? You'll be reduced to a pile of ashes before you could hurt me and besides, I'm immortal," Isaac said as his pupils became black as night while the remainder of his eyes turned yellow. Owen could even see a tiny hint of flames emanating from his eyes.

A sinister smile formed on Caine's face. "The good thing about fighting an immortal is that even if they die from the excruciating pain that I fondly put them through, they will be reborn just to experience it again and again."

"Enough!" Abigail screamed, which startled the entire group as they quickly turned their attention to her. "You're not going to kill or torture anyone here," she said sternly to Caine. He went to speak but she pointed her finger at him as her stare became more intense. Caine firmly closed his mouth to restrain from arguing with her. He then huffed and nodded his head as the blood-red color vanished from his eyes.

Abigail then turned her attention to Isaac, who already followed Caine's lead and transitioned back to human. "You don't have domain over the entire world. You must allow us to have the freedom to make our own choices and trust us. The entire world is not the facility." Her demeanor remained the same as how she acted toward Caine.

"But he's a vampire," Isaac commented.

"I don't care if he's the Loch Ness Monster. Caine has not only been very helpful, but he is also our friend," Abigail countered.

"It's true," Owen added as his arms finally lowered. "He has not only fought with us and assisted us the entire way during this mission, but he has also saved lives. Mine and Avery's life to start with."

"He didn't just save my life…he brought me back to life," Avery energetically added as she smiled.

"How, exactly did he do that?" Isaac inquired as his eyes narrowed.

"He gave me his blood," Avery replied.

"Long story short, he slipped some of his blood into her drink before we left for the condo tonight because he and I both had a bad feeling that Olivia…Astrid would kill her. Ever since Avery killed one of her close friends during an attempt on the gem, your daughter has targeted her ever since," Owen explained.

"Interesting. Avery, would you please do me a favor and transition so I can see your eyes?" Isaac requested.

Avery shrugged and transitioned and sure enough, Owen saw her purple eyes again. The group stared at Avery to the point that she began to fidget. "What is it?" Avery asked while she took out her phone and looked into the camera. "Oh, my eyes are so pretty!" Avery exclaimed as a large smile appeared on her face. Then, something else caught her attention. She raised her upper lip to unveil her fangs. "Awesome!"

Owen chuckled from not only her reaction but also from the fact that she spoke while her upper lip was still raised, making her look and sound hilarious. The rest of the group smiled to some extent from her reaction as well. He then heard a click come from her phone while she posed.

"Really?" Bailey said while she shook her head.

"What? It will be fine. If anyone sees it, I will just say it was some filter I found," Avery responded in a carefree manner. Bailey shook her head again and smiled.

"I have heard of this before but typically, it doesn't work," Isaac muttered.

"Typically, it doesn't. You have a higher chance of success with low-level creatures since the magic doesn't burn through the vampire blood in the person's system as fast. I wasn't sure how long it would last in her system since she has an uncommon creature but luckily it lasted long enough to do the trick," Caine said with a hint of a smirk.

"So, am I like a vampire-cyclops hybrid now?" Avery excitedly asked as her eyes lit up.

"I'm afraid not for much longer. I'm surprised it has lasted this long," Caine responded. Avery pouted as she transitioned back to human.

"Hey, just be grateful that it worked and you are alive," Bailey commented.

"Alive is always a plus," Avery said as she smiled.

Isaac approached Caine, who stood his ground and had a deadpan expression and extended his hand. "Thank you for saving their lives and assisting with this mission. I appreciate it and I apologize for my behavior earlier. I will be sure to tell Marcus and the others that you are a part of this group and to be treated as such." Caine grinned and gave Isaac a quick nod before he shook his hand.

Owen let out another sigh of relief. He wasn't sure who he was more proud of...Isaac for understanding that Caine was different and allowing him into the group, or Caine for not ripping Isaac's arm off. The proud moment didn't last too long. The adrenaline between the battle and the recent questioning of Isaac seemingly was wearing off as the pain became more noticeable. He began to moan through his gritted teeth and his face crinkled from the pain he felt throughout his body.

"Are you okay?" Abigail asked.

"Been better," Owen replied. He then surveyed the room and his friends either were already back in transition or doing so at that time. The only people that were not in transition were himself, Caine, Isaac, and interestingly enough…Avery. He quickly concluded that it must be the vampire blood in her system that had already healed her wounds. Once things died down, that is when Owen realized again that Avery was alive.

He hobbled his way over to Avery and refused to transition because he wanted to be fully himself when he reached her. As Owen grew near, Avery turned and her face lit up. This instantly made Owen smile and when he was close, Avery threw both her arms up to hug him. As she wrapped her arms around his neck, he slid his arms around her waist, with his hands coming to rest on her lower back. Then, without thinking, he went to kiss Avery on her lips. As he leaned in, Avery stood up on her toes and her lips began to pucker.

At the last moment, Owen realized what he was about to do and diverted his head just enough to kiss her on the cheek. He then moved one of his hands to the middle of Avery's back and continued their hug as he rested his chin on the top of her head. He wanted to kiss her on the lips but he felt the timing wasn't right. He wanted their first kiss to be not right after a life-and-death situation. Besides that, he felt he still needed to first come clean about his knowledge of how she felt about him. Only then, could they be honest and discuss their feelings toward each other.

"I thought I lost you," Owen whispered while he hugged her. His voice cracked and his eyes watered from the emotion as his mind decided to revisit the image of her death.

"If it was anything close to how I felt when I watched you die back at the mountain, then I'm sorry you had to go through that. At least I wasn't gone for too long," Avery responded as she continued to hug Owen.

"It felt like a lifetime to me," Owen muttered. He could feel Avery squeeze him harder and nestle her head into his chest. He pressed his lips tightly together as his face grimaced and his muscles tightened while a slight moan escaped his lips.

"Is something wrong?" Avery asked.

"Oh, nothing. Just my bones cracking even more," Owen jested. Avery released their hug and as she did, Owen held his side as he smiled.

"Why didn't you say something sooner?" Avery inquired as she cringed.

"Because the happiness I felt having you in my arms outweighed the pain," Owen replied as he grinned.

Avery smiled and glanced away momentarily before she looked back at him. "I thought you were more…sturdy," Avery commented. Owen chuckled, which caused his pain to increase. This made them laugh even more.

"Well, some of us don't have the benefit of having vampire blood in their system," Owen mocked.

Avery smirked. "True. At least transition some to take the edge off. I'm surprised you haven't already."

"I guess I had other things on my mind," Owen said as he winked. His comment caused Avery to briefly divert her eyes and blush. He decided to finally transition to phase one to help with the pain and accelerate the healing. He could have transitioned more but he felt bad since he knew the others couldn't transition like how he could. Besides, he was in no danger if he didn't heal rapidly. Owen then looked around to see what the others were doing. He noticed that everyone else was huddled around Isaac.

"I hope they are discussing what to do about Astrid," Owen commented.

"Hopefully. Let's go find out," Avery responded.

The two of them made their way over to Isaac. As they walked, Owen had his arm around Avery's shoulder while she kept her hand on his back. As delighted as he was that Avery was alive, he was even more eager to know what the new plan was to stop Astrid.

Especially now, since she was in possession of the gem that housed the djinn. When Avery and Owen reached the group, the current discussion ceased as they turned around and stared at them.

"I didn't mean to break up the party," Owen sarcastically said.

"Not so much of a party. After some introductions between Isaac and my friends that he didn't know, we just started to discuss the current situation that we're in," Abigail replied. Owen then noticed a smile appear on her face. "So, um…you seem to be doing good," Abigail playfully added as her eyes briefly went from him to Avery.

"Yeah…yes, I'm doing okay," Owen stuttered. His eyes bounced around within the members of the group, but not before his eyes opened widely as he quickly gave Abigail a look that implied for her to hush. "I'm just thrilled that Avery is alive," Owen added after he let out a nervous laugh. His friends nodded to his sentiment. He then removed his arm from Avery and glanced over to Hailey. Owen could see her give him a half-smile before she looked away.

He hoped Hailey fell for his ruse. Even though he meant what he said about Avery being alive, he didn't want Hailey to see his true feelings for Avery. Emotions that he thought he would need time to figure out, but after the recent events, it was quite clear to him. He did have feelings for Avery that surpassed them just being close friends. Not only did they share the same feelings for each other, they unfortunately also shared the same hesitations. The main one standing just five feet from them. At some point, he knew he must talk with Avery about their feelings for each other, but when? They were constantly on the go with this mission, to the point where it was hard to find enough time to have normal conversations that were not about the mission.

"From the looks of it, you, along with everyone else, appear to not be well," Isaac said as his eyes moved from Owen and scanned the remainder of the group. "At this point, I would not trust any of the safe houses in or near this city. Even the facility is not safe for us to travel to. I suggest we take a little journey over to a safe house that is near the mountains. Some of you are already familiar with it. It's in the town where you had your celebration due to your win over Marcus back during your training," Isaac commented as he glanced at Owen, Avery, Bailey, and Hailey.

"That's quite a trip to take at this moment. Why did you pick that location?" Bailey inquired.

"To my knowledge, it's the closest place that stores vampire blood and even phoenix tears. Does someone else know of a closer location where we can have access to those items?" Isaac asked as his eyes panned the group.

"Not to my knowledge," Cedric quickly, yet calmly responded.

"I agree. I can't think of anywhere close to here either," Owen added. As Isaac looked away to see if anyone else had a different response, Owen slightly turned his head to look in Cedric's direction. Cedric smirked before he gave Owen a small nod. Owen nodded his head in return, but he didn't enjoy that he just lied to Isaac. However, after Isaac's initial response to Caine, he could only imagine how he would react once he was inside the club.

"Well, I guess it's settled then. It works out too because that will put us closer to the facility," Isaac said as he started to walk away from the group.

"What about Astrid? We need to not only figure out what we are going to do about her but also Marcus and the Amarok as well," Owen blurted out.

"The latest update about Marcus and the Amarok hasn't changed since Hailey and I left to come here," Isaac responded as he turned around and approached Owen.

"Which is what?" Bailey asked as she shrugged her shoulders.

"During the battle, the Amarok killed a lot of my daughter's forces but also sustained heavy injuries as well. Nothing life-threatening but enough for it to take refuge within a densely wooded area a mile or so from the facility's entrance," Isaac replied.

"What if it decides that it wants a snack?" Abigail inquired.

"The forces that I mentioned it killed…well, some of them became food so after everything that the Amarok devoured, I believe it should be fine for some time," Isaac responded as he smirked. Owen grinned at Isaac's response since not only did it take care of the Amarok problem, but it also gave Owen something to tease Anders about later. The rest of the group either smiled or crinkled their face with disgust before Isaac continued. "Marcus is continuing to maintain a wide perimeter to make sure a random hiker doesn't make their way to it by accident. As he does this, he is also clearing the area to hide the evidence of everything that transpired to avoid any unwanted attention."

"Well, hopefully, Anders will revert to his usual, charming self soon," Owen sarcastically said. "The bigger issue is Astrid. Can you be involved in this mission anymore?" Owen inquired.

"Excuse me?" Isaac responded as his brow crinkled.

"I'm not trying to be rude but at the end of the day, Astrid is your daughter. Even with you on our side, can you be objective? What if the only way to stop her is to kill her? Even worse, what if you had to kill her? Unless something changes, you and Hailey's creatures seem to have the best chance by far to stop her," Owen explained while he remained calm. It was a hard question to answer and he wanted to be as sensitive as possible.

Isaac opened his mouth, but no words came out. Instead, he gently exhaled and looked away from the group. After a few moments, he turned his attention back to them. "I know she is a threat and must be stopped by any means necessary. If this was anyone else, killing would be an option. My daughter is not the same person she used to be. She has changed and I see that. Still, I feel like her core remains the same. She's good but if I am wrong, she is still my daughter. I don't think I am capable of killing her." Isaac hung his head, but not before Owen could see a single tear roll down his cheek.

"Understandable, but here's another question. Would you stop us if we decided she had to die?" Bailey calmly asked.

"I think if I knew there was no other way and I wasn't there, then yes. Anything less than that, I fear my fatherly instinct would kick in and I would save her," Isaac responded as he looked up and wiped the tear from his cheek.

"If that's the case, then you are a liability," Caine casually commented.

"What did you just say?" Isaac asked in disbelief as he slightly shook his head. Owen could see that Caine's remark caught Isaac off guard.

"A liability. Not being rude, but I bet I am saying what the rest of the group is thinking," Caine added and as Isaac was about to counter, Caine raised his pointer finger in the air to stop Isaac from talking. "Before you retaliate, just answer me one question. If Owen said he wasn't sure if he could finish any mission due to whatever annoyingly nice-guy reason he gave, would you keep him on the mission, or would he be removed?"

Isaac's eyes drifted down before he answered defeatedly. "Be removed."

"Then I think we all have our answer then." Caine was smug with his response.

"But only after I sat down with him and had a long talk to see if there was any way that he could complete the mission. Either directly or indirectly by supporting the ones that were in the mission. If none of those options worked, only then would he be fully removed," Isaac added in defense of his previous statement. Caine simply rolled his eyes at Isaac's rebuttal.

"We can discuss the politics of this later. Right now, we must recover and figure out where Astrid could be," Abigail suggested in an assertive tone with her eyes narrowed toward Caine and Isaac.

"She could be anywhere," Owen commented as he shrugged his shoulders before he turned to Cedric. "Can you check with your

13

people to see if anyone has eyes on her? That, or at the very least what direction she flew off to?"

Cedric nodded. "I'm on it. Just give me a few moments to get in touch with everyone." Owen returned the nod and grinned. Cedric turned around and walked away from the group and toward the door that led from the warehouse to the office. He didn't go through but gained enough distance for him to be able to talk without any distractions.

"Do you have any idea where she could have gone?" Hailey inquired.

"No idea. It's been so long since I have last seen her and she has changed so much. Now that her true identity has been revealed, she doesn't have to play games anymore. She can go and do whatever she wants. It would be as if we had to start the recon from scratch again to determine her whereabouts and resources," Isaac replied.

"She said she can use the djinn to get as many wishes as she wants between herself and her followers. Probably due to either loyalty, fear, or desperation…but still, is that possible?" Owen asked as he walked up to Isaac. The rest of his friends gathered around Owen and Isaac, minus Cedric who was still on the phone.

"Not only is she smart and resourceful, but she is also determined. If she puts her mind to something then she will find a way to achieve it. The fact that she has all these followers indicates to me that she has proven herself enough to be capable of performing such a task," Isaac replied.

"Great! Now that she has the gem, she has all the things she needs to gain control of the djinn. I can only imagine what terror she is going to unleash upon us. She will be able to do whatever she wants and as sadistic as she has proven herself to be, I am afraid for us and the rest of the world," Bailey said as she crossed her arms over her stomach. Owen could see her nerves rising within her as she began to fidget and, in his opinion, for good reason too. Then, he heard Cedric chuckling behind them.

14

"I'm sorry, but what's so funny?" Bailey lashed out as she whipped her body around to face him. Her brow was knitted as she stared at him with her fiery eyes, awaiting an answer. Owen and the rest of his friends turned around to see why Cedric laughed.

"She doesn't have everything she needs," Cedric responded with a crooked grin.

"What do you mean?" Bailey asked as her face relaxed. Silence overcame the group as everyone awaited his response.

Cedric's smile grew as he raised his phone in the air and slightly waved it around. "We have her witch."

CHAPTER 2

Owen looked around at the rest of his friends as his brow crinkled, and they also shared his confusion. However, Isaac was the only person not fazed by Cedric's news. This made him wonder what Isaac knew that the rest of them were unaware of.

"She has a witch? That's a scary thought," Abigail muttered.

"Had," Cedric said as he smirked.

"In order for her to take control of the djinn, she would have to transfer it from the gem to some other object. The magic within the gem is too strong to allow her to do anything with the djinn, so it makes sense for her to need a witch to complete the task," Isaac commented while his eyes bounced between everyone within the group. Owen felt relieved once he knew this was the reason why Isaac didn't react earlier to the news about the witch.

"If that's the case, then she is missing one of her key components to perform the spell. The gem is essentially useless. That's great news!" Hailey exclaimed.

"Yeah, but I'm sure she can retain another witch to assist her. It's not like they're rare. Don't get me wrong, it's good news but it's more of a delay than anything substantial," Bailey countered.

"For whatever reason, Astrid trusts this witch enough to involve her in such an important aspect of the ritual. She wouldn't just go grab a random witch to replace this person," Isaac commented.

"Either way, I'll take a delay over nothing any day of the week. Who knows, maybe we can get some information out of her as well," Owen said before he took a few steps toward Cedric. "Where is she now?"

"A few of my associates have her restrained at her apartment back in the city. If you give me the address to wherever that safe house is in that small town, then I can have her brought there. Blindfolded, of course," Cedric replied as his eyes drifted back and forth between Owen and Isaac. His confident smile never left him as he spoke.

"That sounds like a legitimate plan to me. The quicker you move her the better because I'm sure Astrid has already contacted her and once she realizes she is taking too long to reply, then my daughter will seek her out. I'll give you the address once we leave. Good job," Isaac said as he nodded in Cedric's direction. Cedric returned the nod before getting back on his phone to text his associates about the upcoming plan.

"How will you ensure that the witch won't use her magic at any point during the transportation?" Selena inquired.

"We have our ways," Cedric said before he winked at Selena.

"Hopefully, a painful one," Caine added as he smirked. Selena simply rolled her eyes and shook her head.

"What? If she is involved with Astrid then she deserves nothing less," Caine added matter-of-factly.

"We don't know if she is working with Astrid because she is forced to or if it's of her own free will," Selena politely retorted. Caine just smiled and shrugged his shoulders at her response. This caused her to let out a small smile as she turned away from him.

Abigail clapped her hands to get everyone's attention. "I hate to break this up but we should get moving. It will be dawn soon and we still need to recover from this night. Even more now since time is of the essence with the capture of Astrid's witch."

"Indeed, but we need to get the proper transportation first. Hailey and I flew over here so we, unfortunately, can't help with that," Isaac said.

"We all fit in that large SUV when we drove over here. It might be a tight squeeze but we can use that," Avery suggested.

"Awesome. Let's get moving then," Owen directed.

The entire group exited the building and followed Cedric toward the fence. At first, Owen wondered how they were going to get over the fence until he noticed one area of the fence was torn apart. He presumed one of them used their strength to rip through it besides the stealthier method that Owen used. They reached the large, black SUV and they all piled in. It was cramped but doable. Isaac got into the passenger seat while Cedric sat in the driver's seat. Isaac gave Cedric the address but right before he was about to pull away, Isaac put his hand on Cedric's shoulder.

"Why don't you let me drive? You are just as injured as the rest of your friends and could use a break. I'm the only one not physically harmed so it makes sense for me to drive. Is that okay with you?"

"I'm good with that. Thank you," Cedric said as the two got out of the car and switched seats. While this was going on, everyone else situated themselves in the other seats.

The SUV's first backseat row had two seats with a space in the middle that was claimed by Bailey and Hailey. The next row was a three-seater bench, so Owen pulled the lever and pushed it back as far as it would go to provide them with the most legroom. Avery and Selena took the window seats and Abigail took the middle seat. Caine and Owen bunched a few blankets and sat on the floorboard, with Caine near Selena and Owen near Avery. However, the two of them were too bunched up to try to relax.

"To avoid playing footsies, why don't one of you squeeze in up here and the other can stretch out and claim all of the blankets down there," Abigail suggested.

Owen looked at Caine and gestured for him to sit in the seat but Caine shook his head. "You sit up there, Owen. I've rested on far worse surfaces than this plenty of times in my life."

"Thank you," Owen said as he squeezed in between Avery and Abigail. Caine then bunched some of the blankets against the door so he could stretch out and sit up at the same time, all while resting his head on Selena's leg. Once everyone was situated, Isaac drove off.

The drive was long and quiet. Owen, who could barely keep his eyes open, watched as they passed through the city and out into the open road, with nothing much around. Just the soothing sound of the pavement as the car drove. It was dark, with a hint of orange off in the distance as dawn slowly approached. Avery, who was asleep, had her head peacefully on Owen's shoulder. He glanced over and noticed both Selena and Caine were asleep. That is when he noticed Abigail turned her head and looked at him before she leaned over and glanced at Avery. She then looked back at Owen and smiled as her brow raised quickly a couple of times. Owen firmly pressed his lips together as he smiled so he wouldn't laugh and just shook his head. Abigail shrugged and then laid her head on Owen's shoulder and closed her eyes. At that point, Owen laid his head on Avery's and fell asleep.

Owen's head jerked up, along with Avery's. His eyes were squinted as he looked around to figure out what was going on. As he rubbed his eyes, he could see they were parked in a driveway.

"We're here," Isaac announced.

Everyone slowly exited the vehicle and stretched their arms and back. As the fogginess in Owen's mind began to clear, he noticed they arrived at a house. The house seemed to be on a hill a few miles from the center of town. It was a two-story colonial-style brick house, with white shutters and a green door. The large house appeared to sit on at least a few acres of land. The green grass and bushes were all landscaped beautifully and the paved driveway was in front of the garage. The garage itself was attached to the right of the house. There was also a paved walkway that led to the front door, but before Owen followed that path, the white garage door opened. A dark blue sedan then pulled into the driveway and straight into the garage. Isaac waved everyone into the garage as he walked in himself.

Once everyone was inside the garage, Isaac clicked the button on the wall to close the door. As soon as the door closed, two men and a woman got out of the car and one of the men walked over to the backseat door that didn't open.

"Let's go," the man said after he opened the door. He held the person's arm and hovered his hand over their head as they exited the car. It was a woman that had a hood over her head that came down to her shoulders, with her crimson hair slightly poking out from underneath. What caught Owen's attention was the necklace that she was wearing. It was a thick metal chain, with a metal pendant in the shape of a pentagram enclosed in a circle. He also noticed symbols etched into the metal throughout the circle and the chain, but not the pentagram itself. The group then entered the house and into a laundry room.

"The first door on your left leads to a basement. You can bring her there and secure her until we come downstairs," Isaac suggested as he pointed toward the hallway.

"You heard the man. Feel free to begin finding out what she knows," Cedric ordered and then grinned. His facial expression made Owen feel uneasy since he wasn't sure what tactics they would use to get the information out of her. Even though she was associated with Astrid, he hoped they wouldn't take things too far. Something just didn't feel right.

The three people escorted the woman to the door. Right before they headed down the steps, he could see one of the men take her hood off. Owen couldn't get a good look at her due to the open basement door she was by. He only saw more of her partially wavy hair before the door was closed behind them. The entire time, she did not resist or say a word.

"Follow me," Isaac said as he waved everyone on. The group followed Isaac into the kitchen.

"Just from the little bit that I have seen so far, you have a very nice house," Avery commented. Owen thought it was a nice house as well as he glanced in the other rooms that had warm colors on the walls and furniture, real cherry-wood floors, and the rooms were very clean. Despite the coziness of the house, the kitchen seemed very modern with the stainless-steel appliances and the marble countertops.

"Thank you. I don't come out here as much as I would like to," Isaac replied.

"Why's that?" Bailey asked.

"Because he doesn't live here. This place is more of a front than anything else," Owen commented.

"Why do you say that?" Hailey inquired.

"Because I have seen Isaac's office and it is filled with various personal and meaningful items from his travels. Memories that he wants to never forget. Look around. There are no pictures on the walls or any mementos anywhere. It's just a house," Owen responded.

"Very good work, detective. You are correct," Isaac said as he patted Owen on the back. "I usually only come here for business-related things. I have a service that comes here to tend to the house and lawn since I am not around a lot. Still, I do enjoy this house and its location. Now if you excuse me, I will retrieve your long-awaited relief. Please feel free to help yourself to whatever is in the pantry and the refrigerator." Isaac then turned around and walked down another hallway and vanished into a room.

Owen grabbed a bottle of water from the refrigerator and a couple of protein bars from the pantry while everyone pillaged what they could. As he began to eat, he looked around and noticed a couple of people were missing…Caine and Selena. Before he called their names, he glanced around again and saw Selena back in the laundry room, so he headed toward them.

"There you are…well the both of you. Why are you hiding in here?" Owen asked.

"I'm keeping him company," Selena politely responded. Owen's brow knitted as his head tilted. He couldn't figure out what she meant until it dawned on him.

"Sunlight," Owen muttered. I'm sorry, I was so out of it I didn't even think about it. How did you make it in here?

"Luckily, I had this blanket from the car, or else it would have been an interesting, yet painful experience getting in here. It was the same blanket I used at times when we drove here. As glorious as being a vampire can be, it has some unfortunate and annoying side effects. So, unless I want to look like an idiot and walk around with this blanket draped over me, then my only other option is to be trapped in a room with no sunlight," Caine grumbled.

"Can you do me a favor and ask Cedric if he brought Caine's blood bag?" Selena asked with a hint of a smile.

"Sure. I doubt Isaac has any of those lying around," Owen added.

"I could just get it right from the source," Caine said with a crooked grin while his eyes briefly became red.

Owen scoffed and then turned back to Selena. "I can ask Cedric to also get you something to eat and drink as well," Owen offered.

"That is sweet of you. Yes, please. Thank you," Selena responded as the two of them gave each other a quick smile.

"No problem. I will also see if there are any windows with blinds or curtains that we can close, even though most of the windows seem bare," Owen said before he turned to Caine. "I presume she is speaking for the both of you so…you're welcome. I'll even be generous and ask Cedric to bring the blood bag inside and not just leave it on the porch," Owen added before he winked at Caine. He could see Selena smile out of the corner of his eyes and Caine just slowly shook his head before he looked away.

Owen walked back to the kitchen and relayed the information to Cedric. "Ay, yes. It's in a cooler out in the car. I'll go get it for him," Cedric said.

"Thanks. Can you also please bring some water and food to Selena? She is staying in the laundry room with Caine," Owen asked.

"Can do," Cedric responded as he nodded his head and left the room.

"How do you think it's going in the basement?" Avery asked Owen as she walked up to him.

"That's a good question. It's been quiet down there, or at least I think it's quiet. There is too much noise up here for me to hear anything," Owen responded.

"Yeah, too quiet," Avery quickly countered. "It's starting to make me feel uncomfortable."

"Same here but no one else seems to be worried, or they are and they're not showing it. I guess for now we presume no news is good news," Owen said as he shrugged.

"I guess unless something terrible is going on down there and we don't know it yet," Avery said as her worried eyes shifted to the basement door.

"Hopefully not but if we don't hear anything soon then I am going down there to check it out," Owen added as he looked in the same direction as Avery. He did his best to mask how worried he was since he didn't want to panic anyone just yet. They were only downstairs for a short while so he didn't want to rush to conclusions.

Not too long after Cedric left, he noticed him come back into the house holding a blood bag similar to one that a person would find at a hospital. He walked into the kitchen and grabbed some

23

refreshments for Selena and then made his way to the laundry room. A few moments later, Isaac came out of the room with a small bottle with an eye dropper as a cap to it.

"Hailey, would you be so kind as to reach above to the top cabinet behind you and pull out enough shot glasses for everyone please?" Isaac asked. Hailey nodded her head, retrieved the glasses, and laid them across the kitchen counter.

"Thank you. Now everyone, please take a glass and fill it with whatever it is that you are drinking," Isaac directed.

"I only got water so I think I need something with a bit more flavor," Owen announced as he began to search for an alternate drink.

"No need for that. Your water will be fine. Trust me," Isaac said as he gave Owen a quick wink. Owen, who was perplexed by his response, followed his suggestion. However, he wasn't looking forward to drinking watered-down vampire blood. Once everyone had their shot glasses ready, Isaac walked to the center of the kitchen.

"Phoenix tears," Isaac announced as he held the bottle up in the air.

"Freshly squeezed? Is that why it took you so long to get them?" Bailey sarcastically asked. Owen couldn't help but snicker at her question.

Isaac laughed. "No. They were from a while back but preserved. It just took me a bit to retrieve them from the secured location within the house." Then, he went to each person and put one drop into their shot glass. Once Isaac put the drop into Owen's glass, he quickly gulped the mixture down.

Almost instantly, he felt revived and all the pain and soreness he felt quickly vanished as his wounds healed just as quickly. Not only that, he felt wide awake and full of energy, but not jittery. It was more than what the vampire blood normally did. Owen's positive energy showed as he smiled before he surveyed the room. It appeared others had experienced the same result due to the smiles on their faces.

"Wow! That's amazing! You need to cry more often," Abigail joked.

Isaac laughed. "Well, now that everyone is feeling better, I guess we should go downstairs and see how our guest is doing."

"Before we do that, there is still one important question that still needs to be answered. What happened to make your daughter turn into the person she is today?" Owen asked.

"I'm sure it's not easy, but understanding the dynamic between you two may help us with the mission," Hailey added. The group now huddled around Isaac, including Caine and Selena who stood in the hallway, but close to the kitchen.

Isaac let out a long exhale as his shoulders dropped. "Our story spans over a thousand years. When I met Olivia, it was your classic love at first sight. We were inseparable. Before we got married, I told her the truth about what I was and she was very accepting. Likewise, that was when she confessed to being a powerful psychic. After we were married, our running joke was that she made me do it," Isaac smiled as he let out a light chuckle. Owen, and the rest of the group, smiled along with him. After a brief pause, Isaac continued.

"We traveled around for a while before settling in at a facility located in Sweden. She understood how important my work was and wanted to be a part of it. She did many things but eventually settled on teaching the new recruits about the various types of creatures out there. That, and identifying the creatures that the recruits had within them before the third day arrived. Basically, what you saw Livia do. Then, one day she wanted to go out locally to see if she could find any other recruits. She brought me a crystal and asked how to stop it from glowing so she could bring it out in public to check for new recruits."

"She didn't know she was one of the chosen ones. Did you know?" Abigail asked.

"Neither of us had any clue. Once she understood the implications of that crystal glowing, she wanted to be in my world...entirely. She wanted to choose a gem." Owen, along with everyone else, was captivated by his story, to the point that they were all silent. Nobody knew a lot about Isaac's past.

"However, as much as she wanted to, I was able to convince her to hold off. There were still many things that we wanted to do and if she didn't make it, then we would both miss out. I didn't want her to do it at all. Not ever. Whenever she tried to bring it up, I would always find an excuse. I was selfish and I didn't want to chance losing the love of my life. Eventually, we did the one thing that we both truly wanted and that was to have a child. Once Astrid was born, the discussions about the gem ceased and we were both fully invested in raising our daughter. Astrid was headstrong, intelligent, happy, and just so full of life. She loved us both equally and we loved her with all our hearts. Early on, we knew not only that she was a psychic, but also her bloodline made her a chosen one as well."

"Did she know?" Avery inquired.

"We told Astrid about her psychic ability because that was hard to hide and without proper training, a child with that ability could be dangerous and not even mean to be. As for her bloodline, we kept that a secret. We decided to tell her when she was older so she could comprehend and make the decision for herself," Isaac explained. As he talked, Owen felt it was like Isaac was the oldest member of their family telling them stories.

"This is great and all, but when do we get to the part when she decides to not play nice anymore?" Caine coldly asked, followed by a quick elbow to his arm by Selena while she glared at him.

"One day, Olivia came to my office and she was trembling. After talking with her I discovered she chose a gem. She said she used her psychic ability to help ensure she picked the right one but I knew that didn't make a difference...not when it came to that. However, I didn't tell her that. Instead, I told her that it would be okay and I would be by her side the entire way," Isaac paused as his voice cracked from the emotion from the memory of that day.

"So, she knew what creature was inside the gem?" Abigail asked.

"No, she said it was more of a connection she felt with the gem. Anyway, at that point, we decided to tell Astrid in case Olivia didn't make it. She was only ten years old at the time so we explained it as either she will turn out to be like Daddy, who has a creature within me, or she will turn into a creature and Mommy will be inside of it. At first, Astrid became upset so we reassured her that her mom would be alive either way. We added that if she did turn into a creature, there was a chance to bring Mommy back to normal." Isaac paused to drink a sip of water.

"I know we weren't totally truthful with her but she was so young and at that time, it was rumored that there may be a small chance that the human's essence remained within the creature. This rumor had merit because the human's essence can't be sensed anymore and the creature can't revert to a human. However, when the creature dies it becomes a human again. This meant there may be a chance to bring the person back. So, with the combination of hope and my distractions of showing off my abilities to Astrid, we spent the next two days spending as much family time as we could. On day three, Olivia kissed Astrid on her cheek and told her how much she loved her. She then asked her to wait on the other side of the facility since it could get loud. I then kissed Astrid on the top of her head and told her that I loved her and that I would stay with her mom. I then told her to go play because it could be a while."

"What happened?" Owen softly asked.

Isaac let out another deep exhale. "Astrid was not strong enough to identify the creature within Olivia and since there was no one around that could, Olivia went into one of the larger holding cells. While inside of the holding cell, she tried to identify the creature but there was too much chaos inside her mind to do so. We kissed and told each other that we loved each other and as I was about to leave the cell, I locked the cell and accompanied her. She begged me to leave but I told her that I promised I would be by her side and when she tried to argue, I reminded her of my immortality. From that point, we just talked about anything to keep our minds off what was to come. I tried to remain hopeful that she would not fully transition, not just for her, but for me too. I lost track of time but at some point, the pain instantly struck her. She began to scream and roll around on the floor. She thrashed around so much that I had to stand back. I kept talking to her in hopes that my voice would keep her from fully transitioning. Unfortunately, it didn't work and she did end up fully transitioning."

"I'm so sorry," Avery whimpered as both she and Hailey briskly approached Isaac and put their arms around him. Owen glanced around and could see that Selena's eyes were glassy. The rest of the group, even Caine, just stood there solemnly.

"What did she turn into?" Cedric finally asked. His words cut straight through the silence within the room. Isaac didn't answer. Instead, he just stared off into the distance as tears rolled down his cheeks.

"Isaac," Owen politely said as he gently grabbed his shoulder. The gesture snapped Isaac out of his trance.

"What was the question?" Isaac asked while he wiped the tears from his face.

"What creature did your wife fully transition to?" Owen inquired.

"A wyvern," Isaac softly responded as his head sank, but then he scoffed.

"What is it?" Avery asked.

Isaac shook his head and briefly closed his eyes before he replied. "The wyvern was green."

"That explains Astrid's choice for her second creature. Wyverns and dragons are within the same general family. The fact that they both happened to be green is just icing on the cake," Cedric commented.

"There are some images that are just burned into your memory. My wife's face and the wyvern she became are just a couple of them. The wyvern had dark green scales all over its body, except for its underbelly. There, it was more of a tannish-green color. It had large black talons on its two hind feet, with a single large, thick black claw where the wings bent. Those claws were sturdy enough to use as its front legs. The wings were like the ones you would find on a bat, but what was more shocking was how large the creature was. It may have only been around fifteen feet tall but its body was solid. Not stocky, but just seemed as if there was solid muscle under those scales. At that time, it was hard to tell how big its wingspan was, but it had to be quite large since it seemed cramped in the room and couldn't fully extend its wings. Its dual green horns, which were straight and extended from the head toward its neck, were surrounded by multiple tinier horns. Then, there was a smaller line of spikes that led from its neck, all the way down to its tail. The tail itself had a two-foot-long thick green spike at the end of it. I remember it roaring before turning its head and staring at me with its yellowish-green eyes."

"How did you escape?" Owen inquired.

"It wasn't easy," Isaac replied.

"What happened next?" Avery asked.

"It began to easily destroy the cell it was in, so we evacuated that section of the complex and sealed off the exits the best we could. It took a while for it to break through the lower-level floors until it reached the main area. That area was similar to the main garden area in the facility, but not as big. I observed it as it entered the main area and spread its wings. Its wing span was impressive," Isaac replied.

"I'm guessing I know what comes next," Bailey commented.

"Now that the wyvern was contained, I sought out Astrid and broke the news to her. She was devastated, but I promised her that I would do all that I could to protect her mom and see if I could get her human form back," Isaac responded.

"Wait, what? You didn't kill the wyvern? I thought that was an unbreakable rule until recently," Owen said as his head slightly tilted.

"It wasn't back then and besides, that creature was my wife and Astrid's mother. I had to do whatever I could to bring Olivia back. In fear of hurting someone, especially Astrid, I knew Olivia wanted me to kill whatever creature she turned into if she lost the battle. The thing was, I couldn't do it. I know I saw the wyvern and history showed that if a person fully transitioned on day three, they would not revert to human form again, but I didn't care. I was immortal. I had the time and resources to try to prove that theory wrong. Call it selfish, but I had to try."

"Still waiting for the part where your little girl learns to loathe you," Caine coldly said from the background. Isaac ignored his remark and continued.

"I researched and tried every method known to man and beyond, to no avail. Even powerful psychics could not sense her anymore but I had to keep trying. Every day, I would watch Astrid come down and talk to it in one of the secure areas and every time it would ignore her. I made sure to feed it before she came down or else it would have attacked her and I didn't want her to think her mom was trying to kill her. Instead, I would just tell her that mommy is stuck and we are trying, but she can hear you, she just has no control over the wyvern. So, we would spend time together with the wyvern, talking to it about our day. I know it seems silly, but it made Astrid feel better. Heck, at times it even made me feel better. About a decade and a half later, the past seemed to repeat itself when Astrid came to me shaking."

"She touched a gem," Hailey softly said.

"Indeed. She said she needed to live longer in order to be able to help her mom. As you all know, she survived the trial and was delighted that she was a vampire, due to their immortality. I taught her the ropes of being a hybrid and even though she lost part of her psychic abilities, she didn't care. She was focused on the task at hand. Together, we continued the research. About seventy-five years in, that is when it happened."

"Finally," Caine remarked, which caused Isaac to almost lose his concentration.

"The wyvern escaped. Not only that. It wiped out an entire village. Once it remembered the taste of human flesh, its appetite was insatiable. Luckily, it did not have the ability to breathe fire. Also, its ability to fly was hindered by its lack of use of its wings since it only had a small amount of room to fly about in its area. Those are the only aspects that kept it from killing even more people. However, the lore about it having a poisonous tail was quite true, for I witnessed it during its rampage. Our hybrids on hand were having trouble containing it, so I had to step in," Isaac said as more tears entered his eyes and his voice cracked.

"You killed the wyvern," Caine said with a hint of a smile as he now saw the direction of the story.

"Yes…yes, I did. I slapped my hands onto its chest and began to incinerate it. I had to stop it. I already failed Olivia by not only keeping the wyvern alive but then allowing it to kill all those innocent people. I don't know what haunts me more, the painful roar of the wyvern or the screams of Astrid begging me to stop killing her mother," Isaac's lip quivered as he took a few deep breaths to control himself from fully breaking down and crying. For a moment, Owen could have sworn he noticed the phoenix's eyes and not Isaac's.

"Oh no…she witnessed it. I'm so sorry," Selena commented from the background.

Isaac shook his head as he wiped his eyes. "Yes, she did and what made it worse was that once the wyvern was dead, not too long after, Olivia's body appeared. That made the wyvern's death seem even more like her mom's death. I don't blame her. Even I couldn't help to think that I killed my wife, a person I loved so deeply. We had a funeral for her and then shortly after, Astrid left, but not before she proclaimed her hatred for me. So, in the end, I lost my wife and my daughter." At that point, Isaac couldn't even lift his head due to the intense emotion he was feeling from that sad, horrific time in his life. Owen put his hand on Isaac's shoulder while Avery, Hailey, and Selena came up and put their arms around him for comfort. The rest of the group remained quiet and somber.

"That explains the rule of not leaving a day-three fully transformed creature alive," Owen remarked as he walked away from Isaac.

"That also explains her actions," Cedric commented.

"It definitely explains her hatred and maybe even who she is today, but not her actions. Why put so much effort into obtaining this gem?" Bailey pondered out loud.

"If she had the djinn back then, she could have wished for her mom to not fully transition on the third day," Caine said as he leaned against the wall in the hallway.

"Exactly," Isaac muttered. "I presume she wants that power now out of principle or for some other unforeseen idea she has."

The room fell silent again and that is when Owen heard a muffled scream that originated from the basement.

CHAPTER 3

Caine and Owen looked at each other through the corner of their eyes. "I heard it too," Caine commented. Owen nodded while everyone else looked at Caine and Owen with dumbfounded expressions.

Owen wasted no time as he rushed to the basement door and quickly pulled it open. By then, everyone was just following him to see what was going on. He rushed down the creaky wooden steps until he reached the bottom and when he turned to view the entire basement, that is when his eyes grew wide.

He saw the witch bound by her wrists and ankles to a chair, with a hint of burnt flesh in the air. Owen squinted his eyes and noticed some faint smoke around the witch. She also had duct tape loosely attached to her mouth. Cedric's people shot up from being startled while their heads whipped around to see who came down the steps.

"Is everything all right?" Owen inquired. His brow furrowed while his eyes drifted between the witch and the three people.

"Everything is fine minus the fact that she is being stubborn," one of the men commented in a carefree manner as he approached the group.

"What's going on here?" Abigail asked as she walked to the side of Owen.

"Just trying to get some information out of her. All that we received so far is that she can't tell us anything. She fears what Astrid will do if she finds out. I keep trying to convince her that she will suffer more with us if she doesn't tell us more," the man said and before Owen could react, he uttered a word in Latin.

Immediately after, an orange glow appeared from the symbols etched into the metal, followed closely by the witch's muffled scream. Owen could see the smoke emanating from her flesh as tears rolled down her cheeks as she screamed in pain.

"That's enough! There is no need to torture her like that and besides, how can she respond with tape over her mouth?" Owen screamed as he got within inches of the man's face. The man had a smug expression before he uttered the same Latin word again. This word seemed to deactivate the magic in the chain as well. The woman was breathing hard and crying as her body was wavering around from exhaustion.

"We take the tape off when we think she is ready to speak. When she doesn't tell us anything we can use, we just keep repeating the process until she gets it through her thick head that it is better to talk to us," the man replied.

"You are not going to get anything out of her like that. All you are doing is making yourself worse than Astrid," Owen said through his teeth.

"Anyone associated with Astrid deserves nothing less. Do you have a problem with it?" The man asked as his eyes transitioned to almost entirely white. The other man and woman stepped up to either side of him as their eyes transitioned as well, but their eyes were more animal-like.

"Yes, I do actually," Owen said as his eyes transitioned and flames surrounded his hands.

"Stop!" Cedric bellowed as he stepped onto the basement floor. By this time, the rest of the group stood to the side or behind Owen, except for Caine who stood near the bottom of the steps.

"I said to interrogate, not torture. There is a distinct difference!" Cedric yelled as he stormed past Owen and stopped in front of the three people. They dropped out of transition immediately after Cedric stopped and towered over them.

"I know but just look at what Astrid has done so far. Imagine what she can do once she gets this person back, or finds another witch," the man explained.

"And look at what you have done," Cedric loudly countered. Before any of them could respond, Cedric raised his hand to stop them. "The three of you will go back to the car and head back to the city. Once you arrive, you'll remain there and do nothing until I say otherwise. I will deal with you later. Do I make myself clear?"

"Yes…yes sir." Owen could see the fear in them as they scurried upstairs. Once they left, Owen transitioned back to human.

"Thank you for handling that," Isaac said as he patted Cedric on his back.

"No problem and I'm sorry it got out of control like that. She was supposed to be just questioned only and at most, maybe some light torture from the chain, but nothing more," Cedric responded before he turned to look at the witch.

"What exactly does that chain do? Is it just some torture device?" Avery asked.

"No. The chain and pendent are made of iron and the symbols etched into it make it like an anti-witch device. Basically, it prevents the witch from being able to use magic. Only a non-witch can put it on or take it off a witch. If she were to do a handstand right now, the magic from the chain would keep it from falling off. That same magic, when activated, will burn any witch that is wearing it," Cedric calmly explained.

"Fantastic," Owen sarcastically said. He then walked over to the witch. When he got close to her, her emerald eyes widened as she reared back in her seat.

"I'm not here to hurt you. I'm first going to take off that duct tape around your mouth so we can talk. Is that okay?" Owen asked as he squatted down in front of her. The woman nodded her head in agreement. Owen gently smiled as he nodded and slowly reached for the duct tape. Luckily, it was already loose so he was able to get a grip on it and gently removed the tape. Even then, he had to apologize a couple of times when she flinched because her skin was so raw. Sure enough, once he removed the tape, he noticed a red rash from where the tape irritated her skin.

"Can someone please get her some water?" Owen asked his friends.

"I'll get it," Isaac quickly answered as he rushed up the stairs.

"What's your name?" Owen inquired.

"Alyssa," the woman weakly responded. He saw that the burns were severe enough that the flesh around the chain was either completely burned away or charred and stuck to the chain itself. The site was gruesome enough to make Owen cringe and even feel pity for her.

"Here you go," Isaac said as he handed the water bottle to Owen.

"Thank you," Owen said as he took off the cap and turned back to Alyssa. He gently brushed her hair away from her face and then held the bottle up to her lips and slowly poured some water into her mouth.

"Thanks," Alyssa weakly said.

"I'm sorry this happened to you but we need to find out whatever we can about Astrid, Olivia, or whatever she is calling herself," Owen said as he stood up.

"Astrid, and if she finds out I divulged anything to you, the consequences would be dire. Besides, why should I trust you?" Alyssa slowly asked while she wavered in her chair from being exhausted.

Owen turned back to Isaac. "Would you mind making one more trip upstairs to help out Alyssa?"

36

"Of course," Isaac said as he partially smiled and went back upstairs.

"You are going to heal her?" Cedric asked.

"Yes. After how your men treated her, she isn't going to speak to any of us. Even more when you factor in the fear that Astrid put inside her mind. Heck, I wouldn't trust any of you after what Alyssa has gone through. At the very least, it's the humane thing to do. Besides, she hasn't caused us any harm so we don't need to drop to Astrid's level," Owen replied.

"Exactly!" Avery blurted out. She then put her arm around the crook of Owen's arm and stood firmly beside him. Abigail and Bailey stood on the other side of Owen to show their support as the rest gathered near him.

"Fair enough, but be mindful. A witch can be very powerful and deceiving," Cedric countered.

"Sounds like me," Caine jested as a devious smile formed on his face. His comment caused the group to smile and even Selena to let out a small chuckle.

Isaac made his way downstairs with another shot glass and handed it to Owen. He patted Isaac on the shoulder and smiled before he turned around and walked back to Alyssa. "Take this. I promise you that you will feel a lot better once you do." Alyssa glared at Owen but eventually shook her head and allowed him to pour the liquid into her mouth. Seconds later, he could see all her wounds disappear and her strength return as her eyes brightened and a smile formed on her face.

"Well, I can see that you are doing much better than before. Do you now finally trust us enough to talk?" Owen asked while he smiled.

"As much as I appreciate you healing me, what's to say that you won't just torture me again or kill me once I told you everything? Besides, if Astrid finds out…"

"What did Astrid say to make you fear her so much?" Owen interrupted as he took a few steps closer to her. Alyssa didn't respond. She only shook her head and looked away. Owen paused as he tried to think of some way to make her trust him enough to talk. He glanced around the room and all he saw were blank faces and shrugs. Finally, an idea popped into his head as a smirk appeared.

"What are you thinking?" Hailey inquired as her brow arched while she crossed her arms. Owen only winked at Hailey and quickly took out his phone and sent a quick text to Caine, *"Be ready for anything."* He then looked in his direction and saw the puzzled look on Caine's face as he pulled out his phone. He then smirked and nodded at Owen. For what Owen was about to do, he needed the fastest and deadliest person in the room to be ready in case things went wrong. Owen repositioned himself in front of Alyssa.

"If you feel you can trust us and that we can even help you, will you talk to us?" Owen asked.

"Yes, but good luck with that," Alyssa sarcastically replied.

Owen reached toward Alyssa's neck, which caused her to flinch. He paused for a moment before he slowly continued and gently grabbed the chain necklace with both of his hands.

"Owen...are you sure about that?" Cedric questioned while he reached one hand toward Owen.

"Yeah, like really sure," Bailey added as her eyes widened.

"To gain trust you must give trust. Don't worry, everything will be all right," Owen said as he quickly glanced at Caine. His eyes flashed red as a hint of a smile formed. Owen then looked into the eyes of Alyssa.

"Please don't make me regret this," Owen whispered. She gave him a slight nod, accompanied by a faint smile. As he began to remove the necklace from around Alyssa's neck, she cringed and squinted her eyes. He presumed she braced herself in case she felt more pain, so Owen quickly, yet carefully removed the necklace and placed it on the ground next to him. He then snapped the plastic ties around her wrists and ankles and took a few steps back.

"Thank you," Alyssa said as she stood up while she rubbed her wrists. "Still, that was a bold move to give a witch that you just tortured all her power back," Alyssa added with no expression on her face.

"First off, I didn't torture you. If anything, I stopped you from being tortured. Secondly, I want you to trust me so we can help each other out. My name is…"

"Owen," Alyssa interrupted.

"I guess you overheard someone call out my name," Owen rhetorically commented.

"Not so much that, but Astrid did show me the pictures she has of everyone in this room. All the way down to the vampire hanging out in the back of the room. Here's a tip, witches are usually good at sniffing out vampires and other unnatural creatures," Alyssa remarked and her deadpan expression became smug. Caine's only reaction was a crooked grin while he shrugged.

"Pictures of us. Yeah, that's not creepy at all," Avery commented.

"Pictures and intel about each one of you to be precise. I just arrived in town a week ago and I've only met up with her once for her to catch me up to speed. She then told me to stay put until I heard from her. I guess that didn't happen. In fact, I should get moving," Alyssa commented. She then started to walk away but Owen stepped in front of her. Alyssa let out a large sigh and then put her hands on her waist and stared at Owen.

"Sorry. I don't want to hurt you but at the same time, we can't let you leave until we find out more about the spell to control the djinn," Owen said as he crinkled his face.

"You really want to play that game with me?" Alyssa countered while she glared at Owen and took a couple of steps toward him.

"I wouldn't mind playing that game with you," Caine commented while he approached her with a devious smile on his face. Right as his eyes turned blood red and Alyssa clenched her fists, Selena stepped in front of Caine.

"Everyone, just take a moment and breathe," Selena calmly expressed. She glanced at Caine, who stopped as the red from his eyes vanished. Selena then turned her attention to Alyssa, who seemed tense and rigid. Her eyes were filled with rage while her fists were still firmly closed. "Please, let us help you. From what you previously hinted, you fear Astrid for whatever reason. I'm sure I am not alone when I say this, but we all fear Astrid to some level. However, we find solace in being together while we try to find a way to stop her," Selena pleaded. Alyssa's fists unclenched and her face became solemn.

"Whatever horrible fear my daughter placed inside your mind; we can get through it together. I can't promise that everything will work out, but at the very least you will have more control over your destiny. Hopefully, that notion alone brings you some comfort," Isaac added as he smiled and placed his hand on her shoulder.

Alyssa paused before she spoke as her eyes scanned the room. "If I don't fulfill my oath to assist her in releasing the djinn to be under her control, then she will kill my entire family. Not just my parents and little brother, but all my relatives. They will all die and I will live to suffer the loss of them and for me, that pain is worse than death itself."

"An old, but effective tactic," Caine muttered as his eyes drifted off while he grinned. He then noticed everyone was staring at him with a variety of expressions from shocked to disappointed. "Sorry. Just reminiscing," Caine added before he turned to look at Isaac. "It's a monster thing," Caine said and then winked. Isaac scoffed before he returned his attention to Alyssa. Owen didn't know about everyone else, but he had to hold back a smile from Caine's last comment. He found it oddly amusing.

40

"Why did you give such an oath?" Selena kindly inquired.

"She saved my life a while back and I said I was in her debt. Afterward, we had a long conversation and that is when she asked for help," Alyssa responded.

"She told you everything upfront?" Hailey asked.

"Not at first. She said she was working on a project and may need me to perform a transfer spell of some sort. She didn't tell me the details but at least reassured me that the transfer didn't involve anything between humans. That's all I wanted to hear so I agreed to help her. It wasn't until I arrived in the city that she revealed the transfer was to move a djinn from a magical object to an ordinary object. She even had the ingredients and spells that I needed. She just needed me to perform the ritual. When I expressed my concern about the djinn, that is when she made the threat against my family and reminded me of my oath. My family means everything to me, even more than my own life, so I agreed," Alyssa replied as she wiped the tears from her eyes. Selena put her arm around her, but Alyssa only accepted the comfort for a few seconds. She then nonchalantly shrugged Selena's arm off her and walked forward a few steps.

"It was probably Astrid who put your life in danger so she could save you," Abigail commented.

"Maybe so but it's a moot point now. As much as I don't want to help her, I must, or else my entire family will be slaughtered. Now, if you can come up with a foolproof plan to stop her and keep my family alive then I am all ears," Alyssa said while she raised her arms out to her sides as she waited for a response from anyone.

"We could kill you. You said you valued your family's life more than your own. This way they are saved and Astrid doesn't have all the ingredients anymore. Problem solved," Caine suggested, followed by a crooked grin.

Before anyone could respond to his solution, Alyssa did. "That saves my family but only delays Astrid. She will just find another witch. Like I said, she already has the spells and ingredients."

"What are the ingredients?" Owen inquired.

"In general, a bunch of common items found within magic such as herbs and animal blood. Those items are then mixed together and used to draw very specific symbols on the ground. Those symbols are then infused with magic by a spell. Next, the gem is placed within one of the symbols and whatever object she chose to be the new vessel for the djinn, will be placed in a different symbol. That object just has to be anything that can be opened and closed. It also must be performed during a celestial event, such as a full moon. There happens to be a full moon coming up soon but if she misses that, it just delays her a month. Then, of course, a witch to perform the spell and that's it. The only items that are rare and would cause her an issue are the gem and the spell. If she was smart, which she is, she would have multiple copies of the spell in different locations just in case the original was taken from her. That just leaves the gem, and I'm sure she will keep it secured. I guess you could try to kill her, which I'm sure will be easy," Alyssa sarcastically responded. The group stood there with blank expressions on their faces as they searched for answers.

"You're a witch. Can't you just snap your fingers and kill her or at least immobilize her so we can snatch the gem away from her?" Cedric blurted out.

"It's not that easy. First off, I don't want to kill anybody." Alyssa went to continue but was interrupted by Caine's scoff.

"Oh great, a witch with a conscious," Caine commented.

"It's not so much that, but the fact that killing can easily lead a witch down a dark path, and that is something I don't ever want to experience. Dark magic will not only change your powers but over time, it changes your soul and it is hard to stop once you start," Alyssa countered.

"Can you at least weaken her so we can kill her?" Cedric asked. Owen noticed Isaac look away momentarily. He could only imagine how hard this conversation was for him to partake in.

"Yes, but only once my oath is fulfilled. Witches take their oaths seriously," Alyssa replied.

"But once you perform the ritual you can stop her without killing her?" Owen softly asked while he was thinking through scenarios within his mind.

"If I wanted to I could, especially since she will be weakened for a while after the spell. However, I fear she will go after my family in retaliation," Alyssa responded.

"You know she may not hold up her end of the bargain and release you and your family once it's all done. There's a chance she will want to employ your services for even longer, using your family as leverage," Avery mentioned.

"I hope not but if she does, I will cross that bridge when I get to it, but for now I have to presume she will honor our agreement," Alyssa responded.

Owen pondered what could be done. It seemed like every suggestion had a negative response to it and things were becoming bleaker by the second. Before they had a chance, but now that Astrid has the gem, nothing can stop her. Holding her witch was just a speed bump on the road to victory. Still, Owen refused to believe Astrid was unstoppable. There had to be a way. The room was silent until Owen finally broke the silence.

"Then we let her finish the ritual," Owen mumbled.

"We what?" Bailey exclaimed.

"Let her complete the transfer. She will be at her weakest and Alyssa will be free of her oath. We just need to find a way for me or a few of us to be close by when it happens. Maybe like prisoners or something so we can strike when she is down." The more Owen revealed his plan, the bigger the smile that grew on his face.

"That could work. Also, she would not be able to use the djinn until the next phase of the moon, so that would give us seven days between the full moon and the waning gibbous phase," Alyssa added. A legitimate smile formed on her face for the first time, but it vanished before she continued. "However, if your plan backfires, you will have only a week to figure something out. Maybe steal the object and run, because once the new moon phase arrives, she will have the power to do almost anything she wants."

"It's risky, but it may be the only solution that is available to us," Isaac commented as he rubbed his chin.

"Risky is putting it nicely," Bailey grumbled. "Whoever signs up to be her prisoner has a slim chance, at best, of making it out of there alive."

"The chances of survival will increase if we send people that she is less likely to kill," Isaac countered as he continued to rub his chin and stare off into the distance.

"You are the only one with a phoenix inside of them, so you'll make it out alive, but not everyone else shares that luxury. Their chances are slim, at best, due to your lovely daughter," Caine commented as he leaned against the wall.

"Not only that, Astrid most likely has a plan in place to defend against any of our attempts toward the gem," Abigail added.

"Well, we must try something and time is not on our side, so if someone else has a better suggestion then please say it now. If not, then this is the plan we are going with," Owen sternly said. He couldn't stop his frustrations from showing at this point. He was also tired of Astrid and all the death, pain, and drama that she had caused over her endeavor to gain control of the djinn.

"How about we gather everyone that we can and just attack her head-on?" Bailey suggested. Owen could sense the confidence in her voice as she spoke calmly yet her eyes narrowed with determination.

"If we don't get to her quick enough and she feels her or the gem is in any danger, she will flee. She proved that when she tried to fly away during our last encounter," Hailey responded. Owen could see Bailey shake her head in frustration as she pressed her lips firmly together, but Hailey did have a point. After that, the room was silent again. Everyone seemed to be deep in thought, except for Isaac who had just recently begun to look at his phone and text whomever he was talking to.

"None of these plans will work if we don't even know where she is," Avery said before she turned to Alyssa. "Do you know where she could be?"

"I have no idea. She was going to notify me where to go once she had possession of the gem and when she was ready to begin the ritual. I haven't looked at my phone since I was taken so I have no idea of any updates," Alyssa replied matter-of-factly.

"I believe your phone was left behind at your place so that you could not be tracked," Cedric added.

Avery scoffed. "Great, she can be anywhere."

"I know where she is," Isaac said with a grim expression on his face.

"Where is she?" Owen slowly asked. He feared what Isaac's response would be.

Isaac sighed before he responded. "According to Marcus, she has breached the facility."

CHAPTER 4

The news shocked Owen as his jaw dropped while he stared at Isaac. Bailey, Avery, and Hailey shared his expression while the others in the room were less shocked. "What?" Owen softly said. It was the only response he could formulate after what he just heard.

"The facility. I remember you telling me about it a long time ago but I can't recall exactly what it is used for. Is it one of the bigger safe house locations?" Cedric inquired.

"No, it's the main headquarters located on the East Coast," Abigail responded.

"All that work to defend it and she still found a way in," Bailey commented.

"Marcus couldn't stop her?" Avery asked.

"He was preoccupied with the Amarok when she, accompanied by a handful of her followers, infiltrated the cabin and gained access to the elevator that leads to the facility itself," Isaac quietly responded while his eyes remained on his phone.

"I hope everyone inside is okay," Avery commented.

"I hope so too. I haven't received any texts or calls from anyone else and Marcus's phone is still working so the communications have not been disabled. She hasn't been inside long, but I already dread what she has done and fear what she will do," Isaac replied. He then cringed and had a look of both disgust and even nausea on his face before he turned and briskly went back up the steps.

"Isaac…" Avery called out but he did not respond.

"Give him some time. This must be very hard on him considering it's his own daughter," Owen said as he put his hand on her shoulder.

"I know. I just hate to see him like this. You are not the only one who sees him like a grandfather figure," Avery said as she crossed her arms over her chest. She then frowned and leaned onto Owen.

"Well, he is just another person to me and if you do decide to execute your plan, Owen, you can't let Isaac go. No matter how much he desires to go, you must find a way to keep him behind. He is too close to this and if he goes, the plan will be doomed before it even begins," Caine mentioned while he approached Owen.

"As cold as it sounds, I agree with Caine," Selena commented as she frowned.

"How do you stop a father from protecting his daughter?" Abigail asked.

"You don't," Owen softly replied.

"Then you are doomed," Caine softly said with no expression on his face.

"You mean the plan, not Owen…right?" Hailey asked.

"I meant Owen, but yes…the plan would be doomed as well," Caine replied.

"Why is Owen doomed?" Hailey inquired as her brow knitted.

"Do you really think Owen is going to volunteer to be the one to sit back and let others do this mission? To miss the chance to sacrifice himself to save his friends…never," Caine sarcastically responded.

"He does have a point but I am sure a lot of people will be volunteering to go. Nobody wants to see anybody get hurt or even worse, die," Abigail countered.

"Then it comes down to one thing. Who is Astrid least likely to kill?" Selena asked.

"We should discuss this with Isaac," Avery suggested.

"If anything, he is the last person to be included in this discussion," Caine rebutted.

"It's his daughter. How could he not be involved in the conversation, no matter how difficult it will be for him?" Avery countered.

"Then by all means, make the mission harder than it should be," Caine sarcastically replied while he turned and extended his arm toward the steps. Avery went upstairs first, followed by everyone else.

"Isaac," Avery called out when she reached the top of the steps. There was no answer so she and Bailey looked around for him.

"I can't find him on this floor," Bailey mentioned to Owen as he reached the top of the steps.

"He's not upstairs either," Avery called out as she walked down the steps. At that point, everyone was back in the kitchen, with Caine lingering in the doorway to the basement.

"Maybe he's outside or in the garage," Alyssa said and then began to make her way to the door.

"Hold up," Owen said as he softly grabbed her shoulder.

"Calm down. I'm not going to try to escape," Alyssa loudly said as she shrugged his hand off her shoulder and glared at him.

"It's not that. I just feel it would be better if you stay indoors and away from the windows in case Astrid or one of her followers are watching the premises. Just for a while until we develop the plan more. Please," Owen calmly responded. She seemed on edge and short-tempered, and he wasn't sure if that was her personality or the situation she was in. Either way, he had to make sure she didn't lose his trust, which was built on the hopes that Alyssa didn't lie about anything.

Alyssa huffed. "Very well." She then sat in the kitchen chair and looked at Owen with discontent.

Cedric peeked into the garage. "He's not in here."

"Hopefully he's outside," Owen remarked while he headed toward the front door, followed by Avery, Bailey, and Hailey. They walked outside and that is when Owen could hear a faint metal-creaking sound on the side of the house. He followed the sound and as they reached the side of the house, Isaac was sitting on a wooden bench swing. He was using his feet to gently make the swing move back and forth, with the rolling green hills as his view. Beyond that, was the town. The house was far enough away to be quiet enough for Owen to hear the birds chirping off into the distance.

"Whenever I am here, I like to take some time to just sit here and enjoy the view. The scenery relaxes me, which in return, helps me think," Isaac mentioned while he continued to admire his view.

"I don't know if I would be thinking or sleeping with how tranquil it is," Avery commented as they approached. Isaac finally turned his head and smiled before he scooted over and patted the seat adjacent to him. Hailey was the first to sit down. Owen noticed this and stopped dead in his tracks. He took out his phone and mindlessly flipped through it as a ruse to avoid sitting next to Hailey. Avery slowed down and looked at the last available seat and then back at Owen.

"Ladies first," Owen said with a small smile while he gestured for her to sit. "Besides, I wanted to check the weather. I see some dark clouds in the area." He was relieved that he was able to think of a reason to explain his behavior.

"How is it looking?" Hailey asked.

"How's what looking?" Owen questioned. His mind went from the next steps of the mission to awkwardly being in the same area as Hailey and Avery. So much that he began to sweat.

"The weather...how does it look?" Hailey slowly asked as her brow crinkled while both she and Avery giggled.

"Oh…that. Yes, sorry. Looks like it may also rain in a little bit," Owen stuttered as he wiped his forehead.

"Pull it together, Owen," Avery jokingly added before she and Hailey turned around. Owen responded with just a nervous chuckle. She was more right than she knew, Owen thought. He knew he needed to focus more on the mission but the social dynamics were currently awkward.

Isaac cleared his throat. "I'm sorry for my abrupt exit earlier. It's just…"

"She's your daughter and it's tough. We understand," Hailey interjected.

"Very tough, but I am also supposed to be your leader and need to…"

"Need to what, not act like a human or a father and just be a robot. No one can do that nor should they," Avery sternly, yet politely said as she interrupted Isaac this time. Isaac smiled and nodded in agreement.

"True and I wish I was half as wise as you two when I was your age," Isaac replied and then turned his head to face Owen. "Do you want to…"

"Interrupt you as well. No sir, that would be rude," Owen quickly talked over Isaac, followed by a wink. Isaac scoffed in amusement and turned back around.

"My head is clearer now. Thank you for understanding. We should head back in before the rain comes," Isaac said as he glanced around at the sky. Owen looked up and only saw one large dark cloud making its way over to their location.

Isaac, Hailey, and Owen began to walk back to the house when Hailey turned around and noticed Avery was still sitting on the swing.

"Are you coming inside?" Hailey called out to Avery.

"I'll be there in a few minutes. I just want to enjoy the view a little while longer," Avery responded as she looked over her shoulder.

"Care if I join you?" Owen asked.

"I rather you not," Avery coldly responded. Owen was speechless from her shocking response and as he slowly began to turn around, he heard Avery call out to him. "I'm just messing with you. Come on over!"

Owen turned his head and noticed her beaming smile and couldn't help but smile himself. "Caine's blood needs to leave your system sooner rather than later," Owen teased. As he was about to sit down on the swing, he noticed Hailey and Isaac were almost back at the house already. He sat down close to, but not right up against, Avery. His leg began to bounce as the nerves entered his mind about the conversation that he still needed to have with her. The part that made him nervous the most was the unknown. How will she react when she finds out he remembers what she confessed to the chimera? That, and will their talk lead to them becoming a couple, or would it drive a wedge between them if they decided they shouldn't become one?

"Weren't you the one who told me to enjoy the moment?" Avery asked as she nudged Owen's arm.

"Yeah, why?" Owen inquired as he was snapped back to reality from being deep in his mind.

"Then follow your own advice and get out of your head before you bounce me off the swing," Avery replied as she winked.

Owen quickly shook his head and stopped bouncing his leg. "Sorry about that. I can see why Isaac enjoys this spot." Owen paused as he mustered up the courage to discuss what had been weighing on him. "There has been something I have been meaning to talk to you about for a while now but the timing of it never worked out."

"Gee, I can't imagine why. This mission has been crazy," Avery playfully commented.

"Well, while we have a few moments before the craziness picks back up, I figured we could talk now," Owen said with his heart in his throat.

"You know you can talk to me about anything whenever you want. I'm always here for you but as you said, the craziness is about to pick up. This moment may be the only tranquil time we will have for who knows how long. If you really want to talk about something then sure, but if it can wait, I say we just enjoy the moment," Avery suggested as she turned to face Owen.

"It can wait," Owen replied with a fake smile.

He felt it was an important subject to talk about and he could feel the weight of this conversation baring down on him. If the past taught him anything, the future was never certain; however, he could sense Avery wanted to just relax. A notion that he too felt was probably the better option to choose since they were about to face Astrid again. Owen leaned back and put his arm around Avery as she snuggled in and put her hand on his leg. He could feel his fake smile phase into a genuine smile. They didn't say anything and just viewed the scenery in front of them as they slowly rocked on the swing.

Only about five minutes passed before large raindrops began to fall on them. They quickly scurried off the bench and bolted toward the front porch. Due to his speed, Owen put his hand on her back and purposely kept the same pace as Avery since he didn't want to leave her behind. Unfortunately, they only made it halfway to the house before it began to pour. By the time they reached the front porch, they were both drenched. They began to laugh over what just happened.

"We're soaked!" Avery exclaimed while she tried to wipe the excess water off her arms.

Owen scoffed with amusement. "I don't know how you can see anything with your hair in your eyes." He moved closer to her and brushed one side of her hair away from her face. This caused Avery to stop what she was doing and affectionately smile at him.

"I know…I'm a mess. I can only imagine how ugly I look right now. You may need to divert your eyes," Avery joked yet her smile left her.

"I don't think that's possible for you to not look beautiful," Owen replied as he gently moved the other side of her hair away from Avery's face and gently smiled at her.

A flirtatious smile formed on her face as she moved closer to Owen. His hand slid down her cheek, and then down her arm until it reached her hand. The two held hands while he stared into her eyes and softly smiled as she stopped right in front of him. He noticed she gently bit her bottom lip right before she began to lean up to him. He felt his lips being drawn to hers as he began to lean toward her as well.

"I was wondering if you guys got caught in the rain," Bailey blurted out as she whipped the door open. Both Avery and Owen yelled and their bodies jerked as they quickly stepped back from each other.

"Sorry, I didn't mean to startle you guys," Bailey added while she chuckled.

"Dang it, Bailey. I'm glad I have good bladder control," Avery asserted while she briskly walked past her and inside the house.

"Are you coming in or do you prefer to stand outside and be wet and cold?" Bailey asked and then smirked. Owen, who couldn't tell if his heart was racing from the kiss that almost happened or from the heart attack that Bailey almost gave him, started to walk toward her.

"My bladder control is not as good as Avery's," Owen jested as he winked at Bailey. She laughed and moved out of his way. As Owen entered the house, Selena handed him a towel.

"Thank you," Owen said. He then took the towel and began to pat himself with it until he noticed Isaac make his way to the center of the living room with his hand raised. The room became quiet in anticipation of what Isaac was going to say.

"I know there is much to discuss and it all revolves around my daughter. It appears with each passing moment, the mission becomes increasingly more complex, thanks to her. I suggest we first take some time to clean ourselves up and have nourishment that is more than just the snacks in the pantry. I know everyone feels refreshed, but your stomachs are empty and no one here smells…fresh. No offense, of course," Isaac said as he grinned and panned the room. Owen smiled because as funny as the comment was, it was also true.

"There are multiple bathrooms throughout the house and many closets full of clothes to accompany them. Please freshen up and find a suitable change of clothes and meet back downstairs when you are finished. I know some local, delicious places that deliver so I will place some orders for the food to arrive later," Isaac added.

It didn't take long for the group to scatter and head toward the bathrooms. Owen let the first wave of people go first as he slowly made his way to go upstairs. He noticed Avery seemed to be one of the first ones to make it to the master bathroom downstairs. Owen wondered what Avery's thoughts were about what almost transpired on the porch earlier. Especially, since she didn't look at him the entire time once they entered the house.

"We can always share a shower if you can handle it," Abigail teased as she brushed passed Owen and playfully winked.

"I don't think I am coordinated enough to shower with someone else. I would probably end up accidentally elbowing them or something. Thanks though." Owen stumbled through his response since he was caught off guard. Abigail smiled and shrugged her shoulders before she proceeded upstairs. He too, made his way upstairs and when he reached the top, he could hear people in the other rooms chatting and rummaging through the closets and drawers. He had too much on his mind to deal with that so he made his way into an office. The room appeared to be the opposite of Isaac's office at the facility.

As Owen toured the room, there was a standard wooden desk, with a computer monitor and printer on top of it, along with random pieces of blank paper and pens. Owen didn't see any personal items or pictures within the office, which made it feel bleak. He sat down in the standard office swivel chair and let out a large exhale. He began to replay the events that happened between Avery and himself over and over in his mind. At first, he was bummed that the kiss did not happen, but then he felt relieved. He felt the conversation still needed to occur first before anything else happened because he didn't want any secrets between them. To Owen, it felt unfair that he knew something that she didn't expect anyone else to know.

As the noises from the hallways and bathrooms dwindled down, he knew it was his turn to take a well-needed shower. To his surprise, the water was still hot the entire time he was in the shower. He would have stayed in longer to relax his muscles, but the phoenix tears removed any soreness he had. Once he was done in the bathroom, he wrapped a towel around him and headed over to the closest bedroom. This was apparently a mistake because it contained all female clothing. He left and went to the adjacent room and luckily, that room contained male clothes.

He sifted through until he found a comfortable pair of mesh shorts and a plain cotton t-shirt since he figured they were not leaving tonight. However, in anticipation of leaving to go to the facility, he laid out a few outfits and even some general supplies for later. As soon as he was done, he could smell the food downstairs. Owen proceeded down the steps and into the kitchen and by the looks of it, he was the last one to join his friends.

"I wasn't sure what to get everyone so I ordered from a few different places. Hopefully, you will find what you like," Isaac remarked. Everyone thanked him and began to line up to get their food.

Owen noticed different types of pizza, deli sandwiches, salads, pierogies, whoopie pies, and a variety of drinks to wash it all down. He grabbed each type of food, took his drink, and scanned the area for a place to sit. It appeared that people were sitting either in the kitchen, dining room, or on a bar stool at the counter. Owen saw Avery, who gave him a quick, closed-mouth smile while she held up her pizza. He smiled because she had enough pizza in her mouth that it made her look like a chipmunk. Unfortunately, she had Bailey and Hailey on either side of her and Alyssa and Isaac on the other side of the dining room table she sat at. He then caught Abigail waving him over from the counter. He walked past Selena, Caine, and Cedric at the kitchen table and put his food next to Abigail's plate.

"It seems we share the same chimera hunger," Abigail commented as she pointed back and forth between their piles of food.

"It looks like it, but my pile seems to be a wee bit higher than yours," Owen replied while he smiled.

"Yeah, but that's because you are a super chimera so it stands to reason you would also have a super chimera appetite. Probably accompanied by a super chimera metabolism," Abigail joked and then rolled her eyes. This caused Owen to scoff in amusement. "Are you just going to stand there and not sit down?"

"I'll stand. I don't mind standing and eating sometimes. I guess it's a habit I picked up over the years," Owen replied before he began to scarf down his food. Abigail shrugged and continued to eat.

Once everyone had finished their meals and conversations, the group adjourned to the living room and found a spot on either one of the couches or chairs, both equally soft and comfortable. Owen sat at the end of one of the couches and noticed as Avery came into the room, looked around, and chose to sit in a nearby chair. He didn't expect Avery to be attached to him everywhere he went but after what happened on the porch, he couldn't help but worry. He was concerned that their near-kiss added another layer on top of her current thoughts and hesitations about them. Maybe, that extra stress freaked her out, Owen wondered. However, he couldn't dwell on it but he did kick himself for not talking about it with her earlier on the bench. As Owen tried to divert his thoughts, Abigail sat next to him.

"Any progress between you and Avery?" Abigail whispered as she leaned toward him.

"Does making it worse count as progress," Owen whispered back.

Abigail scoffed in amusement. "Just like a man to make things worse." Owen grinned as he shook his head. "At least you realized that there is a problem and you must do something to fix it. That's better than most men," Abigail added as she continued to whisper.

"Thank you...I think?" Owen whispered back as his brow knitted.

He then observed the last two people, Isaac and Alyssa, enter the room. Of course, Alyssa was smiling and giggling at whatever the two of them were talking about. Leave it to Isaac to make anybody, even technically a prisoner, feel welcome. Alyssa found a seat on the other side of Abigail as Isaac made his way to the center of the room.

"Everyone, may I have your attention please." Isaac's announcement caused everyone to become silent and look at him. "A quick recap of where we stand. My daughter has acquired the gem that contains the djinn, along with all the other ingredients except for Alyssa. Not only that, she and a handful of her followers have seized control of the facility. Marcus, who must be worn down by now, is still watching over the Amarok that is lurking around a couple of miles away from the facility. It's nursing its wounds but it's still just as deadly as before. Luckily, a couple of our wilderness trainers were outside when Astrid took control. They are safe and Marcus has recruited them to assist him in watching over the Amarok. That leaves us with three days, after tonight, until the next full moon. It was suggested that one or a few of us escort Alyssa to the facility and let her perform the ritual to save her family. Also, to take advantage of my daughter's vulnerable state once the ritual is complete. Thoughts?"

"Fortify our position here and wait out the next three days. Astrid can't get mad at Alyssa for being captured and it will also give us an extra month to figure something out," Cedric suggested.

"It's not guaranteed that Astrid will forgive Alyssa. She may end up blaming her for the delay and punish her family anyway," Avery countered.

"Also, she may send another wave of people here and even if we fend them off, it's another location destroyed and we have to move elsewhere…again," Hailey added.

"There are also the poor people inside that we must figure out a way to save. I can only imagine what they must be going through," Selena mentioned.

"Are there people inside the facility capable of rising up against Astrid?" Caine inquired.

"Not really. Maybe some of the trainers but that is it. We didn't bring in any new recruits due to all the fighting and time away from the facility," Isaac replied.

"How long does the ritual take to set up and perform?" Bailey asked.

"Half a day. Maybe a day to set up if I really take my time and drag it out, but that may be obvious since she will have everything that I require already there. The setup may even go quicker than half a day depending on how prepared everything is for me. As for the ritual itself, not long at all. A few minutes at most," Alyssa responded.

"What if we go there as we originally planned but the night before the full moon? That way, she will be there, but unable to perform the ritual in time. It gets her and our team in the facility quicker, keeps Astrid from coming out here, and doesn't fault Alyssa. All that and we get an extra month to stop Astrid," Abigail suggested.

"Provided Astrid doesn't see right through that ruse and kills Alyssa and whoever else is with her, along with Alyssa's family. I know I would," Caine casually mentioned. Silence filled the room as everyone tried to think of a plan that would cover all the angles.

"Then we go with the original plan. Alyssa and whoever else is going with her will leave tomorrow or the next day and let the ritual happen. Then, while Astrid is down, we kill her or steal the object with the djinn and use that power to our advantage against her. Either way, we end this madness once and for all," Owen blurted out.

"I still like the delay idea better," Abigail retorted.

"Well, maybe if anyone on the team that is going has an opportunity to sabotage the ritual, safely, then why not. That way, the delay can't be pinned on Alyssa. If not, then that team sticks to the original plan," Owen replied.

"That sounds good to me. Does anyone object thus far?" Abigail asked and was met with no objections. "Great, now the biggest question of the night...who's going?"

CHAPTER 5

Hands began to raise across the room in response to Abigail's question. Owen knew everyone's hatred toward Astrid but seeing how quickly his friends raised their hands proved it even more. If they felt anything remotely like how he felt, then they were ready to lay their life on the line to see Astrid stopped for good.

"Everyone's bravery is always refreshing to witness. However, as much as I want to choose each of you, too many people will seem more like an assault mission rather than an escort mission," Isaac commented.

"Let's narrow it down by stating who shouldn't be going. For starters, Avery," Bailey suggested. Avery huffed at her comment.

"Remember the last time you went when it was suggested that you stay? Sorry, but she has it out for you. You will be killed on sight. Sorry," Owen added. Avery didn't respond. Instead, she sat back in her seat and pouted.

"Selena," Caine announced.

"There could be people wounded at this facility and what if she harms anyone on our team? They would need to be healed. I am capable of handling myself and I think I would be a great asset to the team," Selena sternly commented.

"You're quite capable but your generosity when it comes to healing others is not only annoying, it's also enhancing that target on your back. If it wasn't for you, the number of people within this room would have dwindled. She would be foolish to not kill you solely to have an important player off the board," Caine replied in the same stern tone as Selena.

"Caine has a point, which also means Hailey can't go," Isaac calmly remarked.

"Because my creature is strong enough to kill her. I understand but that also means you can't go as well since your creature can kill hers as well," Hailey softly said as she turned her head to look at Isaac.

"I'm afraid I will have to pull rank and insist that I go," Isaac politely countered.

"You're the last person that should be going," Caine added.

"I agree, not only is your creature strong enough to kill hers with ease, but you are too close to this. Sorry, but I don't think you can go and not end up jeopardizing this mission. After all, she is your daughter. I get the impression that you don't seem like the kind of man that would let his own flesh and blood suffer or perish…especially at your own hands," Cedric calmly said.

"I understand your, well everyone's fear, but I feel I must be there. Not only am I the strongest of anyone here and I would imagine over there, but I also have the power to heal. That, and I feel she will be less likely to try to kill me. As evil as she has become, I'm her father and I still feel there are some lines she won't cross. However, if she is that far gone then my daughter has truly vanished and the monster that took her place will have to be dealt with." Isaac's response became more solemn the longer he talked. "Besides, I am the only true immortal around here," Isaac added. He was upbeat in his response and even smiled, but Owen felt his happiness was all an act.

61

"You're only immortal when in transition. Don't forget that," Bailey quickly mentioned.

"She's right unless you have forgotten how close I came to killing you back at the mountain." Owen was direct, yet calm, and he only slightly turned his head in Isaac's direction when he talked. He noticed his response must have been more blunt than he realized due to the vast number of jaws that dropped.

"It was close, but I'm still alive. Remember, I have been around long enough to be able to get a read on a person or a situation. Unlike typical males, I am quite observant." Isaac's response converted the room's silent gape-mouthed expressions to ones of giggles, chuckles, and smiles.

"Well, Caine obviously can't go because this entire operation can't solely be done at night," Abigail said and then turned toward Caine. "Also, I don't think you will last more than two seconds before you want to rip her head off. No offense," Abigail added as she shrugged her shoulders and then smirked.

"None taken," Caine responded with a devious grin.

"She didn't know Cedric and Bailey that well so that wouldn't make any sense either. Owen can't go since he went after her multiple times trying to kill her so that just leaves me," Abigail added while she leaned back in her seat.

"I agree, except for me not going," Owen quickly countered. He didn't see much reaction from Bailey or Cedric, so either that was because they agreed or he didn't give them enough time to respond. Regardless, he felt he needed to speak up. Before Abigail could speak, Owen continued.

"All of us have tried to kill her and the fact that I tried multiple times and still failed means I'm no threat to her. If anything, I feel she finds me unique and interesting due to my control over the chimera. Honestly, I feel like you should go too because before everything went down, you seemed to have a good relationship with her." As Owen talked, the tension in his face eased. He believed in what he was saying and wanted to convey that feeling to Abigail and the rest of the room.

"It's settled then. Me, Owen, Abigail, and of course, Alyssa will head over to the facility," Isaac announced. His attention shifted to Avery when he noticed that she partially raised her hand, accompanied by grumbling from around the room. "I'm sure you and the others have some reservations about this decision and for good reason. There is no correct answer here. Each of us has a reason to not be selected so I have based my decision on what everyone else was worried about the most…who would be the least likely to be killed," Isaac added.

"When do we leave?" Alyssa inquired.

"The morning after tomorrow. I feel we will all need some rest and I prefer to arrive there during the daytime. The thought of entering that area at night with an Amarok roaming around is unsettling, even to me. Also, I need to communicate with Marcus about our plans while he gathers as much intel as he can. My plan is to exchange information and then have him take the vehicle back here so he can recover properly," Isaac responded.

"It's too bad he is too worn down to join your team," Bailey commented.

"I already know he is going to insist on joining us and regardless of his condition, I am going to decline. He indeed needs to recover but he is also very protective, which is usually great, but not in this instance. For this, we don't need anyone who will be too quick to challenge Astrid or seem overprotective. I'm sure that will instantly annoy her to the point of her acting rashly," Isaac replied.

"Well, unless there is more to discuss at this moment, I am going to turn in for the night," Avery said as she stood up and stretched her arms out.

"That is a good idea. I'm afraid I don't have beds for everyone so if you don't feel comfortable enough to share a bed with someone, then there are couches and recliners throughout the house. If it helps, they are quite comfortable," Isaac mentioned to the group.

Before Owen could even stand up, Avery briskly went upstairs. Slowly behind her were Bailey, Hailey, Selena, and Abigail. Owen could hear them chatting among themselves as they proceeded up the stairs. Alyssa viewed the master bedroom but then turned to look at Isaac.

"It's all yours," Isaac said as he motioned toward the room.

"Thank you," Alyssa said as she grinned and headed into the room.

"It looks like we are roughing it boys," Caine sarcastically said as he stood up and proceeded out of the room.

"Where will you sleep?" Owen asked.

"I noticed a recliner in the basement that should be adequate enough," Caine responded.

"I'm sure there is plenty of room around here. Don't worry, we don't have to share a couch," Cedric jested.

"I'm sure there is but I prefer not to wake up to the smell of my burning flesh," Caine responded with a crooked grin while he tapped on the windows. He then exited the room.

"I wouldn't mind waking up to the smell of his flesh burning," Cedric mumbled as he winked toward Owen and Isaac.

"I heard that," Caine yelled from the hallway near the basement door.

"I figured you would," Cedric yelled back and then chuckled to himself. Both Isaac and Owen snickered as well.

It didn't take too long for everyone to get ready to go to sleep and the three remaining men were able to find separate couches and recliners to sleep on. There was not much talking going on, which surprised Owen after the discussion that was just held. Instead, the lights turned off quicker than he imagined and the house became silent, minus the faint whispers he could hear coming from upstairs.

He gave up trying to eavesdrop on them and decided to tune out the noise instead.

Regardless of how hard Owen tried to fall asleep, the thoughts of Avery's reaction after the porch plagued him. He could easily tell she was ignoring him but he was unsure as to why. There were so many reasons it could have been and he went through each one, with painstaking detail, in his mind. He wanted so desperately to talk to her but he didn't want to make an obvious scene about it. However, he had to find a way to talk to her before he left to go to the facility. For good or for worse, he wanted to talk to Avery and get everything out in the open. Even with the fear of leaving her on not the best of terms, he didn't want any more secrets between them. Eventually, due to mental exhaustion, he drifted off to sleep.

Owen awoke early the following morning. The room was just barely illuminated as dawn approached. He wiped his eyes while he slowly sat up on the couch, put his hands on his hips, and leaned to stretch his back. He then moved his head back and forth to loosen his neck. The couch was comfortable, but not being able to move around too much made him stiff. When he was done, he noticed the couch that Isaac slept on was empty. Owen's brow arched as he stood up and quietly walked around in search of Isaac.

He peaked out the window and saw Isaac leaning against one of the trees outside and he seemed to be just staring out into the distance. If he had to guess, Isaac was looking toward where the sun would rise. Owen slid on a pair of flops and walked outside and was greeted by a slight chill in the air. Isaac never turned around as Owen walked across the yard and to the left of him.

"You're up pretty early," Owen commented.

"I had trouble sleeping so I figured I go take in a peaceful sunrise," Isaac replied as he slightly turned his head toward Owen.

"I don't blame you. I'll let you be," Owen said as he patted Isaac on the back and began to walk away.

"You don't have to go. I could use the company," Isaac quickly said, causing Owen to stop.

"Is everything okay?" Owen asked while he returned to his original spot next to Isaac.

"You mean besides the fact that we are about to go on a dangerous mission that could result in the death of my daughter? Sure…everything is okay," Isaac responded while he continued to look toward the skyline.

"Maybe we will find a way to stop her without killing her," Owen optimistically countered.

"I truly hope so but if not, I am going to trust in whatever you decide," Isaac replied.

"Wait, what? Why me?" Isaac's statement made Owen flustered.

"Are you good with keeping this conversation between just the two of us?" Isaac inquired.

"Of course. What's going on?" Owen asked as his brow arched with curiosity.

"I don't know if I can kill Astrid. I would like to think that I could if she is that far gone and evil, but I don't know. My wife asked me to kill the creature if she fully transitioned and it took how many years and innocent lives lost before I was able to do it? I fear that the love I have for my daughter will cloud my judgment. I would remove myself but I feel that I need to be there. I am responsible for the facility and everyone inside of it, not to mention the safety of the people on this mission and…" Isaac responded but then paused.

"And what?" Owen asked.

Isaac finally turned around enough to completely face Owen. "And to see if I can get my daughter back. The real one. The one that used to be a daddy's girl and had such trust, respect, and love for me. Not this dark shadow of her former self that you encountered. Deep down, she's a good person. I would have done this sooner but she has been so elusive that even I could not find her." Owen could hear

66

Isaac's voice crack sporadically throughout the conversation while his eyes were glassy. It bothered Owen to see Isaac tortured like this.

"You are trusting me to decide on how to handle Astrid if you can't do it with a clear mind?" Owen asked. He had a feeling that was where Isaac was headed and it was confirmed when he nodded his head.

"I can do it but why me?" Owen inquired.

"Because from what I have seen, you are the best of us and I don't just mean your control over the chimera or your skills in battle. You have been able to make the tough decisions time and time again and you have put the lives of others before your own on multiple occasions. I am quite impressed by your character. In all my years on this Earth, there are few people that I have encountered who match your integrity and how brave you are to do what is right. It's something I admire about you," Isaac responded while he put his hand on Owen's shoulder and smiled.

Owen half-smiled before he took a step back and scoffed. "Cassandra said something similar to me before we made our way to the mountain."

"I wonder how many more people will have to tell you before you believe it," Isaac commented and then winked.

Owen scoffed again. "Look, I really appreciate it but I'm not anywhere near the high standard that you, or others, see me at. If anything, I look up to you because what you describe about me is what I see in you. I feel like I have made too many mistakes to earn such admiration."

"Thank you but I hope that is just you being humble and not because you can't see what I, and others, see in you. The potential for greatness. We all make mistakes. Heck, I've made thousands of them, but it's how we handle ourselves afterward that is one of the many things that define us. So yes…if I can't make the right decision, then my mind will be at ease with whatever you decide to do, regardless of the outcome," Isaac said and then smiled.

"Thank you. I'll do my best," Owen replied. He was honored that Isaac felt that way about him, to the point that a smile broke through, but the weight of the responsibility was heavy. Being the one to decide Astrid's fate quickly made its nerve-racking appearance as his mind began to think about all the possibilities of things that could happen when they reached the facility.

"If I may be so bold, I feel that you and Avery would make a lovely couple." Isaac's comment caught Owen off guard, causing him to momentarily choke on his spit.

"What…what makes you say that?" Owen stammered.

"I may be old, but I'm not blind. I see the spark between you two," Isaac replied while he grinned.

"It's that obvious, huh?" Owen inquired as his head sunk between his shoulders while his face crinkled from embarrassment.

Isaac sighed. "Owen, if you haven't realized it already, your life is unconventional, to say the least. Don't let conventional thinking stand in the way of you and your happiness. There is nothing to overthink here. You have spent a lot of time with her and you seem to like her very much. With Hailey not in the picture anymore and the fact that you have obviously moved on, there should be nothing holding you back. Just talk to her. I'm sure she feels the same way but nothing will happen if nobody talks," Isaac replied and then shrugged.

"I already know how she feels but how did you know about Hailey and I," Owen asked as his brow knitted.

"We were side-by-side in battle on numerous occasions and during the few moments of rest that we received, we talked. I asked her what was bothering her since I could tell her mind was preoccupied with other matters. That is when she opened up about what happened between you two. She meant everything she told you; however, she was still dealing with the emotion of the tough decision that she made. In any case, I'm glad Avery told you how she felt about you. What's the holdup then?" Isaac asked.

Owen let out a long exhale while he awkwardly looked away for a moment before he responded. "She didn't tell me. She told the chimera back at the farm."

"And Avery must not have realized that you have access to the chimera's memories. On top of that, you apparently have not informed her of this fact yet. Fascinating," Isaac said and then began to chuckle to himself.

"What?" Owen was dumbfounded by Isaac's response and laughter.

"It amazes me how you find ways to make your life harder than it should be. If you only talked to her sooner, you would not be in your current predicament." Before Owen could respond to his remark, Isaac raised his hand to stop him. "I'm sure you had your reasons. Still, you should talk to her soon. Preferably today since we leave tomorrow."

Owen smiled. "Thank you and you're right. I'll talk to her today."

The two stood there, in silence, as they watched the sun break the horizon. Not too long after that, the two of them stepped back inside. By then, Cedric was awake and in the kitchen looking through the refrigerator and the pantry.

"Is the king going to cook for his peasants?" Owen jokingly asked.

Cedric chuckled. "Well, I have to keep the commoners happy." Isaac and Owen both smiled at his comment. "Seriously though. Isaac has been gracious enough to play host to us so it's the least I can do."

"I appreciate it. Do you need any assistance?" Isaac inquired.

"I got this but thank you. Besides, that would defeat the purpose. If I need help, I will recruit some lucky bystander," Cedric replied as he gathered the items he needed.

Moments later, Cedric began to cook, and the smell must have traveled quickly since everyone else began to make their way to the kitchen. Their eyes beamed at the assortment of eggs, bacon, sausage, toast, and pancakes that Cedric prepared. Bailey and Selena jumped in to help with the rest of the preparations, including drinks, so that everyone could eat. Similar to the previous night, everyone found a spot to eat but unlike last time, it was quieter. Owen presumed it was due to his friends still feeling sleepy.

As people finished, they thanked Cedric, Bailey, and Selena and proceeded to get cleaned up and ready for the day. Besides waiting, Owen took the opportunity to get himself ready first. He knew he had just today to talk to Avery and he didn't want to waste any time. Once he was done, he awkwardly roamed the house and made small talk until he knew Avery was finished. As he wandered about, he ran into Alyssa.

"Hey there. How are you feeling about tomorrow?" Owen asked.

"Nervous. I would be lying if I said otherwise. You?" Alyssa inquired.

"Same. There is so much that could go wrong or change. I also fear how Astrid will react when she sees us," Owen responded.

"True. I just hope that whatever happens, my family is spared. To me, that is what matters the most," Alyssa mentioned before she paused and crossed her arms as her eyes narrowed. "However, messing with me and especially my family doesn't sit well with me. Once my family is safe, if there is any way we can make her pay, then I am all for it."

"I'm sure there will be but until then, try not to worry about your family. I will do my best to ensure your family stays safe," Owen said as he gave her a quick pat on her arm and a heartfelt smile.

Alyssa smiled back. "Thank you and I feel like you would. Just remember, if you don't, that spell that turns people into frogs is a real thing." She winked while she passed him and walked toward the master bedroom.

"You're joking…right?" Owen called out but Alyssa didn't respond and just kept walking. "I hope she's just kidding," Owen mumbled under his breath before he proceeded upstairs. As he walked into the room where he changed the night before, he was startled. Sitting on the edge of the bed was Avery.

"Sorry, I didn't mean to scare you," Avery said with a slight grin.

"No, no…it's all right. It works out because I have been searching for you for a while now. You are not an easy person to track down and the chimera can actually do that," Owen responded as he grinned. He then turned around and closed the door. He hoped his response masked the immense fear he felt inside, coupled with the anxiety from knowing they were finally going to talk.

"Before you say anything, I just wanted to tell you that I'm sorry about being distant after what almost happened on the porch," Avery quickly said while she stood up.

"It's okay. Actually…" Owen partially replied before Avery cut him off.

"No, it's not okay. Especially now that you are running back off into danger. Here you are, trying to talk to me, and I hid and ignored you like a child. I'm sorry. You see…I have been bottling up something for a while now…"

"I know, you…" Owen tried to speak but was unsuccessful.

"No, you don't know. I haven't told anybody and it has been something that I have been struggling with myself for some time now. I need to tell you this and I'm sure I will stumble across my words and it won't be anywhere near as perfect as it is in my head, but I need to tell you everything. I mean…I died. You even died as well, but we were both lucky enough to come back to life. How many more times do you think we will have such luck? So, I have these feelings and of course, nothing can be simple and…"

"Avery!" Owen interjected. This caused her flustered speech to come to a halt.

"You did tell someone," Owen softly added. Avery's brow knitted as her head tilted sideways. "You told the chimera."

"How…" Avery stuttered to just get that single word out.

Owen took a deep breath to calm his nerves. "Even though I can't control the chimera, we still share memories."

Avery stood still for a moment, then her eyes grew wide and her jaw dropped. "Oh my gosh. So, this entire time since the farm, you have known how I felt and said nothing?"

"I tried, but the timing was never good," Owen responded.

"Timing was never good. 'Hey Avery, got a moment. Just wanted to let you know that I heard what you told the chimera and I care enough about you to want to talk about it now. I don't want this to continue and you find out later that I knew the entire time and you end up feeling like a fool.' Gee, that took less than thirty seconds!" Avery's tone became more and more aggressive the longer she spoke as her eyes glared at him.

"I'm sorry. I should have told you sooner. I wanted to but I also needed time to process everything you said, along with all my feelings as well. Then, things just became crazy with the mission and I didn't want to try to quickly squeeze in an important talk. I was also afraid I would possibly mess up your concentration, which could've gotten you…"

"Killed. Yeah, well that happened anyway," Avery blurted out which interrupted Owen's frantic speech. She then stomped past him with a frown on her face and a furrowed brow and reached for the doorknob. Avery opened the door and proceeded to leave.

"I don't know how much time I have left!" Owen called out. Avery stopped just past the doorway but didn't turn around. "I don't want us to part ways like this. Not until you know that I too share similar fears and hesitations as you do. Not only that, but I also share how much I care for you…in the same capacity that you care about me. To use your words…I like, like you."

Avery scoffed in amusement as she turned around, her frown now replaced with a smile, accompanied by glassy eyes. She took a few steps back into the room to stand near him. "What about all the fears and hesitations?" Avery softly asked.

"All I know is that I want to be with you. Someone who has always been there for me. A person who makes me smile and feel good about myself, even when I don't believe it. Someone who is as beautiful on the inside as she is on the outside," Owen softly replied as he slowly moved closer to her. He then put his left hand on her hip and used his right hand to brush away a stray tear that ran down her cheek before he placed it on her hip as well. "To be clear, I am talking about you."

Avery laughed and then wiped her eyes and moved her hair away from her face. She then placed her hands on his arms. "I would hope so. Also, I feel the same way about you." Owen noticed her eyes phased to the sky-blue color of her cyclops.

"Your eyes," Owen muttered.

"I know, I know. Don't tease me. Some of us aren't lucky enough to have such control over our emotions like you," Avery light-heartedly responded.

"I meant your eyes are blue again," Owen softly responded.

"Oh," Avery replied as she cringed from embarrassment. "It happened late last night. It's a shame because I was beginning to enjoy the new color."

"It's okay. I'm fond of the original color anyway," Owen said and then winked.

"Thank you," Avery replied and then smiled before she briefly turned her head. She looked back at Owen and as she did, her eyes transitioned back to human. Then, her hands moved around the back of his neck while they locked eyes. They affectionately gazed upon each other as Avery raised herself up until she was on her toes. At the same time, Owen slightly bent over to be within inches of her face.

"I don't want to be afraid anymore," Avery whispered.

"Neither do I," Owen whispered back.

Their lips slowly grew closer and closer, as if each of them was waiting for the other to stop them. Then, they smiled right before their lips gently touched and their eyes closed. Their kiss was soft and passionate as they pulled each other even closer until their bodies met. Owen was overwhelmed with joy. With her, he felt whole and he knew in his heart she mattered the most to him. As the kiss continued, it slowly became more intense as their passion built.

"What!" Owen and Avery were startled while they stumbled away from each other. It was then that Owen realized the door was wide open. As the two of them looked in the direction of the doorway, they saw Hailey.

CHAPTER 6

Hailey's jaw dropped and her brow furrowed while she slowly shook her head in disbelief. Her lips then began to quiver while tears formed in her eyes as she started to take a few steps back from the doorway.

"Hailey." Avery was only able to get out one word before Hailey shook her head faster and then walked away.

"Hailey!" Avery shouted as she chased after her. Owen didn't move from his spot for he was still in shock at what just occurred.

After a few seconds, Owen shook his head to snap out of his trance and then he scurried down the hall in the direction that he heard a door slam. As he was about to pass the steps, he heard a commotion downstairs. There were too many people talking at once for him to know what was happening. He was frozen, not knowing if he should continue to the bedroom to help smooth over the current drama that he was a part of or go downstairs to see what was wrong. His head whipped back and forth while he fidgeted in place as he struggled with his decision.

"We got a problem!" Bailey yelled.

"Dang it," Owen muttered to himself before he ran down the steps. When he reached the bottom, he noticed everyone but Caine and Alyssa gathered around the front door. Caine stood anxiously in the hallway while Alyssa stood up against the family room wall to remain out of sight. Before Owen could say anything, he heard a scream from outside. It was Cedric.

Owen maneuvered his way past everyone until he reached the doorway and witnessed something that took his breath away. There was a large black sack lying on the porch with the heads of the three people that Cedric told to go back to the city positioned on top of it. To make it worse, there was blood splatter all around them. It was a horrific sight. The eyes of all three heads were still opened in terror and the necks were not severed cleanly. The torn, dangling flesh around the bottom of the necks indicated they were torn off their bodies. Cedric was on his knees, distraught, while Selena leaned over him with her hands on his shoulders, trying to comfort him.

"Did you see who did this?" Owen inquired.

"No. There was a quick knock at the door and by the time I got here, whoever did this was gone," Bailey replied.

"It was obviously Astrid's doing, or at least one of her followers," Abigail commented.

Owen glanced over to Isaac and noticed his eyes narrow before he leaned over and uncovered a piece of paper lodged under the sack. Owen could see Isaac's shoulders slouch and a frown form as he read. He then handed the note over to Owen, who read it out loud.

"Bring me Alyssa tonight or else I will add more heads to this sack."

"What do we do?" Owen asked Isaac while he handed the note to Bailey.

"We stick to the plan, but we leave soon. I don't want any more unnecessary bloodshed," Isaac replied as he stared off in the direction of the mountains.

"We'll be ready. I will inform Alyssa," Abigail said. She then patted Owen on his shoulder as she passed him to go back into the house.

"Everyone else back inside and I suggest, for safety reasons, that we don't venture outside until we are done. I will stay out here with Cedric and Selena and take care of this," Isaac solemnly said. Everyone nodded and quietly went back inside.

"Where are Avery and Hailey?" Bailey asked as her eyes panned the area.

"I presume they are still upstairs," Owen replied.

"All right. I'll let them know what's going on," Bailey said and as she turned around, Owen grabbed her shoulder.

"I would wait until they make their way down here," Owen suggested while his face cringed.

Bailey's brow knitted for a moment. Then, she put her hands on her hips. "What did you do?"

"Nothing!" Owen blurted out but Bailey did not change her expression. "I don't know...everything. All I know is that they need some time to talk and as much as I want to go up there and be a part of that discussion, we now have our current predicament in front of us," Owen added as he raised his hands briefly before letting them flop down on either side of him. Bailey's lip curled upward but then she put her hand on his shoulder before she walked toward the stairs.

"Where are you going?" Owen asked.

"They aren't mad at me," Bailey responded and then winked before she continued toward the stairs. Owen gulped while his heart sank to his stomach.

"They aren't upstairs," Caine interjected.

"Where'd they go?" Owen asked as Bailey stood to the side of him.

"While everyone was out front, Hailey stormed out the back door with Avery hot on her trail, pleading for her to stop. Hailey seemed quite upset so I am going to take a wild guess and say that is because of you," Caine responded as he smirked.

"It's one of my talents, unfortunately," Owen said before he turned to Bailey. "Do we go after them?"

Bailey jogged over to the back door and opened it. She then glanced around for a bit before she came back inside and closed the door. The entire time, Owen felt as if the air had left his body as he waited in anticipation.

"There's no sign of them," Bailey mentioned while she approached Owen.

"I should go look for them," Owen replied and as he began to walk away, Bailey grabbed his wrist to stop him.

"Whatever it is, let them work it out. Besides, you don't have time for this. I'm sorry, but you need to leave soon."

"I need to help make this right. Besides, I don't want to go without saying goodbye," Owen frantically responded.

"You don't have a choice," Bailey softly responded. Owen pressed his lips firmly together and clenched his fists. He wanted so badly to go after them, but Bailey was right.

"Who knows, maybe they will get back in time. If not, I'll talk to them and explain everything. It's probably better that I talk to them anyway before you make things worse," Bailey joked as she gave Owen a firm pat on his arm while she smiled.

"Probably so," Owen meekly replied with a crooked smile.

"It will be okay. Now, before this moment gets too girly, I need to take care of some things," Bailey said and then walked away.

"It won't be okay unless you get your head in the game," Caine mentioned as he leaned against the wall in the hallway with his arms crossed and a crooked grin.

"My head is in the game," Owen countered.

"No, it's not. It's on the sideline, participating in whatever drama that you caused. So, unless you want to see them again, I suggest you focus on the mission. I don't care how you do it. Killing Astrid, completing the mission to get a gold star from Isaac, staying alive for your friends…it doesn't matter. Pick one and use that as your motivation," Caine sternly responded as he removed himself from the wall and moved just enough forward to not be in the sunlight.

"You're right. I didn't realize you cared so much for my well-being," Owen mocked.

"No, I just want Astrid dead, but whatever floats your boat," Caine responded as he smiled and walked away.

Even though Owen knew what to do, he still didn't like it. He felt both frustrated and anxious at the same time. He finally thought he was in a good place but now everything was up in the air again. Owen wanted to make sure Hailey was okay and to apologize about how she found out. Even more, he wanted to talk to Avery again to make sure that she was good...that the two of them were good. He so desperately wanted to tell her goodbye and hold her again for he didn't know if that opportunity would present itself after today. He wanted to speak to them in person and not over a phone call or a text message. It seemed their phones were left at the house anyway so he couldn't even text them to at least come back. For a while, Owen paced around the house, looking out the window from time to time in hopes he would get a glimpse of them, but to no avail.

Eventually, Isaac, Cedric, and Selena came back inside after they handled the unfortunate situation on the porch. He overheard that since the bodies were missing, they did a quick ceremony and burned the heads of the victims. Cedric sat down at the kitchen table and grunted as he slammed his fist on the table. It sounded so loud that Owen was surprised the table didn't break. Isaac put his hand on Cedric's shoulder before he sat down next to him to talk. Selena walked past the table and headed toward the basement steps.

Abigail walked up to Owen, who was between the kitchen and the family room. "What do you think we should bring with us?"

"Nothing," Isaac blurted out before Owen could respond. "If we can get into the facility, then all the supplies we will need will be in there. If not, we will be back here quicker than we planned. Carrying extra supplies will just be a burden, especially if we are having to fight for our lives. Also, leave your phones here. We don't need Astrid gaining access to those and besides, she won't let us keep them anyway."

"Well, I guess it won't take me long at all to get ready. I will let Alyssa know," Abigail said and then walked toward the master bedroom.

Owen decided to go as well to get himself ready for the upcoming journey, which was nothing more than a quick change of clothes and some nourishment for the road. He felt weird not bringing anything else. He was so used to having at least a backpack fully stuffed with various items, even when just traveling from one safe house to another.

"We need to leave soon," Isaac announced from the foyer. It didn't take long for Owen, Alyssa, and Abigail to make it over to him. The rest of the group, except for Caine, Hailey, and Avery, joined them too. Then, numerous farewells began among everyone.

"Good luck out there. Bring justice to all those that have fallen because of her," Cedric said as he gave Owen a firm handshake.

"Will do," Owen responded. He turned around and was met by Selena.

"Be safe and don't let your hatred of Astrid cloud your judgment. I wish I could offer more than just my words. Just don't lose sight of yourself." She gave Owen a sympathetic smile before she hugged him.

"You've done so much already and I will remember your words," Owen replied. The two hugged for a few moments longer and then smiled as they backed away from each other.

"Why do you find ways to make it hard for me to have your back," Bailey commented from the right side of Owen.

"You will already have my back when you talk to Hailey and Avery whenever they get back," Owen remarked as he glanced around the area. "I wish they were here. I hate to leave like this."

"I know, but you need to get moving and do more of that hero stuff that you do so well. I will keep things in check here," Bailey said as she grinned.

Owen rolled his eyes and chuckled. "I don't know about that hero stuff but thank you…for everything. I'll miss how you always find a way to keep me grounded and how you have always been there for me."

"You act like you aren't going to see me again. Don't worry, even without my sweet, insightful advice you will survive," Bailey teased.

Owen snorted. "Yes, so sweet." He then extended his hand. Bailey looked at his hand and then pushed it aside and hugged Owen.

"I was trying to do you a favor since I know you hate hugs," Owen commented.

"I'll let it slide this time," Bailey replied before she let go and walked away. Out of the corner of his eye, he noticed Caine standing in the hallway so he made his way over to him.

"You're not going to get all weepy on me now, are you?" Owen sarcastically asked.

"No, but I am going to give you some advice, and as much as it pains me to say it, Selena is right. Don't lose yourself. You already tried that back at the warehouse and if I didn't swoop in to save you, your head would be on her mantle right now. Trust me, I would love to tell you to slowly, yet painfully rip her deceitful heart from her chest and bring it back to me, but I won't. You can't beat her in a straight-up fight. You need to be smarter than her. You must be strategic, even if it takes breaking some righteous codes that you may have. It's the only way you will gain her trust and be left standing victorious at the end," Caine said as he stared intensely at Owen the entire time.

"Then I would lose myself, wouldn't I?" Owen countered.

"True, but it's only temporary so it's okay," Caine retorted and then smirked.

Owen scoffed in amusement. "Thank you for the advice and, I can't believe I'm going to say this, but for also being a good friend. Something that I wasn't expecting, but glad it happened."

"Likewise," Caine replied. Owen then shook Caine's hand and walked away.

"Owen," Caine called out. He stopped and turned around to see what Caine wanted. "Now, if there is a chance that you can bring me her heart, as a gift for a good friend, I would appreciate it," Caine added as a devious smile formed.

Owen smiled. "I'll see what I can do." He then turned back around and headed out the door to meet the others outside.

When Owen was outside, he noticed that Isaac, Abigail, and Alyssa were already in a truck that had a trailer attached to the back. In the trailer, there were two ATVs that could fit two people each. He walked up to the truck and saw that Isaac was driving, while Alyssa was in the passenger seat and Abigail was in the backseat. Owen grabbed the door handle, but he didn't open the door. Instead, he looked at the house one more time in hopes that he would see Avery, but there was no sign of her or even Hailey.

"Goodbye," Owen whispered before his head sunk into his chest. Shortly after, he got into the truck and Isaac drove away.

"It will be a few hours before we reach the point that we will have to switch to the ATVs. Even then, it will take some time to reach the facility because we are not going to drive straight to the cabin. We will stop a mile out and travel the rest of the way by foot. That way, not only will we not bring attention to ourselves sooner than we want, but it won't startle the Amarok. Until we reach the ATV point, I suggest if there is anything about the mission that we can discuss now, then we should. Once we reach the point of the ATVs, it will be too loud and quite frankly too late to strategize anything," Isaac suggested while he kept his eyes on the road.

Silence filled the truck for a moment before Owen spoke. "Is there any spell you can cast that will disrupt Astrid's psychic abilities?"

"I don't know of a particular one geared toward psychic abilities. Maybe a form of a confusion spell if I had the proper ingredients. That could cause a similar result. Why?" Alyssa asked.

"I'm curious to know as well," Isaac added.

"I was taught that a person could not survive having two creatures within them. That the brain could not handle it, but then Astrid informed me that it could be done if a person was a strong enough psychic. So, maybe if we disrupt her abilities, it would weaken her...or worse," Owen replied.

Isaac scoffed. "What my daughter told you is true, yet misleading."

"Shocker. Astrid lied," Abigail sarcastically said.

Owen shook his head. "Can you clarify? What is misleading?"

"It is true that only a powerful psychic can handle having two creatures inside their mind. Anyone else would go insane and eventually die as their brain would just shut down. However, it's near impossible to survive a second gem's third-day transition," Isaac responded.

"Why?" Owen asked.

"There are multiple factors involved. First, you would have to be lucky enough to choose another gem that is compatible with you. Next, the energies between the two creatures would have to be in sync. Finally, the hardest obstacle, you would have to get past the gem's fail-safe magic against this," Isaac explained.

"What do you mean by that?" Alyssa inquired.

"To prevent people from becoming too powerful, the gem's magic prohibits humans from having multiple gems within them. If a person were to grab a second gem and be fortunate enough to pass the first two obstacles, the gem's magical fail-safe would trigger on the third day and kill the human and both of the creatures," Isaac replied.

Alyssa shrugged. "Without examining one of these gems further, I can only conclude that either she found a way to remove the fail-safe or…"

"Dark magic," Isaac interrupted.

"Exactly," Alyssa remarked. Owen's eyes grew as he turned his head to look at Abigail, who shared a similar expression. As he was trying to absorb everything he just heard, Isaac continued to talk.

"That is my fear. I know it's been ages since I have seen her but I know my daughter. There was something off about her. I don't think she is consumed by darkness, but it has changed her somehow."

"After talking with you and getting a read on everyone back at the house, I agree. You and Abigail's auras are similar. Owen's as well, but his is different. Not in an evil way. It's intriguing as to why since I never came across an aura like his before," Alyssa commented before she glanced at Owen in the rearview mirror.

"That's because he's the chosen one," Abigail mocked as she winked at Owen. This caused him to scoff in amusement.

"Long story short, I went through a transition and now the magic of the gem is a part of me. I am truly a hybrid, not just one formed by magic," Owen explained. He paused for a moment before his eyes grew wide. "All this happened without any kind of dark magic," Owen blurted out.

Alyssa smiled. "I didn't think so, but thanks for clearing that up. Now, with Astrid, her aura is similar to another person that has a creature within them. The person's aura will change slightly depending on the type of creature, but that's about it. However, Astrid's aura does have shades of black, which indicates she has darkness within her. It doesn't mean she is evil, but I should have listened to the uneasy feelings I had about her, or else I may have not been in this predicament."

"So, you think all her actions derive from whatever dark magic she partook in?" Abigail asked.

"As much as I wish I could say yes to that, I can't. I'm sure part of her actions are driven by this darkness, but not all of it. The majority is probably due to centuries of pain that started back when I had to kill her mother…the wyvern. If anything, I bet the darkness is feeding off her pain," Isaac solemnly replied.

"Wait, what happened?" Alyssa loudly asked. Isaac then took the time to retell the story that he told the rest of the group to Alyssa. To pass the time while Isaac talked, Owen mindlessly stared out the window. It didn't take long for his mind to wander over to Avery but as much as he hated leaving how he did, he knew Bailey would explain everything to Hailey and Avery when they returned. It wasn't perfect, but Bailey's explanation was better than nothing at all. Then, a small smile came forth when he realized he and Avery finally talked and got everything out in the open. Even more…the talk went well. Sure, he wished he could have gone into greater depth about his feelings and talked to her more about hers. Maybe even spend more time alone with her, but at least they talked and had their moment. Now, he hoped to not only complete the mission but also to make it back to Avery alive.

Once Isaac was done explaining Astrid's backstory to Alyssa, everyone remained quiet as the town became smaller and smaller until it was no more. In return, the mountains grew bigger and bigger with each passing moment as they grew closer.

"What's an Amarok? I have heard that name a few times already. I guess it's some creature?" Alyssa inquired.

"A large, powerful wolf from the Inuit mythology. It's a lone wolf, standing around thirty feet tall," Owen answered. Alyssa scoffed.

"What is it?" Abigail asked.

"Do you have any idea when it will transition back to a human?" Alyssa asked.

"No one knows since it is very unpredictable. Why's that?" Isaac asked.

"Because I think I just found a possible way to delay the ritual," Alyssa said as her smile grew.

"Well, don't keep us in suspense. What is it?" Abigail inquired.

"The ritual must be performed outside so the moonlight from the full moon is shining down upon the symbols on the ground that I will have to make." Alyssa paused with her brow raised while her eyes bounced from each person in the truck, waiting for someone to see her point.

Owen chuckled to himself. "The Amarok," Owen muttered.

"Exactly. I need direct moonlight so I presume there aren't too many places for that where we are going, so all you have to do is lure the Amarok to that area. It will be hard to perform the ritual if there is some monster-wolf attempting to eat everybody," Alyssa added as her smile grew.

"That may just work. From what I understood from Marcus's last message to me, she hasn't left the facility. That, and the Amarok hasn't strayed far from its position. Therefore, she may not realize that there are limited options as to where it could be held. She may think that the ritual could be held far enough away from the Amarok to not warrant any concern. Without any recon, she won't know the area as well as we do," Isaac commented. The group smiled at their new plan.

The rest of the trip was filled with discussions about the details of the plan to prolong the ritual. They discussed which places near the facility would be open enough to have direct moonlight shining through. They also talked about the various ways to coax the Amarok to the location that was chosen for the ritual. Luckily, the locations that Owen and Isaac could think of were near each other so it wouldn't take much to detour the Amarok if needed. The locations were on or near a clearing on a cliff so that added complexity to the plan since there were fewer escape routes. Although Astrid could fly, the plan was geared toward delaying Astrid, not killing her. At the same time, the Amarok could kill Astrid if it got ahold of her.

As they talked, Owen became more hopeful. He understood the great risks involved and how easily the plan could go wrong, but it was the only hope he had so he needed to hold onto it with all his might. As they drove, the roads became more undrivable with a standard vehicle as the terrain became rockier, and there were more slopes and trees. Just as the planning ended, they arrived at their checkpoint.

As everyone exited the truck, Abigail asked a question to the group. "What happens if everything goes downhill and the ritual is completed?"

"Then it's like I mentioned before. If the spell is completed you will have a week before Astrid can summon the djinn. Also, don't forget that right after the ritual is over, Astrid will be very weak and vulnerable, but only for a short time," Alyssa replied and then turned her head to look at Isaac. "I'm sorry, Isaac. I didn't mean to sound cruel. It's just…" Alyssa paused as she searched for the best way to finish her sentence.

"It's just something that must be considered. I understand. I hope it doesn't come down to that, but I understand what you are trying to convey. It's okay," Isaac responded and then gave Alyssa a sympathetic smile.

"We will drive the ATVs from here. I will take the lead and Alyssa can ride with me. Owen and Abigail, you can ride in the other ATV. Help me get them off the trailer," Isaac said as he waved everyone on to follow him. It didn't take long to unload the trailer and secure the truck before they were ready to leave. Isaac and Alyssa got into the lead ATV and as Owen was approaching the second ATV, Abigail tapped him on his shoulder.

"Why do you get to drive? Is it because you want all the fun or is it because you think a girl can't handle one of these," Abigail teased.

"If you want to drive then have at it. That way, if this thing flips it's all your fault," Owen said and then winked as he tossed her the keys. The two then got inside the ATV and once everyone was secure, Isaac drove off with Abigail not too far behind him.

As they drove, Owen could tell they were still going deeper into the mountains, but it didn't seem they were directly headed toward the cabin. He tried to guess where they were going to end up but it was hard for him to concentrate with the rocky, uneven grassy terrain and the tree branches slapping against the ATV as they drove. He glanced over and could tell that Abigail enjoyed driving the ATV by her smile that went from ear to ear. His grip on the rail next to him tightened from both fear and trying to keep himself steady while she drove without caution. Regardless of her driving, he couldn't help not to smile from the obvious enjoyment she got from driving the ATV.

To Owen's relief, Isaac began to slow down and came to a stop in a partial clearing within the woods around them. Everyone got out of their ATVs and stretched their arms and backs from the long, bumpy journey. "Next time, I think Isaac should ride with Abigail since he is the only immortal here," Owen announced. Abigail turned around and gasped at his comment. Owen winked, which caused the two of them to smile at each other while Isaac and Alyssa laughed. Then, they each had some snacks and water to sustain them before they continued to the cabin. As soon as they were done, Isaac got everyone's attention by clearing his throat.

"It's midafternoon and I figured we would have made it to this point around late afternoon so we are making good time. We are about a couple of miles out from the cabin."

"Isn't the Amarok that same distance from the cabin," Owen mentioned as he glanced around with his eyes wide open.

Isaac smiled. "No need to concern yourself with the Amarok yet. We are positioned behind the cabin, whereas the Amarok is to the right of the cabin." Owen let out a sigh of relief.

"What's the plan?" Abigail inquired.

"The plan is that we are going to travel by foot until we can see the cabin. Then, we will stop and I will venture on to find Marcus and the trainers and inform them of what's going on. You, Owen, and Alyssa will stay put. After I brief them, Marcus and I will coax the Amarok over to where we think the ritual will occur. The trainers will be instructed to make their way over to your group. Once the Amarok is in position, Marcus and I will head back and meet with the rest of you. From there, Marcus and the trainers will head to the ATVs and then make their way to the truck. Marcus knows the location of the house back in town so there is no issue there. The rest of us will head to the front of the cabin and find a way to get my daughter to come outside. When it's time to talk to her, I will discuss the terms about us entering the facility. The Amarok will be just far enough away so Astrid won't see it," Isaac responded.

"What if the Amarok leaves before the ritual starts?" Alyssa asked.

"It's territorial and I presume it has claimed the entire area that the cabin is in and then some. We are probably in its territory now. With some food, and if it's still injured, it may not wander far. Besides, even if it did, the ritual will cause enough noise to make it come to investigate. Especially, if it's already near the site," Isaac replied.

"Sounds like a plan. We should get moving soon," Owen suggested. The rest of the group agreed and left soon after.

Isaac led the way with Alyssa behind him, then Abigail, and then Owen following up in the rear. There wasn't much of a path so the group had to mind their footing on the rocks and sticks on the ground. As they hiked, they pushed away the branches from the smaller trees and brush that covered the area while they walked. The closer they got to the cabin, the sparser the vegetation on the ground became. Even the ground was now easier to walk upon as it became more even and the consistency was more dirt, with some gravelly spots.

The entire time, Owen didn't have to transition in order to keep the pace up. He enjoyed being able to admire the hike without the chimera's senses. It was quiet, with the occasional birds chirping in the distance. The warm air became cooler the deeper they entered the mountain, especially in the shaded areas. Then, without warning, Isaac threw his hand up and made a fist, which caused the rest of the group to stop. He then calmly waved everyone to come closer to him. The group approached and there it was, the cabin.

"It seems so quiet," Owen whispered.

"Okay. Everyone wait here until I return. I'm not sure how long or how difficult this will be but you must stick to the plan," Isaac loudly whispered. Everyone nodded their head so Isaac gave a quick smile and then turned around and left. Owen watched him as he cautiously walked and then disappeared as he went over a hill.

"So, do we just stand here or do we find a place to sit and relax until he gets back?" Alyssa asked. Before Owen could respond, there was a loud growl off in the distance.

"I guess Isaac found the Amarok," Abigail mentioned.

"Yeah, but that was too quick. I hear something else," Owen commented as he stared off into the woods.

Shortly after, they heard screaming, followed by Isaac, Marcus, and the two trainers sprinting toward the front of the cabin. Not too far behind them, stood the Amarok.

CHAPTER 7

Owen stood in awe at the sight of the beast. It stood almost as tall as the highest trees in the area. The Amarok's fur was all black, which made its pale-yellow eyes stand out. He could see scars on its snout, along with dried blood, and there were some additional scars on its legs as well. Its fur had some sporadic patches where there was little to no fur present. For a beast that obviously went through a war, it didn't show any signs of weakness. It took one step toward Isaac's group but then stopped and turned its head toward Owen's group. It snarled, revealing its white, sharp fangs.

"Change of plans. Regroup with Isaac, but slowly. Don't stare at it either," Owen said as calmly as he could. They began to cautiously walk toward Isaac's group. He could see Isaac standing far out in front of Marcus and the trainers and was in transition, with flames around his hands. Marcus stood his ground and glared at the Amarok with the dark eyes of the gargoyle, yet he was wobbly. The two trainers stood behind Marcus and were shaking.

Owen watched the Amarok with his peripheral vision as he walked. His plan wasn't working as the Amarok began to stalk them. He then noticed the Amarok stop and crouch down. "Run!" Owen yelled.

Abigail grabbed Alyssa's hand but Owen didn't follow. Instead, he turned to face the Amarok, and not a moment too soon as it pounced at them. Due to the Amarok's size, it was as if an eclipse occurred. Owen transitioned and threw his hands up toward it but with its size and speed, it was already right above him.

Instead of shooting fire at it, Owen dove out of the way moments before the Amarok's powerful jaws snapped where he once stood. As soon as Owen landed on the ground he turned and shot flames from both of his hands toward its face. It reared its head back as it snarled but then swiped at Owen with its razor-sharp claws. He rolled out of the way and then quickly stood up and bolted toward his friends.

Owen didn't look behind him since he already sensed the Amarok was pursuing him. As he grew closer to Isaac and Abigail, who were now side-by-side while Alyssa stood with the trainers, they both raised their hands and projected fire over Owen's head. He ran to the side of Isaac and slid on the gravel to a stop, turned around, and projected flames as well. He could feel the intensity of Isaac's flames, which far surpassed his own in both distance and heat. The Amarok stood at the edge of the forest line, growling as it stared at its prey over the wall of flames.

"Make sure you don't catch the trees on fire. We don't have the resources to extinguish the fire and we don't need another problem on our hands," Isaac called out.

"I can't keep this up for much longer," Abigail yelled. Owen could see the intensity on her face as she gritted her teeth and narrowed her eyes. She was breathing heavily and transitioning deeper and closer to phase three as her human characteristics were fading away. Isaac too was showing similar signs, but he appeared to have more control and he wasn't struggling or breathing as heavily as Abigail was. However, more red feathers formed on his skin, with a small flame encompassing them. On the other hand, even though the chimera's intensity was fierce, Owen didn't feel the strain like the others.

"Marcus! Bring the trainers back to drop point Delta and head back to town!" Isaac ordered.

"I'm not going to abandon you guys. I can fight!" Marcus loudly replied.

"Just do it! Trust me!" Isaac yelled.

"Yeah, go ahead and trust him, Marcus. See how far that will get you," Astrid said as she emerged from the cabin, along with a couple of her followers. She had a smug look on her face while the other two men had stern facial expressions.

"Isaac!" Abigail called out as she began to tremble.

"Both of you stop your flames when I tell you," Owen directed. He had an idea. It was risky, but it was the only solution he could think of to save them.

"Now!" Owen screamed. The wall of fire vanished as Owen dashed in front of them and toward the cabin. As the Amarok started to move forward, Owen shot a burst of flames at it. He then stopped and stared at the Amarok while he growled and showed his fangs. This provoked the Amarok, which caused it to raise its lip and expose more of its fangs as it growled. He then roared at the Amarok and that made it snarl and then charge at him. Owen turned and sprinted toward Astrid. Her eyes widened as Owen and the Amarok quickly approached her. Astrid darted into the air, along with one of her followers, as the other one was knocked over when Owen slid into him. As the two were falling, he could see the large paw of the Amarok just passing over them.

The two were now wrestling with each other under the chest of the beast. He cringed when he looked into the man's eyes and noticed that he had multiple pupils. Owen then heard a low growl and as he and the man looked up, they saw the Amarok's eyes staring at them. They quickly pushed off each other and scurried in opposite directions just in time before the Amarok snapped at them.

Before the Amarok could choose which one of them it wanted to pursue, Isaac hit it with another blast of fire near its hip, but only enough to get its attention. Owen knew Isaac could truly injure this creature, if not kill it, but inside, Anders still existed. As it yelped and turned around, it was ambushed from above by Astrid and her other follower. Both her flames and the shots from his pistol hit the Amarok's back. It whined and was now in distress as they continued their assault. Isaac flew into the air and sent a wave of fire at the two of them with both of his hands.

Astrid was far enough away to move in time but the man had to fly below the flames to avoid them. He aimed his gun at Isaac but before he pulled the trigger, the Amarok stood on its hind legs and snatched the man out of midair. The crushing strength of its jaws, accompanied by its sharp fangs, ended the man's life swiftly as blood squirted out from various parts of his body. The Amarok landed near Marcus and the rest of them, which caused them to scatter. It dropped the limp body onto the ground and growled at anyone close to him.

The man that Owen wrestled with took the opportunity to charge toward the trainers and Alyssa while Marcus was out of position. As the man approached, he flung his hand forward, and what appeared to be a web, shot out from his palm and toward Alyssa. The web struck a piece of a broken log that one of the trainers picked up from the ground. The man yanked the log from her hand and then made a fist with the same hand that launched the web and severed the line. Right before he flung his hand forward again, Owen rammed his shoulder into him. The man stumbled off to the side from the impact.

As the man tried to gain his footing, Marcus appeared and sent his fist through the man's chest. While the man convulsed with Marcus's hand around his heart, Marcus sent his other set of claws into the man's throat. In one motion, Marcus bellowed and thrust his arms to either side of him. The body fell to the ground while the man's head was in Marcus's left hand and his heart in his right hand. The blood poured from the body and was splattered all over Marcus, who stood there with a hardened face. His eyes shifted up to Astrid, who was in shock from his actions, while she floated above everyone. Marcus then released the heart and the head at the same time, while he kept his eyes fixed on Astrid. Owen's face crinkled when the severed head rolled to a stop and the face had a shocked expression still on it.

"You're insufferable," Astrid huffed. She then flew down and grabbed both trainers, one in each hand. They struggled until they felt her claws around their necks. At this moment, the Amarok had finished its meal and was becoming agitated by the people nearby.

"Come along, Alyssa," Astrid said as she repositioned the trainers to face Alyssa. Owen's heart dropped. He knew Astrid would have no reservations about taking a life and no one was in a position to free them from her grip. In addition, there was no time to think of a plan with the Amarok ready to attack again. He turned to look at Alyssa, who he thought took cover once everyone scattered, but Owen was wrong. He could see she was doing something to the soil and her lips were moving but he couldn't make out what she was saying. His eyes continuously bounced between Alyssa, Astrid, and the Amarok.

"Get over here now, Alyssa, or I will demonstrate what I will do to your family when you don't do as I ask," Astrid demanded.

"Don't do this Astrid," Isaac pleaded but before she could respond, the Amarok lunged. With its size and the proximity it was to everyone, the Amarok didn't have to move far for its next meal. Its eyes were fixated on Astrid and the trainers but when it went to chomp down on them, it yelped and jerked its head down to view its front left paw. The Amarok's paw was entangled in vines that sprouted from the ground. That is when Owen concluded that Alyssa was working on a spell.

"I can't hold it for long," Alyssa strained while she had her hand pressed firmly on the ground. The Amarok's attention was now on its paw as it tried to pull it away while it gnawed on the vines. Everyone was able to move further away from the Amarok, but Alyssa. She was now the closest to it, so the Amarok in its frantic state, snipped in her direction. Luckily, she was to the left of it so the Amarok couldn't get the angle to come anywhere close to her.

"You better think of something quickly because if that thing gets loose, I am going to use these two people as dog treats," Astrid called out in Owen and Isaac's direction.

Under duress, Owen and Isaac exchanged looks before Isaac spoke out. "Take us! Let the trainers and Marcus go and you can have the rest of us. That trade obviously favors you. What do you say?" Astrid's eyes narrowed while she contemplated the offer.

"It's too strong. I can't hold on much longer!" Alyssa cried out. Her face crinkled as she gritted her teeth while her arm and hand shook as her fingers dug into the soil. Owen could see with the immense straining and sweat on her face; it was only a matter of moments.

Astrid smirked before she talked. "Isaac, go to Alyssa. When I tell you, grab her and fly her into the cabin. Owen, go open the cabin door and be ready to shut it once we are all inside." Isaac nodded and flew high over the Amarok, landed near Alyssa, and put his hands on her shoulders to help put her at ease.

Owen bolted toward the cabin and as soon as he was inside, he poked his head around the door. While he waited, he had one hand on the doorknob and one on the door itself, ready to slam it closed when needed.

Alyssa yelled through her teeth as more and more of the thick vines snapped around the Amarok's paw. Being on the brink of freedom, the Amarok growled as it continued to yank and chew on the vines.

"Where do you think you're going?" Astrid called out to Abigail who was now headed toward the cabin.

"Didn't you just agree to take us as captives?" Abigail loudly responded with her arms raised to either side of her while she continued to walk.

"I didn't agree to anything," Astrid harshly replied. Abigail stopped and everyone's eyes diverted to Astrid. "However, I do have a counteroffer," Astrid added with a devious smile. No one responded. Instead, Abigail, Owen, and Isaac glanced at each other. The only sounds that could be heard were the sounds of vines snapping, a growling Amarok, and Alyssa moaning.

"Isaac and Owen stay with me. You, Marcus, and these two people will stay out here and be a distraction," Astrid added. Everyone, except for Astrid, gasped. Then, she released her grip and shoved the two trainers forward. The force of the push was hard enough for them to get within range of the Amarok as they stumbled to the ground. The Amarok's attention was on the vines, but not for long as it was almost free.

"No!" Owen yelled. He was worried not only for the trainers that were now in harm's way but also for Abigail's safety. Marcus was fortunate to be currently out of the Amarok's line of sight.

Abigail's lips pressed firmly together as her face crinkled while she looked back and forth between Owen and the trainers. "I got this!" She called out and then looked at Owen who was slowly shaking his head. She gently smiled at him before she ran toward the trainers.

"Now!" Astrid yelled as she flew toward the cabin. Isaac snatched up Alyssa and flew toward the cabin as well. As soon as Alyssa's hand left the ground, the dark green vines turned brown and became limp. As a result of the sudden change, the Amarok stumbled back from trying to pull away from the vines. Marcus, who was behind the Amarok, had to dive out of the way to avoid it.

Astrid flew directly into the cabin; whereas, Isaac and Alyssa landed in front of the cabin door and briskly entered. "Close it!" Astrid loudly directed. Owen hesitated as he watched Abigail sprint toward the trainers while she projected fire above them as a shield. The Amarok already gained its footing, so Abigail used her other hand to send fire toward it. Owen was torn. He desperately wanted to help Abigail and the rest of them but he also knew going out there could not only endanger the mission but also the lives of the people within the facility.

"Owen," Isaac softly said while he put his hand on his shoulder. Owen sighed and slammed the door shut in frustration.

"Don't pout. Do you really think Marcus could have fended off that mangy beast alone in his condition? If anything, I did you guys a favor," Astrid commented while she had a crooked grin on her face. Owen's eyes narrowed in on Astrid but his attention was quickly diverted to the weakened Alyssa who struggled to walk. He and Isaac quickly helped her into the elevator. Once inside the elevator, Owen could hear yelling and growling coming from outside the cabin, but it was silenced when the elevator door closed.

The elevator ride down felt like an eternity. No one talked or even looked at each other. The entire trip, his thoughts dwelled on the ones left outside with the Amarok. He wondered how they could escape such a huge and powerful creature. He feared more for their safety than the change in the mission. Isaac and he were capable enough to carry out the mission without Abigail. He just hoped Abigail, Marcus, and the trainers would make it back to the house unharmed. Finally, the elevator reached its destination and the doors opened.

"Welcome home," Astrid said while she exited the elevator and extended her arms out to either side.

"Thank you, but I think I'm good now," Alyssa said as she briefly patted Owen and Isaac's shoulder. She then slowly walked out behind Astrid, with Owen and Isaac behind her. Owen could hear the familiar faint sounds of the waterfall within the vast peacefulness of the main room. Owen scoffed. He didn't realize how much he missed this place until he arrived there. Not only was it tranquil, but there were many fond memories attached to it. Enough for a faint smile to appear on his face.

Astrid strolled over to a nearby nook and sat on a bench. She then waived the others over to her while she grinned. The group reluctantly did as she requested and sat down on the other benches around her.

"How are you feeling?" Astrid asked while she turned toward Alyssa.

"Worn out, but I just need some rest and I will recover," Alyssa responded.

"Well, I hope you recover quickly because I will need your help in a couple of days," Astrid countered and then turned her attention to Isaac and Owen. "I'm guessing you two are planning to find a creative way to steal the gem back."

"We wanted to make sure everyone here was unharmed and I wanted to talk you out of this insane idea you have regarding the djinn," Isaac responded.

"It's only insane to you because you are afraid of the unknown…of change. Afraid of what I will do once I have control over the djinn. Your fear is clouding your mind, so you are unable to see all the potential that this could bring," Astrid retorted while her face beamed.

"It won't bring back your mother," Isaac softly commented.

"Don't you dare bring her into this!" Astrid snapped at Isaac as her brow furrowed.

"Sorry. If it's of any consequence, I do believe your plan is brilliant. I just feel the way you are going about it is all wrong and I'm afraid that you will misuse this power. If we work together, we can use the power of the djinn properly. There's so much good that we can do with it," Isaac replied and then showed a sympathetic smile.

"No!" Astrid yelled while her eyes transitioned to the green dragon for a moment. Out of instinct, Owen growled and shot up from his seat, and then moved closer to Isaac. He glared at her with his chimera eyes. Isaac held his hand up to calm him down and

Astrid didn't even pay Owen any attention. Instead, she continued to look at Isaac. Owen let out a long exhale as he transitioned back to human and sat down again. Alyssa remained quiet and awkwardly looked away.

"You had your chance. With Mom, with me, and with countless others at your precious facility…and you have failed. So now, it's my turn," Astrid said without emotion.

"I'm sorry that I have failed you, and even your mother but I hope there is still some slim chance that I will get my daughter back. It may not be right away, but it's something that I have always wanted after that tragic day," Isaac remained calm in his response with a hint of a tear that formed in his eye. He then smiled again. "Regardless of our past, I know deep down you are a good person. Please don't continue down this path."

"Look at me as I am now and not as you remember me," Astrid briskly countered.

"Why? Because of your recent evil acts or because you let dark magic corrupt you in order to house two creatures within you?" Isaac gently responded. Astrid's eyes grew wide and then she turned to look at Alyssa. In response, Alyssa's eyes widened and she began to shake her head but before she could respond, Isaac spoke. "She didn't tell me anything. I figured it out after Owen's confusion of thinking that you solely had to be a powerful psychic to be able to control two creatures."

Astrid's eyes shifted back to Isaac and then a devious smile formed. "Both. Now before you try to continue to bore me with these pathetic attempts of humanity, I have other items to attend to. Speaking of which, would you be so kind as to give me clearance for everything within this facility? My hacker friend could only do so much so we have some access, but not everything. That, and of course there are all the hidden nooks and crannies I bet you have throughout this place. Any chance you can tell me where they are too?" Isaac only shook his head in disappointment.

"I didn't think so. No matter. In time, I will find everything else but for now, I have access to what I need. As for you and Owen, you two are free to roam anywhere you please on this floor, but this floor only. If you roam too far, I will start killing your precious employees. Alyssa, you come with me. We need to revive you since we have a lot to plan and prepare for in a short period of time," Astrid said as she grinned while she sat up.

She waited for Alyssa to shuffle her way over to her and then the two walked down the path that led to the other side of the main room. Owen presumed that she was going to take her to the medical area of the facility. The same location that he went to the first time he arrived at the facility. Before Owen and Isaac could say or do anything, two men walked past them and into the elevator. Owen figured they were to either guard the cabin, scout for the Amarok, or both.

"What do we do now?" Owen asked.

"We stick to the plan," Isaac responded. Owen's brow crinkled. "We are inside, Owen. It may be without Abigail and we are now separated from Alyssa, but we are inside. So now, we walk around to make sure everybody is okay and to see if they have any information they can give us. As we do it, we try to gather intelligence of our own. Since it's later in the day we won't be able to check on everybody, so we will talk to who we can and the rest will be tomorrow. The staff's quarters are in a separate, closed-off wing so if we are to play by Astrid's rules for now, we can't venture down there. That means only the ones we meet while we scout the main room are fair game. Tonight, we will formulate what to do next. Also, remember to eat and rest when you can and gather any supplies you need. We must be at our full strength."

"I wish I had your calm state of mind right about now. Mine is all over the place, but okay, let's do this," Owen replied. Isaac patted him on the back and they were off.

The two of them began their journey around the main garden area. As they walked, Owen had an eerie vibe about the facility. Things were the same but felt different. It was quieter than usual for this time of the day, minus the sounds of nature. Owen couldn't help but think about the memories he had of the facility while he walked. All of them were centered around his friends, both the good times and the rough times. Regardless, they were always together. It felt like it was only yesterday that he met a bunch of strangers who would end up being a large part of his life.

Owen's thoughts were interrupted by a slight nudge to his arm by Isaac's elbow. He followed Isaac's eyes and noticed one of Astrid's followers patrolling the garden area. During their walk, they noticed a few more scattered around the garden area, down the other open hallways, and in the common areas. From what they counted, there were half a dozen more followers, some human, some not, that patrolled the area. With the two that died outside and the two that went to replace them, plus possibly more elsewhere, that meant more of them must have entered after the first wave of people.

As they entered the cafeteria location near the garden, they saw a lot of the crew eating, quietly. However, when they saw Isaac and Owen, they became happy and cheered. They all ran to Isaac but the ones on the outside of the large circle around him filtered to Owen. As they did, Owen noticed one of the guards swiftly making his way over while on his phone. Then, he stopped, put the phone away, and just observed. He wondered if Astrid told him to stand down.

Next, multiple questions were quietly asked throughout the gathering. So many that Isaac raised his hand in the air to silence them all. "Listen. We can't talk much but we wanted to make sure everyone was okay. Also, to let you know that we are working on a way of freeing you from Astrid and putting a stop to her plans. I don't know how long it will take so remain strong and know that Owen and I are here for you." Owen could see the smiles of relief appear throughout the group. It made him feel good knowing that they now had hope, but also nervous because that hope relied on Isaac and himself succeeding.

They spent time talking with everybody within the group and everyone had the same information about Astrid and her followers. Unfortunately, all the information they received was nothing that they already didn't know. During this time, they decided to eat as well since their last good meal was back at Isaac's house. Afterward, the group dispersed, so Isaac and Owen surveyed the rest of the garden's main room, as well as most of the other hallways. Except for seeing guards from time to time, everything appeared to be untouched. Then, they came to the final hallway where Owen and his friends lived during their stay at the facility.

Before they started to walk, a couple of more people came up to Isaac. Owen decided to continue down the hallway while they talked. As he slowly made his way down, the weight of remorse was almost too much to handle. Most of the doors felt like headstones. He passed rooms that used to belong to Cassie, Amelia, Joshua, and Michael. His eyes welled up and he felt slightly nauseous. This feeling grew as he glanced at Avery, Hailey, and Bailey's doors. He hoped their rooms wouldn't become memorials themselves. As he stood in the middle of the hallway, he was startled by Isaac's hand on his shoulder. He whipped around and wiped his eyes.

"I'm sorry. It is as hard for me to be in this area as it is for you. I would suspect even harder for you since you spent more time together with them. Your group was one of the most tight-knit groups I have seen pass through this facility in quite some time," Isaac commented while he stood next to Owen. His eyes shifted from door to door.

"How do you deal with it? The loss of friends and loved ones. In your position, you must have seen it countless of times. I mean no disrespect by this but do you become numb to it over time?" Owen quietly asked.

"No. You never become numb to it and the hurt of losing them never goes away. The trick is to keep moving forward, for them. To live for them and never forget them as well. Eventually, one day it becomes second nature. The loss is still there but you have learned how to deal and cope with it," Isaac responded and then he put his hand back on Owen's shoulder. He didn't respond to Isaac. Instead, Owen just smiled, but even that was tight-lipped as he continued to hold back his emotions.

"If I may be so bold as to give you some friendly advice, remember the good times you had with them. Those fond memories you hold will give you strength when you have none," Isaac added. He then gave him a sympathetic smile when Owen glanced at him.

"I remember one of the last things Cassie told me was that she was thankful for being a part of this group. That, and she didn't want me to blame myself if things went wrong during our first transition. She knew I would have hated myself but she was kind and smart enough to tell me that. I will admit, it worked. Then there was Amelia, who was full of life. You couldn't help to always smile around her because of that. Well, that and her obsession over vampires," Owen said as he chuckled to himself. "Then there was Michael, who despite living in video game land, was such a loyal, and good friend. Of course, there was Joshua. He…" Owen paused because he was choked up over his memories of him. "He and I were like true brothers. I'm not even sure what else to say other than that."

"Those are the memories you want to keep close to you to help shield you from the pain of their loss," Isaac commented.

"How long will these rooms remain unchanged?" Owen inquired.

"Typically, they would have been changed out already. When new recruits make it out into the field, the rooms are remade in order to receive future recruits. Anybody from the field that comes back to the facility is housed in an entirely different wing, one that we don't have any access to at this time," Isaac replied.

"I guess I know where I am staying tonight. How about you? We can stay in the same room if you like. It will be cramped but it will do," Owen suggested.

Isaac grinned. "I know those rooms are not big at all so I will take one of the vacant rooms that was never assigned to anybody. They contain general supplies and clothes so I should be fine. I don't know what tomorrow will bring so try to get at least some sleep tonight."

"I'll try. Have a good night," Owen said.

"You too," Isaac responded as the two gave each other a partial hug. Owen then walked over to his room and went inside.

As he entered his room, it looked the same as how he left it. The only way he could tell that someone was in his room was by the lack of dust on his furniture. Owen showered and got ready for bed. During this process, he thought about the mission. Their only hope was for the Amarok to stay in the area long enough to foil the ritual. There was no other plan left to delay the ritual long enough for them to stop Astrid unless they went after the gem. If they could somehow get possession of it again, then they didn't even have to break out of the facility. They could just throw it through the portal, which would make it nearly impossible to find. At the very least, even as determined as Astrid is, it would give them enough time to find a way to stop her.

Owen plopped himself on the bed. At first, he wondered if Abigail, Marcus, and the two trainers made it back to the house all right. He feared for their safety and just hoped they found a way to elude the Amarok and make it back safely.

Then, his concerns shifted to Avery and Hailey as his mind was flooded with thoughts about them. He wondered if they resolved the issues they had between them or not. Thoughts also entered his mind about how Hailey felt towards him as well and would it be something he could fix? In addition, he hoped they understood Bailey's explanation as to why he had to leave without saying goodbye. He wished he was back at the house and with Avery but once again, fate had other plans for him. He hoped that trend wasn't going to last much longer, but first…he had to make sure his door didn't become another grave marker.

CHAPTER 8

Owen woke up early the next morning and quickly got himself ready before he rushed out of his room. Their time was running out and he didn't want to waste any of it when it came to finding a way to stop Astrid. When he entered the hallway, he didn't have to figure out which vacant room Isaac was in since he was already sitting on a nearby bench.

"Well, I guess I don't have to worry about waking you up," Owen remarked.

"I haven't been out here too long and I wanted you to rest as much as you needed," Isaac replied as he stood up.

"With two days left and no idea how to stop her, our only plan to stall her is the hope that the Amarok stays in the area we wanted it in. Of course, who knows where it could be since the last time we saw it, our friends were battling it. So yeah, not anxious to get this day started at all," Owen sarcastically responded.

Isaac smiled. "Let's go get something to eat and we can discuss it then."

The two walked down the hallway and made their way to the cafeteria. After they both went through the line to grab their food, they found a place in the far corner of the cafeteria to eat. As they sat down, Owen noticed his plate was piled a lot higher than Isaac's plate. Even Isaac stopped to gawk at Owen's plate, which was piled high with eggs, bacon, sausage, toast, pancakes, and other breakfast assortments.

"I would blame this all on the chimera's appetite, but there is definitely some stress eating going on here," Owen commented as his lip curled from embarrassment.

"That is an impressive plate. It's good that you have the chimera's strength to carry it," Isaac joked. The two smiled and began to eat their food. As they ate, the two began the discussions to formulate a plan.

"Our current situation is that we don't know where Alyssa, the ingredients for the ritual, and the gem are located. Killing Astrid would be the easiest way to stop this but you are the only one strong enough here to do it. Even if she is weakened, it's not guaranteed that I can kill her. Let's be honest, even as a last resort, you won't be able to kill her so that card is off the table. That's fine and I understand, but that leaves us with one option, the gem. She can find other ingredients and Alyssa is going to help her to save her family so the gem is the only option. It will also keep your daughter alive too. My concern is what if the Amarok isn't around to stall them if we can't find the gem? What's our next move?" Owen asked.

"You are correct to presume that the gem is the only option left to us. As for the Amarok, if that creature can't delay the ritual, then we have no other backup plan," Isaac paused and raised his hand to stop Owen from speaking. "Unless, as soon as the ritual is over, I swoop in and grab whatever vessel that the djinn will be in and fly away. Especially with her weakened, I will be quicker than her and no one else here would be able to stop me."

As Owen thought about Isaac's plan, a smile began to grow. "That's brilliant."

"Thank you but there is a flaw. When I leave, you will be left alone among a group of people who will not be happy, to say the least. You may literally have to claw your way out of that situation," Isaac countered.

Owen's excitement over the plan did not falter after Isaac's comment and his smile remained. "Stand and fight or stay behind to protect. Either way, I can handle it and it will be worth it to get the djinn as far away from Astrid as possible. This may be our only option if all else fails."

"Great. We have a plan we are both content with. Now you can enjoy the rest of your food in peace," Isaac said as he leaned back in his chair.

"I thought I was going to enjoy my food," Owen muttered as his smile disappeared. He then directed his eyes to behind Isaac. He followed Owen's eyes and turned his head to look behind him. That is when Isaac witnessed Astrid walking in their direction.

"Morning gentlemen. I'm glad to see everyone is up early. Hopefully, the two of you slept well. I know I did," Astrid cheerfully said as she stopped in front of their table. Owen did not react to her and Isaac only showed a small grin before he spoke.

"Morning Astrid. You seem to be in a delightful mood this morning," Isaac remarked.

"And why shouldn't I be? I have all the items needed for the ritual. I have my witch, I have my ingredients, and I have my gem," Astrid replied. She then reached into the top of her shirt to pull out the pouch that was attached to the silver necklace she wore. Owen and Isaac's jaws dropped while their brows raised. Astrid's smile grew larger when she noticed their reactions.

"Judging by your expressions, retrieving the gem was part of whatever plan you were trying to conceive over there to stop me. Well, let me save you some time. Please, go ahead and take it," Astrid added as she leaned forward to let the pouch dangle from her neck.

The two of them paused. What was she up to, Owen thought. After a few seconds, Isaac carefully reached out his hand to grab the pouch. As his hand got closer to the pouch, Astrid didn't flinch. Instead, she watched Isaac while she had a smug expression. Owen noticed Isaac's hand was almost an inch away from it when it stopped. "What's wrong?" Owen inquired.

"There is some unseen force that is preventing me from touching it," Isaac responded as he pulled his hand away while he shook his head.

"I had Alyssa ward the pouch that the gem sits inside of. See, if you look close enough, you can see a bunch of these cute little markings burned into the leather pouch. Also, those streaks you see on the pouch are Alyssa's and my blood. This ensures that only we can touch the pouch. I figured the two of you would try to do something so I am simply removing the temptation from the situation," Astrid proudly said.

Owen's shoulders dropped while he sighed. He was becoming more annoyed about how she was always a few steps ahead of them. "What do you plan to do with us?" Owen asked.

"I haven't fully decided yet. I heard you met a lot of people last night and I presume you will talk to the rest today. After your safety checks, there is no reason for me to keep you here or alive. Well, unless I decide to do something like having the two of you do my bidding. That, or releasing both of you so you can relay to the world the power I possess. Of course, I could just keep you around for comic relief as I watch your pathetic plans fail time and time again," Astrid replied and then smirked.

"I'm glad we can be of amusement to you," Owen sarcastically said.

"You will be of more use than that tomorrow. I can't exactly do the ritual with an Amarok roaming about so you are going to assist the few followers I have remaining here and relocate it far away from here," Astrid commented.

"How does one relocate a large mythical beast?" Owen asked.

"Have it chase you, kill it, lead it away with doggie treats, I don't care. I just want it far away before tomorrow night," Astrid countered. "Now if you will excuse me, I have much to plan for. I have guests arriving in a week and I need to also prepare for this ritual. You know the rules and when you do go back outside, you better listen to my men if you know what's good for you." She stood up and gave a fake smile before she turned around and walked away.

"I think your plan is looking better and better," Owen whispered to Isaac, who nodded his head in return.

"Come on, Owen. Let's finish our food and talk to everyone else. If she does recruit us to help move the Amarok then we will help lead it away. With our new plan in place, the Amarok is more of a distraction now and a reason for Astrid to keep us around longer. Especially, if she feels that she needs more people around to keep the Amarok away during the ritual," Isaac quietly said. The two finished their meals and ventured off to find the remaining people they had not talked to yet.

Apparently, there were more people than Owen anticipated, which was fine because it allowed them to stay inside longer. Also, it made him feel better that not only were the staff safe, but that they received hope from Isaac. He was impressed by how calm and collective the group remained and how eager they were to stand up and fight. Isaac had to defuse multiple people to keep them from acting against Astrid. He appreciated the loyalty but valued their safety even more.

They were finally done around late afternoon and to their astonishment, there was no communication from Astrid or any of her followers. They didn't even see her. To avoid having to go out in the dark, they quickly ate dinner and headed back to their rooms.

"Do you think Alyssa is still on our side?" Owen inquired as they walked down the hallway to their rooms.

"What makes you question her loyalty?" Isaac countered.

"I don't know. It's just we don't know much about her and we haven't seen her from when we first entered. It just makes me wonder about her allegiance. Even if she is a good person and is telling the truth, it may not take much from Astrid to convince her to turn on us. Especially, if her family is in danger," Owen rebutted

"True, but I like to think I am a good judge of character and I feel she does want to work with us. We just don't need to give her any reasons to doubt us or else all our hope goes out the window," Isaac responded.

"Well tomorrow should be fun," Owen said as he rolled his eyes.

"Between the Amarok and the ritual, I'm sure we will be quite entertained," Isaac responded as he smiled.

The two patted each other on the back and parted ways. Once in his room, Owen didn't waste any time getting himself into bed. Even though he wasn't tired, he forced himself to lie there with his eyes closed and refused to think about anything. He needed his rest and for his mind to be sharp, for tomorrow was the day they hopefully stopped Astrid.

His plan didn't go as smoothly as he wanted it to go. After hours of tossing and turning, he decided to get up and meditate. It wasn't something he had done in quite some time, so it took longer for him to reach his ideal state of mind, but eventually, it was achieved. When he was finished, he realized it was early in the morning. The session cleared his mind and made him relaxed enough to doze off until his alarm went off a few hours later. As Owen was finishing getting ready, he heard someone banging on his door, so he walked over and opened it.

He saw two men standing at his door with stern faces. Just a few feet behind them stood Isaac. His brow was lowered as he stared off into the distance. Owen presumed he must have been deep in thought about something.

"Astrid wants you to meet us at the elevator in thirty minutes. We are going outside to handle the Amarok situation she discussed with you yesterday," the man informed. Owen only nodded his head in response. The two men turned around and walked away.

"Personable characters, wouldn't you say," Isaac mocked as he approached Owen.

Owen scoffed in amusement. "Very, so what do we do?"

"We play the part and help relocate the Amarok," Isaac responded as the two of them slowly walked down the hallway. "The thing is, Astrid doesn't realize how vast the creature's territory is. Now that it has discovered the area by the cabin, it won't give it up so easily. We may be able to chase it away, but it won't take much for it to come back. There is still a chance it could delay the ritual."

"Let's hope so. We need all the help we can get at this point," Owen replied. The two reached the cafeteria and had a quick bite to eat before they continued their way to the elevator.

Once they reached the elevator, the two men didn't say a word. They only opened the door and everyone entered the elevator. Owen noticed the two men were carrying semi-automatic rifles. They appeared to be dressed like the mercenaries that he fought in the past. After a long, silent ride up to the cabin, they exited and were greeted by two other individuals who were guarding the cabin itself. Both were armed with the same type of weapons as the other men and were even dressed similarly. Once again, Owen presumed they were mercenaries.

"How's it going?" The man asked the cabin guards.

"Quiet. Happy to be in here and not out there with that beast," the cabin guard replied.

"Have you seen it lately?" The other man inquired.

"No, but we can only see so much from these windows," the other cabin guard responded as he peaked out the window. One of the men turned and waved Owen and Isaac to follow him. The two men, along with Owen and Isaac, exited the cabin.

Owen slowly surveyed the area but there was no sign of the Amarok. He paused as he listened but the only thing he could hear was the sound of birds chirping off in the distance. If he didn't know any better, there was no sign that a battle even occurred the other day. He hoped his friends were able to escape the Amarok because he grew weary of losing people he cared about.

"Search the perimeter and if nothing pans out, then keep extending your search until we tell you otherwise," the man directed. Owen and Isaac nodded their heads and began to walk off into the distance.

"Whoa. Don't you think you need to walk more carefully? You are making enough sound to wake the dead," the other man loudly whispered.

"It's not around here. If it were and we didn't see it, we would then definitely hear it," Owen responded while he tapped his ear.

"Are you going to be joining us?" Isaac asked since the two men hadn't moved from their location yet.

"We will but we'll be further back. Consider us your support team, so don't try anything funny," the man replied. Owen and Isaac nodded again, turned around, and continued.

"Support. More like chaperones," Owen said under his breath.

"At least they are keeping their distance. Gives us a chance to talk in private if needed," Isaac whispered.

Both Isaac and Owen transitioned to enhance their vision and hearing as they continued their search. The two of them searched for hours, in all directions around the cabin, and could not find the Amarok. They found traces of it from footprints, animal carcasses, and even some fur…but no Amarok.

"Break time," one of the men announced. At this point, due to exhaustion, the two men walked further and further behind them, with the breaks becoming more and more often. Owen and Isaac felt tired, but nowhere near the two men since being in transition gave them more endurance and stamina.

"How can a thirty-foot-tall wolf be this hard to find?" Owen remarked as he leaned over and rested his elbows on his knees.

"It may just be outside the area we searched in. There are still miles of unsearched terrain, so it could be anywhere. Especially, if it found a new area to explore after it chased off Marcus and the rest of them," Isaac replied.

"I hope they are alive," Owen commented as his head sank.

"They are," Isaac casually responded.

Owen's brow lowered as his head quickly raised. "How can you be so sure?"

Isaac chuckled. "Owen, you really need to pay attention to your surroundings." Owen glanced around their area and then shrugged his shoulders. "Not this area. We passed the area where we parked the ATVs and they were gone. In addition to that, I didn't see any evidence that the Amarok caught up to them. From the tire tracks and paw prints, it didn't pursue them for long."

Owen's head tilted. "We checked the area?"

Isaac smiled. "Yes. It was one of the first areas I checked since I had the same concern as you."

Owen let out a huge sigh of relief as he smiled and his face lit up with joy. "That's awesome!" He could feel a weight lifted from his chest for his worries turned into glee.

"Hey, can't you just fly around and see if you can find it that way? It would be a lot quicker than this," one of the men remarked off in the distance.

"Yes, but with all the leaves on the trees, I might not be able to spot it if it's lying down somewhere," Isaac responded.

"There's not that many leaves and with your eyesight, you would be able to spot a mouse," Owen quietly commented.

"True, but they don't need to know that," Isaac quietly responded and then winked. Owen smiled at Isaac's ruse. "Besides, having it still out here increases the chance of it ruining the ritual," Isaac added.

Isaac turned his attention back to the men. "However, I can fly up and scan the area to see if I see it or any noticeable movement."

The man gave Isaac the thumbs up so Isaac briskly flew into the air and above the tree line. He then slowly turned in a circle to scan the area. On his second time around, he stopped and Owen could see his eyes narrow in on something.

"I think I see some movement but I need to get a closer look. It's maybe a mile past the cabin, but the other side of the cabin, not our side," Isaac called out.

"You're strong, so why don't you carry us and your friend can follow by foot?" One of the men suggested.

"I can't. My creature is pure fire so when I fly, my hands…well my entire body, becomes very hot. The skin on your hands would be charred before we even got close. My counteroffer is for you two and Owen to follow me while I fly so I don't lose track of it." Isaac said as his bird-like eyes stared down as red feathers formed around his eyes. Owen even saw a hint of a thin flame, emanating from his eyes, slowly moving in the breeze.

The men's eyes widened from Isaac's remark about the outcome of their hands, while Owen's brow crinkled. He was unaware that Isaac's body heated up to that extent when he transitioned, but it made sense considering his creature.

"Fine, but don't fly too fast. We need to keep an eye on you," one of the men said as he and the other man stood up.

Isaac slowly glided over the trees while the others on the ground either walked or jogged depending on how well they kept up with Isaac due to the terrain. For Owen, it was a breeze, but he had to slow down to keep up with the stumbling, exhausted mercenaries that were struggling to keep up. Eventually, they reached their destination.

Isaac slowly surveyed the area and then called down to Owen. "Come on up here, Owen. Help me search the area. I will scan the areas further away while you check out the areas closer to us. I am having some trouble finding it now."

"Sure thing," Owen exclaimed and he used his claws to assist his climb up the sturdy, thick tree. About ten feet up he turned and looked at the two men on the ground, who were now sitting on a rock. "Care to join me?" Owen asked before a crooked grin formed on his face.

"We can see you from down here, thanks," one of the men called out. With that, Owen climbed the remainder of the tall tree until he reached the top. He turned and faced Isaac.

"I didn't know your body generated that much heat while you transitioned. That's got to be annoying," Owen commented.

"It would be if it were true," Isaac said and then smirked.

"Aren't you the mischievous one today," Owen said while he smiled.

"Well, my body does get warm but it doesn't get hot unless I either make it or transition very close to phase three," Isaac said. He then lifted his pointer finger, which had a flame on the tip of his finger, and blew it out.

Owen chuckled. "I didn't know you had this side to you. I like it."

Isaac smiled. "Well, it's good to have many different sides to oneself, especially when you are trying to conceal a secret conversation." As Isaac finished talking, his eyes shifted over Owen's shoulder. Owen turned his head and gasped, for he wasn't prepared for there to be another person in the tree next to them…especially Anders.

CHAPTER 9

Owen quickly looked down at the two mercenaries but there was enough leaf covered to obscure their view and the tree was tall so their words didn't reach the men on the ground. He looked back at Anders and of course, he was only wearing the special bio-shorts. Minus his hands and feet being filthy, the rest of him didn't appear to be that dirty…or injured.

"It's good to see you but I didn't know an Amarok, or even a wolf in general, can climb a tree," Owen teased; however, his light-hearted response masked his nervousness. Anders's presence had now changed everything.

"They can't and I'm not too fond of it either," Anders replied with a disgruntled look. Owen pressed his lips firmly together to keep himself from laughing.

"When did you transition back?" Isaac whispered as he floated closer to Anders.

"My concept of time is not fully with me yet, but I think it was late last night or early morning. I was maybe a quarter of a mile out from the cabin so I figured I would come back to get up to speed and help some more if needed. To my surprise, I walked back to a bunch of strangers and you guys were all gone. Then, as I was thinking of a strategy to take out the patrols and enter the facility, I saw some blonde peek her head out the cabin door," Anders replied.

"Must have been Astrid. What made you climb the tree?" Owen asked.

"There was not a safe spot for me to stake out the facility on the ground so I climbed this tree. I've only seen patrols every so often and they don't stray far from the cabin. Only the blonde…Astrid, walked out further and she seemed to be interested in the clearing right over there," Anders whispered back and then pointed toward a clearing not too far from where they were. "Who's Astrid? Is that their leader?"

"Leader and my daughter," Isaac replied.

"Your what?" Anders loudly whispered as his brow lowered.

"My daughter. There is a lot to explain. Just go to my house back in town and the rest can be explained to you. I filled everyone in about Astrid and Marcus may even have additional details about her from our many conversations over the centuries," Isaac calmly replied.

"I can stay and help," Anders offered.

"Thank you but you need to regroup back with the others," Isaac countered.

"Maybe he could fully transition when the ritual starts. It works out because now we don't have to worry about whether the Amarok will show or not. Anders can just walk in the area and fully transition," Owen suggested while he grinned.

"I see how you would be excited over your suggestion, but our original plan was off the table as soon as Anders became human again," Isaac responded.

"What do you mean?" Owen asked.

"Astrid isn't stupid and will be able to tell that the Amarok was staged. Also, Anders just transitioned back to human. Even though I'm sure he would transition back into the Amarok again, it's unfair and too risky to restart the clock on when he will transition back. It's also not common to perform back-to-back transitions so quickly. It could cause issues with who has control…Anders or the Amarok, since the mind can only take so much," Isaac explained.

"Are you sure?" Anders inquired.

"Yes. Besides, Owen and I have an alternate plan," Isaac responded.

"Well, do you see it or not," one of the men yelled.

"We narrowed the movement west of here. Just give us a few more moments and we will have an update," Isaac replied and then turned his head back to Anders. "We need to move fast because we don't have a lot of time here. Once you see us go back into the cabin, then make your move to one of the dirt bikes on the other side of the cabin. Walk it as far away as you can before you start it. I doubt they have done an inventory of everything so they will never know it was gone."

Anders huffed. "Fine. Good luck to the two of you. I hope your refrigerator is full because I'm hungry."

"You're hungry?" Owen quietly blurted out.

"Yeah, why?" Anders asked.

"No…no reason. Good luck to you too," Owen quickly responded. He hoped his response didn't raise any questions with Anders.

"Good luck and it's good to see you again. I'm thankful for everything that you helped with in this mission," Isaac added. Anders gave him a quick smile and nodded his head. Isaac then turned his attention to the mercenaries. "We're coming back down."

Isaac floated down while Owen gracefully dropped from branch to branch before he used his claws to climb the trunk the rest of the way down. When the two were back on the ground, the mercenaries approached them. "Well, did you see it?"

"No. Turns out it was a large black bear. I do not see the Amarok anywhere. It's possible that it may be miles away by now and it may or may not return," Isaac replied.

"Okay. Let's report back to Astrid. Follow us," the mercenary directed. As they walked back to the cabin, Owen and Isaac exchanged a quick look. He tried to match the same level of serenity that Isaac displayed regardless of how much of a panic he was in. Even though they had a plan if the Amarok didn't show, the fact that it is now off the table has put all the pressure on their one remaining plan. As they entered inside, the two cabin guards, along with Astrid, were sitting inside waiting.

"I was about to send out a search party for the search party. I hope that means you found the Amarok and dealt with it," Astrid said as she stood up, followed by the two cabin guards.

"There was no sign of the beast," one of the mercenaries responded. His head then lowered and his eyes shifted. He seemed nervous about Astrid's response.

"No sign. How could none of you not locate a massive, growling creature?" Astrid asked through her teeth while her eyes narrowed.

"We checked all around the cabin, and for miles, so it must be further out," Isaac commented as he stepped in front of the mercenaries. He then began to slowly walk around the side of the cabin and toward the back. Owen followed his lead, for he knew why he was moving. All eyes were now on Isaac and not the window, leaving Anders a clear path to the dirt bikes. "I would presume its territory goes for miles past where we searched," Isaac added.

"So even though we couldn't locate it, the Amarok must be far enough away to not be a threat…provided it doesn't wander back," Owen commented. He hoped his comment would add hesitation in performing the ritual tonight.

Astrid huffed. "No matter. The ritual happens tonight. I will just add some extra security to cover the perimeter to be safe. The ritual shouldn't take that long so if it's still around, we should be long gone by the time it comes back." Her face was hardened with determination before a grin broke through when she heard the elevator.

The elevator door opened and Alyssa walked out and her brow crinkled at the crowd in front of her. "Sorry. I didn't mean to intrude. I was going to start drawing the symbols outside."

"You're not intruding. We were just wrapping up. The supplies you need are near the front door and since no one was able to track down that beast, one of the cabin guards can watch over you while you work," Astrid responded.

"Thank you," Alyssa said. She gave Owen and Isaac a hint of a smile as she walked past them.

"I'll see you all again in a few hours for the big show tonight," Astrid said before she turned around and took the elevator back down.

"I guess we'll take the next one," Owen muttered. Isaac grinned but no one else reacted since they didn't hear him.

The two mercenaries, Owen, and Isaac took the elevator down afterward. It was another silent ride down and when they left the elevator, the two mercenaries walked away without saying a word. Owen and Isaac went back to the cafeteria to eat and rest from their Amarok search efforts. Afterward, they found a quiet area within the garden. They spent most of their time planning what to do once the ritual ended, which included where to rendezvous.

No matter how detailed the plan became or even the backup plans to it, the same basic goal remained. Once the ritual was completed and Astrid was drained, Isaac would grab the vessel and fly away. Once Owen was alone, he had many options to pick from. One idea was to battle the entire group to give Isaac more time to escape. Another idea was to grab Alyssa and make a run for it, which not only would save her but also bide Isaac time to escape. Then, the least likely scenario…kill Astrid while she was weakened, provided he was strong enough to do it. Unfortunately, Owen wouldn't know what to do until the time arrived. While the two chatted, Owen saw Isaac's eyes shift behind him. He turned around and saw Alyssa,

Astrid, a dozen of her followers, and a few facility staff standing together carrying crates.

"My big moment has arrived. This is centuries in the making so you don't want to miss it. The ledge that overlooks the gorge closest to the cabin. I'm sure you are familiar with it. Let's go," Astrid said as she smiled. Alyssa never looked over to Owen or Isaac and instead, stared at her feet. Owen presumed she acted that way because of her nerves.

Due to the number of people, Owen and Isaac took the last elevator up together by themselves. As the door shut, Owen turned to Isaac. "I hope this plan works. There is so much that could go wrong."

"Just like in your other experiences, once the action starts, you will know what to do. Just trust your instincts. Also, we have a plan. Heck, we have a plan with multiple backup plans and we talked about them immensely. There is nothing left to do but wait for the right time to act. My part is easy…grab the vessel and fly away. However, I don't envy your role in this plan," Isaac said and then winked with a hint of a smile.

Owen chuckled. "I don't envy it either, but I will be able to handle myself."

"Remember that confidence when we get up there," Isaac commented as his smile grew more. Owen nodded as he patted Isaac on his back.

"What do you think the crates are for?" Owen inquired.

"My guess is to put the finishing touches on the symbols. You can only do so much prep work with a big spell. The rest usually must happen either right before or during the casting of the spell," Isaac replied.

The elevator reached the top and the two of them exited out and left the cabin. They made their way toward the ledge that Astrid mentioned. It wasn't a far walk and if he stared, he could see a hint of the cabin off in the distance. Owen only saw a couple of her followers and presumed the rest went to scout the perimeter. It appeared that the ones with the guns scouted while the other two were unarmed. This made Owen feel that the two unarmed people were hybrids. He saw three of Isaac's staff of which two were the trainers that were with Marcus. Owen remembered the other person from the supply room off the main garden area, who provided anything they needed besides clothes. He then saw Alyssa and Astrid talking with the crates all around them.

"What do you mean? There is moonlight! What do you think is allowing us to see where we are walking?" Astrid yelled. At that point, Owen and Isaac rushed over to them, along with the two guards in the area.

"I'm sorry, but there must be direct moonlight, or else the spell will fail. There are just too many clouds in the sky," Alyssa replied in a panic.

Astrid got within inches of Alyssa's face. "If I find out this is a trick, I promise you I will kill each of your family members slowly and in such a disturbing fashion that the images will haunt your memories forever," Astrid said in a low, intimidating tone.

"I promise this is not a trick. I wouldn't dare risk my family's life!" Alyssa pleaded.

Owen scoffed in amusement. "All this to be stopped by some clouds."

Astrid glared at Owen. "You think this is funny?" Owen shrugged in response. A smug expression formed on Astrid's face. "Well, it's a good thing I have an alternative plan." Astrid turned a gave a quick nod to her two nearby followers. Without hesitation, they walked over to Isaac's staff members and one grabbed the supply person while the other grabbed the two trainers. All three struggled to escape their grasp but were unsuccessful.

"What are you doing?" Isaac quickly inquired as both he and Owen frantically looked back and forth between the three.

"One doesn't wait this long and not have another plan in case the first one didn't work," Astrid responded as she approached Isaac and Owen.

"What's the other plan?" Alyssa inquired.

Astrid didn't turn around to respond to Alyssa. Instead, she continued to stare at Isaac and Owen. "You see, basically there are two parts to this ritual. The first part is to free the djinn from this gem," Astrid said as she raised the pouch in her right hand. "The second part is to imprison it within this locket," Astrid continued as she raised her left hand which revealed a gold, oval locket. "Now, since we can't do the first part, we will have to find another way," Astrid said as a sinister smile appeared on her face.

"Don't do it. They are innocent," Isaac exclaimed.

"Do what?" Owen asked.

"She is going to place the gem on one of them and when the third day arrives and they transition, the djinn will appear," Isaac replied and as he did, Owen could hear the three staff members mumbling to each other.

"How is she so sure that they will not survive? I thought all the people that worked here were the ones that didn't want to become a hybrid," Owen said as his eyes bounced between Isaac and Astrid.

"Tell him, Isaac," Astrid instructed.

"Because not all the staff members were the chosen ones. Some were just ordinary people who stumbled across a hybrid and were offered to work here," Isaac answered as he looked at the staff members with pity.

"Very good, and these three here are as plain as a human can be. Granted, this method is a lot more dangerous and unpredictable than the first plan, but I have faith that Alyssa will be able to pull off such a feat. Especially, since the spell for this alternative plan is very similar to the spell we were going to perform tonight. Now, if you'll excuse me," Astrid said as she strolled over to the three staff members. As she got closer, they began to struggle and cry as they pleaded for her to stop.

Owen frantically looked around for options, but only one presented itself to him. He roared and charged Astrid. She never turned around but instead, kept walking toward the staff members. Owen quickly found out why as one of the followers holding just one of the staff members threw his hand up and projected a flame toward him. He was too close to dodge it so he went to unleash fire of his own to stop the blast, but Isaac jumped in front of him. As he did, Isaac raised his fiery hand and effortlessly absorbed the flames.

At this point, Astrid turned her head and her eyes widened. She diverted her attention back to her two followers. "Both of you...kill them!"

The two men pushed the staff members to the ground and stepped toward Owen and Isaac. The one that continued to keep his fire stream on Isaac now had both his hands ignited and his eyes were pure fire. The other one transitioned and his eyes seemed to be made of crystal-clear water, to the point that Owen could almost see his reflection in the person's wavy eyes. The same man's hands had a small pool of water that surrounded them. The water around his hands did not drip and was wavy as well.

"Fire and water elementals. I will handle them. Save the others," Isaac directed and then sent a stream of fire at the water elemental. He lifted his hands and put up a small water barrier in front of him. As the fire collided with the water shield, the steam produced was loud. Both the fire and water elemental hybrids' faces crinkled from straining. Even Isaac's face began to strain as he pushed his way toward them.

Owen didn't waste any time. He sprinted toward Astrid, who already had one of the trainers by her shirt and had a portion of the ruby protruding from the pouch. He dove and tackled Astrid from the side of her and they tumbled across the ground. Owen positioned himself on top and took a couple of swipes at Astrid with his claws,

126

but she already transitioned and his claws merely scraped against her scales. He could see an orange glow from her mouth so he flung himself off her just in time as she spewed flames from her mouth.

He turned and looked at Isaac, who was now fully engulfed in flames and had both hybrids by their necks as they struggled. At a quick glance, he saw Alyssa standing by a nearby tree, staying out of the fight. Owen then turned back to Astrid and noticed the pouch with the gem was on the ground. It was easy to spot with the chimera's vision. He lunged for it but Astrid grabbed it first.

Before he could move off his stomach, Astrid kicked him over to his back and drove her hand that held the pouch toward Owen's face. "You want to be the martyr so badly, well here is your chance," Astrid grunted as she placed all her strength behind the gem. Owen transitioned deep into phase three to help counter her attack. It worked but the gem was still moving slowly toward him. Her green, dragon eyes stared into his lion's eyes as he roared. His mouth began to glow but she only smiled. He knew that his flames were not hot enough but he had to try. Before he could attack, the three staff members rammed their shoulders into Astrid. The impact sent her flying off Owen.

She quickly got to her feet and reached for one of the staff members, but Owen punched her in the face. She quickly countered with a backhand that sent him back a few feet. As she went toward him, she was pelted by a rock by one of the trainers. She was then hit over her back with a log by the supply person, followed by the other trainer who hit Astrid in the back of her head with a rock that he held. She shook it off and began to fight back as she front-kicked one trainer into the other and hip-tossed the supply person into the ground. She went to touch the supply person with the gem, but Owen pulled her off and flung her into a tree. As she stumbled forward, Owen grabbed her from behind and bear-hugged her. He squeezed with all his might as he roared. He knew he could only hold her for a few moments before she broke free. "Knock the gem out of her hand," Owen shouted.

The staff members used rocks and small logs to hit Astrid with. She wiggled violently back and forth to avoid her hand from being hit. As she did, they hit her arms, as well as Owen's arms. She flung her head back and smashed it against Owen's face, which caused him to hold his face and fall back into the tree. She then punched one trainer and quickly backhanded the other trainer before she finished with an elbow strike to the supply person. All three were bruised and on the ground, as they struggled to get up.

She turned to Owen and picked him up off the ground by his throat. He was still dazed but began to come to when she pinned him against the tree. She raised the pouch with the gem poking out of it and roared as she thrust the gem toward his face. However, the gem never reached Owen, for Isaac swooped in and tackled Owen to the ground.

Due to the proximity and force, Astrid got spun around and stumbled back a few feet before she regained her footing. Owen, who was slightly dazed by Isaac's heroics, narrowed his eyes to figure out what Astrid was doing. She was frantically looking all around and that is when he noticed that the pouch was empty. Owen began to scan the ground to see if he could locate the gem. As he looked, he did see the two hybrids that Isaac fought, or what he presumed were the two hybrids since they were burned beyond recognition. As he went to look back at Astrid, Owen found the gem…attached to the skin on Isaac's back.

CHAPTER 10

Astrid and Owen gasped as they dropped out of transition. They stood there, in shock, as they stared at Isaac. Owen was in such disbelief that he couldn't speak or move. All he could do was continue to stand there and hope what he was seeing wasn't real.

"What is it?" Isaac hastily asked while his head whipped back and forth between Owen and Astrid. He was still in transition, and with all his clothes, minus his specially made shorts, burned away from his previous battle. Owen noticed patches of red feathers scattered throughout his body.

"The gem. It's…" Owen softly spoke but he couldn't finish his sentence for the reality of what he was about to say was too painful.

"It's what? Where is it?" Isaac asked.

"It's fused to your back," Owen softly responded as his eyes began to swell up.

Isaac's eyes and mouth became wide open. "Maybe if I go deep enough into transition, it will dislodge itself."

His body was quickly engulfed in flames that were so hot that Owen had to shield his face with his arms as he shuffled back a few feet. Through the flames, he saw Isaac's body almost fully covered in red feathers. He was still on his hands and knees trying to push his transition as far as he could without fully transitioning. Isaac grimaced while his talons dug into the ground as he strained to keep control. Between the flames, feathers, and intense heat, it was difficult for Owen to see if the gem was still attached or not.

Then, Isaac reared up, but still on his knees, and flung his arms out to either side of him as he let out a high-pitched screech. The screech turned into a scream as the flames slowly died out and his feathers transitioned back to skin. Owen noticed the phoenix's eyes flickering until the rest of Isaac was human, and then they too vanished. As Isaac screamed, Owen had a clear view of the gem, or at least where it used to be. The ruby had already absorbed into his body and red vein-like lines were branching out from the point of impact. Not too long after, those lines disappeared and Isaac fell face-first on the ground, unconscious.

"Isaac!" Owen yelled as he grabbed him and flipped him over, but there was no response. Owen lowered his head toward Isaac and to his relief, he could hear his heartbeat. He smiled, but it was short-lived as he turned his head toward Astrid. His face hardened while his brow lowered. "Are you happy? Did you get what you want?" Owen yelled at Astrid.

Her facial expression didn't change from when Owen first saw her reaction to the gem attached to Isaac. Then, without changing much of her expression, she calmly spoke. "Take him inside."

"What?" Owen asked as his face crinkled from the shock of her response. At that point, the patrols arrived and their brows furrowed while they tried to figure out what was going on.

"Take him inside! I want everybody inside, now!" Astrid hollered and then turned her back to everyone.

Owen scooped Isaac up, with one arm under his shoulders and the other under his knees. Alyssa assisted the person from the supply room while the two trainers used each other to be their strength and hobbled alongside Alyssa. The patrol party escorted the group back inside the cabin, down the elevator, and back into the main garden area. Owen laid Isaac down on one of the benches while the injured staff sat on a different bench, with Alyssa sitting on the arm of the bench. From what seemed to be a lifetime of waiting, Astrid finally strolled over to them.

"Take these three injured staff members down to the medical wing," Astrid directed toward a couple of the patrol members. They nodded their heads and assisted the staff off the benches and down the hallway. As they walked, the staff members looked over their shoulders at Owen.

"Concentrate on getting better. I will stay with Isaac," Owen said and then gave them a hint of a smile. He didn't want to tell them that everything would be okay because he honestly had no clue if it would or not.

"Alyssa and Owen, follow me and bring Isaac as well," Astrid added with a deadpan expression.

Owen and Alyssa exchanged looks before Owen scooped up Isaac again and the two followed Astrid out of the garden area. After a few corridors, Owen realized where they were headed...the transition area. Sure enough, they came to an electronic steel door. Astrid motioned for Owen to come forth with Isaac. When he walked up to her, she grabbed Isaac's hand and placed it on the scanner, but it beeped and flashed red. Astrid tried a few more times but the result remained the same.

Astrid scoffed. "Clever."

"What's clever?" Owen asked.

"Isaac should have access but it's not allowing us in and the reason why is because he must be using his fingers while in transition. Just the slightest transition will change your fingerprints. He did it that way to avoid what we are trying to do now. No matter, let's see if I can figure out the code," Astrid replied. She then began to key in different combinations of numbers, all with the same result. Finally, the last one worked and the screen turned green and the door unlatched. Astrid scoffed again.

"What?" Owen inquired.

"He used my mother's birthday as the code," Astrid softly answered without looking at Owen. She then turned to him. "I want you to take the lead and bring us to the large transition room and no funny business if you know what's good for you. If I know Isaac, he always had to have a large room in case the creature was too big for the standard rooms."

Owen sighed. "Follow me."

They continued to walk until they made their way to where the recruits transitioned. It was hard for Owen to walk past the rooms, knowing that was where Amelia, Cassie, and as far as he was concerned, Joshua died. His lips tightened to hold back his emotions as they walked to the next door. This door, he knew all too well. It was the door that led to where he and Hailey transitioned. As they reached the large room, Owen glanced around and everything looked the same. It was cold, quiet, and eerie.

"This will do nicely. Bring Isaac to the middle of this room and lay him down," Astrid commanded.

Owen complied, but he felt obligated to speak up for Isaac. "There are cots, clothes, and supplies in the other room. Can we not place him there and then bring him back later?"

"I can't take a chance of him escaping or the ritual going wrong. I have one shot at this and I intend to make it count," Astrid responded.

"Show some mercy…he's your father and you are the one who put him in this situation!" Owen snapped back.

"Enough!" Astrid's eyes flashed green as she yelled. "I will show him the same mercy as he did for my mom…for me."

Owen's eyes narrowed as he approached her. "He still loves you! He has been trying to find a way, despite everything you have done, to save you besides killing you or letting us kill you. He also loved your mom and did everything he could to save…"

Astrid slapped Owen across his face before he could finish his sentence. "You have no right to talk to me about my family history, especially since you were not there and you know only his side of the story. You don't know what I went through," Astrid commented as her eyes became glassy.

"Then explain it to me," Owen nicely requested.

Astrid smiled. "I'm not going to allow you to distract me. If you want him to have all the comforts of home, then you fetch whatever he needs, but do not leave this level unless you want to experience true pain." Astrid then turned to Alyssa. "I will bring back everything you will need to do this new ritual and we can discuss the variances between the two when I return." Astrid wiped her eyes, turned around, and briskly exited the room.

"Do you think what Astrid said about this new plan will work?" Owen asked.

"I don't know the details but conceptually, yes. I would imagine there would have to be some barrier spell to contain the creature, but for the ones she is discussing, I don't know if I have enough power to pull it off," Alyssa responded.

"Do you think you can pull the djinn out of Isaac instead as if it was the gem?" Owen asked out of desperation.

"Human anatomy can be tricky but even if I could, I would need the direct light from a full moon. I'm sorry," Alyssa replied and then put her hand on Owen's shoulder. He hung his head and closed his eyes tightly.

He then took a deep breath. "Can you please stay with Isaac until I get back with the supplies for him?"

"I can but don't forget about yourself as well. It looks like Astrid did a number on your face," Alyssa commented.

With everything that was going on, Owen forgot about the pain he felt on the bridge of his nose and around his eyes. He shook his head, gave her a quick smile, and scurried off. After taking a few extra minutes to get his bearings, he found the room that contained all the cots and supplies. While he was alone, he decided to transition to heal his face. As he did, his breathing became heavier and all the rage that he suppressed was unleashed in a mighty roar that echoed through the room. He then grabbed a cot and flung it across the room before he turned around and got a hold of a chair. Owen slammed it into the ground and then tossed the crumbled chair off to the side. He roared again, but his roar transformed into a scream as he transitioned back to human. He then dropped to the floor and cried. Another one of his friends, one that was not just family, but who he saw as a grandfather figure, was going to die and he couldn't think of a way to prevent it.

Owen rubbed his face and wiped his eyes before he stood up. He then grabbed a mattress off one of the cots and brought it back to Isaac's location. After he repositioned Isaac onto the mattress. He made three more trips back to that room. Two were to bring a mattress for him and Alyssa and the last trip was supplies for all three of them. Owen laid the two mattresses down on the side of the large transition room. He then carefully relocated Isaac and his mattress to near his own mattress. Owen wanted to keep Isaac near him and the supplies so he could make sure he was okay. There was no need for Isaac to be included in any spell preparations yet, Owen thought. Alyssa laid hers down in the same area, but not right next to them. Alyssa dozed off quickly while Owen strained to keep his eyes open since he wanted to be awake when Isaac woke up. His plan did not work as his mental and physical exhaustion got the better of him.

Owen abruptly woke up and noticed Isaac was missing. He glanced around and quickly noticed he was standing, fully dressed, not too far from him. "Isaac, what are you doing?" Owen asked as he wiped the sleep from his eyes.

"Stretching my legs and allowing the two of you to sleep," Isaac responded as he smiled and approached Owen. He diverted his attention briefly from Isaac to Alyssa, who was still asleep.

"How do you feel?" Owen asked while he looked Isaac over.

Isaac scoffed in amusement. "Human."

"Really. How so?" Owen inquired as he grinned.

"I don't have any access to the phoenix's powers and I don't hear it in my head or feel its presence. I can't transition or anything. It's like the creature, or I guess I should say creatures within me are in hibernation. After living for thousands of years, I had almost forgotten what it feels like to be human. Oddly enough, to feel this ordinary is liberating in a way," Isaac explained and then smiled when he was done.

"Human or not, I don't think anyone could ever call you ordinary," Owen remarked.

"Thank you, Owen. I appreciate that. Catch me up to speed. What's been going on since I have been asleep? Heck, how long have I been out?" Isaac inquired.

"Everything happened late last night and it's late in the afternoon now. I'm surprised that you are already awake. That's good because it gives us more time to figure everything out," Owen replied.

"Such as," Isaac countered.

"Such as, gee…I don't know. Figuring out how to keep you from dying. Then, try to figure out how to escape this place, all while keeping the djinn away from your daughter," Owen responded as his brow crinkled.

Isaac gave Owen a sympathetic smile. "There's nothing that can be done to save me," Isaac calmly said.

"No, I don't believe that. There must be a way. Maybe Alyssa can do something with her magic to stop it, remove the djinn from you, or even just delay the transition. There must be something. Maybe the phoenix will counter everything and keep you alive," Owen frustratingly responded as his eyes began to water.

Isaac's calm demeanor didn't change. "Remember a while back when I told you nothing is immortal and there is always a loophole? Well, this is it…the loophole. The magic from the gem binds the phoenix's essence to me. Without me, the essence is not bonded and will simply fade away. Typically, the creature would remain but

135

when the magic from two different gems is mingled together, everything dies. Look, I'm sure there is some ancient cure locked away somewhere out in this world, but we don't have the time or the resources to find it. Alyssa isn't powerful enough or experienced enough to even make the attempt." Owen went to speak but Isaac raised his hand to stop him. "I have accumulated a lot of knowledge over the years and seen a lot of things, and yet I have never seen anyone delay a transition or successfully transfer a creature from a person. It will be okay."

"No! It will not be okay. I refuse to believe it. This isn't fair and I'm so tired of losing good people. People I consider family. You don't deserve this," Owen strained to get his words out as he wept while he talked. He looked down and rubbed his hands over his eyes and that is when he felt Isaac put his hand on his shoulder. He looked up, with tears around his eyes and cheeks, and saw Isaac still smiling. "How can you not be upset or even angry? How can you keep a smile on your face?"

"Because I have lived, Owen. Over three thousand years. I have lived countless more lifetimes than the average person. I don't welcome death, but I can accept it," Isaac explained as he gave him a reassuring smile.

Owen smiled and a small chuckle burst from him as he wiped his eyes. "Your annoying optimism and tranquility are something that I will miss." The two smiled and hugged each other and that is when Owen noticed Alyssa was sitting on her mattress.

"How much of that did you catch?" Owen asked as he and Isaac walked over to her.

"Enough," Alyssa replied as she stood up. "I'm sorry for what has happened to you Isaac and I wish I could help. All I can offer is that once I know my family's lives are safe, I will do what I can to help stop Astrid."

"Any assistance you can offer would be most welcomed," Isaac responded. At that time, everyone was startled by the echo of the door being unlocked. They turned and saw Astrid, along with a few of her followers, bringing carts filled with various items.

"Leave the snack cart near their mattress setup over there. As for the remaining items, bring them to the center of the room," Astrid ordered as she continued her way over to them. "I'm glad everyone is awake. There will be no time for any delays. To make sure everyone has their strength, mainly you Alyssa, I have brought some food and drinks to hold you over and I can bring more if needed. I also noticed there is a bathroom in that observation deck and there is a lift that will bring you up there so yay for no messes. The door that leads out of here is secure so don't get any ideas. I need to take care of a few quick things, including preparing for all the new guests. Once I get back, we will start the preparations."

"New guests?" Owen asked.

"Yes, I have some recruits of my own, which reminds me that I will need to know where your secret gem location is. I also have the people that have done my bidding so therefore, I will hold my end of the bargain and offer them a wish. So, you kids have fun and I will see you shortly," Astrid replied and then smiled before she and her followers left the room.

During Astrid's absence, they took care of whatever they needed to do before they split up. Alyssa made her way to the center of the room and inspected the items on the cart to get an idea of what the new ritual may involve. On the other hand, Isaac and Owen did not plan or strategize. They simply talked, which included reminiscing about their times together at the facility. During this time, even if it was just for a fleeting moment, Owen forgot about the predicament they were in or Isaac's fate. Their conversation came to an end when the door reopened to reveal just Astrid entering the room.

"Okay, it's time to prepare for the ritual. This means it's time for some girl time Alyssa," Astrid announced. Owen noticed Alyssa's brow crinkled as she fidgeted in her spot. Astrid looked at Owen and

Isaac and pointed to the side of the room. As they walked away, Astrid strolled over to Alyssa.

"What can you hear?" Isaac whispered to Owen. They were far, but not too far for Owen to hear them. Owen nodded and transitioned.

"It's hard to pick up everything they are saying but I think I can at least make out parts of it," Owen whispered as he turned his ear in their direction and listened. "They need to make a circle. One big enough to contain the creature, but not too big that it can easily move around. The more it can move or use its powers, the greater the chance it can break the circle and ruin the ritual. Now they are talking about how they are going to ward the circle to contain the creatures." He paused as they went into the details, but one detail caught his attention. "Blood link," Owen whispered.

"Blood link? What does Astrid mean?" Isaac inquired.

"She said she would explain it later. Now she is talking about making a small line that will connect the large circle with a smaller circle that will contain the locket. She is now discussing how to make the connecting line and the smaller circle. Astrid must have really done her research. She is very detailed and knowledgeable about this. You will be in the center of the large circle and everyone else must be out of the circle before the ritual begins or else, they will be trapped inside. She is unsure how the creatures will appear but the second part of the spell starts as soon as the djinn reveals itself. It's apparently a small window and that is where the blood link comes in. It seems to give Alyssa the power she needs to pull this ritual off while containing the creatures. However, she will need an additional power source...Astrid."

"Power source. What do you mean?" Isaac asked. Owen could hear the concern in his voice.

"One of the ingredients used is Astrid's blood, in the large and small circle, as well as the connecting line. Once the djinn appears she will cut her hand and place it in the smaller circle and it will remain there until the ritual is complete. She is debating if she wants to transition to a vampire for the immortality aspect or the green dragon for its immense power. Seems like transitioning to a vampire is the winner. Its immortality will not only fuel the spell, but it will enhance Astrid's chance of survival. Oh no," Owen softly said as his eyes widened.

"What's wrong?" Isaac asked.

"Access to the djinn will be available once the ritual is complete," Owen replied and then looked at Isaac.

"It makes sense. If the moon is not involved then there is no waiting period until the next phase," Isaac commented.

"What do we do? We can't get out of here and now the locket will be active as soon as the ritual is done. Wait...maybe I can grab the locket while Astrid is weak and wish for me and Alyssa to be back at your house. That, or maybe I can find a way to trap her in the circle along with the creatures," Owen said as a smile formed.

"That may work, but there are a few potential flaws to it. First, you don't know the nature of the djinn. It will either grant you your wish exactly how you said it, or it will twist it around for its own personal entertainment or revenge. Especially, for being imprisoned within the gem for however long, just to be transferred to another prison within the locket. It wouldn't surprise me if it was trapped in one or many vessels before its time inside the gem. Second, you don't know how Astrid will react. She may kill everyone at the facility. You would need to somehow get her to give you her word that she won't harm them. Her word seems to be quite important to her. Finally, if she does make it out of the circle, she will kill you and whoever else she wants," Isaac responded.

Owen's smile disappeared. "So, that's it. I just sit back and watch you die while she gets everything she wants. There must be something or else the mission will be a failure. This is more than just a mission. She will become infinitely more dangerous than she already is."

"Try to reason with her. Appeal to whatever sliver of goodness is still within her. She must have some thread of humanity left because I refuse to believe my daughter is totally gone," Isaac said and then paused as his eyes drifted. He sighed before he looked back at Owen. "I know she is still there, deep inside. I just wish I could have lived long enough to see her forgive me. To know that there is still a drop of love for me within that empty well inside of her. It would bring me such joy, but such is life. We don't always get what we wish for. At least I still have fond memories of her when she was young and was full of love for both me and Olivia." Isaac grinned as he glanced over to Astrid.

Owen felt defeated. He didn't know what else to say or do. Isaac had accepted his fate and there was no way to stop the inevitable. His only hope depended on either him reaching the tiny light within Astrid's sea of darkness, or taking advantage of some opportunity to get the locket away from her. Both seemed just as horrendous as the other and neither would save Isaac.

Isaac and Owen sat back and watched Alyssa and Astrid use chalk to draw the circles, symbols, and the bridge between the two main circles. Owen was surprised about how much detail went into what they drew. So much detail that it took hours to complete. They then mixed various herbs and other natural ingredients into a paste. Once they were mixed, Astrid transitioned into a vampire and then cut a small slit in her hand. He figured the vampire's blood was used for the same reason why Astrid would transition into a vampire later…to add more power behind the spell. She then squeezed her hand tightly, which caused the blood to flow more effortlessly into the same container as the paste. It was mixed again and the consistency was similar to paint. They then used the mixture to brush over the chalk outlines on the floor.

Once it was finished, Alyssa touched the bridge and began to repeat the same unknown words over and over until the circles, bridge, and symbols flashed red and became dry. Astrid approached

140

the area and inspected everything once again. She then transitioned just enough to access the green dragon's claws and dragged it over the drawings, which Owen found odd. She then sent a quick blast of fire on it.

"Remarkable. It's perfect. Good job," Astrid commented to Alyssa.

"How do you know it's correct?" Alyssa inquired.

"If it wasn't, I would have been able to scratch the lines or burn them away but as you can see, they remain intact. That's how I know it's perfect," Astrid replied. She then stood up and turned around. "Come on over Isaac and make yourself comfortable in the center of the larger circle. This is where you will stay for however long you have left in this world," Astrid nonchalantly announced.

CHAPTER 11

Isaac and Owen looked at each other before they proceeded toward the circle. Once they reached the edge, they stopped and viewed the design. "Keep moving. You can look at the pretty pictures once you're inside. I can't take the chance of you transitioning early," Astrid instructed. Isaac hung his head and took a deep breath as he entered the circle. Owen followed immediately after him.

"I said only Isaac. There is no need for you to be in there too unless you fancy dying," Astrid commented, but her face did not show any concern...only coldness.

"I'm just here to keep him company until the end," Owen responded as he stared Astrid down. She simply shrugged her shoulders and turned back to Alyssa.

"I would like to make a final request," Isaac called out to Astrid.

"Oh, this should be good. And what is your final request?" Astrid asked as she turned around and arched her brow.

"Six pieces of blank paper, accompanied by six envelopes and one pen please," Isaac requested.

"Final words via paper. Archaic request but I will grant it," Astrid replied and then turned and scanned the area. She flew up and into the observation deck and shortly after, she flew back down with the requested items.

"I figured as modern as this area was you would have your old-fashioned ways still scattered about," Astrid sneered as she handed Isaac the supplies he requested.

"The commentary wasn't needed," Owen remarked through his teeth. Her heartless attitude toward Isaac was wearing on his patience.

"It wasn't needed, but it made me feel good to say it," Astrid countered as she smirked. She then left the circle and went back to Alyssa.

"It sounds like they are going over the ritual. You want me to relay what I hear?" Owen asked.

"No thank you. There's no point since we have all the information we need. They are just going over specifics. Besides, I have more pressing matters to tend to," Isaac replied and then gently smiled. He then sat on the cold, metal floor and organized his supplies.

"Was Astrid correct when she mentioned something about your final words? If so, I would think you would need hundreds, if not more, of these letters. Addresses too unless your mind is a steel trap. I can barely remember just a few addresses," Owen commented as he sat down next to Isaac.

Isaac laughed. "You're close. I do have a protocol in place in case I ever did die, which is all the letters that I have in a secure place are to be delivered to everyone. Both Livia and Marcus are aware of this, as well as what to do in my absence. They will be in charge once I am gone. As for these letters here, I would greatly appreciate it if you could deliver them for me, please."

"Of course. Anything you need me to do," Owen quickly accepted.

"Even though they have letters already, I feel a special letter is needed for Marcus and Astrid. The remaining ones go to the people whom I haven't had a chance to write anything yet. That is Bailey,

Hailey, Avery, and you. These letters are to be opened only after my death. Understood?" Isaac asked.

"Yeah, I understand," Owen responded as he felt his heart drop to his stomach. It was bad enough he had to deal with the death of Isaac, but to tell others…to relive it over and over, made him feel nauseous. Regardless of how he felt, he would honor his request. It was the least he could do and he knew it meant a lot to Isaac.

"If you excuse me, I will need some privacy and time to write these letters," Isaac politely mentioned.

"No problem. Just let me know when you're done," Owen said as he stood up and walked to the outer edge of the large circle. He wanted to give Isaac his privacy but at the same time, remind him that he was still there for him.

Owen watched as Isaac took his time with each letter he wrote before he folded and sealed it within the addressed envelope. He wondered what he wrote for him and was both curious to read it but also dreaded it, for he could only imagine the emotions it would stir within him. More time passed as they entered day two. Isaac didn't seem worried that he potentially had one day left to live, which he admired. He wasn't sure if he could stay as calm as Isaac. He just wished there was something he could do that was more than just delivering letters.

"All done. You can come back over," Isaac called out.

Owen squinched his eyes due to tiredness as he wandered over to Isaac. He was determined to be awake if Isaac was because he didn't want him to be alone. Astrid made Alyssa go to bed a while back to get some rest, for she would need it for the ritual. At first, Astrid would pop in from time to time to make sure everyone was behaving properly and there were no signs of Isaac transitioning. Lately, due to fear of missing her one chance, she stayed in the room. She was either in the observation deck or resting on one of the mattresses.

Owen took the letters. "I will lay these down over by my stuff so it doesn't get damaged by the ritual. I promise I will deliver these letters. Now, I am going to get us some coffee." Isaac didn't respond. Instead, he was staring in the direction of Astrid. "Isaac," Owen said as he moved his hand across Isaac's line of sight.

Isaac shook his head. "Yes, coffee would be great. Thank you."

"I'm going to talk to her. See if I can get her to nicely talk to you or at least hear your side of the story, along with your feelings. I'm sure she will come around," Owen said and then smiled and put his hand on Isaac's shoulder.

"I appreciate it but there is no need. If she wanted to come over, she would have done so by now," Isaac solemnly responded.

"I wasn't asking for your permission," Owen countered and then winked.

Isaac smiled. "You are a good person, Owen. I consider all my recruits, really everyone at the facility, to be like an extended family to me, but you I will admit had a place closer to my heart. Even after you snapped my neck, nothing changed," Isaac added as he smiled.

Owen burst into laughter. "I'm glad that minor incident didn't change how you felt because I feel the same way toward you. In case I don't get a chance to say it later, I wanted you to know that and to thank you for everything that you have done for me. You saved my life. Not just earlier with the gem, but when you accepted me into your facility." They both smiled and then hugged.

"Love you," Isaac whispered.

"Love you too," Owen whispered back as a tear rolled down his cheek.

Owen turned around and walked away toward where the coffee was kept, wiping a tear away as he did. As much as he was upset and angry over Isaac's fate, as well as nervous about the unknown future in front of him, he felt some peace. He was able to at least say a proper goodbye to Isaac, which meant the world to him. He reached the coffee station but paused. An idea formed in his head. He made two cups of coffee based on his memory of what people liked and strolled over to Astrid.

Her brow crinkled while she sat on the mattress. "What is it?"

"I got two coffees. One for you and one for your dad and you are going to take both and head over there and talk to him," Owen directed as he extended the coffees toward her.

Astrid slowly stood up and approached Owen until she was only inches from him. She glowered at him. "Don't you dare tell me what to do, especially when it comes to him." Her voice was calm, yet laced with fury.

"Someone must. That is your father out there who, because of your obsession with that gem, is going to die soon. Isaac told me the story behind what happened with your mom and I'm sure you have your version of it in your head. You may even have a legit reason to be upset with him, but either way…it doesn't matter anymore. All I know is that man out there loves you, regardless of all the evil things you have done. If you are looking for punishment, Isaac's death won't do it. He has already been punished. Not only by the guilt and pain of losing your mom, his wife, but also by how everything went down regarding that. He then suffered for centuries with the thought that his daughter didn't love him anymore. Trust me, you have punished him long enough," Owen sternly countered in the form of a loud whisper. He wasn't going to let her intimidate him. He needed to stand up for Isaac. Astrid didn't respond. She continued to glare at him, but her eyes became glassy.

"Take it from someone who has lost both of their parents. If I had the chance to speak to them again, or at least go back in time and get a final goodbye, I would grasp that opportunity with all my might and never let go. Please, for your sake as well as Isaac's, talk to him while you still can," Owen added in a sympathetic tone. Astrid huffed as she shook her head before she grabbed the two coffees and marched over to Isaac.

"What are you up to?" Alyssa whispered to Owen.

"Trying to allow Isaac to have some peace before he dies," Owen replied.

"No, I understand that, which I admire, but why are you in transition?" Alyssa asked.

"Part, so I can make sure she isn't cruel to him, and part so I am in the loop in case there is anything said that I can use later. Besides, I want to know if Isaac will get his long-overdue reconciliation. It would mean the world to him and I truly hope he receives it," Owen responded as he turned his head so his ear was facing Isaac's direction. Alyssa smiled and placed her hand on Owen's shoulder for a moment.

"Here. Owen thinks we need to reconcile," Astrid frustratingly said as she held out Isaac's coffee.

"Is that something you would want?" Isaac gently asked as he took the coffee from her.

"I don't know what there is to reconcile. You gave up on Mom and killed her. You could have found a way to capture the wyvern and keep your efforts up but no, you chose to kill her instead! There are not enough apologies in this world to make up for that," Astrid scornfully replied as her eyes became watery.

"You don't know the full picture, and I blame myself for not finding a way to let you know everything," Isaac calmly replied.

"I know enough!" Astrid snapped back. "Not only did you not love her enough to keep her alive, you didn't love me enough to keep trying. You made me a promise and then lied. Not only did you kill her…I had to witness it. No child should ever have to see or go through what I did, but hey…it's made me the person I am today. I hope you're proud," Astrid said with a softer voice and a smug expression, yet her eyes were still glassy.

"It's my love for you and your mom that created this mess," Isaac remarked.

"Spare me whatever pathetic excuse you are about to give me because…"

"Your mom wanted me to kill the creature!" Isaac loudly said. His words silenced her while she stood there, with her mouth slightly opened, and stared at Isaac.

"What did you just say?" Astrid asked in one soft breath.

Isaac took a deep breath. "She begged me to kill the creature as soon as you weren't around if she did transition on the third day." Astrid's eyes began to swell up. "I told her I would but when the time came, I couldn't do it. I couldn't bring myself to kill the woman that I loved...the mother of my child. I also didn't want you to feel the devastation of the loss of a parent as well. I just wasn't strong enough to see you that heartbroken," Isaac continued, but his words were strained as he fought back the urge to weep. He wiped the tears from his eyes and sniffled before he continued.

"So, in my weakness, I decided to try to find some way, any way to bring your mother back and nothing worked. I tried...I searched every ancient scroll I could find and had others scouring the world for any clue and we couldn't find anything. The day the wyvern escaped and killed those people was the day that I realized that I failed. Not only did I not obey your mother's final wishes, but my disobedience also allowed her fear to come true...the death of innocent lives because of her. I was fortunate that the wyvern didn't kill you too, but the damage was already done. Not only that, but my child, whom I loved and adored, had to watch me kill the creature that she saw as her mom. For that, I am sorry. I'm...so sorry," Isaac added as his voice cracked and tears ran down his face.

Astrid was speechless. Her only expression during Isaac's explanation was her lips quivering and tears ran continuously down her face. She finally mustered up enough strength to speak. "Why did you never tell me that?"

"Because I didn't want you to lose any hope and after the wyvern died, you never gave me a chance to explain. Your rage took hold of you and you wouldn't let me get a word in. Eventually, you left without saying goodbye," Isaac answered.

Astrid's lips pressed firmly together as she looked away and wiped the tears from her face. "Even if I were to forgive you, it's too late. I have done horrific things over the centuries and even if you could look past that, how can you forgive someone who has sentenced you to death?" Astrid asked as her head dropped and she began to weep.

Her head raised to reveal her face full of tears. He went to hug her but put his arms back down and smiled instead. "There is nothing to forgive. What happened to me was an accident. As for everything else, you are my daughter and I love you…no matter what. I just wish I was there for you more."

"I wish I would have allowed you to explain everything to me all those years ago," Astrid commented. She then took a few steps forward and buried her face into his chest while she wrapped her arms around him. Then, Astrid began to cry. Isaac wrapped his arms around her and laid his head on top of hers. "How can I be worthy of your love after everything I have done, and don't say because I am your daughter," Astrid spoke into Isaac's chest but then looked up at him afterward.

"Because you brought me coffee," Isaac quickly replied as he smiled. A chuckle burst from Astrid as she smiled and wiped her eyes.

The two then spent hours catching up and to Owen's surprise, there was a vast amount to discuss that had nothing to do with the evil acts that she committed. They both shared experiences that they had from their travels around the world. At one point, Isaac and Astrid even talked about her childhood, which included the fond memories they had with not only each other but with Olivia as well. During this time, Owen didn't hear anything negative or even hear anyone get upset, only laughter and smiles could be witnessed.

At first, Owen relayed what he heard to Alyssa, but then he stopped when she decided to go over the spells and the procedures needed for the ritual. Even he could not just sit there and listen the entire time, so he would take breaks to move around or take care of personal needs. Then, as he was stuffing a satchel that he found with Isaac's letters, something caught his attention. The tone of the conversation had changed.

"I'm sorry. I wish we had more time and I wish everything we talked about we could have experienced together. If only…"

"Don't do that," Isaac interrupted Astrid. "I would wish for a lot of things myself, but we can't always dwell in the past. Besides, being able to talk to you and see you smile again has been the best thing that has happened to me since you were young."

"I love you, Dad," Astrid said as she smiled.

"I stand corrected, that was the best thing that has happened to me in a long time. I love you too, Astrid," Isaac replied and then smiled.

Astrid turned her head and arched her brow as she grinned. "Do you remember when I was a kid and you would light my birthday candles by using your finger? I enjoyed that immensely every time you did it and have missed it ever since I left. To the point where I am debating about finding some cake in one of the cafeterias and bringing it back down here for you to do that again. What do you say?"

There was no response so Astrid turned her head back to look at her father and he was still looking at her and smiling, but his expression didn't change nor did his body even move from when she saw him moments ago.

"Dad?" Astrid said loudly as her smile vanished but there was still no response from Isaac. Then, his skin began to turn grey. Owen shot up and took a few steps closer to investigate, with Alyssa right behind him.

"Daddy?" Astrid said as her voice cracked. Once again, no response but now tiny parts of his grey skin began to flake off and float away. Her eyes swelled up and she put her hand over her mouth as she began to sob.

"It's starting," Owen muttered as his eyes began to water.

"She's still in the circle. I can't do the ritual with her in it," Alyssa blurted out as she began to run to Astrid until Owen grabbed her arm. "What are you doing?"

"Think about it. You can still do the spell but she will be locked in there with the creatures. There's no way she can survive between the two of them," Owen quickly responded.

"But what if she does? I can't risk my family's lives on that," Alyssa countered and then raised her arm that Owen had a grip on. He regrettably shook his head and released her. She bolted over to Astrid with Owen by her side.

"Astrid! You need to get out of the circle before I finish the first part of the spell," Alyssa called out but she did not respond. She continued to look at her dad and cry as bigger flakes drifted away and now Owen could see hints of orange glowing where the skin used to be.

Alyssa began to chant. Astrid stood up and slowly backed away while she continued to look at her father. He saw Alyssa raise a small blueish vial in the air and as she chanted, she looked at Owen and then back at Astrid as her face strained. Owen darted toward Astrid, grabbed her, and in one motion, swung her out of the circle but held his grip so she wouldn't fall to the ground. Owen could already feel the heat being generated from Isaac as a white light began to emanate from his entire body. Alyssa finished her chant and threw the vial into the large circle. It burst and the outline of the larger circle began to glow a pale blue color. This happened just in time as there was then a large explosion, accompanied by a white flash that filled the entire circle.

After shielding his eyes, Owen turned and his eyes widened as he stood in awe of the massive phoenix within the circle. It was covered with red feathers, but only briefly as they converted to flames. The entire creature became a bird of fire as the red and orange flames forcefully flowed throughout its body. Even its eyes converted to yellow flames and its talons and beak had flames around them, but Owen could still partially see the black color within the flames. The phoenix was a lot larger than Owen imagined, for it stood around forty feet tall. It expanded its wings but couldn't fully do it because of the size of the circle. Owen could see the flames bouncing off the invisible wall that encased the circle. The phoenix let out a screech that was so loud that Owen had to cover his ears. As he did, he could see nothing but flames in the back of the phoenix's throat. However, the screech became duller as the creature began to fade away.

As soon as the phoenix disappeared, the steam from the floor began to whirl around the entire circle before it began to close in within the circle itself. The steam vanished and was replaced by what appeared to be a combination of a shadow and grey smoke, that started to swirl. This motion quickly formed a tornado that was only about ten feet high. Owen could make out a faint outline of the djinn's arms and long, skinny fingers. More definition formed with outlines of its broad chest and what he presumed was its face with its defined cheekbones. Two red eyes formed next and looked down and began to glow. As they did, the floor began to crack and the blue glow around the circle began to fluctuate.

Owen turned to Alyssa, who just finished chanting, and handed a second, reddish vile to Astrid. "Do it now," Alyssa screamed.

Astrid took out a knife and cut her hand and grabbed the vile with the same hand. She then transitioned deep into phase three of her vampire creature. She phased so much that Owen almost couldn't recognize her as her skin turned pale and her eyes became blood red. Even her facial features changed and her hair turned black. She screamed and slammed the vial into the smaller circle.

The circle glowed red, and that same glow followed the bridge and entered the larger circle. The red glow covered the djinn and the wind stopped as the red glow became more intense. Meanwhile, Astrid continued to scream as her muscles tensed and her nose began

152

to bleed while she kept her hand on the smaller circle. Then, there was an enormous red flash and everything within the room went dark. At the same time, Astrid stopped screaming and crumbled to the floor. Owen observed that the locket that was in the small circle began to glow red for a few seconds before it stopped. The chaos that was once within the room briskly switched to darkness and silence.

CHAPTER 12

The silence continued to fill the room, even after the lights flickered back on. Owen stared at the larger circle that not only just recently contained a phoenix and a djinn, but also Isaac. All the markings on the floor had vanished. The intense heat from the phoenix had turned the steel circle into a variety of colors, such as orange, red, yellow, and even blue. Near where the markings were, the floor was cracked and crumbled. This made Owen wonder how much longer the circle would have lasted before the djinn broke free. He wiped his eyes before he turned his head and saw Astrid still lying on the floor, face down, but she had already transitioned back to herself. She reached her quivering arm out and dragged the locket over to her. He wanted to grab it from Astrid, but he was scared that she would quickly make a wish that would not end well for him. He glanced over and saw Alyssa on her knees, breathing heavily.

"Are you okay?" Owen asked while he walked over to Alyssa and helped her to her feet.

"Yeah," Alyssa responded with a strained voice as she stood up. She then held onto Owen's shoulder to steady herself. "That spell took more out of me than I thought it would." She then shuffled her way back to her mattress to lie down.

He turned his head and saw Astrid sitting near where the larger circle once was. Her back was turned and she was holding the locket in her hand. Owen transitioned and slowly approached her. He had the element of surprise and if he moved swiftly enough, he could snatch the locket from Astrid. Even better, he could rip her heart out while she was weak and in human form. He crept up behind her, raised his hand high in the air, and extended his claws. Right as he was about to thrust his claws through her back, he heard her softly crying and sniffling. He tried to push past it as his hand began to shake, but he couldn't go through with it. Instead, he transitioned back to himself and walked alongside her.

Astrid was startled and veered from him as she quickly put the locket around her neck. "If you try anything, I'll kill you." She tried to transition but could barely make it to phase one as her eyes transitioned back and forth between the green dragon and her human eyes. He could hear the weakness in her voice.

"Yeah, you look like you can put up a fight. Besides, if I wanted you dead, I would have done it when I was standing behind you earlier," Owen commented.

"Then why didn't you?" Astrid asked as her brow furrowed.

"Because I know what it feels like to lose a parent and I wouldn't wish that on my worst enemy. That and Isaac wanted me to try my best to find a way to stop you without killing you. So, in memory of him and for your recent loss, I am calling a truce…at least for a day," Owen responded as he reached out his hand for her to grab. Her furrowed brow remained as she took his hand and allowed him to assist her to her feet. Owen escorted her over to one of the other mattresses and helped her sit down. He then sat on the same mattress as Astrid and leaned his back against the wall.

"Thank you," Astrid said as her face eased and she even had a hint of a smile. Owen nodded his head and responded with a slight grin of his own before he looked forward. Even though he despised her, he also felt pity as he heard her softly crying again.

As she mourned, his mind wandered from Isaac to his own parents. Memories of them flashed through his brain and not just the fond memories, but also the memories of the pain he felt when they died. He pressed his lips firmly together and clenched his fists while he squeezed his eyes shut. He thought he buried those hurtful feelings long ago, but they apparently resurfaced. Owen breathed slowly and tried to clear his mind, but it was not working. In addition to that, the pain of Isaac's death was now entering his mind again. He tried to focus on happier thoughts about them, but Isaac's death was too recent and the image was still fresh in his mind.

He decided to not fight it and to allow himself time to grieve, which he needed. Finally, Owen lowered his wall and allowed his emotions to rise to the surface as he wiped tears from his eyes while he wept. At first, his sorrow was driven by just the emotional pain he was feeling. He never thought he would outlive Isaac and even though he knew his death was imminent, the thought of never seeing him again hurt him down to his core. Eventually, he took comfort that unlike his parents, and even other loved ones who died, he was able to tell Isaac goodbye. Even though his tears still ran down his cheeks, fond memories of Isaac began to enter his mind. Not only for him but for his parents as well.

Astrid and Owen sat only a foot apart on the mattress. He could hear her sniffling, but he didn't look over at her. Instead, he laid his head back against the wall as the tears continued to flow and he too, occasionally sniffled. He must have dozed off because his eyes opened to the sight of Astrid asleep on his shoulder. His face squinched at the sight, but he didn't shrug her off him. Instead, he remained civil and slowly slid away while he supported her body and head until she was lying on the mattress.

Owen rubbed his eyes but was still exhausted. Then, he noticed the satchel on the other mattress. He went over and opened it up. He removed his and Astrid's letter and then sat down on the same mattress. He was hesitant to open his letter because he was unsure if he could handle crying again, but Isaac wrote it for a reason and he wanted to respect it. He was about to open the envelope but he noticed the flap of the envelope was ripped and not sticking as well as the other envelopes. He thought it was odd but nevertheless, he opened the envelope and removed the letter. His eyes strained to see the writing since the room wasn't bright, but he was still able to read it.

"Dear Owen,

Hello. We just had a long talk and covered so many things that I am going to go about writing this letter differently. First off, I apologize if you had to witness my demise. I know it was hard for you to know it was coming but to witness it must have been challenging. My advice is to not remember me as I was today but to remember me when I was alive and well. Remember our times back at the facility and at Duncan's cabin. Those are the memories to cling to. The ones that will help drive away the unpleasant memories of today. I know it's been a hard road for you and I appreciate everything you have done. Remember, when times get rough, you are not alone. You still have good friends, both new and old, that are your family. There is a great strength that can be harnessed from that.

I want to make sure this is clear since you have a tendency to think this way, but you have nothing to blame yourself for. Not for today, yesterday, or any other day. You are a wonderful individual who people look up to. Continue to be that inspiration for them…even my daughter, and if that doesn't work out, guess what…that's not your fault. I know you try and put your heart into everything so if something doesn't work out, it's not because of lack of effort on your part. Remember, even though I am gone, I am always with you as long as you keep me in your thoughts.

Be strong, be kind, be courageous, be brave, and above all…be yourself. Also, I approve of you and Avery as a couple. I'm surprised it didn't happen sooner.

Love,
Isaac

P.S. While you were walking around, I reopened the letter to tell you thank you for convincing Astrid·to come talk to me. Because of you, I got my daughter back. Thank you!"

The tears and his huge smile didn't cease after he finished the letter. Leave it to Isaac to write the perfect final words to him, Owen thought. For now, he folded the letter back into the envelope and returned it to the satchel for safekeeping.

Owen now wondered if he could save Astrid, especially after her breakthrough with her dad. He stood up and turned around and both Alyssa and Astrid were asleep. The idea of sleep sounded wonderful, but he knew he wouldn't be able to, so instead Owen sat back down and decided to meditate. Before he fully committed to the meditation, he did think to himself that Isaac would be proud of him for making a truce with his daughter. Owen smiled before he concentrated on his breathing and not too soon after, he was in his meditative state. After he finished his session, he turned his head and was startled to see Astrid sitting next to him.

"Sorry, I didn't mean to scare you. I didn't want to disturb your meditation," Astrid gently commented.

"It's okay. How are you holding up?" Owen asked.

"As good as one can be after nearly dying and watching their father die all in the same moment," Astrid replied.

"I'm sorry, but that reminds me," Owen said and then reached for Astrid's letter that was near the satchel. "This is from your dad."

"Thank you. I want to read it, but I'm nervous. I'm not sure I can handle whatever he wrote to me," Astrid said as she stared at the envelope.

"I felt the same way but after I read mine, it gave me strength. Your father always had a way with words," Owen responded as he partially smiled.

Astrid smiled. "That he did."

"So, where do we go from here?" Owen inquired.

Astrid didn't respond. Instead, she stared at the spot where Isaac died. Owen didn't want to interrupt her so he turned his head around and that is when he noticed Alyssa was now up and sitting on her mattress. "Up," Astrid muttered while she continued to stare where her father died. Owen's brow crinkled as he tried to figure out what she meant. She stood up and turned to face Owen and Alyssa, so the two followed her lead and stood up as well.

"Gather your things. We are going back up to the main level," Astrid added. She had a hint of a smile as she walked off. Owen and Alyssa glanced at each other with knitted brows and shrugged. There wasn't much to take that wasn't already upstairs. Owen only took his satchel and Alyssa stuffed a few smaller pouches of the herbs used in the ritual into a larger pouch.

"Why are you taking those?" Owen whispered.

"These herbs are very rare and it would benefit me and my family to have these to either use or sell. Astrid won't have any more use for them anyway," Alyssa responded.

The two followed Astrid through the corridors that led back to the garden area. As they walked, no one said a word. During the silence, multiple thoughts roamed through Owen's mind as to what could be next on her agenda. One thing that surprised him was that she didn't try to make a wish yet. Another thing was that her demeanor had changed. It was almost like he was talking to her fake persona Olivia again. He needed to stay focused because as far as he was concerned, she was hard to predict now.

Once they reached the garden area, Astrid turned to Alyssa. "You may go anywhere you like within this area. I will be back for you later."

"When can I leave? I helped you with the ritual and got the djinn so are we good now? Is my family safe?" Alyssa nervously asked.

"Your family is safe, but you can't leave until I test this locket to see if the ritual was a success or not," Astrid replied.

"What's stopping you from making a wish? I'm sure you have thought of which ones to make once you had control over the djinn," Alyssa countered.

"I did, but now I'm not sure which one to do first, so I need time. Recent events have my brain scattered," Astrid replied and as Alyssa was about to speak, Astrid turned to Owen. "Follow me." She then turned and began to walk. Owen glanced at Alyssa who had her arms raised out and her brow was lowered. He shrugged his shoulders before he turned around and followed Astrid.

They made their way through the center of the main room and to the door that led to the offices and medical ward. She opened the door, which didn't surprise him since she did comment about how she already had access to certain areas of the facility. As they walked through and started their way down the hallway, Owen's eyes secretly shifted over to the room that had the secret entrance to the gem depository location. From what he could tell, the room had not been disturbed. He had to hold back a smile from the relief that he felt. The two continued their way down the hallways until they reached Isaac's office.

Astrid stopped in front of Isaac's door and reached for the handle, but she froze. "I know this is his office, but I've never been in here."

"What's holding you back?" Owen asked.

"Emptiness. I am going to walk into his office, and I'm sure it will have all his memories inside, but he won't be in there. It will just be another reminder that he is gone." Astrid paused. "This is stupid.

It's just a door," Astrid blurted out while she shook her hands to shake off her nerves.

Owen gently reached around her, turned the doorknob, and cracked the door open. "The rest is up to you," Owen softly said. Astrid took a deep breath and opened the door the rest of the way and walked in, with Owen right behind her.

Astrid slowly surveyed the room as she strolled around Isaac's office. The office was exactly how he remembered it. Owen decided to stay by the door. "Do you want me to give you your space?" Owen asked.

"No, please stay," Astrid replied with a monotone voice as she was still taking in all the wonders of her father's office. Owen stayed and closed the door, but he didn't venture much further. He remembered how much in awe he was in when he first entered Isaac's office. He could only imagine how Astrid must have felt seeing the memories of his travels, let alone just being in her father's office.

She strolled behind Isaac's desk, slowly pulled out his chair, and sat down. Astrid then took out the letter and began to read it. Owen observed her as she smiled, cried, and even both at the same time. At the end of her letter, he noticed her brow crinkled.

"Did something in that letter surprise you?" Owen asked.

"He said there is a surprise for me in the filing cabinet on the side of his desk," Astrid muttered as she stood up and glanced over to the tall filing cabinet.

She quickly walked over to the filing cabinet, opened the first drawer, and glanced at its contents. "Just papers," Astrid commented. She then opened each remaining drawer and each yielded the same result. "Still, all papers. I don't get it. Am I supposed to try to locate the needle in the haystack?" Astrid said as she slammed the drawer and then put her hands on her hips, frustrated that she couldn't quickly locate what her dad wanted her to find. She opened the top drawer again and began to skim the papers. "Look at all these papers.

I can't imagine how long it will take me to…" Astrid stopped talking as she pulled out a piece of paper. Her eyes narrowed as she examined it, but then, she gasped. Astrid rifled through the remaining papers in the entire filing cabinet, skimming as fast as she could.

"What is it?" Owen asked. He was intrigued so he strolled over to the desk.

"They're letters. All of them and each one is addressed to me," Astrid said as her voice cracked, but she didn't turn around.

"What do they say if you don't mind me asking?" Owen questioned.

"Each one seems to be a birthday letter. The dates start on the first birthday after I left and the last one is dated this year," Astrid responded as she looked over her shoulder with glassy eyes. "He wrote me a letter on every birthday I had over all these centuries," Astrid added and then smiled as her eyes lit up. She turned back and began to read them.

Owen couldn't help to smile at Isaac's sweet gesture over all these years. He walked over to a nearby couch and sat down to allow Astrid to have her privacy and time to go through all the letters.

At first, he thought she may just read only a few from each drawer, but to his surprise, she appeared to be reading every birthday letter he wrote to her. He wanted to get up and leave the room, but she asked him to stay so he had to think of something to occupy his time. Owen surely didn't want to spend hours sitting on the couch, with only the thoughts of Isaac and the mission to entertain him, so he stood up and began to wander around the room. After he exhausted every means available to him to pass the time, he sat back down on the couch and closed his eyes. He didn't think he would be able to sleep, but to at least rest his eyes would be of some benefit.

He jolted awake and to his surprise, a few hours had passed. He looked at Astrid, who was sitting on the floor next to the filing cabinet and appeared to be near the end of the letters. It took a few extra minutes, but the grogginess finally left Owen. When she finished reading, Astrid stood up. He got up as she turned around. She had a deadpan expression as she shuffled toward him, but she didn't make it far before she grabbed a chair and threw it across the room while she screamed.

Owen took a step back and raised his hands as his eyes widened. Her sudden, unexpected action startled him. "What's wrong?" Owen shouted but she did not respond. Instead, he watched another heavy chair tumble across the room that she threw, followed by a couch that she kicked. She became hysterical.

Astrid grabbed his office chair and raised it in the air and as she was about to slam it on top of his desk, she paused as her eyes narrowed. She lowered her arms, allowing the chair to fall to the floor to the side of her. She rested both her hands on Isaac's desk, and then she slowly reached for a picture frame that was sitting on the desk. Her lips began to quiver as more tears flowed from her eyes. She marched over to Owen, with the picture in her hand, and hugged him. She then began to ball.

He hugged her back, but he wasn't sure how to feel about it. His emotions were mixed. He felt sorry for her and could imagine her pain, but he didn't like her. At one point, he wondered if it was wrong to feel like she deserved the pain she was feeling. For the truce, the promise he made to Isaac and his own humanity, he would hold her as long as she needed.

Astrid took a step back and handed Owen the picture and then began to pace around the room. He looked at the picture and saw it was an old sketch of what appeared to be Isaac, Olivia, and Astrid when she was a child. Even Owen was choked up from the sketch. He cleared his throat and gave a quick wipe of his eyes before he placed the picture back on Isaac's desk.

Astrid whipped around. "He wrote me a letter on every single one of my birthdays and he didn't miss one…not one. Each letter was different too. Not just a generic happy birthday letter, but each one was unique. Whether it be reminiscing about my childhood, telling me how wonderful I am, or trips that he went on and the things that he saw that he knew I would like. The only thing that was the same in each letter was 'I miss you. Happy birthday. Love, Dad.' Then, at the end of each letter…" Astrid was already crying as she spoke, but she became even more upset and took a moment to compose herself enough to continue. "He drew a picture of a cake with a candle on it and next to it was a picture of a hand with a flame on its finger. When I was a kid, on every birthday he would light the candles on my cake with a single flame from his finger and it never got old. I always enjoyed that so much."

"That explains why you got upset when you saw me in the restaurant when I lit that little girl's birthday cake with my finger. You weren't acting…that was real," Owen commented.

Astrid shook her head in agreement. "And now I don't know what to do anymore. Before all this, I had a plan. I knew exactly what I wanted to accomplish and what needed to be done to achieve it, and that's what I did. No matter what it took, I did what had to be done. I even knew what my next dozen wishes would be. I had it…I had it all planned until my father's encounter with the gem. I will admit that the thought of my dad being the sacrifice to make my plan work was unsettling, but I was prepared to do it. I was prepared until he and I had that talk and I realized how wrong I was. I spent all those years hating a man that didn't deserve it. All that time I could have spent with him was wasted. Now, I'm an orphan and it's all my fault! My father is dead and it's because of me and now, I can't clearly see the path ahead of me," Astrid said as she spoke through her tears.

"Maybe it's time to choose another path?" Owen politely suggested. His initial intentions were pure, but the idea did cross his mind afterward that she could peacefully stray away from the djinn idea.

"I don't know. On one hand, if I don't continue with my plan for the djinn, then I just threw away centuries of my life. Not only that, but I have done so many horrible things to get to where I am today. All that would have been for nothing…my father's death would have been for nothing. On the other hand, I have a new chance at life. With the djinn's power, I can do all the things that would not only redeem myself but also honor my dad as well," Astrid responded as she paced.

"I feel the latter of the two would be the way to go. I can't see your dad wanting you to continue the way you have been going. He would want you to be happy and to do good things in your life," Owen said as he took a few steps toward her and gently smiled.

Astrid stopped pacing and grabbed the sides of her head with both hands. "I can't think. I don't know what to do. All I know is that the pain I feel is consuming me. It's getting worse and it hurts Owen…it hurts," Astrid commented as her crying turned to wailing as she fell to her knees.

Owen ran over to Astrid and kneeled beside her and put his hand on her shoulder. "I've been here. I know it's hard. You just need to breathe and concentrate on my voice and know you are not alone. I will be here for you to help you through this. It will take time, but I promise you will get through this."

"I can't, I can't. I don't know what to do anymore. I just need to find a way to calm down and be able to think and not deal with all this pain," Astrid said as she continued to cry. Then, her crying slowed down as her eyes drifted down to the locket. She lifted her hand enough to allow the locket to lay on the palm of her hand as she stood up.

"No, no, no. Whatever wish you have brewing in your mind you need to stop. You're not thinking rationally. I'm not saying you can't make a wish but at least wait until you have calmed down enough to truly think about what wish you want to make. I can even help you," Owen frantically said as he raised both his hands in front of Astrid to try to keep her calm.

Astrid wiped her face with her hand and sniffled. "You are right about everything you said and I get it. I appreciate you being here for me even though I don't deserve it. I'm sure it's the last thing you want to do, but it does mean a lot." She walked up to Owen and slid her hand around the back of his head as she raised up on her toes. She softly kissed him on his forehead and then lowered herself back down as she smiled and looked into his eyes. Then, without warning, she punched Owen in his stomach. She then grabbed him as he was buckled over and threw him across the room. He landed on the ground and tumbled hard into the wall. His fall was hard enough to leave some cracks in the wall itself. Owen was weary, but he was able to sit up and lean to his side.

"I'm sorry," Astrid said as she raised the locket in the air and rubbed it with her hand.

"Please, don't," Owen weakly pleaded.

"I love you, Mom and Dad, and I'm sorry," Astrid said with a cracked voice as more tears flowed from her eyes before she rubbed the locket. "I wish that I would not feel any type of emotion in regard to my biological parents."

CHAPTER 13

O wen went to speak, but no words came out. He sat on the floor and just stared at Astrid to see if the wish came true. It didn't take long for his question to be answered. She scoffed in amusement as a smile formed on her face. She then took in a deep breath and let out a long exhale before she wiped the tears from her face.

"What did you do?" Owen asked out of disbelief.

"I made myself strong again," Astrid replied.

"No, if anything you made yourself weaker. As good as both your parents were, that bond you had between them made you strong and helped light your path," Owen countered as he stood up.

"I beg to differ. All the guilt of every time I let them down is gone. I no longer feel the pain of their loss. Every fear I had of doing something that would make them ashamed of me has melted away. Any love that clouded my judgment is no more. I see clearer than I ever had before and I feel even better," Astrid retorted while she had a smug expression.

"Your parents would be disappointed in you for what you just did," Owen commented.

"Yeah, that no longer works on me and besides, they're not here to judge me now are they," Astrid said as a crooked smile formed before she headed to the door.

"Oh great, the same Astrid as before but with no moral compass," Owen sarcastically remarked.

Astrid's face phased from carefree to expressionless as she approached Owen. "No moral compass you say. Well, if I am back to being the villain in your story then I guess I need to step up my game. Become the monster you now see me as again," Astrid said as the green dragon's eyes were now staring back at him.

"What do you mean?" Owen asked. His stomach was in knots because of her general comment. She was already capable of so much evil before, but after her recent wish, there was no limit to what evil she could perform.

"Well, you know how much I enjoy being creative. For example, I could wish for all your friends who know your secret to appear in the large transition room. Then, all I would have to do is hit that little red button and drop a mountain on them. What else...I could wish for Avery to appear as myself in Caine's eyes only. As brutal as he is, I wonder how long she would live? I will be generous and say about ten seconds. The possibilities are endless," Astrid replied as a sinister smile formed on her face. She then turned around and proceeded to the door.

"Wait," Owen called out. Astrid stopped and turned around as she crossed her arms and had a deadpan expression. "I'll do anything just please; promise me you won't hurt or kill my friends."

"Anything?" Astrid asked as she approached Owen.

"Yes, anything. Just tell me what you need," Owen pleaded. He felt as if he was going to vomit from how scared he was of what she could do.

Astrid smiled as her brow arched. "I need you, not to put too fine of a point on it."

Owen's brow crinkled as his head slightly tilted. "What do you mean?"

"I mean you, working for me. Face it, you and your friends killed so many of my followers and even the one or two actual friends I had, so it would make sense to begin to replace them. I started that process already; however, to have someone of your caliber on my side would be quite beneficial," Astrid replied.

"And you think I am the person for the job? Don't you think there would be a conflict of interest in that arrangement?" Owen countered.

Astrid chuckled. "I can see how you would think that but look at it from my perspective. Like me or not, you would have to do what I command, or else the deal is off and your friends are fair game again. Who knows, maybe you will have fun trying to fix my moral compass. Besides, it would be refreshing to have some inherently good people around. So, what do you say?"

"Work for you...in what capacity? I need some details," Owen quickly inquired. His nerves were getting the best of him as he could feel sweat beginning to form on his forehead. He quickly wiped it off so Astrid wouldn't notice.

"Here is what I am offering. You work for me, which means your new home is this facility or wherever I go. You will follow my commands and you will do this until whenever I decide to set you free. That could be in a day or in a hundred years. Now, if you can do this and not be a nuisance while you are working for me, then you and your friends will be safe. My followers and I, won't harm them in any way nor will I use my wishes against them. Even after you are done working for me, I will continue to honor my side of our arrangement. Do we have a deal?" Astrid asked as she extended her hand.

"What's the catch?" Owen asked.

Astrid lowered her hand and smiled. "The catch is that you are not allowed to see your friends again. If I find out you have seen them or had any form of communication with them during our arrangement, then our deal is void and everyone is fair game."

Owen's eyes grew wide. "Never again. You want me to walk away from the people I love and care for. I can't do that and even if I did, I would not be of any use to you. I would be a mess. Without them, I would be a lesser person. Please, anything but that. I'm sure we can think of another solution. Maybe we can do the same thing you offered but for a short time frame. Surely there is something else that I can help you with. Please," Owen frantically begged as the thought of her proposal frightened him. He felt a lump in his throat and he truly hoped they could arrive at a different arrangement.

"Well, I was going to but after how I just witnessed the panic attack you just had, I am going to stick with what I offered. Take it or leave it. The choice is yours," Astrid replied and then grinned. Owen exhaled loudly and began to pace the room.

"Oh, come on. You live to be the martyr. So much that even I am surprised you have lived this long. Self-sacrifice runs in your blood," Astrid playfully added. Owen searched for some solution in his head. Trying to find a way out of a horrible scenario.

Astrid grabbed Owen by the arm to stop his pacing. "I am not going to wait all day for you to answer. Take it or leave it. The offer is only good for five more seconds. Five, four, three, two…"

"All right! I'll do it but under one condition. Give me time to say goodbye to them. It will at least give me some closure, which will help you get more out of me. Please," Owen begged as he fought back his tears.

Astrid eyes drifted away as her lip curled. She then looked at her phone. As she did, Owen's brow knitted. He was confused about what she was having to look up to help answer his question.

"You can have until sunset tomorrow to be back here. If you are not inside the cabin before the sun fully sets then our deal is off," Astrid responded.

"It may take almost half a day in drive time alone. That doesn't leave much time to properly tell them goodbye," Owen countered.

"Goodbye, goodbye, goodbye. I just told three people in under five seconds, so you have more than enough time. If anything, I am being too generous," Astrid commented and then smirked.

"What time is it now?" Owen asked.

"That's what I just checked on my phone. I lost all track of time or even what day it was while down here during this chaos. It's eleven o'clock at night," Astrid replied.

"Already," Owen blurted out.

Astrid extended her hand again. "My offer expires in three seconds. Three, two…"

"Okay, okay…I accept," Owen answered as he shook Astrid's hand.

"Excellent, but don't look so glum. In time, you will come to accept your fate and I would be so bold to even say, enjoy it as well," Astrid commented as she smiled. Owen didn't respond. He just simply glared at her with pure hatred.

"For starters, you will adjust that attitude. I am not going to have you walking around with me all day, every day, with anger or despair in your eyes," Astrid added.

Owen sighed and buried his feelings deep to ease the tension on his face. "I'll be back before the sun sets." As Owen turned around and began to walk out, he heard Astrid loudly clear her throat, so he turned back around.

"I don't believe I gave you permission to leave just yet now, have I?" Astrid said as her face grew cold.

Owen closed his eyes briefly and let out a long exhale to help swallow the comments he wanted to make. "May I leave to go say goodbye to my friends?"

"That's more like it and yes, you may," Astrid replied, and then a hint of a smile formed.

Owen turned around and rushed down the hallway, only to remember that he needed Astrid to open the door for him. He turned around and saw her nonchalantly walking down the hallway. She opened the door and told him how to access the elevator that led to the surface. Owen sprinted through the main garden area and took the elevator up.

"We'll see you back here later," one of the two guards commented as Owen walked past them. He figured Astrid must have texted them or else there would have been more of a conflict. Owen didn't respond and kept moving forward and as soon as he was outside, he bolted toward the ATVs. He jumped on it and sped off for time was not on his side.

It was dark and he was tired, but he couldn't waste any time taking a break or slowing down to see better. Instead, he transitioned and used the chimera's sight to help guide him. The transition even provided him with some energy to help him stay awake. He needed his full concentration to navigate through the dark to make sure he didn't get lost or crash into anything. Regardless of his efforts, the journey back down the mountain took longer than usual. Even worse, he didn't have access to a regular vehicle so it would take longer to get back to the house. Owen wasn't even sure if he had enough gas to make it, but then his worries faded away as he smiled.

From a distance, he saw a familiar jeep loosely hidden in the brush at the base of the mountain. He pulled off to investigate and sure enough, it was one of the vehicles he saw at the house. They must have stashed it here for Isaac, Alyssa, and him to use. He checked for the keys in one of the hiding spots he was taught at the facility. As he remembered, the keys were located within the inside left front wheel of the jeep. Owen hid the ATV and drove off.

He was able to make up the time with how fast he drove the jeep. So fast that he almost lost control of it around some turns but he managed to stay on the road and pulled into the driveway around four in the morning. Owen exited the vehicle and then stopped after a few steps when he had to adjust the satchel around him. That was when he realized that he didn't think about how he was going to deliver the news about Isaac. As he stood there, contemplating what to say, he saw someone come around the corner of the house and stop to stare at him. He was too deep in thought and too defeated to transition to see who it was. The person ran toward Owen and as soon as the person was close enough, he could see it was Abigail.

She ran up to him and Owen had just enough time to raise his arms before Abigail wrapped her arms around him and squeezed. He hugged her back and made sure to take in every moment since he didn't know if he would see her again after today. She leaned up and kissed him hard on the cheek. Her smile was wide and her eyes were full of joy as she took a step back.

"I'm so happy to see you! I was worried sick," Abigail exclaimed.

"It's good to see you too. Why are you out here so late?" Owen asked. His smile faded away whereas Abigail was still smiling.

"It's my turn to patrol the house. With everything that was going on we figured it would be a good idea to take shifts so we weren't caught off guard," Abigail replied. She noticed that Owen was only partially listening as his attention was more directed at the house. "You're not yourself. What's wrong? Where's Isaac and Alyssa?"

Owen didn't respond while he continued to stare at the house. He wanted to keep his emotions in check before he replied. "Please wake everyone up. I have a lot to say and not a lot of time to say it."

"You're scaring me, Owen. What is it?" Abigail hesitantly asked.

"Please, just get everyone up. I will be inside shortly," Owen responded without looking at her.

"Sure," Abigail said as she gently rubbed his shoulder before she headed back to the house.

As soon as she went inside, Owen walked toward the house. He had a lump in his throat and a cement block in his stomach due to how nervous he felt about the terrible news he had to deliver. He took long, deep breaths to help calm his nerves and to assist in holding back the tears he could feel forming. Owen stopped by the front door and froze. He could hear Abigail yell for everyone to wake up, but that was all he was able to hear. The rest was the mumblings of his friends waking up. He went to reach for the doorknob, but his hands were shaking so he balled his fists to steady his hand. Owen could hear a large group of people talking beyond the door. There was no more time to waste so he grabbed the doorknob and entered the house. As he did, he noticed everyone had gathered in the family room. From all the yawning and wiping of their eyes, he could tell nobody else was awake earlier.

"Owen," Avery called out, along with everyone else, and then she ran over to him. Owen smiled as he leaned over to hug Avery and with her momentum and strength, she almost knocked him over as she squeezed him tightly. There was so much momentum that Owen ended up twirling around while Avery was holding on to him. It was either that or he would have fallen to the ground. He stood up straight and her arms were still locked around his neck and her feet dangled off the ground. It was the first peaceful moment since the facility and he didn't want to let go of that blissful moment. He wanted to stay in that moment forever, but he had to gently push Avery away from him so he could talk to the group. By then, he didn't have to go far since everyone gathered around him and was either giving him hugs from the side or pats on his back.

Marcus made his way in front of Owen as he looked around. "Where's Isaac?" A few others echoed his question.

Owen immediately lowered his eyes to help hold back his tears while he reached into the satchel. He pulled out the letter for him and held it out while he looked at Marcus with sad eyes. Owen didn't speak, but his facial expression was deafening.

Marcus's eyes became dark and even in transition, tears began to form as he shook his head in disbelief. He raised his hand and then clinched his fist while he grinded his teeth. "That's impossible. He can't be."

"He can't be what?" Hailey cautiously inquired.

Marcus took a deep breath and transitioned back to human. "How?" His voice was calm and controlled when he asked, but his face was still tense.

"How? What do you mean by that?" Bailey blurted out.

Owen kept his focus on Marcus as he lowered the hand with the letter in it. "Astrid was going to perform the ritual but it was cloudy and the spell needed direct moonlight from a full moon for it to work. Since she couldn't do that, she had an alternative plan and that was for her to touch the gem on one of the human, non-chosen, staff members. Once they transitioned, she could capture the djinn that way and not have a waiting period to use its powers. I saved the staff members as Isaac fought some hybrid elementals, but then Astrid got the better of me." Owen's voice began to crack and strain as tears started to run down his cheek. He paused and briefly looked away. He then sniffled as he wiped his face and returned his attention to Marcus.

"Astrid had me pinned and she was about to touch me with the gem, but then Isaac flew in and tackled me out of the way. Unfortunately, when he saved me, the gem accidentally touched his skin. Even in transition, it didn't stop the gem from absorbing into his body. With the gem inside of him, Isaac became human again."

"Don't tell me…is he?" Avery asked as she put her hand over her mouth.

"He's dead," Owen softly said.

Avery, Bailey, and Hailey began to cry and as they did, they lost control for Owen could see the eyes of their creatures. All three of them hugged each other as they continued to weep. Marcus's eyes swelled as a tear ran down his cheek. He stormed passed Owen and outside. There, Owen could hear him scream and he even caught a glimpse of the large rock that sat out front go tumbling across the yard. Abigail crossed her arms and turned away from everyone as a wave of emotion took over her. Cedric and Caine remained quiet and they both looked away from the rest. Selena, whose eyes were glassy, noticed Owen pitifully standing in the middle of the room so she went up to him and hugged him.

"I can only imagine what you went through. For that, I am so truly sorry," Selena whispered while she hugged him. Owen didn't reply, but he did hold her tighter as the memories of that night began to replay in his head.

After a few minutes, Caine cleared his throat. "I am sorry for your loss but there is a big detail missing. Did the ritual work?"

"Caine!" Selena exclaimed in a harsh tone as she backed away from Owen and whipped her head toward Caine. Her stare was so fierce she could have burned a hole through him.

"It's okay. That is the other thing I must discuss," Owen commented as he put his hand on Selena's shoulder.

The room grew silent and all eyes were on Owen. He noticed everyone, even though they were still upset as sniffles filled the room, had transitioned back to human. Cedric called for Marcus to come in, which he did shortly after. His eyes were dry but Marcus's face was hardened.

"The ritual worked. When Isaac died, he disappeared and the phoenix appeared, but it too vanished into thin air. When the djinn appeared, Astrid was able to capture it. The djinn now resides in a locket that she wears around her neck," Owen explained with a shaky voice.

"She captured it but can she make any wishes?" Caine asked.

"Yes. She already made one wish," Owen answered.

"What exactly did she wish for?" Marcus inquired as his brow lowered.

"During our time there, after Isaac became human, Astrid and Isaac reconnected and it was a true father-daughter relationship again. So, when he died, it really shook her up. Partly because she felt responsible and partly because both of her parents were now deceased. She couldn't think straight anymore and the pain was too much for her to handle…so she wished that she didn't have any emotional connection with her parents," Owen answered. He could see everyone looking around at each other, trying to figure out the implications of the wish.

"I presume it worked," Marcus commented.

"Yes. I watched her pain, along with her humanity, just melt away. At one point I thought she would not pursue her plans with the djinn but once she made that wish, now that plan is her main priority," Owen responded.

"Great, I can only imagine what she will wish for next. We need to get that locket from her," Abigail said as she walked toward Owen but her eyes drifted between him and Marcus.

"If we are alive to do so," Bailey muttered.

"According to most of the lore out there, a djinn can't kill someone from a wish," Hailey interjected.

"Most lore, but not all," Avery added.

"Even if it was true, a person could be creative enough to kill or harm someone without making a direct wish about it. I can think of a few right off the top of my head," Caine commented and then smirked.

"You and Astrid are on the same page because she spouted off a few scary possible wishes," Owen said as he began to fidget in his spot.

"Great, it's just a matter of time before we start to feel her wrath. I can only imagine the fun things she has in store for us," Bailey commented and then rolled her eyes.

"She won't," Owen replied.

"Of course, she will. I bet I'm at the top of her list," Avery said as she crossed her arms and leaned into Abigail, who put her arm around her.

"She won't," Owen repeated.

"How can you be so sure?" Bailey loudly asked as her eyes narrowed.

"The better question to ask is, why did she let you go?" Marcus inquired. He then moved to the side of Owen while his eyes narrowed and his arms crossed. The room became quiet again as everyone waited for his response. Owen glanced around at everyone before he let out a deep breath.

"So, I could say my goodbyes," Owen softly replied as he hung his head.

CHAPTER 14

A sea of gasps filled the room. Owen didn't want to raise his head in fear that his friends' facial reactions would upset him. He was already holding back tears from having to break the news to them…for having to say the devastating news out loud. This now made it feel more real, which upset him even more.

"What's that supposed to mean?" Abigail asked in a stern, yet quiet voice.

"What did you do?" Avery added as she approached Owen. Her eyes were wide and full of concern.

"She was going to do the very same thing that Caine mentioned before, so to spare your lives, I made a deal with her," Owen responded as he looked up and scanned the room, but his eyes refocused on Avery.

"What kind of a deal?" Avery asked as her eyes became glassy.

"She, as well as her followers will not harm any of you. In addition to that, she will not use any of her wishes against you in any way…if I work for her," Owen answered. Tears began to run down Avery's cheeks and her lip quivered.

"Why does that require you to say goodbye?" Bailey asked.

"Because as long as I work with her, I cannot see or have any communication with any of you. If I honor that, she will keep her part of the deal. If not, the deal is off and all your lives are in jeopardy," Owen responded.

"Why would you make that deal!" Bailey exclaimed as she threw her hands out to either side of her while her brow furrowed.

"It was the only way I could keep everyone here safe," Owen quickly, yet loudly responded.

"How long?" Avery softly asked.

"For however long she wants," Owen gently responded. Avery began to cry, which made him teary-eyed as well. Mumbling and disagreement could be heard throughout the group as everyone gathered around Owen again. He received hugs from Abigail, Hailey, Bailey, Selena, and Cedric. Marcus and Caine did not move and Avery moved off to the side of the room and sat on the couch and continued to cry.

"When do you have to be back?" Marcus asked.

"Before sundown today," Owen replied as he emerged from the group of his friends.

"We will find a way to get you out of this and to stop Astrid," Marcus said as he put his hands on Owen's shoulders and stared into his eyes with determination.

"I appreciate it and I will look for any opportunities myself while I am there," Owen added.

"Anyone else curious about what happened to that witchy chick…Alyssa?" Caine blurted out.

"She fulfilled her vow to Astrid so her family is safe, but she too seems to be a prisoner there," Owen replied.

"She may be a valuable asset," Marcus commented. Owen nodded his head and then headed over to Avery, but then stopped. He wasn't sure if Bailey was able to smooth things over or not, or even if Hailey and Avery were on good terms again. He glanced over to Bailey and she gave him a discreet thumbs up. He smiled and mouthed the words "thank you" to her and continued his way over to Avery and sat down.

"I'm sorry. I wish there could be some way…any way, for me to not be in this predicament but it was the only way I could ensure your, and everyone else's safety," Owen said. It hurt him to see Avery so upset, even more, because of him.

"No, I get it, and everyone, including me, is devastated that this has to happen, yet also very grateful…but why does it have to always be you? It just hurts that I won't be able to see you for however long she desires. All this while wondering what evil things she will have you doing. What if she gets you killed? If only we could all be happy and together for more than just a few fleeting moments," Avery said in a defeated voice as she stared off into the distance with her bloodshot eyes.

"No men while I'm gone," Owen quietly joked. Avery began to laugh as she wiped her eyes and nose. She then leaned on Owen's shoulder while he put his arm around her.

"No promises. I am quite the catch," Avery commented as she smiled. Owen chuckled and as they sat there, a thought entered Owen's mind.

"Is this okay what we are doing now? I don't know what happened between you and Hailey," Owen whispered.

"Yes, it's okay. After a very long talk, she accepted us as a couple but will need time to be fine around us," Avery whispered back.

"Understandable. At least she accepts it. For a moment, I thought we were going to get zapped," Owen quietly replied. He could see Avery smile as she continued to lay her head on him. He wanted to show more affection toward her but with Hailey in the room, he figured what they were doing now was already pushing it.

"Does anyone else know about us?" Owen whispered.

"I haven't told anyone yet; however, I presume Bailey knows," Avery whispered back.

"That's fine. Probably not the best time to announce it anyway," Owen quietly replied. The two leaned on each other for a while before Owen stood up.

"Isaac wanted me to hand out these letters since they are not part of the group of letters that apparently will be sent out later. These are the ones he didn't have a chance to set up previously, except for you Marcus. He wanted to write an extra one for you," Owen announced and then he handed out the letters to everyone. When he gave Avery her letter, he also handed his letter to her. "Please keep this safe for me."

"I suggest we wait to read our letters until Owen is gone. The sun is rising and he only has so many hours before he must make his journey back. Let's make it a time of joy, not sorrow. I will however notify Livia since she needs to know what has happened," Marcus said. Everyone smiled and nodded in agreement.

Owen, along with everyone else, took turns getting cleaned up before gathering in the kitchen later that morning. From there, they ate, drank lots of coffee, and reminisced about their times together. There were stories shared...some so hilarious that Owen's side hurt from laughing. There was nothing but smiles from everyone. It warmed Owen's heart to see all his friends in such good spirits. These were the memories that he wanted to etch into his mind, for these would be his saving grace once he had to return. The only unfortunate part was that time was flying by quicker than he wanted. After a few hours, people began to break out into different groups. Owen floated between the groups until it was time to find everyone to say his farewells.

He approached Cedric. "You didn't have to do as much as you did, but you have not only been a trusted ally, but a good friend as well. I can see why people follow you," Owen said and then extended his hand. Cedric grabbed it and pulled him in for a hug.

"You're a good man, Owen. I will do whatever I can to free you from her," Cedric said before he let him go.

Owen then ventured over to Selena. "Be strong. You are loved by many who will stop at nothing to see you back here and safe. A heart as big as yours is a rare gift and something to be proud of, for it not only gives you strength but inspires others to be strong as well," Selena said and then she smiled and gave Owen a long hug.

"Thank you. I've been blessed to have such a good friend as you in my life. A person that is beyond kind and pure, yet stupid enough to be hanging out with Caine," Owen jested. Selena giggled as she released from her hug.

"Well, no one's perfect," Selena said and then winked. She then held his hand. "Be safe."

Owen put his other hand over hers and smiled. "You too."

He turned around and bumped into Hailey. "Hey, um…" Owen stuttered and then pressed his lips firmly together.

Hailey smiled. "Even though we are in an awkward place doesn't mean I don't care about you anymore. We have a lot of history that will never fade away. Please be safe and come back to us. I'll miss you."

"I agree. I'll miss you too and I hope to make it back here soon," Owen responded as the two hugged.

As Owen walked away, he noticed Caine leaning against a wall in the hallway so he went up to him. "Try not to kill too many people while I'm gone," Owen said as he smiled and patted Caine on the arm.

"No promises. Try not to be the goodie good hero while you are gone," Caine countered as he smiled and returned the pat on Owen's arm.

"No promises," Owen quickly replied as he continued to smile and walked away.

Owen didn't walk far until he ran into Bailey. "Why do you always have to make it difficult for me to have your back?" As Owen was about to respond, Bailey interrupted. "Actually, I think I'm done having your back. Do you know how painful it was to come back here and deal with all the girly-girl emotions between Avery and Hailey? That wasn't quick either…no. That went on for hours. I did that all for you. I would rather experience the pain of being sliced up by those mercenaries back in the Alps again before having to put myself through any more of that female drama," Bailey said as her eyes flared at him.

Owen chuckled. "Well, now you can take a vacation while I'm gone."

"Thank you," Bailey said as a slight smile broke through and her face became more at ease. "I'd do it again for you," she added as her smile grew.

"Well, in that case, can you watch over them while I am gone? If Hailey, Avery, or anyone else becomes upset, you can talk to them. You can be like the resident counselor," Owen teased.

"I hate you," Bailey blurted out. This caused Owen to burst out into laughter. "No, I'm serious. Why do we both have to be miserable?" Bailey added as her smile grew.

"I will miss you," Owen sincerely said.

"I will miss you too," Bailey said as the two gave each other a quick hug.

As Bailey walked away, he scanned the room for the remaining people he still needed to talk to. He found Marcus talking to Cedric and Selena in the kitchen, but he could not find Abigail or Avery so he ventured upstairs to see if they were there. When he made it to the top of the steps, he heard a noise from one of the bedrooms so he made his way there. Inside, he found Avery.

"I've been looking for you," Owen said as he closed the door behind him. "Everything okay?"

"You mean besides you having to disappear to work for some monster, sure…everything is peachy," Avery replied as she finished putting away the last of the clothes on the bed.

"I'm sorry," Owen gently said as he took a few steps closer.

"No, I'm sorry. We should be making the most of the time that you have left and here I am, cleaning my room just to hide from my emotions," Avery countered while she closed the dresser drawer.

"It's okay. Well, let's change the subject. Something fun to change up the mood. Hey, do you remember…" Owen was interrupted by Avery, who grabbed him and pinned him against the wall while she kissed him hard on his lips.

At first, Owen's eyes were wide open as he was caught off guard by not only the act but Avery's strength. She pushed him against the wall hard enough for one of the picture frames to fall to the ground.

After the initial shock wore off, Owen overpowered Avery as he pushed her back and pinned her against the adjacent wall as he continued to kiss her hard and deeply. They bumped the dresser, which caused more of the items to roll and fall to the floor. The kissing only stopped for a couple of seconds as they both smiled at their actions.

Avery, while she had her arms around Owen's neck, hopped up enough to wrap her legs around Owen's waist as they continued to make out. He then swung her around and the two fell hard onto the bed. There, they continued to kiss each other passionately as their hands explored their bodies.

"Is everything okay?" Abigail said as she opened the door. Her eyes widened as her jaw dropped. "Oh, I'm so sorry!" She quickly turned her head and closed her eyes.

Owen and Avery's blissful moment was cut short as the two jolted from each other and sat up on the bed side-by-side. "To be continued," Owen whispered. Avery quickly nodded as she smiled and then left the room.

"Sorry," Abigail said to Avery as she passed her. She then turned to Owen. "Sorry, with all the commotion going on in here I thought maybe one of Astrid's followers made it into the house. I'm surprised the entire house didn't hear it. If I had known, I would have let you two continue your fun and just turned up the music on my phone," Abigail added and then winked.

Owen took a deep breath to calm himself. "It's okay. It's probably better that it stopped before it went any further. The timing and the circumstances weren't right anyway."

Abigail scoffed in amusement. "Ah, Owen…so chivalrous." She then stood at the doorway and smiled as Owen chuckled. Abigail walked over to Owen and sat on the bed next to him. "You know, you haven't told me bye yet," she playfully mentioned as she placed her hand on his knee.

"Well, I wouldn't want to make too much noise again," Owen teased as he put his hand on her knee.

Abigail laughed. "I see. Hey, didn't you use to think of Avery as your sister?"

"And, we are done here," Owen said as he stood up and started to leave the room.

"It's okay, Owen. In some parts of the world, it's acceptable for siblings to interact with each other in special ways," Abigail said loudly as she smiled.

"Not talking to you anymore," Owen said as he continued out the door. He didn't turn his head so she couldn't see him smiling. Her smile grew as she followed him out the door.

Abigail grabbed Owen's arm and turned him around. Her smile vanished. "I will miss you. More than you will ever know. We will figure out a way to get you back here as quickly as we can. Until then, think of us often. I know you will be in my thoughts." Abigail grinned before she kissed Owen on the cheek and hugged him.

"I don't think it would be possible to ever forget you guys, especially you. I will miss you too," Owen said as he hugged her tightly. The two eventually made their way back downstairs.

He looked around for Avery, but he didn't see her so he made his way to Marcus. "Any words of wisdom before I leave?" Owen asked.

Marcus paused, and then a slight grin formed. "Isaac always thought highly of you. He always had the utmost confidence that you would always do the right thing and succeed in whatever endeavor you faced. My advice is to continue to be the man that Isaac, as well as I, saw."

Owen smiled. "I appreciate it and I will do my best. Thank you, for everything." The two shook hands, which led to a hug and a few strong pats on their backs.

Everyone, including Avery who made it back into the room, gathered and stared at Owen. As he surveyed the room, he could see it was filled with smiles and a few tears. He looked at the time and as much as he didn't want to go, he knew he had to leave. The time he had with them gave him the fuel he needed to survive what was to come next and he was thankful for it.

"I can go with you. I don't even have to get close to the facility. Just most of the way so you won't be alone," Abigail called out as Owen was making his way to the front door. A few others called out making the same comment.

"I don't want to risk your lives. Thank you, but I'll be fine. Each one of you has done enough and I cannot be more honored to have you in my life," Owen sincerely responded. He paused and then gently smiled. "Goodbye." He then turned around and walked out of the house.

As he was halfway to the jeep, he heard the front door open behind him. He turned and saw Avery running up to him. She stopped within a foot of him. "Don't take too long coming back here," she said as she smiled. Owen smiled but before he could respond, Avery stood up on her toes and kissed him on his lips. The two softly kissed for a few seconds before she stopped and slowly began to walk away.

Owen smiled but then noticed multiple of their friends were watching them through the window and the front door. "It looks like we have an audience," Owen nonchalantly commented.

"I'll handle them. You do your hero thing so you can quickly get back here," Avery replied and then winked before she headed back to the house.

Owen scoffed in amusement, got into the jeep, and drove away. The trip went surprisingly faster than he thought. It took the amount of time that he figured to reach the ATV, but the trip didn't drag on as he anticipated. He figured it was due to him replaying all the joyful moments back at the house that he had with his friends. As he drove the final part of the journey, his mind was solely on Avery. He was ecstatic about their relationship and even though he despised how it had to be put on hold, he didn't let that bring him down. He needed to harness every positive memory if he was going to survive working with Astrid. Owen also tried to have confidence that either he or his friends would find a way to swiftly get him back and stop Astrid.

He arrived at the facility as the sun was almost fully set. He began to walk toward the cabin, but he stopped. The sun wasn't fully set yet and he wanted to enjoy the last few minutes of freedom he had, so he stood around and admired the scenery as he took in the fresh air and smiled. The sun was almost under the horizon so he walked up to the cabin door and reached for the doorknob, but he stopped as the door opened. Astrid stood there with a smug expression. "I see you made it back and with only a few minutes to spare." Owen frowned and started to enter the cabin, but Astrid didn't move out of his way. "Don't look so glum. Look…it appears you have a send-off party," Astrid added as she peered over his shoulder.

Owen turned around and his eyes immediately began to tear from the sweet gesture that he witnessed. All his friends, except for Caine, were standing at the edge of the tree line holding hands while gently smiling. He didn't know how they pulled it off, but he was glad they did. Owen smiled and nodded his head as he crossed his arms over his chest to show the symbol of love. His friends did the same thing. With the sun almost set, he pulled himself away, turned back to Astrid, and walked inside the cabin.

Astrid looked at him and smiled as she closed the door behind Owen. "Welcome to your new family."

CHAPTER 15

Owen woke up the next morning and got ready for the day. The only thing Astrid instructed him to do was to sleep since he was up for so long. As much as he hated to admit it, he felt refreshed after sleeping in. It was already close to lunch time so he made his way to the cafeteria and ate his lunch, alone. As he ate, he tried his best to not dwell on how much he missed his friends. However, if he wasn't thinking about his friends then he was worrying about what Astrid had planned for him. Owen's solution was to do what he promised himself. He thought about his friends, but only the fond memories. It not only soothed him, but it also gave him the motivation to find a way to end his employment. Stopping Astrid was the foremost thought in his mind when he wasn't thinking about his friends, especially Avery.

He threw away his trash, returned the tray, and began to stroll around the garden area. He forgot how serene it was. What brought him back to reality was the eerie silence. Typically, during the day more people were talking and even walking about, but not now. He did see people working, but no one was really talking. Owen hoped to change this for them someday. As he stopped to admire the waterfall, he felt a tap on his shoulder. He turned his head and saw Alyssa.

"You're back?" Alyssa asked with a furrowed brow.

"Not by choice," Owen replied.

"Yeah, I understand that. What does she have you doing?" Alyssa inquired.

"Nothing at the moment, which worries me. I can only imagine what she is up to. You?" Owen asked.

"She is making me construct a barrier around the cabin. Maybe like a mile in diameter, but more on the sides and the back of the cabin. It doesn't extend far in the front," Alyssa responded.

"What kind of barrier?" Owen questioned.

"I am not quite sure but it is like the one I used for the ritual itself. Either she wants to keep something out, or in. The further I get, the more she tells me since I need to know what I am doing. I only have a couple of more days to finish it, so I'm about to head out there again to continue. I'm sure I will learn more then. If she allows it, maybe you can check it out," Alyssa responded.

"Yeah, I would like to check it out. My guess, maybe it is to keep other creatures out. After the Amarok incident, she was nervous about that bloodbath happening again. She lost a lot of people to that creature," Owen commented.

"That could be it. I just hope once it is completed, she will let me go. I'm nervous she will keep me around for possible future spells. It's like she is rebuilding her forces and having a witch at her disposal is a bonus," Alyssa scornfully said.

"Hopefully, she will release you once it's done. If I find an opportunity to help with that, I will take it. You don't belong here. You've done what she demanded," Owen responded as his brow lowered.

"Thank you and I will keep my eyes open for anything that will free us while sparing us of her wrath," Alyssa added as the two shook hands while Owen grinned. She then walked away to continue with her task.

Without knowing what to do, he wandered around the garden area and the surrounding halls and checked on everyone to see how they were doing. Everyone seemed to share the same sentiment…they were okay but worried about what Astrid may do next. Of course, the news of Isaac's death traveled quickly throughout the facility, and people shared their remorse with Owen over it. It was hard to continually relive those painful memories, but he knew it would help the staff members to talk about it. While Owen was wrapping up with the last set of staff members, he heard numerous voices in the direction of the elevator so he went to investigate. When he arrived, he saw Astrid and four other people standing by the elevator as it closed.

"Ah, Owen. Just the person I wanted to see. We have four recruits that I want you to meet," Astrid called out while she waved him over and smiled. Owen, without expression, slowly walked over next to Astrid. "Not only have they been helping me out over the past few years, but they are from the chosen bloodline as well."

"How do you know?" Owen inquired.

"When I was a kid, I used to adore those bracelets that had the special crystal on them so for my birthday one year, Isaac gave me one of them," Astrid responded without any emotion. It was disheartening for Owen to see her talk about her father with such callus. "Everyone, I would like you to meet Owen. He will be helping you on your journey." Owen's brow knitted and before he could question Astrid as to what that meant, a large, bulky man approached him.

"Chad," the man loudly spoke before he gave him a hardy handshake. "Whoa, that's one heck of a grip you got there. Nice!" Chad exclaimed as he towered over Owen while he smiled. He took quick notice of not only his height but also his squarish head with a light blonde flattop haircut. His blue eyes were intense, like the look of a football player right before a game. He was wearing blue jeans with a plain white T-shirt.

"Thanks, pleased to meet you," Owen responded as he grinned. He then proceeded to go down the row of people.

"It's nice to meet you. My name is Prisha," she said as she extended her hand and smiled. She wore a burnt-orange tunic T-shirt with black leggings. Her tawny skin and long, straight black hair down to her lower back seemed flawless as she looked at him with her kind, brown eyes.

Owen smiled. "It's nice to meet you too."

"Thank you," Prisha kindly replied. Her kind nature reminded him of Selena.

"Jaxon," a rugged man with loose, wavy dark hair just past his shoulders, said as he stared at Owen with his defined cheekbones and intense brown eyes. He didn't approach Owen. Instead, Jaxon stood there with his arms crossed. He had on black jeans and a grey V-neck shirt. Owen responded with just a partial smile as he nodded his head.

"So, you're one of them, aren't you," an average-built man with short, messy light brown hair asked before he poked Owen's shoulder a few times. He then took a step back and adjusted his vintage horse T-shirt and his light-blue ripped jeans while he continued to examine Owen.

Owen slowly reared back as his brow lowered. "One of...what?"

"Them," the man replied as his light brown eyes squinted while he stared intently into Owen's eyes.

"Sorry, you will have to forgive Aiden, he's a little, out there," Astrid commented.

"Or...what if I'm the sane one and all of you are not," Aiden quickly, yet calmly retorted.

Owen scoffed in amusement. "You may be on to something there. Yes, I'm a hybrid." Aiden smiled as he remained close to Owen. For someone who seemed crazy, Owen admired his wit and how smoothly he talked.

"May I ask what your creature is?" Prisha asked with a hint of a smile.

"Well, since you asked nicely," Owen said and then winked. This caused her smile to grow more. "My creature is a chimera," Owen added as his eyes briefly transitioned.

"That is amazing," Prisha remarked as her eyes widened and her smile remained.

"Dude, that's awesome," Chad exclaimed as he clenched his fists and grinned.

Owen's eyes drifted over to Jaxon, who did not seem fazed by his revelation. What caught Owen's attention more was that Aiden crept over near Jaxon and imitated him. This caused Owen to scoff in amusement.

"When do we receive our gems?" Jaxon asked in a low tone.

"We are headed there next. I just need to talk with Owen for a moment," Astrid replied. She then grabbed Owen's arm and directed him around the other side of the elevator.

"Did you already teach them about all the mythical creatures out there?" Owen inquired.

"Pretty much. They know the main ones from each culture," Astrid replied.

"Good to know. So, what's going on?" Owen inquired with a furrowed brow.

"You are going to start earning your keep around here. First, you are going to tell me where Isaac's hidden gem mine is. Then, you are going to train whoever lives after the third day," Astrid answered and as Owen was about to counter, she laid her finger on his lips.

"Before you go into the ethics of my request or how you can't give up that location, let me remind you of our deal. You will do as I ask and not be difficult about it, or else the deal is null," Astrid added while she glared at him.

Owen sighed. "The small office right before you come out into the main garden. There is a pressurized lock on the back wall that leads to the secret passage down to the gems."

"That's my boy, but you are coming with us so you can guide the way. I wouldn't worry about getting too close to them until you see who is standing once this is over. Let's get back to them," Astrid directed.

"Okay, everyone. Owen and I discussed it and he is going to take over the training as I move more into a supervisory role. Please feel free to go to him or me about anything," Astrid announced as they returned to the recruits.

"Take over...from who?" Owen asked.

"Me. I gave them an overview of what to expect from start to finish, and after...if they survive. They are aware of the risks and are willing to be a part of this life. They even had some training already, in addition to the knowledge I taught them about the creatures out there. Now, it may have not been Isaac's ten-step program, but it should suffice," Astrid replied.

"Who's Isaac?" Prisha asked.

"Former management," Astrid quickly answered. "Everyone, follow me." Owen and the group followed Astrid through the center of the main room. It was a quiet walk as the recruits looked around them with awe. As they walked, Owen wondered how long he could handle working for Astrid. It wasn't even a full day yet, and he already couldn't stand being around her. He wanted to get to know the recruits more, but with Astrid throwing them immediately into the gem mine, he had to put that on pause.

Astrid led them through the door and into the small room. She then turned and looked at Owen and gestured toward the back wall as she smiled. "You're up."

Owen reluctantly shuffled his way over to the wall and pushed on it, but nothing happened. He tried again but in a different spot, but the wall was still motionless. "Sorry, I only saw this one time and

Marcus was the one that did it. I'm trying to remember what he did so bear with me, please. This may take a bit." After a few minutes of pressing in different areas of the wall, he finally heard a click, and the secret door opened.

"This way and watch your step," Owen remarked as he began down the steps. Even though it has been a long time, it seemed like yesterday he and his friends made the journey down this path. Owen led the way and Astrid followed up in the rear. When they reached the first room, he remembered the intensity of the heat from the torches. It made him wonder how these were already lit. Did they always stay lit or was it triggered by the door opening? He turned and noticed the recruits and Astrid examining the room.

"This is epic," Chad commented.

"Wait until you see the next room," Owen mentioned as he waved the others to follow him. As they entered the next chamber, the recruits were taken back by the large marble gate with the creatures' skulls lined all around it.

"Interesting and out of place. Something you want to tell me about this gate?" Astrid asked as she turned to Owen.

"Only a hybrid can open it. If a human touches it, they will die instantly," Owen replied.

"Fascinating. A nice and unexpected defense. Extra points for giving up that information so freely," Astrid added as she smirked.

"Well, it won't hurt you so there was no reason to hold back," Owen nonchalantly said and then grinned.

Astrid fake-smiled back at Owen. "You know, I wished my feelings away that I had toward my parents, not you. I remember, regardless of your motives, how nicely you treated me after Isaac died. I also remember how nice you were when I was 'Olivia,' so keep that in mind as you make heartless comments toward me. I know you don't like me and I don't blame you, but only being mean to me is just going to make me lash out," Astrid whispered.

"I wouldn't mess with the ominous gate. I feel like the skulls are watching us," Aiden called out. Owen whipped his head around and noticed the other three recruits were dangerously close to the gate, while Aiden was a few feet behind them.

"Don't touch the gate!" Owen yelled. It startled the recruits and they quickly took a few steps back.

"Why can't we touch the gate?" Jaxon inquired.

"Only a person that has a creature inside them can touch the gate. Any human that touches it will die. Consider it one of the gem mine defenses," Owen answered.

"I have inner demons, do they count?" Aiden asked as he raised his hand.

Owen chuckled. "No, those wouldn't count. They should, but not for this." Aiden shrugged and walked closer to the other recruits.

"Sadly, I don't think he was trying to be funny," Astrid commented as she walked up to the gate, with Owen right behind her. "I'm glad I wished not to feel any emotions related to my parents," Astrid quietly said to Owen.

"Why's that?" Owen quietly asked.

Astrid pointed toward one of the skulls. "Coincidence or not, that skull there belonged to a wyvern." Owen's brow arched with interest. "Well, if you would be so kind as to open a door for a lady," Astrid added as she did a mock curtsey.

"Don't trust me," Owen commented and then winked. Astrid smiled in return.

As Owen was about to place his hands on the gate, he hesitated. It felt awkward, and a little scary for him to touch it after having what Marcus drilled into their heads about it. It was silly since he was now a hybrid, but still. His face crinkled and his muscles tensed as he touched the gate, but then relaxed when nothing bad happened to him. With some effort, he opened the gate and held it open.

"Once you enter, there is no turning back," Owen announced. The recruits glanced at each other and nodded before they all passed through the gate.

Owen had mixed emotions about their decision. On one end, he felt sorry for them since he knew that meant there was a good chance that someone would die. Also, the ones that survived would have to live with the daily struggle to keep their creature, and their own sanity, intact. However, they were about to embark on a whole new life with endless possibilities. He just hoped Astrid truly told them everything they needed to know.

He closed the gate and the group followed him to the final room. Owen went over and opened the wooden door to reveal the pitch-black veil inside of it. He smiled when he saw the recruits squinting their eyes to see if they could get a glimpse of anything within the darkness, the same thing he did when he was standing where they were.

"You won't see anything, trust me. It's a portal. Once you touch the darkness, there will be a flash of light and you will be in the gem mine. The magic behind this portal will send you to the area where your gem lies. The trick is to close your eyes and feel where it is calling you. Let it lead you to it and only touch the gem that you feel you are being called to. Don't be tricked by the size or beauty of the gem...that means nothing. If you pick the wrong gem, you won't survive the transition. Even the correct one doesn't guarantee you victory, but the wrong one will mean death. Just a reminder, it will hurt as the gem absorbs into you, but it is only temporary. You will awake in a different room as the magic from the mine will automatically transport you there," Owen explained.

"The only way out of the mine is to touch a gem. If a hybrid or the wrong human enters the mine, they will die. Genius," Astrid remarked while she grinned.

"Wait, I am confused. I thought there was only a slight chance of dying but from what Owen just described, the chance is a lot higher," Prisha voiced.

"Yeah…any chance you can reopen that gate," Aiden commented as he started to backpedal.

"Everything will be fine. Just…" Astrid's words ceased and were replaced with a scream. Owen turned his head and saw the reason. Chad rammed a knife into her upper back. Owen froze and his eyes grew wide from the shock.

"I hope that hurts. Maybe then you will feel an ounce of what you took from me," Chad commented with disgust. His demeanor had changed from the easy-going jock that Owen thought he was. Chad twisted the knife in her back while he had his arm tucked under Astrid's chin. She gritted her teeth and moaned in agony. Then, Jaxon walked in front of her. Astrid's eyes drifted up just in time to see Jaxon's fist slam across her face. While she was dazed, Chad removed his knife and as he did, Astrid went limp so he let her collapse to the floor. Chad handed the knife to Jaxon, who then took Chad's knife, and his own, and crossed the blades under Astrid's neck. Owen glanced behind him and both Prisha and Aiden stood motionless with their mouths wide open.

Owen turned back around just in time to witness Jaxon swiftly slice the blades across her neck, causing blood to spew out as she fell forward. Astrid was sprawled out on the ground, face first, in a pool of her blood. Chad smiled in triumph while Jaxon stood over Astrid, not caring that the growing pool of blood was now touching his shoes. Owen smiled and became excited because the mutiny seemed to have worked.

"I'm going to carve out her black heart just to be sure," Jaxon coldly said as he rolled her limp body over.

He then straddled her and raised both hunting knives into the air. Owen squinted and noticed her neck wasn't pouring blood anymore. "She healed her wound," Owen muttered but before he could warn

Jaxon, he drove the blades down. Astrid opened her blood-red eyes and grabbed his wrists before the blades could pierce her skin, and then she flung him off her. As he tumbled to the side, she shot straight up and before Chad could react, Astrid was already behind him. She grabbed his chin and moved his head right before she sunk her fangs into his neck. Owen was shocked to see Astrid drinking his blood, to the point that Chad stopped struggling and his eyes rolled back. She then threw him against the wall and turned to face Jaxon who had made it to his feet. Owen could barely recognize Astrid since she was deep into a phase two transition. With her control, it would not surprise him if she already went to phase three to heal herself as quickly as she did.

"Join me. Together we can take her," Jaxon pleaded to Owen.

"As tempting as it sounds, an entire group of hybrids could not take her down so I doubt one hybrid and one human could. Just stand down. Maybe we can work something out," Owen offered. It was his only shot at keeping Jaxon alive.

"Coward," Jaxon sneered. Astrid raised her lips to expose her fangs as her eyes fiercely stared at Jaxon.

Jaxon yelled while he charged her. He threw a punch, but Astrid caught his fist, so he threw another punch with his other hand and she caught that fist as well. He struggled to break free from her grasp.

"Is that all you got? Pathetic. I'm so going to enjoy tearing you limb from limb," Astrid said as a sadistic smile formed on her face.

"Funny, I was thinking the same thing about you," Jaxon countered as he deviously smiled. Then, his eyes turned red.

Both Astrid and Owen gasped and took a few steps back from the shock of his transition. Owen signaled for Prisha and Aiden to back up, which they did without hesitation. Owen was perplexed. Not just by the surprise attack on Astrid and not just the fact that Jaxon was a hybrid, but the eyes. They weren't a typical vampire's blood-red eyes. His were different in the fact that his red eyes had a slight glow to them.

Before Astrid could react any further, Jaxon ripped his hands free and sent a quick jab to Astrid's face, and then to her stomach. He then kicked her in the side of her knee, causing her to drop down to her other knee, in pain. Jaxon then grabbed her back and flung her into the wall, hard enough for her to shake her head as she attempted to stand up. He didn't waste any time. He grabbed both knives and darted toward her.

Jaxon slashed down at her, slicing the forearm she used to defend herself. He quickly followed up with another slash, but this time it deflected off her other arm. Owen noticed that Astrid was in transition, but now as the green dragon. Jaxon didn't hesitate and sent a front kick at her, but she countered as she grabbed his leg and then swung him into the wall behind her. The impact was hard enough for him to be dazed. She then grabbed him by the hair and sent a powerful punch across his face. Jaxon's head bounced against the wall and then he toppled to the ground.

Astrid was breathing heavily while she stood over Jaxon. "Are you two in on this little plan too?" Prisha and Aiden remained silent. "Answer me!" Astrid whipped her head around and glared at them with her dragon eyes.

"No, no, no," they both fearfully repeated as they backed away from her. At this time, Jaxon used the wall by sliding his back up it for leverage. Once he was standing, he remained leaning against it so he wouldn't fall as he wavered.

"At the end of it all, you will die," Jaxon weakly commented.

"Maybe so, but not today," Astrid said in a raspy voice as she raised her scaly hand and pointed at Jaxon.

Fire engulfed her hand as she smiled. Jaxon didn't move. Instead, he smirked. Astrid sent a stream of fire at Jaxon that blanketed him. After a few moments, she lowered her hand as the fire ceased. Owen could see a figure walking through the smoke and as it emerged, he gasped. Jaxon had transitioned.

The being stood at least seven feet tall and seemed to have a muscular, yet lean build. It was a male that wore black, metal armor on its body, but it was not bulky. The armor fit well enough that it was like an extension of the creature's skin. It had long, white hair to the middle of its back and its skin had a blackish-blue hue. Its pointy ears pierced through its hair as it stared at Astrid with its red, glowing eyes. The creature then slowly panned the room without any expression on its face.

"Dokkalfar," Astrid muttered while she stood her ground. The name sounded familiar but Owen couldn't quite place it. Astrid huffed when she realized he was confused. "Dark elf," she loudly whispered.

It clicked for him as soon as she said it and he felt stupid for not realizing it sooner, especially with the pointy ears. Dokkalfar, from the Norse mythology. He then transitioned, because he knew this type of elf was pure evil.

The dark elf spoke but none of them could understand it because it spoke in Elvish. Owen and Astrid looked at each other and shrugged. He then turned around and both Prisha and Aiden looked horrified.

"Get in the portal," Astrid commanded but none of them moved. "Now!" Astrid sent a stream of fire toward them after she yelled. Aiden, with his eyes wide open, quickly extended his arm and touched the portal, and within moments, he disappeared in a bright, white flash. Prisha rushed over to the portal and went to touch it, but hesitated.

"Your odds of survival are actually better in the portal than in here. Go!" Owen called out. She nodded and pressed her lips firmly together before she touched the portal and seconds later, she vanished as well.

The Dokkalfar didn't seem fazed by Astrid's fire as he strolled over and picked up one of the knives. He examined it and as he bent the blade itself, it snapped. The dark elf slowly shook his head and tossed it aside.

"We are going to have to work as a team to defeat him," Owen suggested to Astrid. He couldn't believe he said it, but they stood a better chance of success if they worked together.

"Better late than never," Astrid sarcastically replied.

Before they could get into position, the dark elf's brow lowered and his lip curled right before he lunged at Astrid and punched her in the chest. Before Astrid could catch her breath, he swung his leg and swept her off her feet. Owen roared and then charged. Apparently, it was true that these beings were fire-resistant, so he had to rely on his melee attacks. He knew this type of elf was also extremely agile, intelligent, strong, flexible, and durable. Even more, they could perform minor magical spells so even though they were both stronger than the dark elf, he was still an admirable opponent, especially with them being hybrids versus a full-fledged Dokkalfar.

Owen slashed at the dark elf but he glided out of the way while he grabbed Owen's arm and hip-tossed him to the floor. Both Owen and Astrid quickly stood up, and looked at each other, while the dark elf stood in between them with a sinister smile. The two charged the dark elf and sent their claws soaring through the air toward him. He leaned just the top half of his body back and watched their claws just miss him. Immediately after, while Astrid and Owen were near each other and were off-balanced, the dark elf sent a telekinetic blast in the middle of them. The blast sent them flying back and they both landed hard on the floor.

The dark elf didn't waste any time as it performed a somersault and as he did, he grabbed the other knife on the ground and sliced Owen's thigh. As Owen grabbed his leg and grimaced, he swung the blade at Astrid. She raised her arm and the dark elf watched the blade deflect off her scales without even a scratch. His brow furrowed and before he could react, Astrid punched him across the face and then followed up with a slash across his chest. Her claws scraped across his armor, leaving marks on the armor itself, but her claws did not penetrate through it.

Owen transitioned deeper into phase two and then lunged at the dark elf and rammed his shoulder into his chest. The impact sent the dark elf tumbling across the floor before it slammed into the wall. The dark elf shook his head as he lifted it and looked at Astrid and Owen as they stood side-by-side. His eyes narrowed in on the two monstrous creatures that stood before him, but then his eyes relaxed as he grinned before he slowly stood up.

Owen growled and as he charged, so did the dark elf, but the dark elf stopped after a few steps and quickly threw the knife, underhanded, toward Owen's chest. He was caught off guard and tried to dodge the knife by twisting his body, but he wasn't quick enough. The knife lodged right below his left shoulder. He grunted as he grabbed his shoulder and fell straight to the floor. Owen grabbed the hilt and attempted to dislodge it from his body, but the pain was too excruciating.

While Owen was on the floor, Astrid ran toward the dark elf and swiped at him, but he ducked under the attack and as he drifted around her, he stuck his leg out and pulled her shoulder forward. This caused Astrid to trip and fall face-first onto the floor. The dark elf grabbed her back and flung her toward the open portal. She landed just a couple of feet in front of the portal and as she was pushing herself back up, the dark elf grabbed her by the back and dragged her toward it. Astrid put her hands against the frame of the portal's door and braced herself as the dark elf put his weight on her upper back and pushed. He even grabbed the back of her head and began to push it toward the portal.

"Owen!" Astrid screamed for help while she strained. She didn't have her feet under her so it was all upper body strength for her. Luckily, the dragon was strong but with the positioning the dark elf had her in, it was only a matter of time. He saw Astrid winning as she pushed further away while she growled, but then the dark elf grunted and pushed her back to her original position, and then some. As this back-and-forth went on, Owen quickly contemplated what to do next. He had to think quickly because, with each push by the dark elf, the closer Astrid's face became closer to the portal.

The dark elf must have seen how the portal worked and knew Astrid would be the hardest to defeat. Using the portal to its advantage, all while not touching it, demonstrated the Dokkalfar's knowledge. He felt confident that he could kill it by himself, so he could wait it out and let the dark elf push her in and fight the creature alone. Another option was that he could ram the two of them into the portal and solve both his issues. The problem was, if he messed up, he could wind up in the portal. Even worse, Astrid could wish herself out of the gem mine and then retaliate toward his friends.

"Owen!" Astrid called out again. She tried to fly away from the portal, but in return, she gave up her strength. This allowed the dark elf to gain an even better position on Astrid. So much, that she became dangerously close to the portal. She had no choice but to hold onto the portal's door frame again for as long as she could.

Owen huffed and then roared as he yanked the blade out of him and dropped it on the ground. He gritted his teeth to fight through the pain as he stood up. At this point, the dark elf looked over his shoulder at Owen and watched him approach. The creature's face strained as he pushed but his eyes narrowed in on Owen. Then, the dark elf quickly flung his hand toward Owen and sent out another telekinetic blast.

Owen transitioned deeper and didn't even bother to dodge it. He braced himself and when it hit him, he bent over and dug his claws into the floor and only slid back a few feet. He looked up at the dark elf and growled as he showed his fangs and raised his claws. Owen wasn't sure if the blast was weaker because the dark elf was getting tired or because he was deeper in transition, but for the first time, the dark elf looked concerned. The dark elf's brow was raised while he quickly looked back and forth between Astrid and Owen.

He continued to walk toward the dark elf but to the side of it. The dark elf's brow lowered as he contemplated what Owen was going to do. When Owen reached the side of them, about a handful of feet away, both Astrid and the dark elf turned and looked at him. Owen raised his upper lip and let out a mighty roar as he charged and shot flames at them. He knew they were both fire-resistant, but the fire wasn't meant to harm them. It was meant to blind the dark elf. He pushed himself off Astrid and waved his hands in front of his face.

With the concern of touching the portal removed, Owen dove at the dark elf while he was covered with fire and couldn't see. He tackled the dark elf and the two tumbled across the floor before they wildly slashed at each other. He was deep enough in transition that he was now overpowering the dark elf. As they grappled, Owen found the opportunity he was looking for and sunk his fangs into the dark elf's neck. The dark elf yelled for just a moment before he stopped and his body went rigid from the venom.

Owen breathed heavily from the intensity that coursed through his veins. He stood over the dark elf and then grabbed the top of his chest armor and raised him to his feet before he slammed him against the wall. Owen drew back his hand and as he was about to thrust it forward, he felt a hand on his shoulder. He jerked his head and saw Astrid standing next to him.

"No, allow me," Astrid said with a deadpan expression as she stared at the Dokkalfar with her green dragon eyes. The dark elf's eyes were wide open and frozen.

Owen moved to the side but kept his hand on the dark elf's chest to keep him from falling over. She strolled over to the creature and put her hand around its neck. He noticed blood beginning to trickle down the dark elf's neck from her claws slowly digging in. She didn't stop squeezing and as she continued, a hint of a smile formed on her face as she looked into the dark elf's eyes. Blood began to spray and pour out and over her hand as her claws made their way deeper into his neck. The neck began to collapse from her continuous grip to the point his head began to bobble from the lack of support. Then, Owen heard the crunching of the dark elf's spine and that is when Astrid yanked the head of the dark elf from its body. She continued to stare into his eyes a few moments longer, as she smiled, and then tossed it to the side. At that point, Owen released his grip and let the headless body fall to the ground.

CHAPTER 16

They both breathed heavily as the adrenaline coursed through their bodies. Due to how deep in transition Owen was, the only emotions he was able to feel were pride and strength from their victory over the dark elf. However, he was also proud that he found the restraint not to turn against Astrid and jeopardize his friends' lives. His attention was drawn away from the corpse when Astrid bellowed.

He turned around and noticed she was in the middle of the room and screaming as she paced back and forth. Owen transitioned back to human, and as such he could feel the exhaustion and soreness become more prominent but he was deep in transition long enough that his wounds had healed. Astrid turned quickly toward Owen and approached him as her brow furrowed.

"How could I not have seen any of that coming? A common human got the drop on me and the other one was a freaking hybrid! A hybrid! Are you kidding me? They were with me for a long time and I thought I could trust them. How could I have been so blind? I mean, I felt like I knew them but nope, two people right under my nose plotting to kill me…one being a hybrid. They almost succeeded. I was a heartbeat away from death," Astrid frantically said before her eyes darted away from Owen as she looked around the room.

"Some people are sneaky and besides, hindsight is twenty-twenty. You can't let it beat you down. You are not all-knowing," Owen responded. His feelings for Astrid were pushed aside as his instinct to help people in distress took over.

"No, but I used to be more proficient in detecting truth versus lies when I was a full-fledged psychic. I have a lot of people coming in just a few more days and it's imperative that I know their intentions," Astrid countered as her eyes refocused on Owen.

"I thought your plan was to gain your psychic powers back before they came so you could make sure they didn't double-cross you with their wishes," Owen commented.

"Yes, but when I already used up my first wish, I thought to myself that maybe I could get by between my limited psychic abilities and the powerful creatures I have inside of me, but it appears I already have my conclusion. I need my full psychic powers back now. Not only for the people coming but for the people that are already here. I can't trust anyone. I wanted more time to craft my next two wishes, but it appears that is not a luxury I have anymore," Astrid responded as she fidgeted in her spot. Her voice was laced with panic.

"What's your plan?" Owen inquired. His curiosity peaked because if she did something rash, then he could possibly exploit it. Before she could continue, they heard a moan from behind them. They turned their heads and saw Chad lying on the ground and barely moving.

"Perfect," Astrid remarked and then smirked. "Grab him. He's coming with us."

"Why?" Owen asked.

"Because I have plans for him. Now fetch him," Astrid sternly replied. Owen swallowed his words before he walked over and picked Chad up. He was still quite out of it so Owen slung his body over his shoulder and went back to Astrid.

"Thank you. Now, back to what I was talking about before," Astrid said and then pulled out the locket from under her shirt and held it in her hand. "It's time to make a wish and hope it pans out well." Astrid took a deep breath and put her hand on Owen's shoulder. "I wish I had my full psychic abilities back."

Within a blink of an eye, the three of them found themselves back in the large transition room where Isaac died. They stood in the center of the room where the ritual took place and from what he could see, the room appeared to be the same as he left it. This quickly made Owen frown as the memories of Isaac's death returned.

"Why are we back here?" Astrid commented as she panned the room.

"Look at where we are standing. I need to back away before Chad and I get caught up in some djinn ritual," Owen said as he carried Chad out of the circle. He found a place off to the side of the room and laid Chad down.

"It can't be exactly like before because this wish can't kill me," Astrid retorted while she stood in the center of the circle.

Silence filled the room as Owen watched Astrid for any signs of her wish coming true. Astrid shrugged her shoulders. He was surprised that the wish was taking as long as it was and he couldn't understand why.

"I don't feel any different." Astrid barely finished her sentence before she dropped to her hands and knees while her face cringed and strained from the pain. She then straightened her back as she sat up and threw her hands out to either side of her. While still on her knees, she looked up and screamed. As she screamed, streams of green and red smoke rose out of her mouth and twisted around each other as they drifted higher. Astrid's body was rigid the entire time as the green and red smoke continued to rise. Once the smoke exited her body, she collapsed back down to her hands and her scream was replaced with heavy panting. Owen stood in amazement as he observed the twin streams of smoke whirling around each other. The smoke then split and formed two separate spheres that were floating side-by-side fifty feet in the air.

The ball of red smoke shot off to the left of Astrid and smashed into the ground. As the smoke dissipated, a woman appeared wearing an older-style lavender dress that had a corset. The dress flowed from the extended hips down to her feet and her brown hair was tied up in a fancy bun behind her head. He watched her quickly look around the room. Owen squinted as he transitioned to get a better glimpse of her and gasped when he saw her eyes were red.

"Vampire, which means…" Owen muttered to himself as he slowly turned his head to the far right of Astrid where the green sphere of smoke had already landed and was filling a large area of the room. He tilted his head back to see the entire circumference of the green smoke. "Time to go," Owen quickly said as he whisked the unconscious Chad up and bolted toward the door. As he passed through it, he laid Chad on the floor, close to the smaller transition room's doorway. With Chad safe, Owen decided to take the opportunity to shut Astrid and the two other monsters in the room and lock it. At the very least he would have to just worry about the green dragon later. Better the dragon than Astrid, Owen thought to himself.

He had to enter the large transition room again so he could grab the heavy door's handle and pull it shut. A thunderous roar took Owen's breath away as it echoed from within the room. He had to move quickly so he ran out the door and as he was about to grab the handle, the room began to become increasingly brighter and hotter. He turned his head just in time to catch a blur of something with flames behind it. Owen flung himself on the other side of the door and held on to keep it from moving. He could feel the sheer intensity of the heat as the fire blanketed the area, so much, that he had to let go of the door.

The brightness and heat vanished, but Owen could hear a growl off in the distance. "Owen, hurry up!" Astrid called out. He looked around the door and saw Astrid and the vampire standing at the doorway. Owen grabbed the door and began to run and close it at the same time, but he happened to see a green horn barreling down on him so he let go of the door and let his momentum carry him as he dropped and slid under the horn. As Owen was sliding, he witnessed the horn slam into the door and jam it shut. He scrambled to his feet and ran a short distance before he stopped. Owen turned around and that is when he got his first true look at the green dragon.

It easily towered over Owen, at least thirty feet tall, and more than doubled that in length. Its batlike wingspan was so long that it couldn't fully extend them due to the size of the room. The dragon was covered in moss-green, armor-like scales, with the underbelly lined with lime-green scales. Its head was covered with moss-green spikes, with two longer brownish-green horns that were pointed back toward its neck. The spikes also pointed in the same direction as its horns. He also noticed more green spikes running from its head, down the spine, to the tip of its tail. Only its moss-green nose horn pointed straight forward. Owen knew that was used more to push foliage around than as a weapon. At least, he thought it was until he was almost skewered with it.

The massive and powerful dragon dug its thick black claws into the steel floor as its green eyes focused on Owen. As it stared at him, the beast then showed its razor-sharp teeth. In this moment, he truly understood why Astrid was so powerful before.

Owen steadily began to walk backward while he watched the dragon continue to stare at him. He quickly assessed his options, which weren't many. The door was jammed shut so he couldn't escape that way and he presumed Astrid wasn't going to get the vampire to try to force it open. He could try to force it open himself, but he would have to find a way to lure the dragon away and keep him away. The room he was in was basically a reinforced steel box, so there wasn't much for him to climb on or hide in, or even use as a melee weapon. He could try to fight it but he would lose, even if he was deep in a phase three transition. The chimera itself was no match for his opponent. He hoped the dragon would become bored of him and leave him alone, but that didn't seem plausible. It was still intently watching him and had now taken a couple of steps toward him.

His only shot was the control center at the top of the room, but the only way up there was by the slow side elevator. Owen glanced over to the elevator and wondered if he could climb his way up the gears and cables, but it would leave him vulnerable to an attack. He needed to get inside the control center. Once there, he could use the Gatling guns, or even cave in the room itself, provided the dragon didn't burn him alive first. He needed a fast way to climb to the control center and one idea did come to mind, a dangerous and foolish one. He needed the dragon's help to get to the top.

He took a deep breath and transitioned to phase three, which caused the dragon to growl. Owen then bolted toward the elevator and as he predicted, the dragon roared as it charged. The elevator was almost within reach, but the dragon was already there as it snapped at Owen. He dove out of the way as he heard the dragon chomp behind him. He stood up and hit the elevator button, but he didn't get on. Instead, he jumped onto the nearby horn on the dragon's snout.

The dragon raised its head and thrashed about while Owen held on with all his might as his claws dug into the horn. The dragon stopped and tried to bite Owen while he dangled in front of its mouth but to no avail. As he hung there, he could hear the dragon taking a long breath inward as the thrashing and biting stopped. His eyes grew wide as he gasped, so he used the opportunity while the dragon was not moving and swung himself over to the top of the dragon's nose. He then crawled on top of its head, using the spikes to stay in place. The dragon released a wave of fire that left a large scorch mark after it impacted against the wall. The beast then lowered its head and went to scrape Owen off with its claws. He saw this and slid multiple feet down its neck, all while trying to avoid the sharp spikes;

however, he didn't miss them all. He received a few lacerations on random parts of his body. The dragon was becoming more agitated, making it harder to stay focused, so he needed to act soon.

As the dragon lifted its head, Owen regained his footing and crouched down while he held onto its spikes. It was too far of a distance for him to make it to the rising elevator, but he saw another way. As soon as he felt the dragon stop moving, he leaped from its neck to the single claw on the crook of its wing that was propped up. Owen landed near the claw on the wing, so he grabbed the claw while his other hand grabbed where the wing was attached to the bone, piercing the wing with his claws. The dragon grunted and to Owen's advantage, and luck, it jerked its wing upward. Using all his upper body strength to stay on, he firmly positioned his feet onto the bone within the wing and leaped using every ounce of power he had.

The elevator shook and clanged as Owen slammed onto the side of it, but he managed to grasp the railing. He had to ignore the pain as he climbed his way to the top of the elevator. He glanced down and noticed the dragon's attention reverted from its wing to all the commotion he just caused on the elevator. Owen made another leap from the top of the elevator right before the dragon's claws shredded the spot he was just at. He was now hanging from the railing on the control center deck. His muscles were getting weak but there was no time to rest. Owen roared as he pulled himself up and over the railing and plopped on the floor. The dragon's claws just missed him again as they ripped through the railing as he rolled away.

He could hear it building up for another fire attack, so he rushed over to the Gatling gun and sent a barrage of bullets at it; however, the dragon already sent a wave of flames in his direction. Owen held the trigger down as long as he could before he had to dive out of the way of the flames. He could feel parts of his skin blistering from the intense heat of the dragon's fire. When the fire vanished, he jumped up and checked to see what the dragon was doing. To his relief, the dragon was a little further back than it was before and not focused on

Owen. Also, he saw multiple small blood spots on its belly. He was thankful he was able to injure it enough to buy him some time.

Owen thought about shooting it again, but he wasn't sure if the bullets would pierce the heavier scales and even more, he was an easy target within the little control room. He needed to find the button that would destroy the room, along with the dragon. He quickly glanced around and there were a lot of options. "A door," Owen shouted when he saw it at the back of the control room. He ran over to it and grabbed the handle but the door wouldn't open and it didn't take long for him to figure out why…there was an electronic lock on the door.

"Why would there be a lock on the inside?" Owen yelled as he tugged on the handle. He tried to remember when Astrid's mom's birthday was, but nothing came to mind.

Then, his head jerked around when he heard the dragon roar. He bolted over to the controls and frantically searched but he couldn't find what he was looking for. After a few moments of panic, as he searched around, he finally saw a nearby desk that had the red button that Isaac and Klayden mentioned. He ran over to it and noticed there were actually two red buttons. One that had a plastic lid over it with a label under it that said "*collapse mountain*" and another red button, without a plastic lid, that said "*collapse room.*"

Owen heard a growl…one that was nearby. His eyes slowly drifted up until he saw the green dragon standing near the control center. It menacingly stared directly into his eyes before it took a deep breath. Owen gasped and slammed his hand on the red button for the room at the same time the dragon flooded the control center with fire. He dropped to his knees behind the metal desk and yelled as he withstood the intensity of the heat as the flames shot between the desks. He heard a loud commotion, filled with loose rocks and falling metal, accompanied by the dragon's roar as it spewed flames into the room…it was deafening. Then, the fire stopped and a higher-pitched roar was heard before it too, ceased. The only sound Owen heard now was the sound of falling rocks and debris and then, there was silence.

Owen laid on the floor as exhaustion took over while he breathed heavily. After a few minutes, he rolled to his side before he slowly rose to his feet. He then walked over to where the control room deck used to be. He stood on the tips of his toes to look over the rubble and he could see the rock and metal mixed together as it covered the entire room. He listened carefully and could not hear anything, which meant the dragon was killed by the collapsed room. If it wasn't for that emergency red button, the dragon would have killed him, Owen thought to himself.

He stayed in transition until his wounds were healed. Once he looked himself over and saw that he was healed, except for the soreness and tiredness, he transitioned back to his human state. He noticed the power in the control room was out, and that was when he saw that the metal door was not only full of various colors from the extreme heat of the dragon's fire, but it was also now propped open. Owen presumed it was open either due to the power outage or from the intense heat of the dragon's fire that short-circuited the door lock. Either way, a smile appeared on his face because he was happy to get out of there.

Owen wasn't sure where he was so he aimlessly ventured down multiple hallways in hopes that he would recognize something. As he walked, he realized that Astrid no longer had the power of a vampire and a green dragon. She was human…a regular, easily killable human. He knew her psychic abilities were now at full strength and there was even a chance she had a vampire on her side, but he didn't care. Owen smiled as he became excited over the thought that he could kill her now and end his misery. He even began to play different scenarios in his mind as to how he would do it.

Owen needed to clear his mind and be stealthy about it. Not knowing the extent of her psychic abilities, including the range, he couldn't go in there and just attack. No, he needed to find the right moment where he could do a quick neck snap, rip her heart out, or simultaneously set her and the vampire on fire. He even debated about using a gun and just shooting her, maybe even using a rifle so he could kill her from a distance. That way, she wouldn't be able to sense his intentions. Whatever he did, Owen had to move swiftly before Astrid used her third wish and countered whatever he had planned.

Owen lost track of time but eventually stumbled upon the area in the lower levels that was familiar to him. The briefing room where he found out what creature he was, the makeshift barracks where he slept, and the smaller transition room that led to the large one he just left. As Owen wandered around, he almost bumped into Astrid.

"Owen, as I live and breathe. You never cease to amaze me," Astrid said as her eyes lit up while she smiled. "I figured if the dragon didn't kill you then the cave-in would, but here you are, my little dragon slayer," Astrid added and then playfully slapped him on the shoulder.

Owen scoffed. "Where is your vampire friend?"

"Funny you should ask. She's in the smaller transition area with the multiple rooms inside. After you," Astrid said as she gestured toward the door that led to that area.

Owen proceeded down the small hallway, all while trying to keep his mind clear of his intentions, but this proved to be much more difficult than he imagined. He had to not think about finding his opportunity to kill Astrid, but at the same time, he had to think about it in order to act upon it. The only way he could think how it could work was if he thought about it in short bursts, but even then, concentrating on that made it harder to think about anything else while he was around her, until he walked into the transition room.

He saw the vampire lying on the floor with a bloody hole in her chest, and what was more disturbing was her heart was lying on top of her bloody hand. He felt nauseous, not because of the dead vampire, but because he knew how it happened. "You made her rip her own heart out, didn't you?" Owen said as he turned around.

"Yes, very observant. I'm impressed," Astrid commented while she smiled before she continued. "Even as she ripped through her chest, whaling as she did, she never stopped or even hesitated."

"Why did you make her do that?" Owen asked.

"I could sense the bloodlust within her so before she became out of control, I decided she would make an excellent test subject to verify if my powers had fully returned. I'd say the experiment was a success," Astrid replied as she moved closer to Owen. Her hand ran through Owen's hair as she sympathetically gazed upon him. "I can sense the chaos in there. The struggle between the fear of losing your friends and ending my life. I can make that all go away."

"I can too," Owen said without expression as he thrust his hand upward toward Astrid's chest. He transitioned as his hand was moving to not give away his intentions.

Astrid smiled as she continued to run her fingers through his hair. His brow knitted as he looked down and saw his claws inches from her chest. He tried to push through the invisible barrier that was between them, but as he strained to push his claws forward, he could not move his hand any further toward her. He dipped further into transition and he still could not conquer the barrier.

"What did you do to me?" Owen asked in a gravelly voice while he stared at his hand.

"I solved your dilemma for you," Astrid softly said as she placed her fingers under his chin and slowly lifted his head.

Owen jerked his arm away and took a few steps back while fire covered his hands. He roared and flung his hands forward, but the fire did not shoot out. He focused in on Astrid yet the fire would not release from his hands. He then pointed his hand toward the wall and the fire launched from his hand and blasted the wall. Astrid did not react, she simply stood in the same spot, smiling. Owen growled and moved his hand toward Astrid, but the fire dissipated when it was near her. He then transitioned back to human and his shoulders stooped while he hung his head. "How did you solve my dilemma?"

"By making it so that you will never kill or cause me any physical harm. Now, you and I can truly work together without me having to constantly be on guard or you always trying to find the right moment to pounce," Astrid replied as she approached him.

"Our deal is still on? Even after I just tried to kill you?" Owen asked as he raised his head.

"But of course. I don't blame you for trying. Heck, I would have tried more times and quicker than you did so if anything, I applaud you for your self-restraint. However, if you continue to find ways to undermine me, I will not be as forgiving as I am now," Astrid responded while she had a hint of a smile on her face.

"Why don't you just re-wire my brain so that I am the perfect employee for you?" Owen inquired.

"For so many reasons," Astrid said as her smile faded away. "I'm not stupid. I have very few friends. Actually, I believe you and your friends killed them so I literally have no real friends. Everyone else either fears me, wants me dead, works for me, or wants a wish. So, even though you currently fit in one of those categories, I hope to change that. Yes, I know...I've done so many horrible things that you would rather die than be my friend, but a girl can hope," Astrid commented as she slightly shrugged her shoulders. Owen chose not to confirm that he would never be friends with such a vile person. He didn't want to push his luck after the failed attempt on her life. He needed to get back in her good graces if he was ever going to stop her.

"Also, any decisions you make will be of your own accord and not because I controlled you, and using our deal as an excuse for your actions will only go so far," Astrid mentioned. She paused as her eyes drifted away from Owen for a brief moment. "In all honesty, another reason is that I just prefer to not be surrounded by mindless drones. I want some relationships to be real or…real as it can be," Astrid added.

"Careful, your humanity is showing," Owen teased. Astrid smiled and shook her head. "Where's Chad?" Owen asked as he glanced around.

"That traitor is with the other two in the barrack location, guarded of course. I'm on my way there now, care to join me?" Astrid asked with a devious smile. Owen nodded and followed her. As they walked, he wondered how Aiden and Prisha were doing and even more, what Chad's fate would be. They entered the room and both Prisha and Aiden stood up while Chad was bound and gagged on his cot with two mercenaries standing guard.

"Are the two of you okay?" Owen asked as he scurried over to Prisha and Aiden.

"Yes, I believe so, but are you okay? You look like you have been through a lot," Prisha said with a sympathetic look.

Owen scoffed. "You have no idea. I'll fill you in later." Owen turned his head to Aiden. "You?"

"I'm peachy, minus the ever-growing list of questions I have in my head. For starters, am I going to die? If so, is there a last meal option because I can go for some crab legs and steak right about now," Aiden nonchalantly responded.

Owen chuckled. "Sorry, nothing fancy like that here. As for dying, I hope not."

"I bet I can answer a question that is on everybody's mind. What creatures do you have inside of you? I know I'm quite curious to unravel this mystery," Astrid commented with an eager smile.

"You can do that? How?" Prisha asked.

"Simple. Just come closer and allow me to peer into your mind," Astrid replied and then stepped toward Prisha.

"Whoa, wait. Doesn't she have to stand in a magical circle to keep things from getting out of control?" Owen quickly asked as he stepped between Prisha and Astrid.

"Does Isaac still use that method? Gosh, he is a stickler for the old ways. You can use that method for additional safety, especially if your psychic isn't as strong as a seasoned one such as me, but it's not necessary," Astrid responded as she gently pushed passed Owen.

"No offense, but it's been centuries since you were at your full psychic power. Are you sure?" Owen asked.

"It's like riding a bike. I mean, look what I was already capable of doing with that vampire and you," Astrid replied while she grinned.

"Vampire?" Prisha muttered as her eyes bounced between Owen and Astrid.

"Owen will explain later. Now silence your tongue and don't look away from me," Astrid said as she stared into her eyes while she placed her hands on Prisha's temples. It didn't take long for both of their eyes to become fixated on each other, without blinking. Owen took a step back when he witnessed Prisha's eyes transition to the creature's eyes for a few seconds. During that time, her eyes were dark in the center, with a light green circle around it.

"Well, that's interesting," Aiden remarked from behind Owen.

Astrid removed her hands and backed away as she shook her head and took a deep breath to steady herself. Prisha mirrored her reaction. "Is everyone okay?" Owen asked. Both Astrid and Prisha nodded their heads.

"What did you see?" Prisha inquired as her eyes grew wide.

Astrid smiled. "Oddly enough it's rare for a creature to line up with the person's culture, but in this case, we have ourselves a winner."

"What is it?" Prisha asked quickly in one breath.

"A creature from the Hindu mythology. It's a naga," Astrid replied. Prisha smiled at her response.

"Are you familiar with the creature?" Owen inquired due to her reaction.

"Quite familiar. It's known not only in Hinduism but also at least in Buddhism and Jainism. There are variations of them but mostly, they are human from the waist up and the other half is a cobra. I presume it's a male since you used the term naga, right?" Prisha asked.

"You're correct and to add to that, I didn't sense it was as powerful as some of the other well-known nagas out there," Astrid commented.

"I'm honored either way. Unless provoked, they're benevolent beings and are known protectors, especially with bodies of water. They have even been known to create water, and the more powerful ones could create heavy rains and floods. They are also immune to poison and venom. The upper half could be straight human or it could have some snake features such as its eyes, fangs, or even the hood of the cobra could be over its head. They are very strong and flexible and can shapeshift into either a human or a snake. Their venom can be lethal and they are as tall as, if not taller than you, Owen. I could go on and on, but that's them in a nutshell," Prisha added. She then smiled as her eyes drifted away. The creature seemed to be a good fit for Prisha, Owen thought.

"Impressive knowledge. Aiden, you're next," Astrid said and then strolled over to Aiden, who froze as his eyes bounced back and forth between Astrid and Prisha. She placed her hands over his temples and once again, not long after, Aiden's eyes briefly transitioned. His creature's eyes had black pupils surrounded by a pale-yellow color. The resemblance between his eyes and Hailey's was almost identical. Astrid grinned as she backed away.

"I haven't seen one of these in ages and I always liked them as a kid growing up. From the Greek mythology, your creature is a griffin," Astrid remarked.

"That bird, lion combo thing. Does that mean I can fly?" Aiden asked as his eyes lit up. He then jumped and strained to fly, even flapping his arms like a bird, but nothing happened. Owen had to put his hand over his mouth to avoid laughing out loud at him while Prisha and Astrid looked as their brows crinkled.

"None of you have your abilities yet. As for your creature, you are correct, sort of. The griffin is half eagle, half lion, with the front half being the eagle and the back half the lion. Of course, it has the wings of an eagle, along with the eagle's talons for the front two feet and the head is of an eagle. The back legs and tail are of a lion, as well as most of its body. Griffins are very strong and can fly and of course, they have sharp fangs, claws, and talons. Like the naga, they are inherently good creatures unless they are provoked. They are known to be loyal protectors of whatever they are guarding and will defend it fiercely. Also, like the naga, anything can kill it, especially fire. But, the naga has you beat when it comes to their lifespan. Nagas can easily live a thousand years," Astrid explained and then began to applaud them.

"We got some good creature selections. Nothing rare, yet nothing common. The naga would have been rare if it was more powerful. I'd say both creatures are uncommon, but closer to the rare side of uncommon so congrats. The two of you will be powerful if you survive the transition," Astrid added.

"That's the part you never really went into detail about," Aiden commented as he raised his hand.

"I'm sure Owen will fill you in, but now, for our last person of the day…Chad," Astrid said and then grinned while she walked over to him.

"What do you mean? He never made it to the gem mine," Owen said as his brow furrowed.

"No, he didn't but that's okay, I have a special treat. Remove his restraints," Astrid commanded. The mercenaries removed the straps and gag from Chad, so he quickly sat up. He then went to stand up, but the mercenaries grabbed his shoulders and pushed him back down. Owen, Prisha, and Aiden followed Astrid and then filtered off to the side of her when she stopped in front of Chad. "It's okay. You may stand," Astrid commented. Chad stood up in front of her while the mercenaries watched him carefully.

Astrid pulled a black, cloth-like pouch from her pocket. It was no bigger than the palm of her hand. She undid the strings and opened it. "Inside here is a gem…an onyx. I want you to reach in here and grab it," Astrid said without expression.

"How do you know that gem will match with him?" Owen inquired.

"I don't. Most likely it will not," Astrid replied with a deadpan expression.

"Then that's a death sentence," Owen blurted out as he began to walk forward but Astrid raised her hand. Owen stopped. "At least give him a chance in the gem mine."

"The traitor will get no such courtesy," Astrid glanced at Owen, who fidgeted in his spot as he tried to think of a way to save Chad without getting anyone killed. "Relax, I was going to give this gem to one of the staff people upstairs as part of my plan, but now Chad will actually be useful." Astrid's eyes narrowed in on Chad. "Take the gem!"

Chad reached and grabbed the pouch. He then slung his arm back and as he was about to throw it; Astrid grabbed his arm. "Stop," Astrid commanded. Chad froze. "Good, now reach in the pouch and pull out the gem." She then let go of his arm and smirked while she opened the pouch to allow Chad to be able to bypass the ward and take the gem.

Chad's hand trembled on its way to the pouch. "I don't want to do it, but I can't stop myself," Chad said through his teeth as he tried to fight her control. Owen and the others watched helplessly as Chad's hand entered the pouch. He then pulled out the onyx, which was slightly bigger than a golf ball. Owen's eyes widened as Astrid's smile grew while Chad stared at the gem. Then, the onyx began to absorb into his hand as he screamed and clenched his wrist with his other hand. The pain dropped him to his knees as he continued to scream. Prisha looked away while Aiden and Owen grimaced. Once it was over, Chad passed out and toppled over.

"I get my revenge all while continuing with my plan," Astrid said in a chipper voice.

"Your plan?" Owen asked.

"It will make more sense if I show you, but let's just say that I will soon have a guardian for this facility," Astrid playfully answered.

"The creature inside the gem…you know what it is," Owen said as his brow arched. Astrid smirked in response to his comment. "Well, what is it?"

A devious smile formed on Astrid's face. "It's a wendigo."

CHAPTER 17

Owen's eyes popped wide open. "Are you insane? What possible plan can you have with such a creature? It will kill everything it encounters, including you. Whatever plan you have cooking up in that mind of yours, change it. Lock him in the transition room and be ready to kill it as soon as Chad fully transitions."

"I'm sorry, a wen-di-what?" Aiden asked. Astrid gestured at Owen to answer him.

Owen sighed. "Wendigo…from the Native American mythology. If you ever had to picture what death would look like in creature form, this is it. It's a person who has been cursed to become this horrid monster with an undying craving for human flesh. Even though it will kill and eat just about anything, it's human flesh that it desires the most. Regardless of how starved this creature may appear, it is quite deadly. There are of course different variations to what it looks like and what it can do, but generally, it's a lanky creature that stands ten to fifteen feet tall, with long arms and fingers. The beast has matted patches of hair covering its decaying grey skinny body, and it smells just as bad as it looks. It has red sunken eyes and a deer skull for a head, that has antlers with many points that spread out wildly. The beast also has sharp claws, yellowish teeth, and even sharp talons on its feet. As for its powers, it is immensely strong and very quick. It is also durable and if it continues to satisfy its endless craving for human flesh, it can regenerate and live forever. They are known for their hunting skills, between their strength, speed, heightened senses, and stealth...they are unmatched. They can even imitate a human's voice to draw their prey in. This abomination can only be killed if it starves to death with the lack of human flesh, or if you burn its icy heart. There are rumors that silver through the heart can kill it or injure it, but most lore suggests burning the heart, if not the entire body, to kill it."

"That sounds terrifying," Prisha commented and then shuttered.

"Yeah, I agree. Why are you so eager to have one of those things?" Aiden asked.

"The project I have Alyssa working on is to create a barrier that no creature can pass through, on either side, of it. The barrier will be around a mile wide, in all directions, around the facility. However, there will be some adjustments for the area in front of the facility. The design will allow only humans to pass through it. For example, not only will it keep unwanted creatures from the outside, like an Amarok, from coming too close to my facility, but it will also keep creatures, such as the wendigo, inside. The wendigo will act like a guard against unwanted visitors," Astrid proudly responded.

"That's great and all but what happens if the barrier fails, or even more...how will you keep this thing fed? I hope you aren't going to just feed it people from here," Owen countered.

"I'm not concerned about it becoming loose and as for its diet, it will eat any animal within its area. That food source will go fast since we can't replenish them. However, it needs humans to survive and we have plenty of that in stock. Either with more traitors, enemies, or random hikers...I'm sure we will find someone. The good thing is that it doesn't kill or eat its prey fast. It slowly eats them over time, especially humans, so it can continue its intake of human flesh," Astrid retorted in a carefree manner.

Astrid turned toward the mercenaries. "Carry Chad back to the infirmary and have him patched up. I don't need him dying before his big day. Tell them that I also want him sedated. Once that is complete, I want him relocated and tied outside in the area that I will have designated for him." The mercenaries nodded before they reached under Chad's shoulders, picked him up, and dragged him away.

She then turned to the rest of the group. "Owen, you will accompany me outside to inspect and test the barrier spell. If that goes well, you can then get yourself cleaned up, join your newfound friends, and stay with them through the third day. As for you two, make yourself comfortable in the barracks, and don't stray too far."

Astrid turned and walked away, with Owen behind her. As he was walking, he turned and began to walk backward. "I'm sorry. I will be back soon. You will be okay for now and we will talk as soon as I get back," Owen said and then gave them a sympathetic smile before he turned back around and left with Astrid.

The two walked quietly down the hall and to the elevator. The silence continued in the elevator ride up until Astrid broke the awkward silence. "Are you always this talkative?" The unexpected comment made Owen chuckle.

"Wow, you laughed at my comment. Look at you warming up to me already," Astrid playfully added. Owen grinned and shook his head right as the door opened and they exited the elevator. They walked outside and were greeted by a mercenary and Alyssa, who were both dragging their feet, back toward the cabin. Alyssa was sweating heavily and covered with dirt as she changed direction and walked toward them.

"Good timing. It's complete," Alyssa said as she continued to catch her breath. He couldn't blame her, Between the distance of the barrier and how hot it was outside, he would have been sweating himself.

"Complete…as in fully operational, ready to go?" Astrid asked.

"Yep, ready to go…like me. Now, can I go back to my family?" Alyssa huffed.

"Great! Let's test it out," Astrid perkily responded. "Was the barrier spell to the specifications I requested?" Astrid asked the mercenary.

"Yes, it goes for around a mile to all three sides of the cabin. In the front, I'd say around twenty to fifty feet depending on where you go, with the pathway you requested. It is outlined with salt," the mercenary replied as he pointed to each area he discussed.

"Salt…outdoors. Won't it just blow away?" Owen inquired.

Alyssa smiled. "Let me explain to you how this works." She waved everyone over to follow her. She didn't walk far until she reached one of the trees about twenty feet away. "In order to construct a barrier spell so vast, I had to build it like a wall…one section at a time. I would pick two trees, regardless of their distance, and carve that symbol you see at the base of the trunk in each of them," Alyssa explained as she pointed. "I would then connect the two trees with a thick line of salt. By the way, I don't know how you were able to come up with so much salt that quickly, but I used most of it. Anyway, once the salt touched the anchor trees, I performed the spell and once it was complete, the markings and the salt became indestructible. Give it a try," Alyssa said as she gestured for Owen to test her project.

He walked up to the tree and transitioned. He then ripped at the tree and the symbol, but he could not even make the tiniest scratch on it. He then tried to set the tree on fire but he didn't see any evidence of burnt wood. Owen took a few steps over and kicked the salt and almost tripped because it was like he kicked a boulder. The salt line, only one to two inches in height, didn't move. He tried to move it with his hand and blew on it, but nothing. Not even another round of fire was able to destroy the line. Owen scoffed. He couldn't believe everything remained. He then transitioned back to human. "Neat little trick there," Owen said and then winked. Alyssa smiled and shrugged her shoulders.

"Neat, but let us see if it does its purpose. Owen, walk past the barrier," Astrid directed. Owen did as he was instructed and walked past with no issue. Astrid waved him back so he crossed the border again without an issue.

"Okay, do the same thing, but in transition. Just phase one, to see how sensitive it is," Astrid said as she gestured toward the border again.

Owen transitioned and walked toward the barrier but when he tried to cross, he hit what felt like an invisible wall. He transitioned back to human and rubbed his face. "Seems pretty sensitive," Owen sarcastically remarked.

"Indeed. Excellent. Now, do the same thing from the other side," Astrid directed.

Owen walked over the line and transitioned again before he walked back over, but this time with his hands up. His hunch was correct when he hit the invisible wall again. Astrid began to clap while Owen transitioned back to human again and walked across.

"Can something fly or jump across or burrow under the border?" Owen asked.

"Nope, since it is, in essence, one giant circle. It allows a barrier to be formed between all the trees, from the very top to underneath the soil and everything in between. It's like an enclosed circle," Alyssa replied.

"What about the pathway?" Owen asked as he looked toward the cabin.

"Follow me," Alyssa said as she walked back toward the cabin. "Since I didn't have any trees to work with here, I created a separate barrier area within the larger one by using these large rocks and placed them about ten feet around the cabin and then for the pathway itself. It wasn't easy, but I was able to chisel the symbols into the rocks."

Owen examined the work that Alyssa did. The pathway was wide enough to fit one to two people standing side-by-side, but what made his brow crinkle was that the pathway stopped short of the exterior barrier by about five feet. Even more, it was closed off by salt at the end of it as well. Then, it dawned on him as to why it was done that way. "The pathway stops short of the exterior and is closed off as added protection. That way, nothing that is already inside the barrier can just come straight inside the cabin," Owen commented while he looked over the pathway itself.

"Very good. That's correct," Alyssa said while she strolled over to Owen.

"Still...nothing is indestructible. There must be a way to bring it down," Owen remarked.

"True. Another witch could remove the spell, or another being that had enough magical force could dismantle or drain the magic away," Alyssa responded.

Owen scoffed. "I hate to admit it, but it's impressive. If it wasn't for the type of creature Astrid is unleashing within here, I'd say it is perfect."

"I agree and bonus points for being a big boy and admitting my idea is a good one. Still, don't get hung up over the creature. You worry too much," Astrid said as she nudged Owen on his arm with her elbow.

"What creature?" Alyssa asked as her brow knitted while she looked back and forth between Astrid and Owen.

"A wendigo," Owen responded.

"You can't be serious. My family and I are very familiar with the lore behind that creature. Your protector is a former cannibal who is cursed to be a hideous evil monster that has a never-ending hunger for human flesh. Really? That's insane and it's too dangerous," Alyssa quickly countered as her eyes widened.

"Will your barrier spell contain it within this area?" Astrid asked.

"Well, yes but that's beside the point. It…" Astrid raised her hand.

"Then there is nothing else to discuss," Astrid countered with a crooked grin.

"Nothing but my family," Alyssa said with a stern tone as she crossed her arms over her chest as her eyes narrowed.

Astrid slowly approached her while she smirked. "You have done an excellent job with both the djinn and this barrier spell. So good, that I need you to stay with me now for the unforeseeable future." Alyssa's brow furrowed and as she was about to speak, Astrid raised her finger to silence her and kept talking. "However, your family is safe. No matter what happens from this point forward, they are safe from me, my followers, and any wishes from the djinn. If you and I have a fallout, only you will be punished. So, if you do what I say and dissociate from your family, you will live a long and painless life. Only, if you accept this offer, of course."

"Why can't I see them anymore?" Alyssa asked.

"Because I don't need a family of witches plotting against me. Also, I have found that family and friends are less likely to attack, in fear of their loved ones getting caught in the crossfire. Besides, I tend to get a person's full attention when they aren't distracted by matters that don't concern me," Astrid replied matter-of-factly.

"Please, I don't want to lose my family," Alyssa responded as her voice cracked and her eyes watered.

"She has done everything that you asked of her. Please, don't do this to her," Owen pleaded.

"Everyone is being so dramatic. I didn't say she will never see them again. Just until whenever I feel I don't need her services anymore. I will even extend her the same courtesy as you and allow her a day to say her goodbyes. I know they don't live near here so I will even give you access to a phone to make whatever arrangements to see them. You can meet them in the same small town you were in before you came here. See…I'm not as big of a monster as you make me out to be. So, do you accept my terms?" Astrid inquired.

Alyssa hung her head and firmly closed her eyes. She then took a deep breath and raised her head as she wiped her eyes. "I accept." Owen could sense the disdain emanating from her.

Astrid smiled. "Good." She then took Alyssa's hand and paused for a moment. This made Alyssa lower her brow and curl her lip. "It may not seem like it now but in time, you and I could become friends," Astrid added before she let go of her hand and took a few steps back. "Alyssa, you earned yourself some rest so feel free to clean yourself up and do whatever you would like…within the facility. You can even go outside as long as you don't stray too far. Owen, I advise you to head back to the recruits and guide them through this process." She motioned for the mercenary to follow her as they went back inside the cabin.

"I'm going to kill her," Alyssa muttered.

Owen sighed. "You can't."

"I don't care what monsters she has in her. I'm sure I can find the proper spell to end her," Alyssa countered as she coldly stared at the cabin.

"She's not a hybrid anymore," Owen responded.

"What do you mean?" Alyssa asked.

"I mean, she made a wish to restore her full psychic abilities. When she took your hand for no good reason, while she was silent, I bet she did the same thing to you as she did to me," Owen replied.

"What did she do to you?" Alyssa cautiously asked.

"She made it so I couldn't harm or kill her," Owen slowly responded.

"She what? She can do that? How can you be so sure she did it to me?" Alyssa frantically asked.

"After she touched me, I tried to kill her and I couldn't. No matter how hard, I couldn't make myself do it. She explained to me afterward what she did. It seems she must touch you for her ability to work for things like that. She had no reason to hold your hand in silence. Think about it, why would she risk allowing an angry witch to be within her ranks without taking precautions? I'm sorry," Owen explained. Alyssa turned and screamed while she clenched her fists.

Owen put his hand on her shoulder. "We'll figure out a way but for now, take the chance she gave you with your family and keep going through the motions with her. At least your family is safe. My friends are still in danger if I don't follow her commands. Hopefully, in time we will come up with a way out of this that protects us and our loved ones."

Alyssa grinned and nodded her head before she patted Owen's hand that was on her shoulder. The two went back inside the cabin and as they made their way to the main level, Owen's thoughts dwelled on Alyssa. He felt pity for her since he understood the hurt and frustration she was experiencing. The only solace he took was that he had a powerful ally on the inside who was in the same situation. He hoped that between the two of them, and possibly Prisha and Aiden, they would find a way to defeat Astrid. He would include Chad, but his fate was already sealed.

Owen and Alyssa went to their separate rooms to get cleaned up. Once Owen was finished, he ventured to the lower level to meet up with the others. He didn't want to waste any more time getting to them since he was in their position before. Owen knew how scary and confusing it could be as they waited for the third day.

As he entered the barracks, he saw the two of them sitting on the same cot, both resting their elbows on their knees. Both of their heads raised simultaneously when they heard him enter the room. It was only them in the room, with two mercenaries standing guard outside the door.

He sat down with them and explained everything that he could think of to help them understand the situation they were in, but before he went into it, he talked about Astrid. Owen explained what and who she was before the gem mine and what happened afterward.

Next, he talked about himself and his group of friends. He discussed everything that they went through from training and the entire mission from start to present. He told them as much information as he could, but Owen did hold back some details about his friends because he wanted to be sure he could trust them.

Prisha and Aiden were shocked by everything Owen discussed, and for good reason. Not only did his story about his adventures keep them intently listening, but it also filled in the holes that Astrid conveniently left out. They were both hurt that they were deceived yet grateful for hearing the entire truth. Once they absorbed the information that Owen conveyed to them, he moved on to what was to come.

"You will have one more day of peace before the third day starts. Before that time arrives, you must go into the transition room because it could start at any point during that day. The room is designed to contain and eliminate any creature that spawns if a person fully transitions," Owen said in a calm tone.

"So, being a chosen one doesn't guarantee our odds of survival?" Prisha asked.

"A better question is why do we have to die? Can't you just wait for us to transition back to ourselves?" Aiden added.

"It increases your odds of not fully transitioning but there is no guarantee. As for your question Aiden, if a person fully transitions during the third day, they cannot transition back. They're gone and only the creature will exist. That is why Astrid is placing Chad within the barrier she had set up. She will have extra added protection against any intruder and keep people petrified of what she could do with the wendigo. She knows Chad's chances of walking away from this are slim at best. She is using him to uncage the wendigo from one prison to another. The fact alone that she must make sure it has an ongoing supply of human flesh terrifies me," Owen explained.

"Does it hurt?" Aiden softly asked as he winced.

"Transitioning in general, no. Transitioning on the third day is a pain like no other I have ever experienced, both physically and mentally. Oddly enough, it's partially masked by your constant will to remain in control. That is crucial…to fight as hard as you can. To think of whatever positive human memories you can to stay in control," Owen replied.

"Why did you phrase it like that? Human memories. What other memories would I have?" Prisha asked.

"Your creature's memories. The more you transition, the more you become your creature. This doesn't end just with the physical aspects, but mentally as well. You will already have a hint of its personality but that personality will intensify the deeper you transition. If you go deep enough like you will soon, some of its memories will creep in too. Meditation before your transition helps prepare your mind for what's to come. If you survive, meditation will also assist you in your daily life as you must deal with your creature's personality and share one mind," Owen explained.

"Is it that much of a struggle afterward?" Prisha inquired.

"It depends on your creature type and well…you. In the beginning, it is a struggle for everyone but you will adjust in time. It switches from a struggle to more of a standard way of life…and if you are lucky, a partnership. The more your mind is in tune, the easier it will be to stay in control when you transition in the future," Owen responded.

"Yeah, that's great and all, but what if you don't know how to meditate?" Aiden asked as he shrugged his shoulders.

Owen paused as it took him a moment to realize they didn't have the same training as he and his friends did. "Prisha, do you know how to meditate?"

"I used to as a kid but I haven't since then," Prisha replied.

"Well, there is nothing else to learn until you survive the transition so let's focus on that. Time for a crash course in meditation," Owen said as he stood up.

They spent a good portion of the day practicing the various techniques. Prisha's prior experience paid off as she was able to swiftly pick up on the techniques. On the other hand, Aiden struggled in the beginning. He couldn't focus because his mind was filtered with random thoughts that he felt needed to be shared. After some testing of Owen's patience, Aiden finally was able to grasp the art of meditation. He also learned that not everything that comes into your mind must be shared.

"I believe this is a good time to stop," Owen announced as he lightly tapped each of them on their shoulders.

"Are you sure? Wouldn't it be a good idea to practice even more?" Aiden asked.

"You could, but it will be better to have dinner, relax, and just have fun. Talk, laugh, or whatever. Just enjoy the moment while you can because after tonight, either way, it will be your last night as a normal human being," Owen responded.

"Well, that's both disturbing and intriguing at the same time," Aiden commented.

Owen chuckled and started to walk away when Prisha gently grabbed his arm. "Where are you going?"

"I figured you two would like to be alone," Owen responded.

"We're not a couple or anything like that," Aiden commented.

Owen grinned. "I meant you two know each other and would feel more comfortable if a stranger wasn't around."

"Aiden and I have known each other for a while now but you are not a stranger. You have been a friend to both of us and have given us hope in what seemed to be a hopeless situation. If we survive, we will need you again. So please, stay," Prisha softly said while she gently smiled. Owen returned the smile and nodded in agreement.

After they ate, they spent the rest of the night sharing stories and laughing. They refused to go to sleep, but at least accepted Owen's suggestion of taking a power nap to help keep their minds fresh for the meditation. While they napped, Owen was lucky enough to find some of the special bio-clothes that they could wear during the transition. After he explained the purpose of the special clothing to them, they were thankful to put them on. While they talked and laughed, it reminded him of when he and his friends sat in this room doing something similar. He was glad Prisha asked him to stay.

Owen glanced at the time and noticed it was close to the beginning of the third day. He looked back over to Prisha and Aiden who were laughing while they reminisced. Owen cleared his throat to get their attention. "I'm sorry, but it's time." The laughter ceased as their smiles faded away. They nodded and followed Owen from the barracks to the transitioning room.

As they walked, he explained how the rooms worked and what they needed to do once they were inside. They followed Owen inside and wandered to the center of the room while Owen sealed the door. The other door that led down the corridor to the large room was closed, even though it didn't matter anymore. Luckily, the remains of the dead vampire were removed and the area was cleaned. Once the door was locked, he turned and waited as Prisha and Aiden finished talking to each other and then hugged.

"Are you ready?" Owen politely asked.

"Thank you, for everything," Prisha said as she hugged Owen and then walked inside one of the rooms. Owen sealed the door behind her and then turned to Aiden.

Aiden smiled and shook Owen's hand and began to walk into the room across from Prisha but he stopped in the doorway and turned around. "So, if this works, I'll be able to fly? Like right away? No waiting period?"

Owen scoffed in amusement. "Yep. Right away."

"Can't wait," Aiden said as he smiled and walked into his room. As Owen sealed the door behind Aiden, he smiled as he thought about Avery and how excited she would be if she could fly.

Both Prisha and Aiden sat on their mats and began to meditate. As Owen waited, he pulled up a chair and placed it between the two rooms. At first, he would look back and forth as he watched them intently but after a couple of hours, he sat back in the chair and only glanced occasionally to see if they were still meditating.

Hours passed before Owen jumped up from his seat, half awake, when he heard Aiden screaming. He rushed over to the glass but felt helpless because all he could do was stand and watch. He yelled his name, but there was no way he would hear him. Aiden's head turned and all he could see were the griffin's eagle eyes, surrounded by white feathers, staring back at him. His talons scraped across the floor and he could see fur growing on his legs, and then a loud screech came out of him. Owen's eyes grew wide when Aiden began to hover, while he continued to strain as his entire body tensed up.

Owen's head whipped around when he heard screaming from behind him. He cringed when he saw Prisha standing on her feet but bent unnaturally backward. The back of her head was near the bend of her knees as she hollered. She then stood straight up and wavered like a snake but her other muscles were stiff. Owen could see her legs were already full of green scales and he also saw the naga's cobra eyes straining under the intensity of the transition. She fell to her knees as the transitioning continued and he could see the more man-like features appear on her face as her voice became deeper

"You can beat this. Just hold on a little while longer," Owen shouted at the top of his lungs. He hoped that they could hear him, but he wasn't sure since they didn't give him any indication that they could. He couldn't tell if they were about to fully transition or not as he quickly looked back and forth between the rooms.

This went on for a few minutes before Prisha's room became silent. When Owen looked into her room, he saw Prisha lying on the ground. She was breathing hard, but she was human. He let out a long sigh of relief as he smiled, for she made it. However, this was interrupted by a loud screech behind him.

CHAPTER 18

He took a deep breath and prepared himself for what he was going to see. Owen slowly turned around and to his amazement, and delight, he saw Aiden lying on the floor, exhausted. He smiled and chuckled to himself. The loud screech must have been the end of the transition before he reverted to himself, Owen thought. He felt exhausted just watching and worrying about them. Owen went and opened both doors before he helped the weary Prisha to her feet and assisted her out of the room. He sat her down on the chair so he could go in and help Aiden to his feet. Aiden put his arm around Owen's shoulder as they slowly left the room. Prisha stood up and hugged Aiden, which made Owen smile from ear to ear. He was ecstatic that everyone made it. As the two hugged, Prisha waved Owen over. He didn't hesitate to walk over to them and join their embrace. Eventually, they left the transition room and made their way to the garden area, near the hallway where the bedrooms were.

"Congratulations again. You don't know how happy and relieved I am that you two survived. All you have to do now is rest. I will check back with you later in the day or even tomorrow to allow you to not only recover but to acclimate yourselves to your new life. Just remember, especially in the beginning, it is harder to stay in control. Even more, if your emotions are high. You may be in transition and not even know it so add some meditation to your daily routine and let me know if you need anything," Owen said but his attention was diverted to Aiden. He stood there and watched Aiden strain as he tried to push his body to go up. "Are you trying to fly?" Owen asked.

"I thought I would be able to fly right away," Aiden commented while he continued his efforts.

"You have the ability but you must learn how to do it. For now, just concentrate on staying in control and not accidentally slashing someone to pieces," Owen urged as his eyes drifted to Aiden's hands.

Aiden followed Owen's eyes until he saw his talons. "Whoa!"

"Breathe slowly and steady your mind," Owen calmly said. After a minute of controlled breathing, he noticed that Aiden's talons had disappeared and his eyes had transitioned back to normal.

"Thanks. Baby steps…got it," Aiden added.

"Exactly. It will take time but we will train and get both of you comfortable in your new life, but for now, you two can take those rooms over there," Owen said as he pointed to rooms that never housed his friends. He wasn't ready to replace the rooms that used to belong to his fallen friends, even though he felt Prisha and Aiden would do them justice.

"Don't forget to pick up your supplies and extra clothes later. I will ask Astrid for permission regarding your clothes since that is in a different area of the facility," Owen added. They both nodded as they continued to their rooms.

After they went into their rooms, Owen realized there was one other transition…Chad. He hurried toward the elevator but before he reached it, he heard his name. He stopped and turned and saw Astrid walking down the main path in the garden area. He walked over to her to see what happened.

"Why are you down here already? What about Chad? Did he…"

"Fully transition? He sure did. Hours ago. A good thing too because man, for a big guy he squeals like a little girl," Astrid answered as the two met. Owen frowned at the thought of his suffering.

"And the wendigo?" Owen asked.

"Just as ugly as you described it. Your description of it was pretty close to what it looked like. Side note, the barrier spell definitely worked. It sure did keep it contained, but not the smell. Wow, that beast stinks. Luckily it sped off into the woods not too long after it realized that there was a human nearby." Astrid replied.

"A human! Do you know who it was?" Owen asked in a panic.

"I do. I compelled one of the mercenaries to begin walking around within its territory as loudly as he could. He didn't last long, but at least the wendigo will be fed for a while," Astrid said nonchalantly.

"You sacrificed one of your own people? An innocent person who will be alive for a while as that thing slowly eats him," Owen commented as his face squinched from disgust at her actions.

"That man was far from innocent. Besides, that's what he gets for allowing an ATV to go missing with no explanation. His slow agonizing death will send a message to everyone else that I don't mess around. Just be thankful it wasn't someone that works here," Astrid countered. Owen paused, for he knew Anders was the reason why the ATV vanished, and even though it was a terrible way to die, he was glad it wasn't someone at the facility. As Owen stood there, Astrid continued.

"So, how did the last two recruits do?"

"They both survived and are now in their rooms, recovering and adjusting," Owen answered.

"Splendid," Astrid said as her face lit up. "Now, not only are you in charge of their training, but I will also need you to stand by my side tomorrow. Maybe a few days after depending on how long everything takes when my guests arrive."

"Guests?" Owen asked as his brow knitted.

"Yes, anyone I promised a wish to will be here for me to deliver on that promise, and of course for me to gain more wishes. I will need you here as added protection in case anything goes astray," Astrid replied.

"Isn't that what your mercenaries are for and don't you have some other hybrids hanging about around here? Besides Prisha and Aiden," Owen retorted.

"I do, but my forces have dwindled and I need them elsewhere to continue protecting and keeping an eye over particular matters. I'm sure I can handle whatever comes my way, but it would be nice to have the additional muscle to make people think twice. That, or if someone does happen to pull a fast one on me, then you will be there to assist me. This is not a request. Figure out a schedule for the recruits and I will see you tomorrow morning. Relax. It will be fun," Astrid said as she winked and then walked away.

Owen shook his head and left. He was too mentally exhausted between the recent events and not getting much sleep the night before. He decided to eat and then head back to his room to shower and get some much-needed sleep. He had a feeling he was going to need all the rest he could get between the training and whatever else Astrid had planned for him.

He awoke the next morning refreshed and eager to meet with Prisha and Aiden to see how their night went and to begin their training. He found them in the cafeteria already eating, so he went and grabbed a tray of food. The two saw Owen coming and waved him over.

"Morning. How has it been going?" Owen asked as he sat down.

"Do you normally eat that much food?" Aiden asked as he examined Owen's tray.

"I have ever since I made it past the third day and my metabolism went into high gear. It happens to everyone, but more with certain creatures," Owen replied.

"Oh good. I thought I was stress eating, which made me stress out and eat more. I then became worried if I was going to eat so much that I wouldn't fit in the elevator anymore," Aiden commented, which made Owen chuckle.

"Besides food, how else is everything going?" Owen asked.

"Surprisingly well. I sense the naga within me, but I feel more at peace than I thought I would be. Especially, when I sat by the waterfall late last night. I felt calm while I admired it," Prisha responded.

"That's a good start. How about you Aiden?" Owen inquired.

"I didn't kill anybody," Aiden mumbled while he continued to eat. Owen paused while he waited for him to say more, but Aiden was done talking.

"Well…that's always a win," Owen responded and then cleared his throat. "Anyway, after we finish here, we can head down to the training hall. We can first sit and discuss exactly what you trained on while you were with Astrid. After that, we can move to a different room and work on your transitioning and specific creature skills. I'm afraid that some of that may be a learning experience for all of us. I don't have thousands of years of experience like Isaac had, but we will figure it out together. Astrid wants me with her when all her guests arrive so at some point, I will have to leave but I will check in on you as I can. In my absence, you can work on transitioning. Don't worry, we will practice that first. Just don't push it too much too soon. You don't want to fully transition on accident. Now, if there are any non-transitioning items we identify during our discussion later, then one of the other trainers here can assist you with that. Sound good?"

"Sounds like a plan," Prisha replied.

"I agree. By the way, I hesitate to ask this but…did Chad make it?" Aiden hesitantly inquired.

"No, I'm afraid not so if you go outside, be mindful of the borders," Owen responded and then went into detail about how the barrier spell worked and what to look for when they were roaming around outside.

The group finished their meals and then walked to the classroom. There, Owen found out exactly what they knew and wrote up a plan of action to train them to the same level that he was trained at. They then moved over to one of the training rooms. He first showed them techniques for transitioning from one phase to another while maintaining control. Owen wanted them to practice just in the first phase of transition and then once they were both comfortable, he would move them to the next phase. The training session lasted the entire morning until they broke for lunch. As they were finishing up their meals, a mercenary approached them.

"Owen, Astrid would like to see you in the training room. The one on this level that is furthest from here."

"Tell her I will be there in just a few minutes," Owen responded. The mercenary nodded and walked away.

"Okay. The two of you are off to a great start. Just stick to the plan and you will be fine. I'm not sure how long I will be gone but I will be back as soon as I can. Good luck," Owen said and then grinned.

"I think you will need more luck than we will," Aiden commented.

"Probably so," Owen said as he curled his lip to one side.

Owen walked down to the training area. He was all too familiar with this area since it was the same location where he and Klayden trained. When he walked in, Owen almost thought he was in the wrong room. Astrid had converted the training room into something that he would see at a convention center. A couple of mercenaries stood next to the door and there was a long red carpet that led to the middle of the room, where a large comfortable chair sat. A few feet to the right of that chair was another comfortable, yet smaller chair. Both chairs seemed to be from Isaac's office. On the other side of the larger chair was a white pedestal with an empty black necklace display on top of it. The room was stripped of any training equipment and replaced with rows of folding chairs on either side of the red carpet. What seemed out of place were the black tarps lying across the floor behind Astrid. As Owen surveyed the room, he heard the door behind him open.

"The guests are lining up at the edge of the barrier line and are about to begin coming inside," Astrid announced while she walked down the red carpet.

"Don't you need to make your third wish for any of this to work?" Owen commented.

"You are correct. I've been back and forth about it for hours and then I realized, why fuss over it when I am about to gain many more wishes. Therefore, I picked a straightforward wish," Astrid commented. She then held the locket in her hand. "I wish for ten million untraceable dollars to be added to each of my off-shore accounts," Astrid said and then took her phone out.

"Really…that's your big final wish?" Owen mocked.

Astrid didn't respond to him as she flipped through the screens on her phone. She stopped on one and narrowed her eyes. "Excellent. It's all there," Astrid remarked and then smiled. She then strolled over to the necklace display and draped the locket over it.

"People will enter this room and fill the seats. One at a time, each person will approach me, starting with the first row. Once they are done, they will leave the same way that they came. Most of the people will get one wish, but a select few will receive two wishes. I will remind them of their wish count as they lift the locket and start the process. The mercenaries are here to back you up, but they will also be directing traffic and other menial work. I also have a couple of followers, that are hybrids, making sure everything goes smoothly inside and outside this facility. As I mentioned before, your role will be to protect me and the locket. I expect you to be on top of it," Astrid explained but then paused while she was within inches of Owen's face. "Mess up, and you will end up watching one of your friends take a stroll out in the woods to meet the wendigo. I'm sure it will be thrilled to have some company," Astrid whispered as her face grew cold.

"Understood," Owen replied as he stared into her eyes.

"Good," Astrid exclaimed and then sat on the large chair. "This one is for you. Come, sit," Astrid added while she patted the arm of the smaller chair.

Owen did what she asked without any comments. He had no choice and he had to now protect her at the same level as he would any of his friends. He could feel his anger bubbling inside of him but he had no choice but to choke it back down to keep his friends safe.

"I'm surprised you are just wearing your normal, everyday clothes. I thought you would be in some fancy gown with a tiara on or something," Owen commented while he sat down.

Astrid smiled. "The thought did cross my mind but I chose not to just in case things get messy."

"Is that what the tarp is for?" Owen asked as his eyes drifted behind her chair.

"Yes, and to make it easier to haul the wendigo's food outside," Astrid replied in a carefree manner.

Owen shuttered at the mental image that she had just given him. Not too long after their conversation, people began to enter the room and fill the seats. Astrid reminded everyone of how it should go and the dangers if anyone were to try to use a wish against her in any form. She also stated that no one could ask for any special powers, which he figured must have been an unpopular statement due to the grumbling in the audience, but Astrid didn't seem to care. Owen wished he had a piece of paper and a pencil to write down all her wishes so he could have a better idea of how to defeat her later. There would be too many to memorize so he wanted to at least make a mental note of the ones he felt were important.

A person would walk down the aisle and grasp the locket with one hand, and Astrid's hand with the other. Owen presumed it was so she could see what their intentions were before the wish was spoken. Many of the people's wishes were to heal or take away sickness from a loved one, followed by money, property, or success in a career. Their wish was always last. Astrid would instruct them what to wish for and exactly how to say it.

The line was moving smoothly with no attempts against Astrid, but he could tell the djinn quickly had enough of Astrid's tactics. With Astrid's guests, the wishes were granted based on what the person's wish was intended, but with any wish related to Astrid, the wish had to specify exactly what was wanted. If there was an ounce of wiggle room for the djinn, it would take it. Astrid's frustration grew when she had to take more time to think about her wish, and even more when she had to waste another wish to fix a previous one. One of Owen's favorite mishaps was when Astrid wished she could breathe fire like a green dragon. She got her wish…literally. Fire would come out of her nose or mouth every time she exhaled. That one made Owen snicker for a few people after, but he stopped when he caught an unhappy glare from Astrid. Then, it finally happened. As Owen slouched in his chair, something caught his attention…silence. He looked over and the person making the wish was straining to talk.

"It appears this gentleman was going to wish that they were more powerful than me," Astrid announced as she grabbed him by the throat and choked the life out of him while everyone watched in horror. Owen hoped this would not continue since he hated to see innocent people, most likely victims or pawns in Astrid's plans, dying for trying to get justice. Unfortunately, this was not the case. The frequency of attempts increased. One woman tried to stab her with a blade she had hidden on her. Astrid took the blade from her and stabbed her repeatedly in the chest. She let the blood spray and flow in front of her as the mercenary removed the body and placed it on the tarps with the rest of the fallen people. She kept the dagger and used it on others when they tried to trick her, either by stabbing them or slitting their throat.

"I'm getting tired of doing your job, Owen," Astrid commented.

"I don't know how to help you. I can't tell who's going to do it and you are killing them before I can even get out of my chair," Owen countered.

"Fair enough," Astrid responded with a hint of a devious smile.

The room was a little over halfway cleared and the last ten people went well, so he hoped it was evident to everyone to not try to sneak anything passed her. Before Owen knew it, she had a dagger up to a man's throat. He was frozen as she stared at him. She then turned to Owen. "Your turn." Astrid turned her head toward the man. "You will not run from Owen, or struggle with him."

Owen grabbed him by the back of the shirt and walked him a few steps forward. Astrid left her chair and walked to the side of Owen. She didn't stand close, but far enough away to get a good view of what she wanted done.

"This man was going to wish that my mind powers did not work on him. Well, I guess he didn't wish it fast enough," Astrid announced to the room. She then looked in Owen's direction. "Kill him."

Owen felt sick to his stomach as he began to sweat. He put his hand around the man's throat while he pleaded for his life. He then put his other hand on the man's head. The man was blubbering and Owen had tears forming in his eyes. He wanted so badly to save him but to do that, he would sacrifice his friends in the process. How many more times would he have to do this today, he wondered. Then, a thought entered his mind. It wasn't pleasant, but he hoped it would work.

"Do it!" Astrid commanded.

Owen transitioned to phase three, which caused people to become uneasy and panic as they stood up. Some tried to leave, but the mercenaries raised their guns and stopped them. Owen put his arm around the man's neck and roared when he sunk his claws into the man's belly. The man hollered, but his screams became more high-pitched when Owen slowly dragged his claws from the man's belly to his chest. Blood spewed out while the man cried. Then, Owen kicked the side of the man's knee, causing it to bulge out while he collapsed to his other knee. He would have completely fallen if Owen hadn't sunk his claws into the man's shoulder. While his claws were in the man's flesh, his hand ignited. The fire charred the skin inside and out as the man's agony-filled screams became gurgled as blood entered his mouth. That is when Owen took his free hand and raked it across the man's throat. While he convulsed, Owen took his hand out of the man's shoulder and roared as he swung it down with all his might and decapitated him. The head rolled forward and came to a stop about ten feet away from Owen, with the look of agony still plastered on the man's face.

The body fell forward as Owen walked over, grabbed the back of the severed head, and held it up. "Do you want to end up like this man? You will not outwit or kill Astrid so just stop or else this will be your fate. A monumentally slow and painful death and I will make it even worse than what you just witnessed. Just do what you were told, get your wish, and go and live a happy life. Push aside whatever she did to make you want to take revenge. The only outcome will be your death and your family and friends mourning you. Your revenge died at the door when you walked in here so just let it be. Do you understand?" Owen sternly asked in a gravelly voice as he shoved the head in people's faces. No one responded. "Do you understand?" Owen yelled and then he roared while he threw the man's head against the wall, causing it to smash like a pumpkin.

The remaining people all agreed at once, with some of them gagging. Owen surveyed the room while he growled. Everybody sat back down in their seats and didn't make a sound, except for the sound of faint whimpers scattered throughout the room. "Move the body so we can continue," Owen directed toward the mercenaries while still in transition. The mercenaries wasted no time scurrying to the headless body and transporting it to the tarps.

Owen could feel the chimera's rage coursing through his veins. So much, it masked how horrible his human side felt. He was afraid to transition just yet in fear of allowing those emotions to surface so he remained in transition as he walked back to his chair. He didn't sit down. Instead, he stood close to Astrid's chair with his blood-stained clothes and claws and glared at the crowd.

Astrid strolled over and stood in front of him. "I'm impressed. You have them so frightened that they wouldn't dare challenge me. Not today…not ever. I can get used to this side of you," Astrid whispered. She gave him a sultry look as she walked away while she gently slid her hand across his chest. She sat down and proceeded with the wishes. Owen had to transition down to phase two to take the edge off so he could concentrate on remembering the wishes. This task was another welcomed distraction, especially since he had to transition down.

Finally, after a full day of wishes, the room was cleared. His plan had worked. The brutal sacrifice of one person saved many more from dying and him having to be the one to do it. Owen was mentally exhausted. Not just from the ordeal he went through or remembering the wishes, but holding the transition as long as he did. Even though he was in full control, it still wore on him as the hours passed.

"All things considered; I believe that went better than I anticipated," Astrid remarked.

"Good. May I be excused now," Owen asked.

"What's the rush? I say we need to celebrate, but not like that. People are gone now so you can transition back to normal," Astrid suggested.

"I will but I figured I would help drag the tarps upstairs first," Owen countered.

"The mercenaries will handle that. Transition back to human...now," Astrid commanded as her brow lowered.

Owen hesitated out of fear. He was afraid he would crumble in front of her but he couldn't delay any longer, so he transitioned back to normal. As he expected, his feelings broke through like a river through a dam. He pressed his lips firmly together while they trembled. His brow crinkled and his eyes had a hint of glassiness in them.

Astrid looked at Owen with sympathetic eyes. "You won't want to hear this, or even believe this, but it gets better over time. You just have to remember it's not your fault. They knew the rules and the consequences. You and I were just enforcing them. You are excused but feel free to find me later if you would like to celebrate with me," Astrid offered and then put her hand on his shoulder before she left to talk to the mercenaries.

Owen rushed out of the room and quickly made his way to the top level. He headed straight for the elevator and ignored Prisha and Aiden, who called his name numerous times. He reached the elevator and frantically mashed the button before the door opened. It took all his strength to not break down in the silence of the elevator while unpleasant thoughts tried to evade his mind. When it reached the top, he bolted out of the cabin and headed toward the nearest open cliff, which happened to be the same spot where the ritual was going to be held. The thought of the wendigo didn't even enter his mind as he walked in and out of the barrier to get into the clear.

Once the cabin was just out of sight and he reached the cliff, Owen leaned over and vomited. After that, plus a few dry heaves, he screamed out into the void before he fell to his knees and began to sob. The thoughts of what he did to that poor man haunted him. He brutally tortured and killed not only an innocent man but one who was probably justified in wanting revenge against Astrid. Now his body, along with the others, will be tossed into the woods for the wendigo to feast on.

It scared him that he was capable of performing such a horrific act. He wondered how could he be such a monster. Yes, he did it to save lives and to prevent himself from killing multiple people, but he took it to another level. Even worse…when he was slowly killing that man, it didn't bother him. He knew that the chimera's personality was more present so it wasn't really him, but it didn't matter. He was in control and still did terrible things to an innocent human being.

He became fearful that Astrid was right…in time, this would be easy for him. He denied it at first, but now he wasn't sure after what he just did. How many other people would he mutilate, and then justify afterward, until it didn't bother him anymore, he fearfully pondered. It frightened him that her influence, over time, would change him into someone that he wouldn't recognize anymore. Owen couldn't get the images out of his mind and for a while, he figured he deserved how horrible he felt. He sat there on the cold slab of rock, in the dark…crying, lost, and utterly alone.

CHAPTER 19

Over the past few months, Owen was able to get into a routine. In the mornings, he would meet with Prisha and Aiden for breakfast and then they would find a quiet area within the garden to talk and laugh about various topics. Occasionally, the topic was serious or upsetting but the three were there for each other and became close as time went on. He was grateful for them because he could feel himself becoming darker without his friends. Especially, while being forced to live and work with Astrid. Prisha and Aiden kept him smiling, even when he didn't think he was able to. They helped replace his thoughts of despair and frustration with ones of happiness.

Since they completed their training with the other trainers, such as firearms and melee combat, Owen was able to focus their training on using their abilities and increasing their control over their creatures. In addition to their training, they would meditate and work out in the gym almost every day. Once they established control over their creatures, the three began to spar.

Prisha progressed well within her training right from the beginning. When she transitioned, she became quite strong and flexible. These traits increased the further in transition she went. In phase two, she was able to use the venom within her fangs, as well as create water. Not much, but enough to fill a bathtub if she transitioned deep enough. Regardless, it was a good ability to have. Even if it was just to have drinking water when none was available. However, Aiden didn't want to drink it because he doubted that it went through a magical water filter. Owen and Prisha couldn't help but tease him about the magical filter from time to time.

To supplement her abilities, she decided to incorporate at least the melee weapons from India. One was a talwar, which is a curved sword like a saber. The other was a koftgari dagger, which is a high-quality steel blade that is slightly curved outward toward the end of the blade. The steel hilt of the blade had designs on it that ended with a tiger's head that curved inward. She also kept a compact revolver on her as well. Owen was impressed by Prisha's great control over her creature and how well she progressed in her training.

As for Aiden, he had a rough start when it came to learning his powers and remaining in control. More times than Owen could count, Aiden's transitioning would quickly escalate and he would have to be calmed down to keep from a full transition. With increased meditation and discipline, Aiden was able to stay in control and once that occurred, his progress took off. He had his talons, strength, and increased eyesight in phase one, and those increased once in phase two, but he also gained the ability to fly.

Without knowing how to fly, Owen went to Astrid for advice. With that advice, he was able to teach Aiden and he went from flying into walls to full control of his flying ability. This brought Aiden much joy. He also used a variety of guns from semi-automatics to revolvers and everything in between. He liked the idea of having the option to fly and shoot his opponents if he felt he couldn't beat them hand-to-hand. However, he enjoyed the idea more once he figured out how to fire the guns if his talons were out.

During the afternoon, Owen would eat lunch and then shower after the intense workout he had with Prisha and Aiden. He would then take the time to make his way around the main level and talk to

Isaac's original staff to make sure they were doing well. While he did this, Prisha and Aiden patrolled the barrier line to make sure everything was okay. They never did get a glimpse of the wendigo, but they would find the occasional blood splatter on the ground and trees.

Owen ate dinner with Astrid each night in a private area she had constructed that viewed the waterfall and surrounding garden area. Astrid demanded that he eat with her so they could go over the training and overall daily happenings with the facility. He felt like her unofficial second in command. At first, he despised going and the only thing that made it tolerable was the food and drink. Astrid used two of her wishes to have a platter that served whatever food she asked for, and a pitcher that contained whatever drink she requested. She allowed Owen to make requests, which he enjoyed.

However, over time he found himself content when it came to seeing her. She didn't always talk about business. She would sometimes talk about her day or ask how Owen's day was. There were times when the two of them would talk about their past or how they were feeling inside. Sometimes, they would even just watch television and laugh. Owen couldn't believe it or stop it, but he began to look forward to their meetings. He didn't forgive her for the things she had done, but his hatred and disgust toward her were not as intense as before.

Once he left Astrid, he would venture outside the cabin. Sometimes, he would stroll along the barrier line to see if he could catch a glimpse of the wendigo. He never did see it, but he would hear the words "help me" faintly off in the distance. He knew it had to be the wendigo mimicking the sounds of that phrase because if he listened closely enough, the pitch was off...usually too high. Either way, it would send a shiver up his spine every time he heard it. He spent most of his time sitting on the ledge of the cliff. It felt secluded and with the leaves changing colors and falling, it was a pretty sight. With fewer leaves, he could see further down the gorge. He wasn't sure how far down it went, but the length of the gap was around two hundred feet if he had to guess. He would sit there anywhere from one to a few hours, just admiring the view or thinking about what his friends were up to and if they were doing well. Even when it was dark and he couldn't see well, he still felt peaceful. He would also meditate out there if he wasn't planning on doing that in his room before he went to bed.

This area, along with the meditation and the help of his new friends, helped him clear his mind and stay positive. His nightmares about the day he mutilated that poor man were intense right after it happened. He would wake up every night screaming and drenched in sweat. Now, the terrible dreams are gone and he is not burdened with the lack of sleep and constant guilt. In some way, he should thank Astrid as well since he used the djinn's platter to stress eat a lot of chocolate cakes. Even though his time at the facility was not as horrible as it once was, he still missed his friends terribly.

He didn't see much of Alyssa since Astrid had her in the scouting parties. Her goal was to find more gems in nearby states where Astrid's research hinted a gem may be located. The mercenaries would follow her like a search party would follow a bloodhound. If she was close enough to a gem, she could sense the magic and once she felt she was over it, the mercenaries would take over and retrieve the gem. They only found a few, but the ones they found Astrid would keep in her private office. When she was in town, Owen and Alyssa would talk about her adventures or they would talk about their friends and family. In the beginning, he could tell she was quite bothered by not being able to communicate with them. She was often quiet and would mope around. After a couple of months, she seemed more cheerful. Owen wasn't sure if she finally accepted it or if their talks began to help, but he was glad to see her in a better mood.

One day, as Owen, Prisha, and Aiden finished their sparring, Astrid walked into the training room.

"Hello everybody. From the sweat, I see everyone had a productive session. If you don't mind, I would like to continue the training session with just Owen. You two are excused," Astrid stated as she looked solely at Owen.

"No problem," Owen responded and then turned to the others. "Good job everyone. I'll talk to both of you later." He half-smiled as the other two did the same and quickly left the room. He couldn't blame them. Astrid had a way of instilling fear into people by merely just her presence.

"What did you have in mind? We can't spar because I can't hurt you and unless you are an expert in chimeras, there's nothing to teach me," Owen commented.

Astrid giggled. "I'm not an expert, but I can teach you something." Owen's head tilted as his brow knitted.

Astrid stood beside him and pointed out in front of him. "I want you to shoot your flames out as far and as intense as you can with your hands only. Even if you must transition to phase three…I just want to see what you've got." Owen continued to stare at her. "Go on, just do it. Humor me," Astrid added as she nudged him in the arm with her elbow while she smiled.

Owen shrugged and transitioned deep into phase three and roared as he flung his hands forward as far as his arms could stretch. Two streams of fire burst from his hands. Owen then moved his hands together so the two flames would form one large intense flame.

Astrid strolled down the flame line, shielding her face from the intensity of the flames. She then began to casually walk toward the flames and as she did, the fire stopped streaming from Owen's hands. With her standing in front of him, his fire ability ceased to work. "Impressive. Transition back to human so I can talk to you and have your full attention." Owen did what she asked and transitioned back to normal.

"I'd say the original blast was around thirty feet, which is impressive, but the fire wasn't as intense as it was later. Shortly after you started, it became hotter, but you lost almost half the distance of your flame. All this is great…better than an average hybrid that has a fire ability, but what if I told you that you could do so much more?" Astrid asked and then smirked.

"I'm listening," Owen said as his brow arched.

"You know you can transition to phase three and have so much more access to the chimera's abilities and power, but you don't go as deep as you could. You're holding back," Astrid replied.

"I don't know about that. I already go pretty deep into phase three, to the point I can feel the chimera's essence about to come forth," Owen countered.

"I'm sure you do, but it scares you because you don't want to fully transition. I get it. You are scared because you don't know exactly how far you could take it before the chimera will appear. I can help you with that," Astrid explained.

"Why do you want to help me?" Owen asked.

"First, because the stronger you are, the more useful you are to me. Second, as a thank you. You spent additional time with me and during that time, we talked and even laughed. If it was real or not, it was good to remember what it was like to have a friend. Now, do you want to learn or do you want me to keep being mushy?" Astrid asked while she grinned.

Owen chuckled. "Teach me, please."

"Okay. Now you will line up as you did before and transition to phase three, but this time I will stand behind you and put my hands on your temples. I will tell you to keep going further in your transition and you need to trust me and do as I say, even if you feel that you have gone too far. Keep going until I tell you to stop. Do you understand?" Astrid asked.

"Yes. I'm nervous, but I will trust that you will not let me fully transition unless you want to be face-to-face with a chimera," Owen responded.

"Good," Astrid said as she placed her hands on the sides of his head. "Proceed!"

Owen stuck his hands out and unleashed the fire. He kept transitioning deeper but he began to stop when he felt he went far enough. "Keep going," a voice inside his head instructed him to do, so that's what he did. Every time he was about to stop, he would hear those same words again. He became nervous but kept following the directions of the voice inside his head. He felt as if the chimera was right under his skin, ready to burst out of him. Owen's intensity was the highest he ever experienced; however, he felt more powerful and confident than he ever did before as well. His arms and hands were of a beast and he could see the flames holding their original distance. Then, without reason, he roared and as he did, fire spewed from his mouth. "Stop," the voice echoed in his head. Owen couldn't help it, the chimera demanded more. "Stop," the voice said louder. Owen tried to stop but he was having trouble. Then, he felt a sharp pain in his head that made him lose his concentration, and quickly dropped down to phase two.

He was breathing heavily from the adrenaline and then he turned around when Astrid released her hands from his head. "What just happened?" Owen asked.

"It depends. So many things happened," Astrid responded with a hint of a smile. "You transitioned deeper than you ever have before without fully transitioning. With that, you became so much more powerful and fearless as more of the chimera came out. Look at the floor. You can tell your flame was more intense and held its original thirty-foot distance by looking at the discoloration on the floor. That is how intense your fire was. Good job."

"Thank you. I've never felt like that before. All that power. I felt, unstoppable," Owen remarked as he smiled. "It's good to know I can reach that level and make it back. It's just unfortunate I can't do that without your help. Even when you told me to stop, I had trouble until you forced me to stop," Owen added as his smile disappeared.

"Chin up. You don't need my help. Why do you ask? Because I planted a fail-safe in your brain," Astrid said with a hint of a smile.

"What do you mean?" Owen inquired.

"I know it must be hard to know when to stop, even when you were told because your creature is doing more of the thinking at that point. You just can't stop, hence why people lose control and fully transition. Even with you being a true hybrid and having control, at some point, you can push too far and lose that control. I was counting on this and waited until the last moment before I intervened and planted that fail-safe. I adjusted your mind so that if you go too far, that pain will slap you back down to phase two. I would have done it back to your normal state, but just in case you were in battle, you don't want to transition down to human. That may have some unfavorable consequences. Also, you can still fully transition if you want to. When your mind commits to that you won't even feel the pain. Consider your mind, upgraded," Astrid explained before a smug expression appeared.

"You not only made me stronger and have more control, but you also took away my fear of losing control. Granted, after what Livia did, I didn't have that fear anymore, except when I transitioned to phase three. Now, that is gone. I don't know what to say," Owen muttered.

"Some people would say thank you," Astrid commented while she shrugged and smiled.

Overwhelmed with joy, Owen hugged Astrid. She didn't move at first, but then she wrapped her arms around him. "Thank you," Owen whispered. He then realized what he was doing and let go and quickly backed away. "Sorry, I didn't mean to just do that."

"No worries at all. In fact, you should do that more often," Astrid playfully replied and then winked at him. Owen scoffed in amusement. "Well, as much as I would like to continue this, I'm afraid that I have some things to attend to. I'll see you later," Astrid added and smiled as she walked away and left the room.

Owen stood there for a bit, confused at what just happened. He wondered if she was getting more under his skin, to the point that someday in the distant future, he may consider her a true friend and forget everything she had done. He couldn't fathom that happening and chalked up today as over-excitement for not fearing a full transition when he was in phase three. However, he had noticed that Astrid had been good lately. No plotting or killing or threats…just acting like a normal human being. One that gives orders, but she was acting more like a person…a person that was tolerable to be around and even sometimes, fun to be around as well. Owen then thought it could all be a ploy to gain his trust, but there was no way to be sure. He had to continue as he was and just be mindful that it could be a trick. If not…if she was truly becoming a good person, he would honor Isaac's wishes and continue to help her on that journey.

Since Astrid was busy and Alyssa was back in the facility, he decided to see if she wanted to eat dinner with him. It had been a while since he had talked to her and he wanted to catch up. After he took a shower and changed, he walked down the hall to her room and as he was about to knock on her door, his hand stopped. His brow lowered and he turned his head sideways while he moved it closer to the door. Owen could faintly hear chanting from within her room, but it didn't last long before there was silence. He waited for a minute to see if he could hear any more chanting or noises coming from her room, but the silence continued.

Concerned, he knocked on the door, but he heard nothing but the sound of his hand beating on her door. "Alyssa, are you okay?" Owen loudly asked as he pounded on the door, but there was still no response. He contemplated kicking the door open, but maybe there was a legit reason. He didn't hear any signs of a struggle and he didn't see any marks on the door from someone forcing themselves in, so he decided to wait. Owen sat down on a nearby bench and watched the door as he waited. About fifteen minutes or so later, he heard her door unlock and Alyssa emerged from her room.

"Hey, Owen," Alyssa said as she smiled, but it quickly went away as her eyes widened. "Wait, why are you here? You should be with Astrid. How long have you been out here?" Alyssa loudly whispered so quickly that her words almost ran together.

"Astrid was busy so I figured I would ask you if you wanted to eat dinner so we could catch up, but you never answered your door. I was worried, especially since I heard chanting and then silence, regardless of how much I knocked," Owen replied.

Alyssa gasped as she looked all around. "Come with me," Alyssa quietly requested and then grabbed Owen's hand and headed back to her room. She walked so fast that she tugged on Owen's arm to make him move faster. They entered her room and then she briskly closed her door.

"What's wrong?" Owen asked.

"I've got a confession and I need you to keep quiet about it. I can only imagine what Astrid would do if she found out," Alyssa responded.

"Found out what?" Owen quickly countered.

Alyssa paused while she fidgeted and then her face crinkled. "That I have been using magic to talk to my family."

"You did what? How?" Owen loudly asked. Alyssa put her finger over her mouth while she intensely stared at Owen.

"Inside voice. I used astral projection," Alyssa replied.

"That's a real thing? Tell me about it," Owen requested.

"Yes, it's a real thing, but I can't just snap my fingers and do it. Stronger witches can do it quickly and however often they choose. I, on the other hand, need assistance from herbs and crystals and can only manage to perform the spell once, maybe twice a week since it really drains me. To the point that it's hard for me to perform any magic the day after. I also can only perform the spell for about ten minutes before I run out of power, but in those precious ten minutes, I can see and talk with my family. I wish I could hug them, but I will take what I can get for now. That short time frame each week for the past couple of months has really saved me," Alyssa explained.

"That explains your mood change. That's amazing and I'm thrilled for you. I'm just surprised you were able to keep it hidden for so long and I'm sorry if I messed up your time with your family earlier. I was just worried," Owen commented.

"Thank you and you didn't ruin anything. My astral body, spirit, consciousness, or whatever you want to call it leaves my body. My body is here, but I can't hear or react to anything since mentally I'm with my family. As for hiding it from Astrid, I take a few precautionary steps because as strong as a psychic she is, Astrid would be able to sense all that mental energy being exerted. I surrounded myself with particular herbs that I burned to help mask any magic in the area. I also wait until you and Astrid are at dinner because not only is she a good distance away from here, but she is also distracted by you. That is why I was so scared earlier. I was afraid with you here, she may have picked up on what I was doing, but I haven't experienced her wrath yet so I'm hoping I'm in the clear," Alyssa remarked as she wiped her forehead.

"Don't worry. Your secret is safe with me. I won't tell anybody here, not even Astrid. She purposely doesn't read my mind because she wants our friendship to be real, so you should be fine," Owen said as he smiled but then he pressed his lips together as he looked away.

"I really appreciate it but what is it?" Alyssa inquired.

"I don't want to get you in trouble or take time away from your family, but…" Owen paused as he tried to push the words past his lips.

"You want me to help you astral project so you can see your friends," Alyssa added as one side of her lip curled.

"It would mean a lot. I miss them dearly. Like I said, I would not be upset with you if you said no. I would understand, but if there was any chance, even if it was just for a few minutes, it would mean the world to me," Owen said with kind eyes and a gentle smile.

"Give me a week or two and we can try. I know how you feel and I don't wish that feeling on anyone…well, mostly anyone. I just need time to recharge and let my family know what is going on. Who knows, maybe you can find out if your friends made any progress on how to stop Astrid or how to get us out of here," Alyssa responded as she grinned.

"Thank you!" Owen exclaimed as he rushed to her and hugged Alyssa. "Sorry, apparently I am extra emotional today."

Alyssa laughed. "It's okay. Let's go grab some dinner." Owen nodded and the two left her room and walked to the cafeteria to eat. After Alyssa and Owen ate dinner and caught up, they began to walk around the garden, when Prisha and Aiden greeted them.

"I see you are hanging out with the commoners tonight," Prisha mocked in a British accent. Owen shook his head while he laughed.

"Well, I always try to keep the little people in mind," Owen teased back in a British accent as well. The group laughed and then Owen explained the change of plans. Then, the group strolled around the garden as they chatted. As Owen was talking, he noticed he didn't see Aiden so he looked around and he found Aiden behind them, floating.

"Why are you floating behind us?" Owen asked as he stopped and knitted his brow.

"Why walk when you can fly, hover, glide, or float? So much easier," Aiden answered. He didn't seem fazed by the question.

"Wow, that's lazy, and I have seen my fair share of laziness. That is really up there," Prisha commented.

"Somebody is jealous. You know, green is not a good color on you," Aiden teased as he put his hands behind his head and leaned back while still in the air.

"As much as I want to fuss at you that your legs are going to become wobbly from lack of use, your control over your flying skills is remarkable," Owen mentioned.

"Don't encourage him," Prisha said as she playfully slapped Owen's arm.

"It's okay, Prisha. Owen sees it. Game recognizes game," Aiden remarked.

"Wow…just, wow," Alyssa said as she turned around and continued to walk. Prisha shook her head and followed Alyssa's lead.

"Yeah…wow…unbelievable," Owen said. He then secretly turned around and smiled as he winked and gave Aiden a thumbs-up. Aiden smiled back as he nodded.

"Astrid gave me a gift," Owen said but purposely stopped talking to make his friends' imaginations go wild.

"Well, what was it?" Alyssa inquired after Owen's long pause.

"She made it so I won't accidentally fully transition when I am deep into phase three," Owen responded. He then explained what happened in the training room and explained more about what was done for him so he would not accidentally transition.

"Can she do that for us?" Aiden asked as he softly landed on his feet.

"First off, thank you for joining us. Second, I think it will only work for me because of the different relationship that I have with my creature and how my mind works now. I'm a totally different hybrid than everyone else. Sorry," Owen replied.

"It's okay. It was worth a shot," Aiden responded and shrugged it off. Afterward, the group discussed various topics as time flew by.

"Well, it's getting late so I'm going to head off to bed," Alyssa commented. Prisha and Aiden were in the same mindset and the group dispersed shortly after. Owen wasn't surprised, especially with Alyssa and the magic she performed earlier.

Owen didn't feel tired enough to go to bed so even though it was later than when he usually went outside, he decided to go anyway.

The air was cool as he walked to his usual location. It was quiet, except for the sound of crickets off in the distance. Between the clouds and the lack of a full moon, Owen had to transition to make sure he didn't trip over anything. He eventually reached his spot. The area was pitch black so besides admiring the view, he decided to sit down and get in some meditation before he left to go to bed. As he transitioned back to normal and sat down, a small flash of light caught his attention.

He scanned the area, but he didn't see the light again. He wondered if it was a stray hiker's flashlight. This worried him because if they wandered into his area, they might run into the wendigo. Owen continued to survey the area for any signs of life and that is when he saw a flash of light again from across the gorge. He slowly stood up and transitioned in order to get a better look. It was difficult, but as he squinted to peer over the void, he saw the outline of what appeared to be a human, but not exactly. The top part seemed human but the bottom half was disproportionate to the rest of its body. Owen was about to transition deeper to get a better view, but he didn't have to. A small, white crackling light appeared and illuminated the area. Owen gasped, and then he put his hand over his quivering mouth. His face crinkled while a tear ran down his cheek. It was Hailey and Avery.

CHAPTER 20

Hailey stood tall while the electricity arched between her fingers on her right hand which she had slightly raised in the air. Squatting in front of her was Avery. Owen wiped his face and smiled before he raised his hand to about chest height. He whipped his head around to make sure no one was behind him, and he only saw trees and boulders. He knew the risk, but he didn't have the willpower to tear himself away. Instead, a flame flickered from his hand to illuminate just his chest and face.

With both of their creature's heightened vision, Hailey and Owen were able to see each other. Hailey smiled and put her left hand over her chest. He looked at Avery and noticed she was smiling but she wasn't staring him in the eyes. She wasn't in transition either because it would have made her vision worse. He understood; therefore, he shuffled a foot to the right so Avery would be staring him in the eyes. Hailey's smile grew when she noticed what Owen did and he could see her relaying his actions to Avery. He then saw Avery giggle and then she used sign language by crossing her hands over her chest to say one word, "love." Owen smiled and he sparked a flame in his other hand. He then carefully crossed his hands over, but away from his chest to relay the word "love" back to her so she could see it. Avery's smile grew from ear to ear as she wiped a tear from her cheek. Owen looked up and mouthed the words "thank you" to Hailey. She grinned and slowly nodded her head in acknowledgment.

Everyone stared at each other for a moment, but Owen didn't want to press his luck so he pointed behind him and frowned. Hailey pointed at her wrist and then to the ground under her feet. Owen figured she was telling him to meet them at the same time and place again, so he gave her the thumbs up. The three waved at each other before Owen extinguished his flames and Hailey's electricity vanished. He stared into the darkness for a few more seconds before he smiled and walked away.

He had to contain the happiness he felt as he passed the cabin mercenaries, and anyone still awake, as he walked through the facility to his room. Once he was in the safety of his own room, an enormous smile appeared on his face. It wasn't much and of course, he wanted more interaction with them, but just that small moment in time was what he needed. He felt revived. When he went to bed, he had the most restful night he had in a long time.

The next morning, he had to stifle his happiness again since he did not want to draw any attention to himself. He also decided to not tell Prisha and Aiden due to the nature of how serious it was if Astrid found out they knew. He wouldn't want them to be punished because of him. After the training was completed but before dinner with Astrid, he sought out and found Alyssa.

"Hey there. What's up?" Alyssa asked.

"Since you trusted me with your secret, I have one of my own. After everyone went to bed I went outside and Hailey and Avery happened to be in the area," Owen quietly informed.

Alyssa's eyes grew wide. "Are you crazy? What if someone saw the three of you together?" Alyssa loudly whispered as she pulled Owen closer.

"It's okay. I was in an area where no one could see us and they were on the other side of the gorge. It was also dark outside and the light sources we used were kept low and we were not out there long. I know it was a risk but I couldn't just turn away from them once I saw them. That little interaction meant so much to me. That is why we are going to keep it up each night for as long as I can. I knew I missed them, but I didn't realize how much until tonight. You of all people should understand that," Owen countered.

Alyssa sighed and lowered her head. She then raised her head and put her hand on his shoulder. "You're right, I do. We can help each other out so we both can keep seeing the ones we care about. I'm sorry if I got snippy. It's just nerve-racking trying to sneak around like this while keeping a powerful psychic like Astrid out of the loop."

"At least we are not alone in this. If we work together, maybe we can stay sane long enough to figure a way out of this mess," Owen commented.

"I couldn't agree more," Alyssa remarked.

The two talked for a little while longer before they parted ways. Owen stuck to his daily routine, including dinner with Astrid. He acted normal and kept the routine going as he always did. The only change was that he went outside later.

Over the next couple of weeks, Owen was able to see them most of the time. The times he couldn't were due to unforeseen Astrid requests or because he couldn't leave Astrid in time without being suspicious. It wasn't always Astrid's fault. Sometimes, Prisha and Aiden caught Owen in the hallways and he didn't want to be rude to them or spill his secret, so he stayed and chatted with them. Some days, Hailey would bring someone other than Avery. Owen was lucky enough to see Bailey, Abigail, Marcus, and Selena as well. After the first few times with Hailey and Avery, whomever Hailey brought with her brought a pair of binoculars to help see Owen, except for Abigail who of course didn't need them.

Every secret meeting Owen had with his friends, he made sure they stayed on the other side of the gorge. A few times in the beginning, Hailey and Avery indicated with hand gestures about coming over to his side, but Owen would always shake his head no. He was too scared to take the chance and get caught. He was also fearful that they may come from a different direction and run right into the wendigo. Eventually, they realized something must have been too dangerous for them to meet Owen face-to-face so they gave up asking. It broke Owen's heart to do it, but he didn't want to take any chances and risk their lives. He began to look so forward to seeing his friends that it was hard for him to concentrate. Then one day, during training, he was having a hard time focusing until something was said that made him stop what he was doing and turn around.

"I'm sorry, what did you say?" Owen inquired.

"That I wish we could track and kill the wendigo," Aiden repeated.

"Why?" Owen asked.

"Because we can't go on missions so why not make up our own mission? We're ready," Aiden replied in a carefree manner.

Owen scoffed. "I don't know what to start with first. The fact that Astrid would have your head if she found out that you killed the wendigo or the fact that you said you are ready."

"She wouldn't know it was us. We could say we found it that way when we did our patrol," Aiden replied.

"So, your plan is to kill her wendigo and then lie about it in front of Astrid, the powerful psychic. Good luck with that," Owen mocked.

Aiden rolled his eyes. "Then we kill it and go on the run. Her forces are thin and by the time she even found out, we would be long gone."

"I can't believe I am saying this but I agree with Aiden," Prisha added.

"Even if that plan did work and you two accepted the life of a fugitive, what makes you think you can kill a wendigo? I wouldn't be able to help you because I don't want to put my friends' lives in danger," Owen commented.

"We're ready. Even you said that we have received more training than you ever did," Prisha rebutted.

"True, but the real world and training are night and day. Are you ready for a mission...sure. Are you ready to take on a powerful creature with just the two of you...no. Back then, I wouldn't be either and when we made our assault on the mountain, I had a team of hybrids with me. Even then, people died or were seriously hurt," Owen explained.

"We can't train forever," Prisha commented.

A devious smile appeared on Owen's face. "You're right. Stay right here, I will be back in a little bit." He left and retrieved three vials of vampire blood and rejoined Aiden and Prisha in the training room. Then, by making use of the wall dividers in the room, he confined them to a quarter of the room's original size. It was still a large area that even had a climbing wall. The entire time, Aiden and Prisha watched, dumbfounded, as Owen prepared the room.

"Why am I beginning to regret everything I said about being ready for a mission," Aiden remarked as he surveyed the area.

"You have nothing to regret if you are ready. All you have to do is convince me that you are ready for a mission. For this test, the only rule is don't kill anybody, so remember, at the end of the day we are all still friends," Owen explained.

"Yeah, that's great and all but I prefer not to spend the next year in the medical wing if this doesn't pan out," Aiden said as he scratched his head.

"That is why I brought us some vampire blood for the end of this trial," Owen responded as he smiled and lifted the small pouch in the air. Then, he walked over and placed it on the side of the room. Aiden and Prisha stood next to each other as Owen approached them again. "Ready?" Owen asked.

"Yes," they both replied and then they pulled out their small, concealable revolvers from behind their backs and pointed them at Owen. "So, when does our first mission start?" Prisha said while the two stood with smug expressions.

Owen chuckled as he raised his hands. "Well, I guess I'm convinced." They lowered their guns, looked at each other, and smiled. "Convinced that you need to show me more," Owen blurted out as he transitioned and shot fire toward them. Prisha and Aiden were caught off guard by Owen's trickery as the flames hurled toward them. Prisha transitioned and bent herself, almost in half, backward to avoid most of the flames. Due to how close they were, some of the flames burned her chest and right shoulder area. The fire also grazed her hand, so she dropped the gun as she grimaced in pain. Aiden transitioned and sprung into the air, but the flames burned his shins and feet as he yelled while he flew toward the ceiling.

Prisha unsheathed her talwar and koftgari as she stood straight up and then swung her talwar down across his chest, but Owen grabbed her wrist and hip-tossed her. However, with Prisha's flexibility, she was able to land on her feet, while her back was parallel with the floor. With Owen still holding her arm, she used him as an anchor to swing her koftgari at Owen as she stood back up. She succeeded as the dagger cut Owen's chest and before he could react, she turned her wrist so the blade was facing Owen and she sliced him across the chest again. Owen staggered back as he held his chest.

He growled as he extended his claws. Prisha raised both her weapons and lined herself up with Owen. Right as he was about to pounce on her, there was a loud noise, followed by an intense pain in his right leg. He grunted and then hobbled a few steps back as he looked up. He saw Aiden hovering about ten feet above and to the right of Prisha.

"Yield," Aiden demanded. Owen growled as his eyes narrowed in on Aiden while he stood up. "Please," Aiden requested as his voice trembled.

Owen spewed fire from his mouth toward Aiden as he jumped toward him. In response, Aiden fired blindly into the flames while he flew further up, but his concentration was directed toward Owen and his flames…not the ceiling. As a result, Aiden smacked his head against the ceiling and plummeted to the floor. His body slammed against the floor as his gun tumbled off into the distance.

Prisha rushed over and helped Aiden to his feet while he held his head. They turned their heads to see Owen lying on the ground, holding his left rib cage as blood poured between his fingers.

"Please tell me you are convinced now," Aiden said while he gained his footing. Owen slowly raised his head and stared at Aiden. Owen then transitioned deep into level three while he continued to stare at Aiden. At this point, Owen had very few human traits left. He had fur all over his body, and his fangs and claws were longer and thicker than before. His face resembled more of a lion than a human. Owen snarled while his breathing became heavier and the blood from his wounds stopped pouring out.

"Oh, I wish I brought the arsenal of guns I originally planned to do," Aiden muttered as his eyes grew wide while he took a step back.

"Owen, calm down…your mind is filled with the chimera's thoughts, not your own human reasoning," Prisha pleaded as a hint of a snake's hiss was within her words. Owen's eyes shifted to her as his lip raised and revealed more of his sharp teeth.

He let out a roar loud enough to echo loudly within the room. Aiden extended his talons as he let out a screech while Prisha raised her weapons and readied herself. Owen charged, which provoked the others to do the same. Prisha thrust her talwar at Owen, but he dodged it and swatted the blade toward Aiden. That made him rear up to avoid being cut. Owen then tore through her arm that held the sword. As she dropped the talwar, in one fluid motion, he sent a strong backhand toward her that landed on her chin. The impact caused her to stumble backward before she fell to the ground.

Aiden advanced as he slashed at Owen, so he raised his arm to block the attack. His talons sliced through Owen's forearm but with him being so deep in transition, the injury didn't faze him. Instead of showing pain, Owen just stared Aiden down, which made Aiden hesitate before he followed up with another slash. Owen caught his wrist and slammed his other hand into the side of Aiden's face, but he didn't let go of Aiden's wrist. Out of the corner of his eyes, he saw Prisha charging him. The roar of the flames around Owen's hands and arms grew louder, but it didn't drown out Aiden's screams as the flesh around his wrist and hand were melting away. Out of desperation, Aiden began to gouge Owen's arm and luckily, Owen let go. As soon as he was free, he flew into the air while grabbing his arm and wincing in pain.

Owen turned his attention to Prisha, took a step forward, and jolted his arms forward as a massive flame was unleashed from both hands. What Owen didn't realize, was that Prisha created a small pool of water near his feet so as he stepped onto it, the combination of the hard floor and water made it slippery. This caused him to lose his balance. The flames shot off to the side of Prisha and then ceased as he regained his balance. He had just enough time to keep himself from falling before just narrowly avoiding Prisha's front kick.

After her unsuccessful attempt at the kick, Prisha was standing right next to Owen. She quickly flung an elbow toward his head, but Owen grabbed her arm and sunk his teeth into it. Prisha screamed and then punched him on the bridge of his nose. This caused him to release his bite and shake his head. She grabbed her arm and repeatedly kept making a fist with her hand. While she was distracted, he sent his own front kick to her chest that sent her in the air a few feet back as she landed hard on the ground.

Out of instinct, Owen quickly turned around and raised his hands as fire projected from them. The flames connected with Aiden as he was in a nosedive toward Owen with his talons stretched out in front of him. The blast from the fire caused him to holler as he flew out of control and past Owen. He landed on his shoulder and parts of his neck and head as he skidded to a stop. Owen ran over to Aiden and kicked him in the face. As Aiden laid on his back, dazed, Owen straddled him and put his hand around Aiden's throat. His lip raised as a low growl came from Owen as he sunk just the tips of his claws into Aiden's neck. Aiden grinded his teeth and his face crinkled from the pain. He went to attack with his talons, but Owen shook his head as his claws sunk a little deeper. Aiden realized his grim situation, stopped struggling, and raised his hands in surrender. Then, there was a gunshot.

Owen looked and saw Prisha barely sitting up with her hand holding her spare pistol in the air. She then lowered it and pointed it at Owen's head. "You forgot that your venom wouldn't stop me. Now, release him!" Prisha demanded as she breathed heavily. Her face strained from the pain, accompanied by adrenaline.

"I didn't forget. I know a naga is immune, but a hybrid, especially one that isn't deep in transition, is not fully immune...just partially. I just needed to slow one of you down enough so I could prove my point," Owen responded in a deep, gravelly voice.

"What point?" Prisha asked as her eyes narrowed.

Owen transitioned down to level two but kept his claws in Aiden's neck. He wanted to be more human for the point he was going to make. That, and not accidentally kill Aiden. His face softened. "If this were real, Aiden would be dead. Once I had him, I waited for you to react. Even if you killed me, Aiden...your close friend, would be dead," Owen added and then he removed his claws from Aiden's neck and went to retrieve the vials of vampire blood. When he returned, Aiden was still lying in the same spot and Prisha had lowered the gun, as well as her head. He handed the vials to them and gulped down the other vial. Within moments, everyone was revived and transitioned back to human. Prisha and Aiden rushed to each other and hugged, and then they sat on the floor next to each other in silence.

Owen approached them and then knelt in front of them. "My objective today wasn't to try to defeat both of you. It was to open your eyes to the harsh reality of this new life. The fact that your friends, from the ones you cherish most in this world to the ones you just met, can die at any point during a mission. Think about it, either one of you could have died and yes…you would have completed your mission, but you will have to live with that hole in your heart where your friend used to be. You think it's bad when it first happens but no, that's not the worst time. The pain doesn't end there…no. The worst parts happen a week, a month, a year, or whatever after when they are not around for any special occasions. That, or something simple…like something funny you heard that they would like but they aren't around to tell them. You live with the daily nightmare of what you could have done to save them, or the painful reminders that life leaves behind so you don't forget that they are gone."

He paused as he watched Prisha and Aiden sit in silence as they both stared at the floor. Owen continued in the same compassionate tone as before. "The two of you were impressive today in your combat skills and as you move on and gain experience, your skills and control will grow even more. I even saw some teamwork; however, you didn't utilize that as much as you should have. We can discuss that more later, but as far as I am concerned, your training is over. Do you want to know what will convince me that you are ready to go on a mission? It will be when either one of you accepts a mission because then, after hearing all this, you decide you are ready for that responsibility. That means you know the cost and yet you still want to go on the mission." Owen then stood up and began to walk toward the exit door when he heard Prisha call his name, so he turned around.

"How did you get past all the losses you experienced so far," Prisha asked and then sniffled. Owen could see her eyes slowly beginning to tear up. Aiden heard her question and raised his head and his eyes were watery as well.

"I never got past it because it never goes away. You just learn how to deal with it and continue with your life. The quicker you learn how to make peace with it and move forward, the better off you'll be. That, and having other friends to lean on while you find ways to enjoy life always helps," Owen softly responded with a sympathetic look. Prisha and Aiden slowly shook their heads before Owen gave them a hint of a smile and left the room.

As soon as the door closed behind him, Owen took a few steps and then leaned his back against the wall and took a deep breath, followed by a long exhale. He felt horrible for the lesson he just taught them, but it had to be done. This way, if they did want to go on a mission, they would truly understand the potential detrimental impact it could have on their lives. In a way, he felt like Klayden when they had their final training. As brutal as it was, it did impact him. He just hoped the impact he had on Prisha and Aiden would be seen as a positive one.

Owen made his way back to his room, cleaned himself up, and left to meet Astrid for dinner. It was a weird feeling for him to look forward to this part of his day, but each day he felt she was more of a delight to be around. This made him feel more hopeful about honoring Isaac's wish. As they ate, Astrid talked about her day and the two joked around about random topics. However, there was silence as they wrapped up their meals until Astrid spoke. "What's wrong?"

"What makes you think something is wrong?" Owen responded but without looking at her.

"Call it a woman's intuition, or centuries of experience, or just the plain fact that we have spent enough time together for me to know you well enough to know when something is wrong. Spill it,"

Astrid said and then stood up and walked over to Owen, and then sat down next to him.

Owen sighed. "Let's just say I drove the point home in today's training session with Prisha and Aiden about being ready for a mission. They kept saying they were ready and I wanted them to understand what their comments entailed. I know what I did was only to help them but still…when it was over, I think I installed true fear into them."

"I'm sure you did. I bet you even transitioned deep into level three as well, didn't you?" Astrid asked as her brow arched.

Owen shrugged a little as his face cringed while he slowly nodded his head. "I also went into detail about dealing with death," Owen commented.

"Geez, Owen. They'll have nightmares for weeks to come," Astrid added.

Owen scoffed. "Not helping."

Astrid smiled, which caused Owen to crack a smile. "You know you are a good person and whatever tactic you used, I'm sure it was whatever you felt was best to keep them alive and safe," Astrid commented as she gave him a quick rub on his knee.

"Thanks, but next time, lead with that and not the nightmare comment," Owen said and then winked as he grinned.

Astrid chuckled. "I'll keep that in mind." The two talked for a little while longer before they parted ways.

Owen walked back to his room to waste some time before he went outside to see his friends. Before he reached his door, Alyssa poked her head out of her room and whispered his name. He turned his head and saw her waving him over to her room. He glanced around and didn't see anybody so he scurried over to her.

"What's up?" Owen asked.

"Do you know what Astrid is up to tonight?" Alyssa inquired.

"She will be in Isaac's office going through more of his papers. She likes to go through them and learn what she can about the facility, as well as anything else gem or facility-related," Owen responded.

"That's good. She will be far away and her mind will be focused elsewhere," Alyssa commented.

Owen's brow knitted. "What are you up to?"

A crooked smile formed on Alyssa's face. "Do you want to talk to your friends tonight?"

"Are you serious?" Owen asked as his eyes lit up.

Alyssa pointed behind her and the area was already prepared. "Yep, but we should start it now to be safe."

Owen's smile grew but then disappeared in a flash. "What about you and your family's time? As much as I want to talk to my friends, I don't want you to sacrifice time with your family."

Alyssa put her hand on his shoulder. "That is sweet of you but it's not a problem. I discussed it with my family last week and they were all on board with the idea of you talking with your friends. They didn't want you to suffer the way I did."

Owen's smile returned. "Thank you. You have no idea how much this means to me. I owe you one." He then patted her hand that was still on his shoulder.

Alyssa smirked. "You're helping me rid ourselves of Astrid, that's more than enough payment. Now, we don't have much time here so let us begin."

Alyssa led Owen over to a circle of teacup candles and had him sit cross-legged in the middle of it. She then lit a large bundle of herbs and walked around the room to allow the small amount of smoke to fill the room before she placed it in a bowl next to them. Owen remembered that part was to help conceal the magic she was about to perform. She then entered the circle and kneeled on a small pillow behind him. Owen began to smile because he was excited and eager for Alyssa to start the spell. He couldn't wait to talk to his friends again.

"Okay, I am going to start the spell. As I do, I need you to focus on one room in that house. Not a person, but a room. The more detail, the better," Alyssa instructed.

"Why not a person?" Owen asked.

"For starters, they may not be in the most ideal place to see you. For example, they could be in the bathroom," Alyssa replied.

"Good point. The room option it is," Owen quickly said.

"Besides, once you are in the room you can call out and see who is around. You need to make the best use of your time. Once I put my hands on your shoulders, the two of us will astral project to that location and you will have ten minutes, at best, before we will end up back here. I'm sorry that I must tag along, but you're basically piggybacking me to get there so I will have to stay relatively close to you," Alyssa explained.

"That's totally fine. I'm ready," Owen said and then took a deep breath.

Alyssa's hands hovered over Owen's shoulders as she began her incantation. Owen closed his eyes and focused on every detail he could think of for the kitchen. He wanted to make sure there was no mistake where he wanted to go and hoped at least one person would be in there. If not, the other rooms were close enough that someone would hear him. Then, without warning, Alyssa touched Owen's shoulders. He expected his mind to travel through space and time to reach the kitchen. Then, for him to be floating and glowing when he arrived, but that wasn't the case.

As soon as she touched his shoulders, within the blink of an eye, he was standing in the kitchen at Isaac's house with Alyssa standing next to him. Owen smiled, for the spell worked but he needed to act fast. He wasn't glowing or floating. It was like he was actually standing in the room. The kitchen was empty but right as he was about to announce himself, Selena and Caine walked into the kitchen. They were startled by Owen's surprise appearance as they gasped and stopped dead in their tracks.

"Owen. You made it back! I'm so happy," Selena said while she smiled and rushed over to Owen but as she went to hug him, she walked right through him. She stumbled and then turned around as her brow knitted as she slowly reached out her hand to touch Owen's chest, but instead, it glided through and disappeared inside his body.

"Well, that's interesting," Owen commented as he looked down. He wasn't sure what was more bizarre to him. The fact that Selena's hand disappeared inside of him, or that he couldn't feel Selena when she walked through him or touched him.

"What's going on here?" Selena inquired as she yanked her hand back.

"Astral projection," Livia commented as she entered the room. Owen and Livia smiled at each other as she approached him. Her eyes then drifted to Alyssa for a moment. "From the looks of things, if Alyssa has to be here to help you with this, then I presume you don't have a lot of time," Livia added.

"Correct, and as much as I want to talk to everyone for a long time, I'm just going to dump as much information as I can before I must go," Owen quickly responded.

"Everyone, in the kitchen...now," Caine called out. Within moments, Owen could hear people rushing down the steps and through the house. Soon, the kitchen was filled with his friends. Marcus, Abigail, and Bailey all stopped and smiled, but before they took a step toward him, Owen raised his hand.

"No time to explain. I just need everyone to listen," Owen blurted out as he passed his hand through Livia's arm. This caused the rest of his friends' faces to crinkle from confusion. "Where are the others?" Owen asked.

"Cedric is back in the city trying to see what he can do to help find a way to save you and Alyssa and stop Astrid. Anders is doing the same by following up on some leads we have. As for Hailey and Avery, they ironically left to go see you," Livia replied. Owen was bummed that people were missing, but there was unfortunately nothing he could do about it. He just hoped that he would see and talk to them soon.

"Speed things up, Owen," Alyssa commented.

Owen nodded. "You're right, sorry. Before I start, I just wanted to say how much I appreciated seeing everyone during our secret meetings. I have immensely missed everyone, so it's helped me more than you know. Anyway, here is what I know." The room fell silent as everyone moved closer to Owen.

"Astrid is not a hybrid anymore. Instead, she is a powerful psychic but her powers seem to work only when she is touching you. I learned that when she hotwired my brain, I could not cause her any physical harm. She made a lot of wishes, but it didn't take long for the djinn to grow tired of her antics and he began to twist her wishes around. Therefore, she had to waste a decent amount of her wishes to fix what the djinn did. To the point she either didn't wish for certain things or she did but settled if it was close enough. Some of the main results of her wishes is that she can project fire from her hands again. However, it's nowhere near the level when she had the green dragon within her. She is very strong and has a high dexterity. She is immortal but only when it comes to aging and sickness. She can heal rapidly. I believe those are the main ones. Oh, she cannot fly anymore. Astrid tried to get that ability but her wishing session had already been going on for a long time. At that point, the djinn was messing with her too much so she gave up on it. At best, she may be able to hover a few feet off the ground. She also has a wendigo trapped in a large magical, invisible cage around the perimeter of the cabin, marked only with a salt line. Creatures cannot cross the barrier lines in either direction, including a person who is in transition. I also made friends with two newly-created hybrids that defected to our side and their names are Prisha, a naga, and Aiden, a griffin. I have trained them both and they have come a long way. Also…"

Within a blink of an eye, Owen was back in Alyssa's room. "Well, that was an interesting experience but thank you so much. Too bad it ended abruptly but at least I got a chance to talk to them."

Owen didn't hear Alyssa respond so he turned his head and immediately gasped as his face cringed while he slightly shuffled backward. His eyes grew wide and his jaw dropped when he saw Alyssa's body lying across some of the teacup candles, and her severed head a few feet from her body. Owen's eyes went back and forth between her head and her body, which was in a growing pool of blood.

He slowly turned his head and looked up when he noticed that somebody was standing next to him. It was Astrid, wielding a bloody machete. "We need to talk," Astrid said with a deadpan expression as she pointed the tip of the machete toward Owen.

CHAPTER 21

Astrid and Owen's eyes locked as he remained frozen and speechless. He didn't know what to say or how much she knew. He couldn't fight her and he wouldn't make it far if he tried to escape, so his only hope was to be able to talk his way out of the potentially disastrous situation he was in.

"What do you have to say for yourself?" Astrid asked through her teeth as her eyes became glassy.

"I'm sorry," Owen softly responded.

"Sorry because you broke a major part of our agreement by interacting with your friends or sorry because you got caught?" Astrid questioned as her brow furrowed.

"Sorry because I upset you," Owen sympathetically replied. Astrid raised the machete above her head. Owen took a deep breath and held it as his eyes remained fixed on the blade. She then screamed while she turned around and hurled the machete across the room. She threw it with enough force that it lodged itself into the wall. Owen let out a long exhale as he was relieved the machete was stuck in a wall and not himself. He stood up at the same time as Astrid turned back around.

"I trusted you," Astrid said as her voice cracked. Owen went to speak but she pointed her finger at him. "I'm not done! I trusted you and now I feel betrayed and stupid, and not because I delivered on everything that I promised, but because I actually thought we were friends…good friends." Owen tried to speak again but was quickly silenced again by Astrid. Then, a tear ran down her cheek.

"I let you in. I dropped my guard and was myself with you…only for you to rip my heart out. In fact, it would have hurt less if you physically ripped my heart out besides betraying my trust. It would have been different if it was anyone else, but someone I cared enough about to consider my friend…that hurts. You know I don't have any other true friends," Astrid added as her voice strained. She tried to fight back her emotions but she lost that battle as more tears ran down her face.

"It wasn't my intention to hurt you like this. Believe it or not, I have enjoyed the time we spent together. So much, that I consider you my friend as well and you know that is something I thought I would never say. We have made so much progress together. I just terribly missed my friends, so when Alyssa presented this opportunity to talk to them, I wasn't strong enough to resist. This was the only time I astral projected. Please forgive me," Owen pleaded.

Astrid wiped her face. "I know it was the only time. I have been on to Alyssa's little game for a while now, but I was having trouble narrowing it down until recently. You can imagine my surprise when I walked in here and saw you were here too. So, what did you talk about with your friends?" Astrid inquired as she folded her arms across her chest. Her face was expressionless, except for her glassy eyes.

"Alyssa said I wouldn't have a lot of time so I had to make it quick. I just told them hello and how I missed everyone. I also warned them about the wendigo in fear that they may try to rescue me," Owen blurted out.

"Is that the only time you saw or spoke to your friends?" Astrid inquired.

"Yes," Owen answered while he looked her in the eyes. He responded quickly, even though his mind was full of doubt. He didn't want to add to Astrid's anger but at the same time, he feared he would get caught in a lie if she already knew the answer or even worse, read his mind. It was a gamble, but he had to remain calm if he was going to sell it and hope their deal would not be null and void after his indiscretion.

Astrid lowered her arms and slowly approached him. She stopped right in front of Owen and then looked into his eyes as she held his hand. It took all his might to remain calm and not flinch. After a few seconds, which felt like years, she let go of his hand. "Did you find what you were looking for?" Owen nonchalantly asked.

"I did, and I never had to peer inside your mind," Astrid responded. Owen's brow crinkled. "You didn't show any fear when I touched your hand, so there was no need to go any further. Besides, I like to keep the promises I make, so I'll take your word that this was a one-time incident."

"So, my friends are safe?" Owen carefully asked.

"It only happened once so I will look the other way this time, but I advise you to not test my limits when it comes to forgiveness," Astrid replied.

"Of course, thank you. I appreciate it," Owen responded as he grinned.

"I'll have someone come down here and take care of this," Astrid added as she gestured toward Alyssa's body. She then turned and headed toward the door.

"If it's okay with you, can you please not feed Alyssa's body to the wendigo? Instead, can she please have a proper burial? Also, can we notify her family so they aren't wondering?" Owen suggested in hopes that Astrid would treat this with respect.

"Yes, to the burial, but you will oversee it. As for her family, no. They will figure it out eventually. Be grateful that I even considered what you proposed and at least accepted one of your requests," Astrid responded.

"Thank you," Owen said as he lowered his head. He was bummed that her family would not know what happened, but felt comforted that she would have a proper funeral. He looked up to see Astrid turn around and grab the doorknob, but she paused.

"You still miss your friends that much, after all this time?" Astrid softly asked without turning back to look at Owen.

"Yes, yes I do," Owen responded.

Astrid was quiet for a moment before she let go of the doorknob and turned around. "Then, let's invite them to a party."

"A what?" Owen inquired as his brow raised.

"A party...more specifically, a ball," Astrid replied.

"Again...what?" Owen repeated.

Astrid chuckled. "A ball...a formal party with ballroom dancing."

Owen shook his head. "I know what a ball is. I'm just surprised you offered it. Why?"

"Can't a girl have her reasons?" Astrid playfully responded.

"Considering how much you are against the notion of me seeing my friends...no, you can't," Owen countered. He was still flabbergasted at her suggestion.

"Well, I haven't been to one in over a century and I've been dying to go. Also, if I want to grow our friendship, I should show acts of kindness. Something more than just sparing you and your friends' lives," Astrid explained.

"I don't know what to say," Owen muttered.

"Say yes and I will send the invitations out tomorrow and we can have the ball in a couple of weeks. It's a quick turnaround but I believe I have the resources to pull it off," Astrid said with a smug expression.

"Yes," Owen said, followed by a smile.

Astrid smiled as she perked up. "Excellent. I will give you the details later, as well as send someone to do a fitting for your tux. In the interim, I suggest you learn how to dance." She then turned around and reached for the doorknob again.

"You're not going to teach me?" Owen asked.

Astrid looked over her shoulder. "Of course not, silly. I have a ball to plan," Astrid responded and then winked before she exited the room.

Owen stood there, perplexed by the sudden change of course in how Astrid felt. So much, it overwhelmed the feeling of excitement that he could see his friends without fear of retaliation from Astrid. He wasn't sure what confused him more...the sudden mindset change or his feelings toward Astrid. Owen knew he wanted to guide her away from her darkness and he did enjoy her company as of lately, but did he really consider her his friend? How could he when he knew he had to get away from her and if needed, kill her? At the same time, he had to be friends with her on some level if he was going to try to fulfill his promise to Isaac. As Owen examined his complicated relationship with her, he was shocked back into reality when he glanced over and viewed Alyssa's body. Owen didn't want to leave and risk a mercenary bringing her to the wendigo, so he sat in a chair and waited.

He must have dozed off because Owen jolted from his seat when the mercenary walked through the door with a wheelbarrow and a tarp. Owen didn't care for the means of transportation of Alyssa's body and head outside, but he understood. There wasn't a stretcher or cart that could make the journey once they were outside and it was probably for the best that people didn't notice a dead body being carted through the garden.

Owen made a stop in the wilderness training room, grabbed an axe, and then followed the man outside. Once outside, Owen directed him over to where Amelia's and Cassie's funerals were held. He picked that location due to the clearing and it was far enough away

289

from the cliff just in case Hailey and Avery were there. They came to a stop and the man adjusted his grip to dump Alyssa's body out.

"Stop!" Owen yelled. The man was startled enough to stop and look at Owen. "If you dump her body out, I promise that I will kill you and use that same wheelbarrow to cart you over to the wendigo for a midnight snack," Owen added as he stood close to the mercenary and stared at him. The mercenary's head sunk into his shoulders as he slowly lowered the cart and backed away. Owen decided to keep Alyssa in the wheelbarrow, instead of laying her on the ground, to keep the bugs from swarming her body. He turned to the mercenary. "Thank you. You may go now. I've got it from here."

Once the mercenary left, Owen fumbled his way around in the dark, while being mindful of the barrier line, before he transitioned to see better. He then began to chop wood for the funeral pyre. By the time he was able to construct the pyre, the sun had just begun to break the horizon. Owen even took the time to carve her name with one of his claws into a piece of wood and place it at the base of the pyre. He wasn't sure what depressed him more...the funeral for Alyssa or the fact that he was becoming an expert at building funeral pyres.

He laid Alyssa's body on top of the pyre and then placed her head where it originally was before Astrid displaced it. He was exhausted and sweating, but he wanted to pay his respects properly and not rush it. Even though nobody was around, he spoke out loud about their short time together and how much he appreciated the laughs they shared and the help she provided. He also promised if he could find a way to notify her family about her death, the funeral, and all that she did to help, he would.

"I'm so sorry things ended the way they did for you, but your death will not be in vain. Goodbye," Owen said and then used his hand to set the wood on fire. The intensity of the fire made short work of the pyre as Owen stood there and waited for the flames to reduce to a smolder. He then shoveled some dirt onto the remains to not only extinguish the rest of the fire but also to bury whatever remained.

He left and dropped the axe and wheelbarrow off before he ate and then showered. Afterward, he went to sleep for a few hours. Once he woke up, he searched for Prisha and Aiden to see how they were doing and to update them on what had happened. They were not in the training room, or in their rooms, so he searched the garden area and he eventually located them near a stream off the wooden path.

"Do you mind if I join you?" Owen politely inquired.

"Please do," Prisha responded as she gestured to a spot in front of them.

Owen strolled over and sat down. "I wanted to check in to see how the two of you were doing after yesterday's training session. I apologize if I was too intense."

"You didn't tear my throat out so, we're square," Aiden commented while he leaned his back against a tree. He only glanced at Owen before he went back to whittling.

Owen smiled and then turned to Prisha. "And you?"

"It was a hard lesson to learn, but a well-needed one, so thank you for being strong enough to teach it to us," Prisha responded and then gently smiled.

"I'm glad. I was nervous I turned two friends against me after that session. I was taught a similar lesson back when I was a recruit, so I remember it being a tough pill to swallow afterward," Owen commented.

"That is sweet of you to check in on us, especially after everything that has happened to you," Prisha said.

"Everything that has happened to me. As in, what exactly?" Owen asked as his brow knitted.

"Astrid informed us about Alyssa's death due to her using astral projection to see not only her family but to also assist you in seeing your friends. She said she let you off with a warning to show that she can be merciful," Prisha explained.

"Yeah. She killed Alyssa while she helped me and I buried her this morning. I think I was spared just because she sees me as a friend. Did she say anything else?" Owen inquired.

"Yeah, that we are to help her with a ball that she is throwing in a couple of weeks and that we could join once we were done. She even read our minds to make sure we weren't involved or had any knowledge about any activities against the rules," Prisha added.

"You mean the trap she is throwing," Aiden remarked while he whittled.

"You think it is a trap?" Owen asked.

"No, I think the evil overlord whom you betrayed is throwing a ball out of the goodness of her heart," Aiden casually responded while his attention remained on his wooden project.

"I wouldn't put it past her. If I were you, I would be very mindful while in attendance at this ball," Prisha said.

"You two make a good point. I will proceed with caution, provided I don't trip over my feet every two seconds," Owen commented.

"You don't know how to dance?" Prisha asked.

"Not any of those fancy dances," Owen replied as he glanced away due to embarrassment.

"I would be honored if you allowed me to teach you," Prisha offered while she smiled.

"I would hate to impose," Owen countered.

"I could teach you if you prefer," Aiden muttered.

"Yeah, you can teach me Prisha. Thanks," Owen quickly said.

Prisha giggled. "Not a problem. It's the least that I could do for everything that you taught me, as well as saving mine and Aiden's life."

"So, you do understand why I didn't tell you about the astral projection plan?" Owen asked.

"Yes, and I wouldn't be surprised if there were other things you didn't tell us about. If you did share, then you would have had a funeral for Aiden and me as well," Prisha responded.

"I'm glad that you understand because regardless of my intentions, I still felt bad not keeping you in the loop," Owen commented.

"Thank you for not sharing," Prisha said as she put her hand on Owen's shoulder and grinned.

"Well, I need to take care of a few things but I will find you later and we can figure out a schedule," Owen suggested to Prisha, who nodded in acceptance.

Owen started to walk off but then turned around. "I didn't know you could whittle."

"I can't. This is the first time I tried it. Everyone always seems so relaxed in the movies while they did it and the final product always looked great," Aiden commented.

"What are you making?" Owen asked.

"I was making a griffin but it appears I have made a canoe instead," Aiden replied as he held up the small piece of wood that only seemed to have a slope in the middle. Owen and Prisha chuckled at Aiden's failed attempt.

The next couple of weeks went by quickly for Owen. He didn't see much of Astrid during this time since her excuse was that her schedule was hectic. She mentioned she was quite involved with the preparations of an event of such royal caliber, under such short notice. His time was spent with Prisha and Aiden, but more with Prisha. She taught him at least the basic ballroom dance moves, and even some intermediate moves toward the end. He thanked her each day for the lessons since he was grateful to not look like a fool in front of his friends…especially Avery. Also, during this time, he was fitted for a tuxedo, which he had never worn before. He felt awkward, yet confident when he viewed himself in the mirror.

The day of the event had finally arrived and the night before, Owen tossed and turned. He was excited about seeing his friends but also anxious about Astrid's true motives behind this ball. Astrid left early that day to make sure everything was in order. She claimed that she received permission from the wealthiest townsman to use his family's house to host the event. This small town, which was the same town where Isaac's house was located, was more popular than Owen imagined. He wondered if it was due to the location and quaintness. Prisha and Aiden left a few hours after Astrid to make it there in time to help before they received guests.

After changing into his tuxedo, Owen left around midday in order to arrive in the early evening. The event began at eight o'clock, but guests were being received starting at seven o'clock to mingle. This meant that only drinks and light hors d'oeuvres would be served. With the butterflies in his stomach, he was only able to eat just barely a normal meal for himself before he left.

He was thankful that there was a driver for him so he could just relax and enjoy the ride, but that didn't last long. Instead, most of the time was spent wondering what Astrid could have planned, if anything. A small part of him hoped that her intentions were pure and if so, it would be a huge stride in a positive direction. One that he could easily work with in his efforts to change Astrid for the better.

Owen could see the mansion from a distance but it was a lot bigger when the vehicle finally arrived at the gate. The tall, iron gate was attached to the stone wall that surrounded the property. The gate was already opened due to the line of cars that were in front of them. He was impressed by the style of the mansion, from the long, cobblestone driveway that looped around a fountain located in front of the mansion, to the modern stone architecture of the mansion itself. As the vehicle grew closer to the front, Owen admired the fountain. The bronze fountain, which had a green hue to it, was placed inside a stone base. The fountain itself had three tiers. The first tier had women sitting on a bench playing different stringed instruments. The middle tier had many designs and the water spouted from each lion's head that surrounded it. The final, smaller tier at the top was held up by horses rearing up. There was even an eagle at the very top of the fountain. Owen watched the water showering down each tier until they reached their stop.

He exited the vehicle onto a red carpet that led to the large cherry doors that were held open, but he didn't see Prisha or Aiden. Owen glanced around and he didn't see his friends and it seemed no one was congregating outside either. He followed the red carpet up the stone stairs, passed the greeters, who handed him a glass of champagne, and into the large foyer of the mansion.

Owen was in awe as he looked all around him at the modern, vast area, of the foyer. Even with the numerous amounts of people, there was still more than enough room to move around and not feel cramped. The floor was marble and the entire room had shades of white and tan, with accents such as the gold railings on the dual staircase in the back of the room. The stairs swung around each side of the room and led to a focal point at the back center of the room. Above the open area of the stairs, was an elegant chandelier.

The men appeared to be all dressed like Owen; whereas, the women wore a variety of different colored dresses. The styles of the dresses varied, but mainly were more fitted above the waist and then flared out below the waist. Some dresses were long enough to touch the floor while others came to their ankles. All the dresses flared out but some were sleeker than the other dresses that had more fluff and frills to them. Even with the similarities between the dresses, the varying styles made each of them stand out. Whether it be off-the-shoulder, long-sleeved, high-slit, or one of many other styles. As Owen stood in the middle of the room, in awe, he began to realize how out of place he felt. He downed the glass of champagne and placed it on a server's tray. That is when he felt a tap on his shoulder.

CHAPTER 22

It was Prisha, smiling and wearing a salmon-colored, long-sleeved dress that had frills that started at her waist. "You have no idea how glad I am to see you. I was one step away from hiding in a bathroom," Owen said as he gave her a quick hug. "The dress looks good on you. You should wear it more often, like in training or something."

Prisha chuckled. "I would but you said we are done with our training," Prisha playfully replied and then winked. Owen laughed at her response before she continued. "Thank you and you clean up well yourself."

"Thanks. Where's Aiden?" Owen asked.

"Over there…mingling," Prisha responded as she pointed.

Owen looked over and saw Aiden talking to a small group of women, who were all giggling. Aiden glanced over and waived at Owen before his attention was diverted back to the handful of women. Owen scoffed in amusement.

"He's not going to be any help to us tonight, is he?" Owen commented.

"None whatsoever," Prisha replied.

"Aren't you two supposed to be working?" Owen inquired.

"We helped Astrid when we first arrived but once we changed, she instructed us to make sure everyone mingles…especially you and your friends," Prisha responded.

"So, I guess we can't all stick together. That makes me feel warm and fuzzy," Owen sarcastically remarked. "Where's Astrid?"

"I'm not sure. I haven't seen her in the past hour or so," Prisha answered.

"I wonder when my friends will arrive?" Owen asked as he glanced around.

"I'm sure they will be here soon," Prisha responded.

"Did you see anything suspicious while you've been here?" Owen inquired.

"Nothing. This may be a wild presumption, but it could be just a fun night out. I mean, there are various influential people gathered here tonight, so she could be using her powers to gain favor from them," Prisha replied but then her eyes narrowed as they drifted over his shoulder.

"What is it?" Owen asked but as he went to turn around, Prisha stopped him.

"Remember when I said I haven't seen anything suspicious…well, now I do," Prisha whispered.

"What do you see?" Owen whispered back.

"I see a large group of people that just entered and they are all looking around. It's like they are trying to find someone," Prisha responded and then smirked. Owen's brow crinkled at first but then lightened up as he smiled and whipped around. Sure enough, his friends had arrived.

Owen smiled and started to run, but quickly reframed and walked briskly instead to maintain etiquette. He saw Marcus, Selena, Avery, Hailey, Bailey, and Abigail slowly walking forward as a group. Bailey was the first to see Owen. She smiled and nudged Avery while she continued to stare at Owen. Avery followed Bailey's eyes and once her eyes locked onto Owen's, a smile formed from ear to ear as her eyes lit up. Apparently, she didn't care about the etiquette as she rushed over to Owen, wrapped her arms around his neck, and kissed him firmly on his lips.

"You have no idea how much I missed you," Avery blurted out as she gazed into Owen's eyes while she smiled and laid her hands on his chest.

"I feel the same way," Owen said as he placed his hands on her hips and gazed back at her while he smiled.

Avery squinted and then used the side of her hand to remove the lipstick that she left on his lips. "Sorry about that," she said afterward.

"Worth it," Owen said and then winked. He then glanced Avery over. She was in a sleek, modern light blue dress, with see-through arms and light blue heels to match. Her hair, which she normally wore down, was up.

"Do I look okay?" Avery quickly asked as she looked herself over.

"Just when I thought you could not look any more beautiful, you proved me wrong," Owen responded with a gentle smile.

Avery blushed while she smiled. "Thank you. You look quite dashing yourself."

"Thanks. I can barely breathe in this thing, but thank you," Owen teased. They both were laughing when the rest of the group joined them.

Owen shook Marcus's hand. "It's good to see you again. I can only imagine how ecstatic you must feel being able to wear a tux. It's like a suit on steroids," Owen jested.

"Well, I do enjoy changing it up from time to time," Marcus replied as he adjusted his bowtie while he had a hint of a smile.

"Where is Livia?" Owen asked.

"She wanted to lay low to stay off Astrid's radar as a strategic advantage for us. This way, we won't show all our cards on the table," Marcus answered.

Owen nodded and turned and hugged Hailey, who was wearing a similar style dress as Avery, but hers was off the shoulder and her dress was white with sparkles, with the heels to match. "Thank you for bringing everyone to the gorge. It helped me more than you'll ever know."

"Of course, how could we pass up a chance to see you? We tried for a while and we almost lost hope when we never saw you. I'm glad we tried a little while longer," Hailey responded and then winked.

"I'm glad you did too," Owen said and then hugged Hailey again. "Thank you for your understanding with Avery," Owen whispered.

"The two of you are very important to me so I'm glad you're both happy," Hailey whispered back.

Owen then turned to Selena, whose dress was royal blue with gold, glittery accents and had more volume and frills below the hip as the dress came to the floor. Her arms were covered and she had a blue choker that matched the dress.

Selena hugged Owen. "I'm glad this time I didn't walk through you."

"That makes two of us. I'm happy to see you again," Owen said as he smiled. "Where's Caine?"

"It's still a little too bright outside and besides, these events aren't really his thing," Selena replied.

"That's a shame but probably for the best. We don't want him to lose his temper and dwindle half the population of this town," Owen joked. The two of them chuckled. He then felt someone standing next to him. He turned and it was Abigail.

She was wearing a red dress, sleek in design but more flowing toward the end of the dress. There were no sleeves since the dress hung from her shoulders down to a low neckline. She wore red, sparkly heels to match.

"I hope you didn't forget about me," Abigail remarked with a devious grin.

"That would be impossible," Owen replied and then winked. The two smiled and then gave each other a long hug. While they hugged, Owen caught of glimpse of Bailey...in a dress. The dress was very similar to Abigail's dress but black, and the neckline was not as low. Also, the dress came all the way to the floor.

"Look at you," Owen said as he grinned while he looked over Abigail's shoulder. In response to Owen's comment, Abigail turned and tucked her arm around the crook of Owen's arm. Bailey sighed and rolled her eyes when she reached them.

"Tell me I am not the only one seeing this," Owen said as he leaned his head toward Abigail.

"I see it, but I wouldn't push it. It's the same woman, just different attire," Abigail playfully suggested.

"Exactly, so don't mess with me, Owen," Bailey said as she glared at him.

Owen grinned and then let go of Abigail and slowly approached Bailey. "Do you have on the matching heels?" He asked while he had a crooked grin.

"Actually, I don't," Bailey replied as she stuck her foot out and revealed she was wearing black sneakers. "It's bad enough I must wear this dress and get dolled up, but I refuse to subject myself to additional torture. Go ahead, get all your comments out of your system...purge."

Owen scoffed in amusement and then hugged Bailey. He then took a step back. "I missed you and you look beautiful tonight," Owen commented. Bailey smiled right before he turned to the other women in the group. "Everyone looks beautiful tonight." As everyone smiled, Abigail passed Owen and he gently grabbed her arm to stop her. "You got a picture of Bailey in the dress to use as blackmail later, right?" Owen whispered.

"Multiple pictures," Abigail whispered back while she smiled.

At that time, Prisha and Aiden approached the group, so Owen introduced everyone. Once the pleasantries were finished, Owen turned to Prisha and Aiden. "I'm about to discuss plans with my friends. You can stay, but that means you are involved and if you get caught, it may not end well for you. Look what would have happened if I filled you in earlier and Astrid read your mind. You may have been wendigo food."

"We are in this, together," Prisha responded.

"How could I say no to a bloodbath that will probably be our own? I'm in," Aiden energetically responded.

Owen patted them on their shoulders. He then caught the entire group up to speed on everything that went on from the night of the astral projection until now, including some odds and ends prior to the night that Alyssa died.

"I hate to break this up, but Astrid wanted Aiden and me to make sure that large group gatherings don't go on for too long, especially with Owen's friends. She wants everyone to roam around and mingle so it doesn't look awkward to the other guests," Prisha informed the group.

"You do realize that she may be planning something," Marcus commented.

"I know, but we won't find out for sure until we play along," Owen responded.

"We will split up. Bailey, Hailey, and I as one group, then Selena and Abigail as another, and finally Owen and Avery. Search around and we will reconvene when the dancing occurs," Marcus directed, and then everyone paired up.

"Make sure Astrid doesn't touch you," Owen added.

"We'll see what we can find out," Prisha said before she and Aiden walked away.

"Are you ready?" Selena asked as she turned and looked at Owen.

"No," Owen replied with a delayed look back at Selena.

"Good luck everybody," Marcus said, and with that, the teams scattered.

It didn't take long for the teams to fan out and find their way through the side doors of the large foyer. Owen and Avery casually walked through the hallways, and individual rooms, for any form of a clue as to what Astrid was planning. All they found were random guests walking around and admiring the mansion. However, they did receive a surprise when they opened a door that they thought led to another room but instead, it led to a closet where a couple were making out. Owen and Avery giggled and excused themselves as they closed the door.

"I don't see anything. Maybe we should head back and see what the others have found," Avery suggested.

"I agree," Owen responded.

"Next time, it would be nice to get dressed up and go on a date that doesn't involve some evil that we have to defeat," Avery huffed.

"Let's try to make the most of it, shall we?" Owen said as he reached out his hand to her.

"What did you have in mind?" Avery playfully said as she took his hand and moved closer to him.

"Well, there is dancing, which I have practiced just so I wouldn't embarrass the two of us," Owen mentioned.

Avery grinned. "That's sweet of you. A fight could start at any moment yet here you are, making sure you don't step on my feet."

"Just trying to prevent a fight from starting," Owen joked, which caused Avery to giggle. "I suggest we walk back, but we do it with your initial intention that you had with that dress."

"What do you mean?" Avery asked as her brow crinkled.

"The dress happens to be the same eye color as your creature. Tell me you didn't transition before you came here to see how it would look," Owen said as his brow raised and he smiled.

She shook her head while she smiled. "It looked great," Avery responded. She then hung her head, yet still smiled. She looked up and she had transitioned just enough to alter her eyes.

"Wow, they do match. Now, let's show them off," Owen suggested as he took her by the hand and began to walk.

"Are you insane," Avery whispered loudly.

"It's just your eyes, trust me…it will be fine and you'll love it," Owen begged.

"Okay," Avery slowly said as she rolled her eyes.

The two walked into a room and noticed a couple admiring a painting. "Excuse me. I'm sorry to bother you but which way leads back to the foyer? It's like a maze in here," Owen politely inquired.

The couple chuckled. "No problem. Go through those doors there and then make a right. Follow the crowd and you will find your way out," the man explained.

"Thank you so much," Avery nicely responded.

"I love how your dress matches your eyes. So lovely," the woman complimented.

"Awe, thank you so much," Avery said while she beamed. The couple walked away while Owen and Avery headed to the door.

"Wow! I love that compliment way more than I thought I would. A girl can get used to this," Avery commented while she continued to smile. During that moment, Owen was reminded about how much he missed seeing her smile and how it was difficult to not be happy around her.

"See, I told you and I get the extra added bonus of seeing you smile," Owen remarked.

Avery held Owen's hand. "Well, let's see how many more times I can smile before we make it back to the foyer." The two walked to the door and opened it, just as Astrid was about to open the same door.

It startled the two of them to see Astrid, with a smug expression, appear at the doorway. "There you are," Astrid said as she smiled and entered the room while Owen and Avery slowly backed up. "I've run into all your other friends except the two of you. Ah, your dress and eyes match…cute," Astrid added.

"Thank you. I was curious if anyone would notice," Avery stuttered as she transitioned back to normal.

"It suits you," Astrid commented.

"Your dress looks good on you. I can see you couldn't resist the dark green color," Owen said as he nodded toward her off-the-shoulder dress that flowed to the floor, with some frills at the very bottom. He also noticed that the locket was around her neck.

"Thank you, and you look good in your tux," Astrid remarked as she smiled. Avery squeezed Owen's hand harder than she realized. He firmly squeezed her hand back to remind her of her strength.

"You outdid yourself tonight. It's a good turnout and a beautiful location, and most of all…I get a chance to see my friends. That means a lot to me, so thank you," Owen said as he softly smiled at Astrid.

"It's the least I could do. Now don't forget…the dancing will begin momentarily," Astrid mentioned as she walked past Avery and Owen to reach more of her guests in the back of the room.

"Well, she ruined the fun with the dress we were having," Avery commented as she put her hands on her hips.

"Sorry. Don't let her get to you. Now, let's go back and meet with the others to see what they have encountered," Owen suggested. The two of them made short work of finding their way back to the rest of the group that was already waiting for them in the foyer.

As he and his friends exchanged stories, they were left with no clues. The only thing in common was that each group encountered Astrid at some point, but she didn't touch any of them. Even Prisha and Aiden stopped by and reported the same story as everyone else. As the group stood and scratched their heads about what to do next, they heard someone tapping a glass over a microphone. The room

304

went silent as all eyes were on Astrid, who stood at the top of the dual stairwell.

"Good evening, everyone. I hope you are enjoying yourselves tonight. Don't worry, I'll keep this brief. I decided to host this event tonight to just bring everyone together and have fun while we become more acquainted with each other. Trust and friendship are very important in a small town like this because, without them, we lose the spirit that makes this place wonderful. Tonight, I've seen some of the biggest hearts around and I thank you for that, as well as your insight. I hope we can all grow together. Now, without any further delay, our main event of the evening…the ballroom dance. We will start the night with a traditional waltz. Afterward, there will be a variety of other traditional ballroom dances. I hope everyone continues to have a good time," Astrid announced and afterward, the guests clapped and then entered the room.

The group entered the large ballroom that had a high ceiling with another chandelier and lights that surrounded the windows, that extended from the floor and came to an oval shape at the top. Avery and Owen walked onto the oak dance floor along with most of the other guests, while the others lined the outskirts of the dance floor.

Owen noticed Avery's eyes kept scanning the other couples on the floor. "It's just us now," Owen softly said. Avery smiled and then the dance began. The two of them were not professionals by any means, but they managed to glide across the floor as their bodies extended and flowed to the music. Regardless of the numerous other couples on the dance floor, Owen and Avery were in their own universe and filled with joy. They smiled as they gazed at each other and even laughed if one of them had a misstep.

The song finally came to an end and the next one appeared to be a jive. Avery smiled as she began to mockingly dance to it. "Maybe it's time to allow someone else to have a turn," Owen teased and the two of them laughed as they held hands and walked off the dance floor.

"Impressive," Abigail remarked as they approached the group.

"Thank you, but the credit belongs to Prisha for teaching me," Owen said as he pointed to Prisha, who smiled and curtsied.

"When did you learn to dance, Avery?" Selena inquired.

"I learned while I was growing up," Avery answered.

Aiden approached the group. "I hate to break up the fun, but Astrid instructed me to have everyone follow me so she can talk to all of you in private."

"Here we go," Bailey commented as the entire group sighed and followed Aiden.

They went through a series of rooms until they reached what appeared to be a private office. They entered and fanned out as much as they could, as they stood side-by-side toward the back of the room, while Prisha and Aiden stood behind them. Astrid, who was sitting at the desk, stood up and walked in front of it.

"Thank you. I'm glad you could join me. Now we can get down to business. I had full intentions of making this a fun evening while finding a way to work together to get past our differences, but unfortunately, I don't believe that can happen. However, since I am a gracious host, I will allow you to leave this party unharmed and even give you time to go back to Isaac's house, pack up your stuff, and leave. Let's say...twenty-four hours," Astrid said matter-of-factly.

"What made you come to this decision?" Owen inquired.

"No need to answer that because I have a counter-proposal," Marcus announced as his eyes narrowed in on Astrid. She remained silent as she stared back at Marcus so he continued. "I propose an immediate surrender of the djinn and the facility you currently inhabit, along with everyone else inside of it, unharmed. Then, your life will be spared if, and only if, you accompany us to a location of our choosing. There, we will assist you to become the person that Isaac, your father, always viewed you to be," Marcus countered in a calm, yet firm tone.

Astrid's face hardened as she looked at Marcus with disdain. "You know Marcus, Isaac may have thought the world of you, but I don't. I don't know what he saw in you but that doesn't matter now. Why…because you're dead."

Marcus went to respond, but the only thing that passed his lips was blood trickling out of his mouth. His face cringed with pain as he coughed up blood. His eyes drifted down and then followed the hand that was driven into his chest to a trusted and close friend…Hailey.

CHAPTER 23

M arcus peered into the cold, eagle eyes of Hailey as he grabbed her arm and wobbled. His face crinkled more, not from pain, but from confusion as he stared back at her. Everyone else was frozen with their mouths and eyes wide open from shock. Then, Hailey sent lightning through the hand that was in his chest. This caused Marcus's body to violently convulse and more blood, and now smoke, to pour out of his mouth and chest. His gurgling scream ceased when she ripped his charred heart from his chest. His body crumbled to the floor while she stood over it. The entire time, Marcus never transitioned. She let his pierced heart slide off her talons and fall onto his body before she casually walked to the side of Astrid. She stood next to Astrid, calmly and with a hint of a smirk, in her blood-stained white dress.

"No!" Owen yelled as he couldn't take his eyes off Marcus. Tears ran down his face from both the loss of Marcus and the betrayal of Hailey. Avery began to ball as she grabbed Owen's arm and continued to stare at Marcus's body.

Abigail and Bailey transitioned and went to charge but Hailey held her hand up while electricity arched between her fingers. Astrid followed suit as she raised her hand that was engulfed in fire. Selena transitioned but turned around to see what Prisha and Aiden were doing. From the looks on their faces, they were in just as much shock as the rest. They raised their hands in surrender so Selena turned back around. At that point, Owen and Avery transitioned and redirected their attention toward Astrid and Hailey. Flames ignited from Abigail and Owen's hands as their intensity grew.

"What have you done?" Owen screamed.

"How could you do something like that? He was a part of our family!" Avery yelled while she cried.

"Because she is a backstabbing traitor," Abigail angrily said through her teeth.

"Well, to be fair. She was on your side, a part of your family as you would say, until about an hour ago," Astrid casually commented while she had a crooked smile.

"What do you mean?" Bailey asked. She was breathing heavily due to the intensity of the werewolf flowing through her.

"When your happy little family spread out to mingle, I took the opportunity to do a little investigation myself. Since I was lied to recently, I needed to make sure I could trust Owen again, so I read Hailey's mind," Astrid said as her smile disappeared. She then turned and looked at Owen.

"I was there and you never touched her," Bailey blurted out.

"Who said anything about me having to be in contact with someone to be in their mind?" Astrid casually asked and then smirked at Owen.

"You made a wish when I wasn't around," Owen commented in a gravelly voice.

"Smart boy. It was early on. Remember when you inquired about my third wish…the one that I needed to make before my guests arrived? Well, I already wished that my psychic power would work without me having to touch someone. Granted, the djinn made it so I had to be near the person to do it, but still. So, I pretended to touch people to keep the ruse going. Don't be mad, a girl has to have some secrets," Astrid explained and then shrugged while she smiled.

"Even if you didn't touch her, when could you have done it?" Bailey inquired.

"When the three of you were in the art room admiring the paintings. You and Marcus walked in front of Hailey, so I walked behind her long enough to make the needed modifications. You two should have paid more attention to her and not the paintings," Astrid explained.

"You played me," Owen snarled. His upper lip raised to expose his fangs as both his, and the chimera's anger, filled his body.

Astrid's smile vanished. "You want to talk about being played. You lied right to my face about your secret nightly meetings with your friends. I even gave you a second chance after I caught you during your astral projection. Not only that, but I spared your friends' lives as well. I even kept my word and didn't get inside your head. After all my generosity, you...a person I thought was my friend, looked me in the eyes and lied," Astrid said in a stern, yet shaky tone of voice as her eyes became glassy.

Owen's eyes diverted from Astrid and he had no response. He lowered his hands as the fire went out and he transitioned back to human. "I'm sorry. I failed both you and your father," Owen commented as his eyes too became glassy.

"You sure did and now you will share my pain. Furthermore, your services are no longer required. I have traded up and at least Hailey won't be deceitful like her predecessor," Astrid said with a smug expression.

"Hailey, snap out of it. Don't you see she is using you?" Avery pleaded.

"Whatever Astrid has done; it was to make things better. Besides, why would I want to go back to a bunch of people that I can't even trust myself," Hailey responded without expression.

"She has twisted your mind around. You don't feel this way. Don't you remember all the horrible things Astrid has done?" Avery asked.

"Can't be any worse than what any of you have done in the past. Besides, all her actions were to make things better," Hailey countered.

"It's pointless to try. Once I found out the truth, I altered her mind to justify anything that I did or said. Also, I may have tweaked her mind to focus more on the emotional pain from the relationships she had with each one of you," Astrid added while she grinned.

"Did you not just hear what she said?" Bailey asked.

"I did, but she changed me for the better," Hailey responded again without emotion.

Selena stepped forward. "Hailey, how do you feel that you killed a close friend and mentor such as Marcus?" Her tone was calm when she spoke.

"I don't feel anything. Well, maybe some relief since now I don't have to worry about hearing him give demands all the time. Besides, if anything, I feel good because if Astrid felt he should be dead, then it was for the better," Hailey replied in the same tone as before.

"We need to leave and regroup," Selena commented.

"No, I'm not leaving her to be some puppet for Astrid," Owen responded while his eyes drifted to Hailey.

"I'd listen to her if I were you," Astrid commented.

"I'm staying with Astrid," Hailey said in a stern voice as she went deeper into transition.

"We can take them," Abigail said as she began to stalk them. Owen followed her lead as he went into transition.

"Hailey, I think you need to fry someone else to prove a point. How about…" Astrid stopped talking when the door behind them slightly opened but no one entered. The entire room turned and stared at the door until Caine strolled through.

"Sorry for the delay, but the mercenary guarding that door decided to allow me to have a snack," Caine remarked with a sinister

311

grin. He then wiped the remaining blood from his mouth and then sucked it off his finger.

"I thought you didn't like parties," Selena said as she grinned.

"Well, I was hungry and I know how much you hate it when I have my meals delivered, so I decided to go out," Caine teased. Selena, as well as Owen and his friends, couldn't help to smile. "So, do I just snap Astrid's neck now so we have time to make it back to the dance, or what?" Caine casually added as his eyes turned red and narrowed in on Astrid.

"Should I just kill them all?" Hailey inquired as she lifted her hands. The lightning around her hands began to grow the more she focused on the group.

"Well, that's a totally different Hailey from earlier," Caine commented.

"Astrid used mind control on her to make her defect," Selena mentioned.

"I wonder if I kill the source if it will kill the connection between them as well," Caine said as his eyes drifted toward Astrid again.

"It won't. Her mind is permanently changed so unless you find a way to re-alter her mind, then she will remain mine," Astrid added. Caine raised his lip to show his fangs.

"Are you sure?" Hailey asked. Owen's brow crinkled because he wasn't sure why she would ask that of Astrid. "If you say so," Hailey added. Owen looked around and noticed he shared the same confusion as the rest.

Hailey grabbed Astrid and flew toward the skylight, but Caine was able to catch Hailey's foot. She quickly lowered one hand and shot a bolt of electricity at Caine that hit him in his neck and shoulder area. He released his grip and grunted while he staggered back to the desk. Hailey then soared, while she held Astrid, through the skylight and vanished into the night sky. Caine moved away quickly to avoid the shattered glass that fell.

"Who was she talking to?" Bailey blurted out to the group.

"Astrid may have been using telepathy to speak to Hailey. If so, Hailey may have confused it with normal speaking," Selena suggested.

"Psychics can do that?" Avery asked.

"One as powerful as her, it's possible. If the connection between the two is strong enough, the telepathy can even extend past the psychic's own capabilities. However, this could be just another wish that Owen didn't know about," Selena responded.

"We can discuss Astrid's capabilities later because I believe we overstayed our welcome," Caine commented. Owen carefully listened and he could hear people coming in their direction. He figured it was probably because they heard the skylight shatter.

"Do we go through the window?" Abigail asked.

"Yeah, that's a good idea. Let's draw more attention to the room filled with blood, glass, and a dead body," Caine sarcastically remarked.

"We may not have a choice," Owen added.

"I have an idea," Aiden shouted. He then ran over to the skinny desk on the side of the room that had a clear fancy glass bottle with a round glass topper, surrounded by a few glasses. Aiden popped the top off and downed a few large gulps.

"Your solution is to drink. Really?" Prisha commented.

Aiden stopped drinking and let out a large breath of air as his face cringed. "That smells like brandy," Caine said as his brow raised.

"Yeah, but it tastes like regret," Aiden replied as he shook his head and placed the glass container down. He then rushed over to the front of the desk, grabbed a piece of broken glass, and braced himself.

"What are you doing?" Owen inquired.

"Creating a distraction," Aiden responded and then slit the palm of his hand. Blood began to pour down it. Prisha ran and grabbed

313

napkins from the skinny table and gave them to Aiden. "Follow my lead, Prisha. The rest of you leave through the front door when the coast is clear," Aiden added as he slung his arm over Prisha.

"Thank you. When you can, go to the large house on top of a hill off to the east, toward the edge of this town. You can't miss it and at least one of us will be outside waiting for you," Owen said as the rest of the group filed in behind Owen.

Prisha and Aiden nodded and walked to the door. By now, the voices were close to the door. Aiden became weak in the knees right before Prisha opened the door. As soon as the door opened, Aiden went into character.

"I'm so sorry. I just wanted my coat from the coat closet so I could get my jacket and leave, but then I saw the drinky drink on the table, and my lips were so dry. Look at them...they are still dry. Even after drinking...dry. Look...see," Aiden slurred as he puckered at Prisha. At that point, the voices stopped and Aiden and Prisha were out of sight.

"Yes, I see they are dry. Let's get your hand bandaged. I still don't understand how you cut it," Prisha commented. The group moved to the door and transitioned to hear better.

"I thought...I thought I saw a spider. So, I threw that ball thingy at the window and I wanted to make sure it was dead. Someone needs to stop cleaning these windows so much because the glass on the ground was very slippery and I fell and cut my hand. Look at all this blood. I should sew...I mean...saw...I mean," Aiden stammered and slurred.

"You mean sue?" Prisha asked

"Yes, that's the word...sue. Thank you...you're so kind," Aiden slurred. Even though the situation was dire, Owen and the others had to put their hands over their mouths to keep from laughing. They could now hear other people talking, but couldn't make out what they were saying.

"No, no need to go in that room. I am going to have a service come out and clean it up and I will notify the host. Apparently, this gentleman also thought the room was a bathroom as well," Prisha added.

"The bidet was a nice touch," Aiden said clearly, and as the people sounded disgusted, Owen had to bite his lip from laughing. Then, the noise went away as it appeared the people had left the area.

"I don't know the guy, but I like him already," Caine commented.

The mood within the room was upbeat but just for that one moment in time until reality sunk in when they turned around and saw Marcus lying on the floor. "We can't leave him here," Owen commented.

"Well, we can't just carry him out the front door now can we," Abigail frustratingly said.

Owen turned to Caine. "Can you please get him out of here? You are fast enough to do it without anyone seeing. Please?" Owen kindly begged.

Caine rolled his eyes, "Fine." He then scooped up Marcus and even his heart and within the blink of an eye, they vanished, with just a hint of a breeze that followed Caine.

The group left the room but stopped when Bailey happened to see the guard sitting in the corner of the room. He was semi-obscured by someone's jacket. "Please don't tell me he is dead," Bailey commented.

Selena rushed over to him and checked his vitals. "No, he is alive, just drained." She then put her fingers on his neck and Owen noticed a slight glow for a few seconds.

"You healed him, why?" Owen asked.

"To hide the evidence that a vampire bit him. Let's go," Selena explained as she hurried along with the group.

They rushed down the hallways and through the rooms until they reached the foyer. Then, in pairs, they calmly walked through the

315

foyer, passed the mercenaries and hybrids that were unaware of what occurred, and out the front door. Once they were outside, they instructed the valet to retrieve the vehicles that Bailey and Abigail took to drive everyone to the event. Once they piled into the vehicles, they left and drove back to Isaac's house.

When they arrived at Isaac's house, Caine was already there and Marcus was lying in the backyard while Livia mourned over him. Everyone got out of their vehicles and stood behind Livia and waited in silence, quietly mourning as they did.

Livia stood up and wiped the tears from her eyes and then more tears appeared when she saw Owen. She briskly walked up to him and gave him a long, large hug. After their embrace, Livia checked on the others. As she talked with them, Caine informed Owen that he got Livia up to speed with what went down at the mansion. Owen made sure to thank him multiple times for bringing Marcus back. He knew he would have to fill in the holes that Caine would not know about, to both him and Livia, but he was grateful that he was able to bring Marcus back.

Everyone agreed to give Marcus a proper funeral, and the pyre was easy to construct since there was a wood pile designated for the fireplace. There was enough wood left over from the previous winter season that they were able to take as much wood as they needed to construct a funeral pyre. Like Alyssa, Owen carved Marcus's name into a log and placed it at the foot of the pyre. He then carried Marcus over and laid him on top of the pyre.

Each person there went up to the pyre and spoke about the good and funny times that they had with Marcus. Tears and smiles filled the faces of each of them as they celebrated Marcus's life. Toward the end, Livia brought out one of Marcus's suits and laid it on top of him. She turned and nodded at Owen to start the fire.

Owen approached the pyre and wiped the tears as they ran down his face. "I would wear your suits for you in honor of your memory, but I don't think I could pull it off as well as you did. I will find a

316

way to stop Astrid. For you, Isaac, and countless others…your deaths will not be in vain. Goodbye my friend," Owen muttered right before he set the pyre ablaze and walked back to his friends.

The light from the fire chased the darkness from the night away as Owen and his friends stood and watched the pyre burn as they cried. Avery and Owen hugged and consoled each other as the others did the same.

Toward the end of the funeral pyre burning, Owen heard a car door close. He turned around and saw Prisha and Aiden walking in his direction. "I hope we are not intruding. We arrived a while ago but stayed in the car so we wouldn't be a bother. Sorry about your friend," Prisha said with a sympathetic smile.

"You two are never a bother and your help in getting us out of there was both hilarious and most appreciated," Owen replied.

Selena reached out and gently took Aiden's hand and placed her hand over his cut. A glow emanated from under her hand and less than a minute later, his hand was healed. "Thank you, but how?" Aiden asked while astonished.

Selena smiled. "My creature is a unicorn."

"And that is one of its tricks. Handy," Aiden commented.

"If you don't mind me asking, what creature did Marcus have within him?" Prisha politely inquired.

"A gargoyle. Why's that?" Owen asked.

"Just trying to figure out why he didn't transition to save himself," Prisha replied.

"In his case, a gargoyle around a bunch of humans that it doesn't recognize, in an unfamiliar area, will become aggressive in self-defense. I presume Marcus didn't want to take the chance of any of us, or an innocent, becoming injured, or worse," Owen explained.

"That, and he probably didn't want to take the chance of the gargoyle being seen. I almost died back in the city not too long ago. I could have easily avoided it if I transitioned but I couldn't risk the cyclops, my creature, to be seen. The last thing we need is for a creature to be broadcast to the world. It would cause a panic, as well as put our lives at risk," Avery added as she approached them.

"True, and as horrible as it is, we must think of the greater good. Even if it puts our lives in danger," Owen commented.

"I understand," Prisha respectively responded.

"Me too. That's some dark stuff, but I get it," Aiden said as he patted Prisha on her shoulder.

"Dawn is approaching. I'll be inside," Caine announced.

"What, are you a vampire or something," Aiden jested, but when nobody laughed, his smile disappeared. "Wait…seriously? Like a full-blown vampire, not just his creature?" Aiden nervously inquired.

"Yeah, but you will be fine as long as you stay on his good side," Owen commented and then smirked before he walked off. Aiden looked at Caine, who flashed his red eyes while he deviously smiled before he went inside.

"You're not going to sleep tonight, are you?" Prisha muttered.

"I will as soon as I find a cross made of garlic and dipped in holy water," Aiden replied.

Everyone else went inside except for Owen, Avery, Bailey, and Livia. They stayed until the fire was almost out and then they covered up the remains of the pyre with dirt. "We should all go inside and get some sleep. We will need clear minds to figure out what to do next. Owen, you can fill me in later with anything else you learned that I don't know about yet," Livia suggested.

The rest agreed but before they walked off, Owen cleared his throat to get Livia's attention. "Alyssa, the witch that helped us, was killed by Astrid a couple of weeks ago. I was able to give her a proper burial, but her family doesn't know and they were close. Is there any way you can find out how to get in contact with them so I can notify them? Please," Owen asked.

"I will find them and even notify her family too. You will have your hands full with Astrid and Hailey," Livia mentioned.

"Thank you. It's weird to hear Hailey's name mentioned with Astrid, but thank you. Please let Alyssa's family know that she died while helping me in what she believed in and that she did receive a proper burial. Also, that she loved them very much and thought and spoke of them often," Owen relayed.

"I will make sure they receive that message," Livia replied.

"Thank you," Owen responded. He felt relieved that Alyssa's family wouldn't have to wonder about their daughter for too much longer. Even though the news they were going to receive would be devastating, at least they wouldn't be in a constant state of panic. That, and they will know she always kept them in her mind and heart. Owen and the rest of the group entered the house and immediately went to sleep.

Everyone woke up around noon and got themselves ready for the day. Owen moved slowly at first since it took him longer to wake up. He had trouble sleeping at first because his mind kept replaying Marcus's death. During lunch, Owen, and the rest updated Livia on everything they knew from last night. Owen then took the time to discuss, in detail, about his time at the facility. Afterward, Owen cleaned up his mess and walked into the family room, along with Avery and Prisha. They were only in the other room for a few minutes, chatting in general, when Owen heard some dishes break, followed by yelling. He rushed in and saw Abigail restraining Selena as Bailey disarmed the knife that Selena was yielding, while Aiden stood between Livia and Selena. Livia, who appeared flustered as she breathed heavily, was also holding her arm from a cut that he presumed Selena caused.

"What is going on here?" Caine loudly asked as he came around the corner and stood in the hallway. His eyes turned red and his face hardened when he saw Selena being held against her will as she grunted and screamed.

"Selena attacked Livia," Abigail announced.

"That's impossible. She wouldn't hurt anybody unless she had a reason," Caine countered.

"I saw it too. She was helping Livia to wash the dishes and then suddenly, she snapped and slashed at her," Bailey explained.

"Then Livia must have provoked it," Caine said as he glared at Livia.

"Really?" Livia said as her brow furrowed while she put a towel around her wound.

"I don't know her that well, but does she normally act like a wild animal?" Aiden inquired. Caine whipped his head toward Aiden and raised his lips to expose his fangs as his eyes turned blood-red. "No offense, but just look at her," Aiden quickly added as he raised his hands in surrender.

Caine, along with everyone else, looked at Selena. Even with Abigail holding her, she was still struggling to free herself while she yelled and her eyes were wild like an animal.

Caine's vampire characteristics disappeared as his brow crinkled with concern. "No, that's not like her at all. What's wrong with her?"

Livia walked over to the restrained Selena, who became enraged when Livia approached her. Owen could see Abigail's face strain to the point she had to transition to keep Selena from escaping. Livia gently placed a couple of fingers on Selena's temples, which caused her to pass out.

"Bring her to the couch please," Livia requested. Abigail carried her over to the family room and gently laid her down on the couch. Everyone, but Caine followed behind Abigail. Owen could see Caine's concern and frustration as he paced around to get a view of Selena, so Owen grabbed a blanket and placed it over one of the windows in the family room.

"It's not much, but I have a shaded area in the family room for you," Owen said and then tossed Caine a blanket. "Here, this will help you get to that spot."

"Thank you," Caine said before he carefully followed Owen into the family room and to his designated location. As they entered, Owen noticed Livia's hand on top of Selena's forehead, while Bailey patched her other arm up with the first aid kit. A minute later, Livia opened her eyes and removed her hand.

"What did you see?" Caine inquired while his eyes remained focused on Selena.

Livia took a slow breath. "Astrid placed a thought in Selena's head to kill me as soon as the opportunity presented itself."

"Which it did when she was helping you wash the dishes and utensils, including that serrated bread knife," Abigail added.

"If it wasn't for me fixing my hair at the spur of the moment, she would have sliced my throat and not my arm," Livia mentioned.

"I can't believe Selena was an assassin this entire time and we didn't know. How could Astrid have done this?" Avery asked. Owen glanced over to Caine who remained speechless as he continued to stare at Selena. His eyes were slightly glassy as he sat helplessly in the corner.

"I doubt she even knew. The seed that was planted in her head didn't germinate until the opportunity presented itself. As for how she did it, Astrid must have gotten close enough to Selena to implant that demand into her mind," Livia responded.

Abigail let out a long sigh while she shook her head and pressed her lips together firmly. "Astrid talked to us briefly but we purposely stood on the other side of this pedestal that had a vase on it. At one point, she leaned over to admire the vase. Her hands were behind her back when she leaned over, but Selena stood right on the other side of the pedestal. They were maybe just a few feet apart at most and she only viewed it for a few moments before she straightened up and spoke again."

"That is when she did it then," Livia commented.

"Dang it...I should have pulled Selena back," Abigail huffed as she stood up and paced the room.

"It's not your fault. None of us knew she could use her powers without touching us and she used that to her advantage," Owen added.

"How far were you from the vase?" Livia inquired.

"I was only a couple of feet behind Selena and to her left. I positioned myself in case Astrid tried anything," Abigail responded.

"I should have snapped her worthless little neck last night," Caine muttered as his brow furrowed.

"It would not have changed anything. Her death won't change any mind alterations she has performed. Besides, it was for the better that you, or any of you, didn't engage Astrid," Livia said as she stood up.

"Why's that?" Bailey asked.

"Because it only takes a second for her to invade your mind. Think of her power like a spider's web. If you get too close, you will be trapped and the spider can do what it wants at its leisure. For example, Caine, if it took you more than a second to kill her, she could have simply thought, 'Kill Selena.' Once she thought it, you would have killed her, or anyone else she picked, without hesitation," Livia explained.

The room became silent as that chilling thought seeped into everyone's mind. "Can you help her?" Caine softly asked.

"Yes, I can. Small alterations like these are relatively easy to remove. It's the deep-rooted ones that are more difficult to unravel," Livia replied.

"She'll be okay," Abigail said as she put her hand on Caine's shoulder and gently smiled at him. Caine nodded but he didn't take his eyes off Selena.

"Before I do, I think I need to check everyone else's mind to make sure Astrid didn't mess with anyone else," Livia added.

Everyone agreed and lined up in the middle of the room except for Caine who stayed in his corner. Livia didn't inspect him since he was never close to Astrid and was only at the party at the very end.

She walked behind each person, besides in front of them for safety reasons, and put her hands on either side of their head. She went from person to person, only spending less than a minute, except for Owen, whom she spent a few minutes with.

"Everyone has a clean bill of health," Livia announced.

"Even me?" Owen asked.

"When it comes to hidden agendas placed in your mind by Astrid, yes...even you," Livia replied.

"Then why did it take you so long to examine me?" Owen inquired.

"Because the thought she hardwired into your mind about not physically harming her made it difficult to examine you. I had to sift through more to make sure nothing else was there," Livia replied.

"Can you remove what she has done to my mind, or will I never be able to hurt her again?" Owen asked.

"I can, but it will be a long and painful process. Are you willing to go through that?" Livia inquired.

"To be in full control of myself again...yes," Owen quickly responded.

"There's one more thing," Livia mentioned.

"What's that?" Owen asked.

"I also noticed she altered your mind so you could transition deeper into level three," Livia commented.

"Yeah. It was one of the few things she did that I was grateful for," Owen replied.

"Well, it's all intertwined so if one goes, the other goes as well. I'm sorry," Livia added. Owen's heart sank. To be free of Astrid's control, he had to give up a gift that brought him not only power but relief from the fear of an accidental full transition.

"Could you add that part back when you are finished?" Owen inquired.

"If I could, I would. Sorry. If it's any consolation, it wasn't foolproof. If you ramped up too quickly you would have skipped right over that security measure," Livia responded and then rubbed the side of his shoulder.

Owen sighed. "Very well. Remove everything."

"I will, but let me take care of Selena first, then I will focus on you since you aren't actively trying to kill me," Livia said and then winked.

Owen scoffed in amusement, "Yes, of course."

Livia kneeled on the floor next to Selena and placed both her hands on her temples before she closed her eyes. Owen noticed Livia's face grimacing while he could see eye movement under Selena's eyelids. Everyone waited patiently, and in silence, as they sat still and watched, except for Caine who paced back and forth in his small little area. Suddenly, Selena's eyes opened wide as she gasped for air while she quickly sat up. Livia's hands flew off her due to the force of her sitting up.

Caine sped over to her and hugged her. "Are you okay?" He asked while he looked into her eyes.

"Yes...yes, I believe so," Selena responded and then smiled, but it was only briefly. She could see his face straining from the pain of the sunlight hitting his skin because he left the blanket behind. Owen could even see smoke rising from a couple of spots. "But you're not. Please, get out of the sunlight," Selena begged. Caine kissed her on her forehead and then sped back to the safety of the shadows. Owen was caught off guard by the open display of affection that Caine displayed but then regained focus as people gathered around Selena.

"You'll be all right. I removed Astrid's poison that she put inside your mind, so there is nothing to worry about," Livia said as she put her hand on Selena's shoulder and gave her a sympathetic smile.

"Do you remember anything from after lunch?" Abigail's inquired.

"I remember everything," Selena responded and then began to sob as tears rolled down her face. She then gently grabbed Livia's injured arm and healed it quickly while she repeatedly said "sorry" while she cried.

"It's okay. It wasn't you in control," Livia said. She then hugged Selena after she was healed.

"I know, but it was still me and I couldn't stop myself. I just felt a violent, blinding rage toward you and wanted you dead and there was nothing I could do. Like I was a spectator watching the horror unfold. I haven't felt that way since I went after those noblemen centuries ago. I'm so, so sorry," Selena said but it was almost too hard to understand since she was crying while she spoke.

After a few minutes, Selena's crying turned to sniffles so Abigail escorted her over to Caine. She sat down next to him and laid her head on his shoulder while he had his arm around her shoulders. Afterward, Abigail took Selena to the bedroom, on the main floor, to rest.

"Owen, I suggest you pick a bedroom upstairs and get comfortable," Livia suggested.

"Why upstairs?" Owen asked.

"Because you won't bother the others as much with your screaming," Livia softly replied.

"I can stay with you," Avery called out.

"I appreciate it but stay here. I'm sure I will need you when I am finished," Owen said with a fake smile.

Avery walked over to him and gave him a quick kiss on the lips before she hugged him. After, Owen slowly walked up the stairs, but not before Bailey patted him on his shoulder as he passed her. He picked a bedroom in the far corner and sat down on the bed. Livia entered soon after and closed the door. She then pulled up a chair next to the bed.

"Lie down and close your eyes. Once they are closed, I will place my hands on your head. It won't hurt at first, but the deeper I go, the more intense it will get. I must warn you, once I start, I can't stop. If I stop before I'm done, your mind will be a mess. Are you sure you want to do this?" Livia sympathetically asked.

"Yes," Owen replied. He then laid down and closed his eyes.

He wasn't sure how long he laid there before he began to feel a headache, which then became more intense by the moment. He squeezed his eyes tightly and clenched his fists as his face crinkled while he tried his hardest to manage the pain. The pain started behind his eyes and slowly spread to his entire head. If he could, he would reach inside his skull and squeeze his brain to make it feel better. Just when he thought the pain was becoming unmanageable, the real pain hit. Owen felt as if someone jammed multiple searing hot daggers into his brain, all at once. He let out a blood-curdling scream as his entire body became rigid. His chest lifted into the air while the rest of his body remained on the bed. For whatever reason, he could not open his eyes, nor hear anything else but the sound of his own screams. Owen hollered so much that he thought he was going to pass out from the pain, but unfortunately, he remained awake through the entire horrific experience. Suddenly, the pain vanished without a trace.

"Open your eyes," Livia said. Her voice sounded distant, but he did hear it. She repeated it a couple more times, and each time it sounded closer before Owen was able to open his eyes.

"There he is. You did well. I'm sorry that you had to go through that," Livia said as she handed Owen a towel.

"Did it work?" Owen inquired as he wiped the sweat from his face and neck.

"It did. Your mind is your own now," Livia responded as she smiled.

"Thank you," Owen said as he repositioned himself on the bed, but then wobbled.

"You're welcome and take it easy. That took a lot out of you. Just take it slow and get some rest, but also make sure you get some food and water. You will be fine," Livia said as she steadied his wobbly body before she got up and walked over to the door. Owen slowly nodded his head. He could feel the lack of energy in his body as he strained to keep himself upright. "I believe you have guests," Livia added and then opened the door.

Everyone entered the room, except for Caine who stood at the doorway. Avery sat on the bed and hugged Owen while Abigail sat on the other side of him and put her hand on his knee. Bailey sat next to Avery and Selena sat in the chair in front of Owen while Prisha and Aiden stood near Livia. Owen could feel the warmth of their compassion as he melted and laid his head on Avery's shoulder. The two leaned back against the wall and she then slowly ran her fingers through his hair. Selena then handed Owen a bottle of water.

"Thanks," Owen weakly said as he sipped his water.

"It killed me to hear you like that," Avery softly said to Owen.

"Sorry, but at least I don't plan on doing that again any time soon," Owen said and then winked.

Avery chuckled. "I hope not. It worked; I presume?"

"It did," Owen replied.

"Good. Now we can focus on how to kill Astrid and get Hailey back," Bailey blurted out as her eyes narrowed.

"But how do we stop someone as powerful as Astrid? We can't even get near her. Even worse, how do we get to Astrid without hurting Hailey?" Livia asked.

"Maybe we can steal the locket from Astrid and use our wishes to solve that problem," Prisha suggested.

"It's always around her neck and I doubt she will just hand it over out of the goodness of her non-existent heart. Besides, there's no way any of us can get past her forces without her knowing," Aiden commented. Owen scoffed, followed by a chuckle to himself.

"What is it?" Avery asked.

"I think I know a way. It's a long shot, but it may work," Owen muttered as he sat up.

"Do tell, what is this grand idea that you have?" Caine inquired.

"It's something that you will not like and something that we can only do if she is comfortable and willing to help," Owen replied.

"She?" Caine slowly asked as his brow lowered.

"Selena," Owen replied and then he turned to her.

"Me?" Selena asked as her head tilted and her brow knitted.

"Yes…and no," Owen said as his face cringed. "It's not only you that we need help from, but the unicorn within you as well."

CHAPTER 24

The blanket that Caine held in his hand dropped to the floor as he walked into the room. His eyes flared wildly at Owen as he approached him. "How dare you ask her to do something of that nature," Caine said through his teeth as his eyes flashed red.

"I wouldn't have asked if the need wasn't dire," Owen calmly said before he looked at Selena. She raised her hand to stop Caine from advancing.

"There's no guarantee that this will work. I'm not even sure if a unicorn can grant a wish. As much lore as there is out there that says a unicorn can grant wishes, there is other lore that says otherwise," Selena commented.

"I know it's a long shot. I'm hoping that since it's such a magical creature, the lore is accurate about it granting wishes," Owen said while he remained calm.

"I hate to break it to you but we aren't the purest people around," Bailey commented.

"Yeah, and it's not like we can borrow someone's child and ask them to make a wish on how to kill Astrid. Heck, there's not even an abundance of children in our circle of friends," Abigail added.

"Those are good points. A unicorn will only present itself in front of someone who is pure. Not only that, a unicorn will only grant a wish if the wish is pure in nature and not evil or selfish. With that said, I doubt a unicorn will grant us a wish on how to kill Astrid, no matter how evil she is. I don't even think it will allow us to steal the locket from her," Avery mentioned.

"There may be another way," Owen muttered.

"What is it?" Livia asked.

"If we ask Selena while she is deep into a phase three transition, she may be able to grant a wish before she fully transitions. She may even have a little wiggle room with the wish than a unicorn would," Owen said as he stared off into the distance while he thought out loud. When he was done speaking, he turned his attention back to Selena to see her reaction.

"I won't be able to hold off a full transition for long. Also, I won't be able to focus on making a wish come true if all my concentration is being used to keep me from becoming the unicorn," Selena countered.

"I may be able to help with that," Livia said as she approached Selena.

"How?" Selena asked as her brow knitted while her head tilted slightly.

"I can stand near you and use my abilities to delay you from fully transitioning. It won't last long, maybe just a few seconds or so, but you will at least be able to concentrate," Livia explained.

"Don't feel obligated to do any of this," Caine remarked.

Selena paused as her head lowered. She then stood up and walked over to Caine and put her hands on his chest. "I don't feel obligated. It's something I want to do." Caine scoffed. He turned his head, but Selena gently redirected his head forward so she could look into his eyes. "I do. Because of Astrid, I almost killed an innocent person. Look at all the horrible things she has done and what she is capable of doing. She even made Hailey kill Marcus. I don't want to live in fear that it will happen to me again, but this time I succeed and kill someone. Imagine if she got to you and I ended up on that funeral pyre," Selena added. Caine's face eased and his eyes opened more when the mental image hit him. "I want to do this. If it works then great, we will finally have a way to defeat Astrid. If not, at least I can say that I tried."

Caine sighed. "I don't know if it's you being noble or stubborn, but if you truly want to do this, then I will be by your side the entire time." Selena smiled and gently placed her hand on the side of Caine's face.

Selena turned around. "Someone please let Cedric know to keep a cell clear in the transitioning room. It's about to have a visitor," Selena commented as she smirked.

"I'll text Cedric the details and tell him we will be there tonight," Abigail said and then took out her phone.

"We can use the car ride to come up with ideas of what the wish should be," Bailey commented.

"Good idea because we will only have one shot at this so the wish has to be perfect," Avery added.

Owen gently put his hand on the side of Selena's arm. "Thank you," he sincerely said as he smiled. Selena placed her hand on his and returned the smile as she nodded her head. Caine didn't look at Owen. As soon as Owen approached Selena, he turned around and left the room.

The group didn't waste any time getting ready to leave. They took two cars back to the city and most of the time was spent brainstorming what to wish for. They each came up with their own ideas and then, while on speakerphone, discussed their ideas with each other. Not only were they selecting which wish to use, but who would be the one to ask it. To enhance their chances of success, the idea was presented to have the purest person in the group ask. After a short debate, Prisha was selected to ask the wish.

They arrived at the club later that night. Cedric greeted the group outside and was introduced to Aiden, Prisha, and Livia. Abigail explained the importance of Livia's involvement in their plan to

Cedric. He understood, so he made an exception for allowing a non-hybrid into the club, provided no one else found out about it. Cedric also made sure to walk with them so they could bypass security without any hassles.

This was Livia's, Aiden's, and Prisha's first time at this type of club so Abigail went over everything they needed to know. Still, they were in awe of everything they witnessed once they went through the red door. Owen couldn't blame them because even though he had visited the club multiple times, he still caught himself staring at some of the spectacles.

Once they entered the training room, Cedric led them to the transitioning room's entrance and unlocked the steel door. "Are you sure you want to do this?" Cedric asked Selena.

Selena took a deep breath. "Yes," she responded and then she held Caine's hand. Cedric nodded and opened the door.

After a couple of minutes of navigating the corridors, they entered the transitioning room itself. They quickly noticed that all the steel cages and cells, large and small, were empty. The room was about the same size as the training room within the club. The ground and walls outside of the creature areas were made of stone, but the inside of each cage appeared to vary. Cedric led them to a caged corral-like area, that was well stocked with hay, flowers, berries, vegetables, and a trough with fresh water in it.

"Business slow?" Abigail commented as she glanced around.

Cedric chuckled. "We just had a creature transition back to human recently and while we cleaned that creature's area, I simply pushed back the people who were going to use this room. A matter of this importance calls for privacy," Cedric responded.

"Thanks. I appreciate it. Everything looks good," Owen commented as he shook Cedric's hand.

Owen turned to Selena. "Ready whenever you are." She nodded her head and gave each person there a hug and exchanged words of encouragement. When it came to Caine, she spent more time with him and they stood further away to allow for more discretion. She kissed him gently on his cheek before she walked over to the cage.

"I'm ready," Selena said and then entered the cage. Prisha, Livia, Caine, and Owen followed right behind her. The remainder of the group stayed outside of the cage, while Cedric held onto the door to the cage with a firm grip. The group went to the back of the enclosure to give them more room to work with, especially with the gate door open.

Owen turned to Caine. "Remember, once she turns you need to run out of here as fast as you can. No offense, but with you being the evilest one among us, the unicorn will target you."

"Well, everyone has to excel at something," Caine casually responded with a crooked grin.

"He's right, Caine. Don't make my last moments filled with worry," Selena commented.

"You have nothing to worry about. I will be here waiting for you when you transition back to human, no matter how long it takes," Caine replied.

"I would hope so. You are immortal so you have time to spare," Selena teased. Caine scoffed in amusement as he stood next to her and held her hand.

Owen turned to Livia. "Okay, you're up."

Livia nodded and stood in front of Selena and placed her hands on her temples, but then shifted her body so that her hands were still in place, but she wasn't standing directly in front of Selena.

"Why are you standing like that?" Owen inquired.

"To lessen the chances of my head being impaled by a horn. Even then, I am still too close for comfort," Livia replied.

"I can hold onto your shoulders and yank you away as soon as she fully transitions," Owen suggested.

"Good idea, but don't touch me until you see the unicorn. Anything sooner and you will be inside Selena's mind and I can't properly control her mind with a passenger on board as well," Livia said as she continued to keep her eyes on Selena.

"Understood," Owen said as he positioned himself behind Livia. He looked over to Prisha, who stood to the side of Owen, but in front of Selena. "Are you ready?"

"I'm ready," Prisha responded as she nodded her head.

"Selena will transition straight into level two and then slowly increase from there, so when this starts, begin to repeat the wish over and over until you see the unicorn. I don't know how long she will be in phase three before she turns, so talk fast," Livia directed.

"Got it," Prisha responded and then turned and stared at Selena.

"Whenever you are ready Selena. Good luck," Livia mentioned.

Selena's eyes narrowed and her brow lowered while she took a few breaths to steady herself. The room fell silent as all eyes were on Selena. Then, her face turned white and her eyes turned fully light brown, with her pupil remaining black but more oval-shaped.

"I wish I knew how to stop Astrid from hurting people," Prisha said loudly and repeatedly.

Selena grinded her teeth while her entire body strained as she grunted and moaned. Her skin quickly turned white, along with her hair. She squeezed Caine's hand hard enough for even him to wince in pain. Livia's face crinkled and her arms and hands were shaking from the intensity as she used all her might to keep Selena from fully transitioning.

Then, Selena began to scream as an off-white, twirled horn began to slowly protrude from her forehead. Owen's eyes grew wide as he placed his hands near Livia, ready to grab her since he felt Selena wouldn't last much longer. Selena stopped screaming and stared at Prisha, without blinking, as her face continued to strain. He then noticed the horn begin to emit a white glow, but then there was silence behind him as Prisha stopped repeating the wish. Owen turned his head and noticed Prisha was smiling as her eyes were glowing white.

Prisha's eyes stopped glowing as she stumbled back the same time he heard a loud neigh in front of him. Owen jerked his head around to see a unicorn standing on its two hind legs as its front two legs kicked in the air.

He grabbed Livia and yanked her aside before the unicorn landed back down. As it did, the unicorn backpedaled while it tossed its head up and down with its ears back while it squealed and snorted. It stopped and looked at each person near it until it saw Caine. The unicorn lowered its head and began to paw the ground.

"Caine, get out of there," Owen yelled. Caine, who fell over when Selena fully transitioned, stood back up, but he squinted at the unicorn as he wobbled. He held his hands up the same way a person would try to look at the sun.

"Get her to safety," Owen called out to Prisha. She nodded and grabbed Livia and they ran out of the corral. He then began to wave his hands and yell at the unicorn, but it did not pay him any attention.

As it was about to charge, Owen heard a loud roar come from the gate, loud enough to gain the unicorn's attention. It was Abigail, deep into a phase two transition. She growled and slowly approached the unicorn, which caused it to take a few steps toward her. As it did, Caine seemed to become more himself, but not fully.

"Go for it," Owen called out to Caine, who was finally able to speed outside the gate within seconds.

"Abigail! Transition back to human and get out of here," Owen said as he slowly backed away from the unicorn.

"Come on! I got your back. Make a run for it," Abigail called out.

"Just do it! Trust me," Owen demanded.

Abigail huffed and transitioned back to human and left the corral. As she did, the unicorn became less agitated. It looked over in Owen's direction, but he remained calm and slowly backed up.

"I know you're scared and confused, but I am not your enemy. I just want to leave, peacefully. We mean you no harm and I know you can sense that," Owen carefully spoke to the unicorn as he stopped. The unicorn snorted, followed by a small neigh as its ears went back up. It turned and walked away from Owen and as it did, Owen walked out of the corral and Cedric closed and locked the gate behind him. Avery hugged him as soon as he was out.

"When did you become a unicorn whisperer?" Aiden inquired.

Owen grinned. "I'm not. I was just hoping that the lore was correct about their nature and how magical they are."

"Unicorns will run from people, except for the ones who are pure, but it will attack anything that is pure evil, hence why it targeted Caine. It's even said that pure evil cannot stand in the presence of a unicorn. This was evident by Caine's reaction," Bailey explained.

"All I could see was a bright ball of white light that made me dizzy and confused," Caine commented.

"Luckily, Abigail caught its attention long enough for you to escape. Vampire or not, the magical properties of its horn could have killed you if it pierced your heart. Anyway, Owen then took it upon himself to test out another theory about unicorns," Bailey added.

"That is what he was referring to before. That they are so magical that they can understand any form of language on this planet," Avery commented.

"Exactly. So once the unicorn understood Owen wasn't a threat and it already knew he wasn't pure evil, it walked away since he is also not pure of heart," Bailey commented.

"I couldn't have said it better myself," Owen said as he grinned and shrugged.

The group, minus Caine, took a moment to admire the unicorn. Its size and physique were similar to a standard horse, and it had a long white, flowing mane and tail as well. Its pure white, flawless coat was amazing and then there was the horn, that spiraled to about a foot or so in length. Owen felt at peace as he watched the unicorn.

"Is anyone interested if Prisha's wish worked?" Caine sarcastically asked the group. Owen shook his head. The unicorn grabbed his attention so much that he forgot about the wish. He and the rest of his friends turned and looked at Prisha with anticipation.

"I could hear a whisper in my mind. It said, 'An iron key within Isaac's office.' I felt like there was going to be more but then the whisper vanished when she fully transitioned," Prisha replied.

"Probably telling us exactly where it was, but no matter...it worked! It's not much but it's more than what we started with," Abigail commented.

"True, but to get it, we have to march right into the lion's den to retrieve it," Owen mentioned.

"Then that's what we will do," Bailey said as she walked toward the others.

"I would've been surprised if it was easy," Avery jested.

"I'll send a handful of hybrids with you to assist in whatever you need. I would accompany you but I am needed here. Sorry," Cedric added.

"You have done more than enough. Thank you for the additional hybrids and for everything that you have done," Owen replied and then shook Cedric's hand.

Owen walked over to Caine. "Are you sure you don't want to come?"

"As much as I would enjoy ripping Astrid to pieces with my bare hands, I promised Selena I would be there when she returned. Besides, without her, I don't trust myself to keep my rage and bloodlust in check. I know that makes me sound dependent and weak, but it's the truth," Caine said as he glanced over to the unicorn and squinted.

"You are anything but weak. Go, be with her," Owen softly said as the two firmly shook hands.

Before the group left, the remainder of them quickly talked to Caine and as they were leaving, everyone stopped to admire the unicorn one last time. "The five-year-old in me is jumping up and down while screaming for joy," Avery commented, which made everyone smile.

Owen and his friends met Cedric's support team right outside the club. They had their own vehicle so they followed the other two cars in the group back to Isaac's house. During that drive, everyone used their time wisely by formulating a plan to get into the facility and locate the key. They also made sure to inform Cedric's people about Astrid and Hailey's abilities so they would be prepared. The obvious question, while they planned, was how to get around Astrid and Hailey. The entire group went back and forth trying to think of a way, but none of the ideas to draw her out of the facility appeared to be a viable choice. Finally, everyone concluded that no plan was going to be perfect and totally safe, so they had to go with something that had the least likelihood of getting themselves killed.

The group made it back to Isaac's house in the middle of the night. As much as they wanted to rush and retrieve the key, they decided to get some sleep so they were fresh for tomorrow's adventure. Cedric's hybrids took turns guarding the house to allow everyone to sleep without fear of being ambushed in their slumber.

It was late morning before Owen finally woke up and got himself ready for the day, along with everyone else. After lunch, Owen sat on the couch in the family room and was joined by Avery, who leaned against him. "It would be nice to just be able to stay here and relax versus running off into danger again," Avery commented.

"I'm guessing once we are past this mess, you will want a vacation that is far away from the mountains," Owen teased.

"You have no idea," Avery responded. At that time, the rest of the group, including Cedric's people, entered the room.

"We should leave soon. By the time we drive there and then make our way to the facility, it will be dark. Have we landed on a plan of action yet?" Bailey inquired.

"I feel like it's an ever-changing plan," Abigail commented.

Owen scoffed. "True, but this is what's concrete. Livia will stay here with two of Cedric's people. The rest of us will head to the facility. Once there, we will recover the key and evacuate all the facility workers that aren't under Astrid's rule and make our way back here."

"What about Astrid and Hailey?" Abigail asked.

"We have to draw them into a fight," Owen replied.

"Does that include me?" Aiden asked as he raised his hand.

"No, you will be on Avery's team. She will lead you and the rest of Cedric's people into the facility to find the key and get everyone out of there. Her team will have everything they need to accomplish this," Owen replied.

"That leaves the rest of us to take on Hailey and Astrid," Abigail mentioned.

"Correct and if we can't draw them out, then we will take the fight to them inside the facility. I don't care if we have to barricade them inside a room. Either way, we will stop them," Owen responded.

"Are you sure my part within your plan will work?" Prisha asked.

"More hopeful than sure," Owen commented.

"That's comforting," Prisha muttered.

"It should work or let's put it this way, it can't hurt. If you can create water and get Hailey wet, it will throw them off. She's smart enough to know she won't get electrocuted because she is the source, but she can't touch Astrid with any form of a charge on her or she will fry her," Owen explained.

"Anybody else feel we are moving too fast? Don't get me wrong...stopping Astrid and Hailey is the top priority, but still. If we just hold off a few more days, maybe we can come up with a better plan. Heck, we may be able to recruit other people from our sister facilities," Livia suggested.

"I'm sure you are right, but every minute Astrid is not stopped is a chance for another wish to be granted or an opportunity to corrupt Hailey even further. We have already delayed enough as it is now. Besides, the sister facilities have their own issues to deal with, some even worse than ours. We need to act now," Owen firmly suggested.

"If that is the case then please, be careful...all of you," Livia said before she hugged everyone, including the people she didn't even know well. Not too long after, the team loaded up the vehicles and the trailers and left for the facility.

The drive was long and tedious, but Owen was used to it by now. So much so, that he was the lead vehicle since he knew the quickest route and the best place to stop before they switched to the ATVs. Night had just fallen when they reached the stopping point for the ATVs. Owen, Bailey, and Abigail were ready as soon as they arrived. Avery grabbed her trusted hammer axe while Aiden and Prisha pulled out the weapons that they acquired from Isaac's house. Oddly enough, there wasn't a large selection at his house, so Prisha took one of the large hunting knives while Aiden took one of the semi-automatic handguns.

"We need to be silent once we leave here so if anyone has anything to say, now is the time," Owen mentioned. Immediately after, Owen approached Avery while she was sharpening the blade of her axe. Right before he tapped her on the shoulder, Avery turned around and Owen had to rear back to avoid being accidentally sliced across his chest.

"Oh, I'm so sorry!" Avery blurted out as she put her hand over her mouth while her eyes grew large.

"If you didn't want to talk, all you had to do was say so," Owen teased.

"Well, I was hoping that death would be a big enough hint to leave me alone," Avery playfully countered.

Owen smiled. "Be safe. We can't go on a proper date unless the both of us are there."

"Then I guess you better stay alive too," Avery said before she gave him a hug and a soft kiss on his lips.

"Enough with the mushy stuff. We are about to go into battle for crying out loud," Bailey sternly commented as she passed them.

"Yeah, stop with all the mushy stuff," Abigail said as she looked at the two of them and winked. Avery and Owen embraced each other for a few moments more before they separated and Owen walked over to Prisha and Aiden.

"I should have asked this sooner, but while there is still time, are you sure you are ready for your first mission?" Owen inquired. They both nodded their heads in agreement.

"Are you sure? If not, there will not be any judgment or disgrace. After our last training session, I wanted to be sure," Owen added.

"I'm ready. I am at peace with the outcome and I feel it's a just cause, considering the horrible acts that Astrid has already performed in such a short span of time," Prisha responded.

"Is there a reward when someone completes a mission?" Aiden asked.

Owen chuckled. "I don't know. This is still technically my first mission that has been going on for a long time now. I guess we will find out together," Owen replied. Aiden pouted in response. "Who knows, maybe you will get a wish from the djinn," Owen added.

Aiden's face lit up. "Now you're talking."

The group was ready and they left for the cabin. As they carefully walked to make sure that none of the patrols discovered them, Owen's mind began to wander. He hoped they could find a way to distract Astrid and Hailey long enough for the other team to find the key. He didn't expect to defeat them, they just had to stay alive long enough to draw them out and keep them busy.

When they reached the cabin area, anyone who had a creature that could see well at night transitioned to help lead the way. It was dark under the trees, but the moon was almost full so the light from that helped illuminate the open areas. They had to come from a different angle to make sure they didn't cross the barrier line. This forced them to have to go around to the front of the cabin. Before they did, Owen signaled that his team would go first while the other team stayed behind. Once the battle started, Avery's team would sneak in.

Owen's team strolled in front of the cabin and waited. The two guards inside came out with their semi-automatic rifles drawn. "Stay where you are! Identify yourselves!" Then, there was a whistle from Avery's team, which caused the guards to turn in the direction of the whistle, but they never fully turned around. Cedric's team shot them in their heads. They had silencers on their handguns, but the guards didn't. As the guards died, one of them squeezed the trigger and shot the ground. The gunshot echoed throughout the woods while the two guards silently laid on the ground as blood pooled around their heads.

"Well, that's one way of drawing her out," Bailey casually commented.

Before Owen could respond, he noticed Avery's team walking fast toward them. Before he could ask why, he saw the reason. Astrid and Hailey were behind them and even worse, Astrid had Aiden by the neck as she walked him forward.

CHAPTER 25

Aiden's face strained from the tight grip she had on him. "So predictable. What's even worse is that we've been watching you for the past ten minutes. I thought about just killing everybody before you even reached this point, but I was curious as to what angle you may have, and I found it…thanks to Aiden," Astrid said as a devious smile appeared on her face. Owen gasped as his anxiety skyrocketed when he feared how much information she may now know from reading his mind.

"It appears that there is an iron key in Isaac's office that will bring you salvation from me, and your master plan is to distract me so they can retrieve it. Seriously…toddlers can come up with better plans than that," Astrid mocked.

"Please, let him go. Don't hurt him," Prisha begged.

A sinister smile appeared on Astrid's face. "You want me to let him go…sure. Aiden, I command you to go find the wendigo and kill it with your bare hands. However, you cannot transition and you can't stop or leave the barrier until the wendigo is dead."

"Are you insane!" Owen yelled.

"No, I'm creative. You of all people should know that," Astrid said while she smiled.

Aiden began to slowly walk toward the barrier line. "Um, I don't want to be doing this, but I can't force myself to stop," Aiden called out as he walked. Prisha ran over, stood in front of him, and grabbed his shoulders to prevent him from going any further. When Aiden couldn't get past her, he grabbed her and pushed her aside.

"I'm sorry. I couldn't stop myself," Aiden sincerely apologized as his face cringed.

"It's okay. You're not in control," Prisha replied.

Owen and Avery began to run after him but immediately stopped as a bolt of lightning cracked in front of them. They turned and saw Hailey's hand pointed in their direction. "No, no, no. Aiden is a big boy. He can do it himself," Hailey said while she had a smug expression.

"So, let's talk about the terms of your surrender," Astrid announced. At that time, flood lights from the cabin turned on and illuminated the entire area they were in. Not only that, but half a dozen mercenaries ran out of the cabin with their guns pointed at Owen and his friends. Cedric's team refocused their aim on the mercenaries.

"Sure thing. Here are our terms," Owen said and then transitioned to phase two. He then thrust his hands forward and projected flames at Astrid and Hailey. Abigail followed Owen's lead and shot fire at them as well. Cedric's men opened fire, killing a couple of mercenaries quickly before they had to take cover from the return fire. Bailey, Avery, and Prisha transitioned to phase two as well.

The flames from Owen and Abigail only grazed Astrid from the combination of a couple of events. First, Hailey used her body to shield Astrid, so their flames hit her in the back instead. She yelled in pain as she fell to her knees. The second reason was unexpected as he watched their flames slam into an invisible barrier in front of both of Astrid's hands. She had them extended out in front of her face and chest. Astrid apparently wished for the ability to produce a psychic shield. It was only the width of the circumference of her fingers spread out on both hands, but enough to block the vital areas on her. Astrid's face strained against the power behind the flames. Before they could react, Hailey spun around and dropped a barrage of thunderbolts all around him and his friends. None of them made a direct hit, but the force was powerful enough to knock everyone back and to the ground.

"Bailey and Avery, take Cedric's people and breach the cabin. We will find Aiden once we deal with Astrid and Hailey," Owen directed.

"I can go find Aiden," Prisha blurted out.

"We need you here. Stick to the plan," Owen countered. Prisha didn't respond and continued to stare off into the woods. "We can't fight them and the wendigo and we need your help here and now or else we will lose," Owen softly added. Prisha turned to Owen and nodded her head. She stared at Hailey and Astrid as she transitioned deeper.

"Well, that wasn't very nice," Astrid remarked as she slowly moved her shoulder that was burned. She then helped Hailey off the ground. Owen could see that Hailey was still in pain as she winced while she moved. He couldn't help but feel bad for her, especially when he could see the burns on her that he caused. Nevertheless, they had to continue with the plan and hope she didn't become even more injured.

"Let's go," Owen yelled as he and Abigail charged Hailey and Astrid while they shot their flames again. Prisha stood up but stayed behind them. Cedric's people opened fire as they followed behind Bailey while they pushed forward toward the cabin.

"Change of plans," Avery called out as she turned and rushed into the woods.

"No! Avery, come back!" Owen called out. She didn't stop but she also forgot about being in transition and slammed into the invisible wall. She fell backward but shook it off. Avery sat there for a quick moment before she stuck her hand past the barrier line. Once she saw it go through, she continued her pursuit. Owen grinded his teeth out of frustration since he desperately wanted to go after her, but he knew he had to continue with the plan.

Astrid and Hailey rolled out of the way in separate directions to avoid the flames. As soon as they stopped, Hailey shot electricity from her hand while Astrid projected fire from hers. The two of them had to stop so they could dodge Astrid and Hailey's attack. As they did, Abigail charged Hailey and they began to fight. As Owen charged Astrid, he could see nothing but a melee of claws and talons slashing through the air. Then, he realized that he was running toward Astrid, so he slid to a stop.

"What's wrong Owen? Afraid that I am going to get back into that pretty head of yours," Astrid mocked.

"You're not getting back in there ever again," Owen spouted.

"I can tell that Livia undid my work and that she is still alive. Maybe I'll visit her and personally express my feelings," Astrid said as she grinned.

Owen could feel the anger brewing inside of him. She was heartless and he had enough of her treacherous and murderous ways. He surprised Astrid by shooting flames from his mouth at her, but he purposely aimed it more to her left. She jumped out of the way but Owen continued his attack as he had the flame follow her. What Astrid didn't realize was that he was leading her toward Hailey. Finally, Astrid shot fire from her hand at Owen to force him to stop, which he did as he dodged her attack.

Abigail, who was conscious of what Owen was doing, leaped back as Hailey's slash just missed her. Owen noticed both Hailey and Abigail had various slash marks on their bodies from their skirmish as they both breathed heavily.

Suddenly, water fell from above and splashed Hailey. It was enough to drench her and soak the ground around her, but Astrid was just out of range. Prisha walked in between Abigail and Owen and stood just past them. Her face was hardened as she glared at them.

"Wow, if you think a little water is going to stop me, then you need to go back and hit the books," Hailey commented as sparks danced around her entire body and her eyes began to glow.

Prisha smiled and when she did, Astrid examined her closer and her eyes grew wide when she noticed Prisha's hands resting near her waist…one was open and one was closed. "Hailey, don't…" Astrid tried to warn Hailey, but it was too late. Prisha opened her second hand and another large volume of water splashed on and around Astrid. The electrical current from Hailey was now able to find its way to Astrid, and when it did, Astrid began to convulse as she was being electrocuted.

Hailey immediately transitioned back to human and turned to Astrid, who was lying on the ground, unconscious with sporadic charred areas on her body. She checked her pulse and let out a sigh of relief when she noticed Astrid was still alive. She looked up at them and glared.

"Feel free to send more lightning our way if you like," Prisha said with a devious smile.

Hailey's brow furrowed before she sprung toward Prisha and as she cleared the wet area, Hailey began to transition. Prisha braced herself but Hailey never made it to her. She stopped and looked in horror as Owen shot fire from both his hands in the direction of Astrid.

"No!" Hailey screamed as the flames blanketed Astrid. She shot bolts of lightning out of each hand toward Prisha, Abigail, and Owen. They were able to dodge the main bolts, but the smaller electrical currents that stemmed from the main bolts did hit them. They fell to the ground, but Prisha immediately got up and pursued Hailey.

Hailey quickly grabbed Astrid, whose clothes were on fire, and rolled her in the wet dirt to extinguish the flames. She looked behind her and saw Prisha coming so she shot another quick bolt from her hand at her. Prisha was able to bend out of the way, but she had to almost come to a stop to do so. Hailey used that time to snatch Astrid up, dart into the night sky, and disappear.

Owen scoffed in amusement. We did it. He and Abigail got up and ran to Prisha and they had a group hug. They smiled, despite their injuries. Owen and Abigail then turned and stood in front of Prisha.

"You did it," Abigail said with excitement.

"Good job and smart move with the second round of water," Owen commented.

"Thank you," Prisha said to them as she tried to catch her breath while she smiled.

The celebration was short-lived. Their eyes drifted toward the woods as they stopped smiling. "We need to help them," Prisha said and as she went to run, Owen grabbed her by the shoulder. She turned her head and looked at him with a furrowed brow.

"You're right, but Abigail and I will do it," Owen directed.

"I can handle it and there is no way I am just going to stand around while others are in danger," Prisha countered.

"You won't. You're going to go inside the facility and help that team find the key," Owen replied and then raised his hand to stop Prisha from talking. "I know you are capable but you can't help us out there. Abigail and I are the only ones that can wield fire, which is the thing that will kill the wendigo. That, and our creature's instincts are to hunt," Owen loudly explained and when Prisha tried to talk again, Owen cut her off. "It is going to be hard enough to kill the wendigo while worrying about Avery and Aiden. Please don't add to that. We will do whatever we can to safely get them out of there, I promise," Owen kindly said as he put his hand on her shoulder.

Prisha gazed into the woods before her shoulders dropped as she sighed. "Fine, please go save them. I'll see what I can do in the facility."

"Thank you and good luck," Owen said.

"Good luck…both of you," Prisha responded before she ran toward the cabin.

"If you can find any vampire blood or phoenix tears, bring them out. I have a feeling we may need it," Owen added.

"Got it!" Prisha yelled while she continued her way to the cabin.

Owen and Abigail jogged in the direction of where they last saw Avery. As soon as they were inside the wendigo's territory and the cabin was out-of-sight, they stopped and began to slowly walk. They also both transitioned to enhance their vision and hearing. Owen wanted to call out to Avery and Aiden, but he didn't want to give up their location to the wendigo or announce their presence to it.

"How familiar are you with a wendigo?" Owen asked as he peered into the woods.

"Very. Once you informed us about it, I did a lot of research on it," Abigail responded as she peered into the woods.

"Good. Then I don't have to remind you how dangerous of a creature this is, or how excellent of a hunter it is then," Owen commented.

"I'm quite aware. Just remember. Fire alone won't kill it. You must melt the thick ice around its heart and then burn the heart," Abigail added.

"Got it. Let's fan out and sweep the area, but keep eyes on each other just in case something goes wrong," Owen suggested.

"Sounds good. Be safe," Abigail said.

"You too," Owen replied before they began to slowly prowl the woods.

They averaged anywhere from thirty to fifty feet from each other, depending on the terrain, as they searched the woods. The area was lit by the moonlight, but the brightness would vary greatly due to the clouds in the area. Owen couldn't get over how quiet it was. There was no sound…not even crickets. The only sound he heard was the slight crunch of the leaves and rocks on the ground as he walked.

"Help me," Owen heard faintly echo in the distance in front of him. The voice sounded human, but unnatural at the same time. Owen felt a cold chill run up his spine as he continued in the direction of the voice. He looked at Abigail who heard it as well as she slowly nodded her head. He began to wonder if the wendigo was trying to lure anything into a trap, specifically them.

Owen became unsettled because this meant there was a real possibility that it knew of his and his friends' whereabouts. He transitioned deeper to allow more of the chimera's instincts to surface. The fear lessened as he transitioned while he scanned the area for any hint of where it could have headed. As he continued, Owen caught a whiff of something foul. He stopped and looked all around him, but nothing.

"Help me," Owen heard again, but this time it sounded closer.

He raised his claws and slowly continued. He glanced over to Abigail, who had her claws raised as well. Then he discovered the source of the stench…the wendigo's feeding ground.

Owen covered his mouth and nose and yet, he still gagged. The putrid odors from the decaying corpses were overwhelming. Abigail came in from the other side of the feeding area and her face crinkled as she immediately buried her nose in the crook of her arm. Even then, Owen could see her gagging. As the two approached each other, Owen couldn't help but look at the blood-stained ground, rocks, and trees where random chewed body parts and bones were scattered about. He also noticed a few bodies scattered throughout the area. Some were intact, but a combination of skeleton and flesh.

"This is awful," Abigail commented as she viewed the area with disgust.

"I know. The sights are just as bad as the smell," Owen added.

"You know I hate Astrid, but surely she didn't know its feeding ground was so horrible," Abigail said as she looked around.

"She knew," Owen muttered.

"What?" Abigail asked as her eyes widened.

"During one of our talks, she told me that she was shocked because it seemed that the wendigo must have killed and eaten its victims quickly because that contradicted the lore. She lied to me. She knew it had an abundance of human flesh to eat since it was eating them slowly. It would have continued to eat the dead flesh, but why would it when it kept receiving a live, fresh body to feed on? She knew this, yet she still sent people out here anyway. She's an unredeemable monster," Owen said as he clenched his fists.

"We need to torch this entire area. Not just to hide the evidence, but to put these poor souls to rest. I don't care who you are…no one deserves to have their remains devoured by some monster. Especially, to be slowly eaten alive over days before that person dies alone and in agony. Well, maybe Astrid," Abigail said as her brow furrowed.

"We will, but after we dealt with the wendigo," Owen replied.

Before they could continue their hunt, they heard a moan, so they followed it to a nearby bulky tree stump. They both were startled when they saw a pale and bruised man who appeared to be jammed under the stump. His eyes were yellow from an infection and his wounds were red and oozing a whitish-green liquid. He laid in a pool of his own blood and filth as ants were beginning to eat away at his flesh.

"Kill me…please," the man weakly begged. Abigail and Owen looked at him with sympathetic eyes. They knew there was no saving this poor man, so they honored his request. They were unable to get a proper angle to end his life swiftly and they didn't want to brutally kill him, so the only thing they could think of was to bleed him out.

Owen leaned over and placed one of his claws near the man's jugular vein. "I'm sorry," Owen whispered as he slit the man's throat. He stood up and the two of them watched his eyes slowly close and not too long after, the man stopped breathing.

"Let's keep moving. I won't allow this to be Aiden or Avery's fate," Owen commented as the two of them continued out of the feeding area. They began their hunt again as they spread out to cover more area. They went deeper and deeper into the woods but yet again, they were met with silence.

"Help me." Owen and Abigail came to a halt because this time, the voice sounded close.

Owen raised his claws as he scanned the area. At first, he didn't see anything, but then he saw movement. He looked at Abigail and pointed in the direction of where he saw something move. Then, he could hear crunching on the ground so he hid behind a tree. The crunch became closer and closer and as it did, he raised his hand higher and extended his claws. He glanced over to Abigail and she was doing the same.

"Who's out here?" A voice whispered loudly in the night. Owen rolled his eyes because he recognized the voice. He came out from behind the tree and sure enough, it was Avery.

"Luckily, not the wendigo," Owen sarcastically remarked as his brow furrowed.

"Well, it was either attract the wendigo or have you accidentally slice my head off," Avery countered.

"Where's Aiden?" Abigail loudly whispered as she approached them.

"Not that far away. Maybe a hundred feet in that direction," Avery replied and then pointed in the direction that they were already headed.

"Why aren't you with him? Is he alive?" Abigail inquired.

"He's alive, for now," Avery commented as her head sank.

"What does that mean?" Owen asked.

"It looks like the wendigo found him first. It clawed him across his legs and chest so now he is lying on the ground, moaning in pain," Avery responded.

"And you just left him there?" Abigail sternly asked.

"The bigger question is why did the wendigo leave him there," Owen added.

Abigail paused for a moment before she rolled her eyes and shook her head. "Because it's baiting us."

"That's what I thought too, so I have been scouting the area for it when I came across you guys," Avery said as she looked back in the direction of Aiden.

"New plan. Abigail and I will spring the trap while you get Aiden out of here," Owen directed.

"He won't go for it. Not with Astrid's command in his head," Abigail commented.

"Then Avery can protect him until we can kill the wendigo and if we fail, then she can carry him screaming safely over the barrier line," Owen quickly said.

"I can fight with you," Avery blurted out.

"Abigail and I are the only ones that can kill it. Besides, it's better that you protect Aiden and help the others get the key," Owen responded.

"Fine," Avery huffed. "Be careful," she added as she looked at Owen and Abigail while she gently placed her hand on Owen's arm.

"You too," Abigail and Owen both said. Owen held Avery's hand for a moment before the three of them headed toward Aiden.

They fanned out again as the three moved quietly toward Aiden's position. Owen planned on being the one to walk up to Aiden. This would provoke the wendigo to come after him while giving Abigail a chance to ambush it, leaving Avery free to approach Aiden.

"Help me." The eerie voice echoed throughout the woods. They pushed past their fear and continued to walk forward.

Owen could now hear the distant groans of Aiden and as they got within thirty feet of him, Owen could see the pain he was in. Aiden held his leg and chest as he slightly rocked on the ground and moaned. The pain seemed more intense than it should have been from how the wounds appeared. Something else was going on, but Owen couldn't figure out what it was.

"Help me." The voice in front of them was now louder and closer. Enough for them to stop and ready themselves. They stood there, motionless and in silence as they stared in front of them. A minute passed by and still nothing. Owen had to remind himself to breathe and eventually, he began to fidget in anticipation of the attack. He decided to slowly walk forward toward Aiden to see if the wendigo would reveal itself to him. Abigail walked forward as well, but she was around twenty feet off to Owen's left and a few feet behind his pace. Avery was located to the right of Owen, and about the same distance as Abigail was, but even further behind.

"Help me." The voice came out from the trees near Owen, maybe just ten feet away. He shot a burst of fire in the direction of the voice, but there was nothing there.

Owen transitioned deeper and listened and that was when he heard the leaves rustle from behind Avery. He jerked his head around and stared past Avery, but there was no sign of the monster. She noticed what he did and turned around and that was when the wendigo slightly growled as it appeared from behind a tree. Even though it looked exactly as Owen thought it would, the fear he felt shot straight to his core. His fear amplified when he realized this horrid creature was only standing ten feet from Avery.

It stood motionless as its red sunken eyes fixated on Avery. The disgusting smell they experienced back at its feeding grounds was now present again. The wendigo's claws began to raise while it slightly crouched down before it growled and lunged toward Avery. She launched her axe at it and the blade lodged itself in the upper left chest area, near its shoulder. It roared as it was knocked off balance and fell to one knee. She turned around and began to run in Aiden's direction while Abigail and Owen ran toward the wendigo. It growled as it yanked the axe out, tossed it aside, and then chased after Avery.

Avery's eyes were wide with fear, but then they narrowed with determination as she ran. The wendigo caught up to her within moments and raised its claws in the air before it slashed at her, and that is when Avery dived toward the base of a skinny tree. It was narrow enough that she could almost grasp the tree with both her hands and have her fingers touch each other.

As her hands connected with the tree, she used her momentum and strength to swing herself around the tree. Avery was close enough to the base of the tree that her body lightly grazed the ground the entire time as she glided around the tree. Luckily, its claws barely missed her as they sliced through the tree instead. She let go of the tree and slid on her knees until she came to a stop. Avery jerked her head around and saw that the wendigo came to a stop and turned its head to look at her. The tree that it sliced fell over while they continued to stare at each other. Avery bolted in the opposite direction of Aiden to not only save herself, but Aiden too. She ran as fast as she could around the trees and over the rocks without looking back. The wendigo didn't hesitate to pursue her.

"Run! It's gaining on you," Owen called out as he and Abigail chased behind the wendigo, who seemed to almost glide through and around the obstacles due to how fast and agile it was.

"She's not going to make it," Abigail loudly said to Owen. He knew she was right, so he flung a ball of fire at it, but it missed and slammed into a tree. Abigail did the same and she shared the same result as they both tried over and over. The wendigo never looked back at Owen and Abigail since it was determined to capture its meal.

Avery abruptly changed direction and ran toward a hill. The sudden change in direction slowed the wendigo down, but only for a moment before it was close behind her again. She tried to slow it down more by weaving her way between the trees, hoping that the spaces were not wide enough for the wendigo to go through. Her plan worked; however, it was still gaining on her, but just not as fast as before. It then extended its long, lanky arms and fingers. Owen panicked because he could see that its claws were almost touching her. The closer it got to her, the more the knot in his stomach grew.

She reached a hill and ran up it, but this caused her to slow down. With the wendigo within striking distance, it raised its claw. Avery reached the top but her foot slid out from a small pile of fallen leaves. She fell and tumbled and as she got up, she screamed and braced herself because the wendigo's claws were already coming toward her.

"No!" Both Abigail and Owen yelled as they reached the bottom of the hill.

The wendigo's claws slashed across her face, but they never touched her. Instead, its claws scratched down an invisible wall just inches from Avery's face. The barrier not only saved her, but the wendigo's momentum made it slam its entire body into the barrier. The dazed monster fell backward and rolled down the hill.

Avery frantically looked around before her eyes drifted down and saw that she was standing on the other side of the salt line for the barrier spell. She let out a large sigh of relief, and then smiled and chuckled to herself. Owen and Abigail smiled at the miracle they just witnessed and he could feel the weight being lifted off his chest now that Avery was safe. Owen held his hand over his heart as he nodded to Avery. She did the same. "I'll get Aiden," Avery called out and then ran back toward Aiden, but she stayed on the outside of the barrier. Now, it was up to him and Abigail.

The wendigo's red eyes glared at them while it slowly stood up and stalked them. Abigail transitioned deep into phase two while Owen transitioned to phase three. Owen and Abigail roared and then charged the beast. The wendigo showed no fear as it snarled while it advanced.

Owen unleashed his fire attack while he charged, which made the wendigo squeal as it ran through the flames. He tried to follow the wendigo with his flames but he couldn't in fear of hitting Abigail. She sent a short burst at it, making it grunt as the fire hit its chest.

The beast then swung its claws at Abigail, but she rolled out of the way. It then quickly spun around and slashed at Owen, who ducked under its deadly claws. Then, the wendigo swatted at Owen, and again, he just narrowly dodged the attack by jumping to the side of it. The beast was quicker than he imagined. Abigail tried to attack, but the wendigo quickly moved from her charging path and swung its claws at her, which she narrowly escaped. The two of them stood next to each other as the wendigo turned its head to look at them.

"Its reach is too long. We can't get close enough to do any damage and it will eventually cut us down to pieces," Abigail commented as her brow lowered while she stared at the beast.

"Then we hack our way through. Just attack wildly, but with purpose and be ready to take whatever it sends our way," Owen replied as his upper lip raised to expose his fangs.

"I think I enjoyed hanging out with you at the fair more than this," Abigail remarked. Owen scoffed in amusement.

They charged the wendigo head-on. Its powerful claws slashed down in between them, but they side-stepped the attack and they both ripped through the rotten flesh on its arm. Owen then lunged at the creature and slashed more decayed flesh from the thin amount it had covering its ribs. The wendigo roared as it turned and slashed at Owen. He smacked its claws away, but due to the length of them, they ended up leaving deep scratches on his arm. Owen growled as he winced and jerked his arm back.

While it was distracted by Owen, Abigail was able to tear through its leg. Its knee buckled but it kept itself from falling. The wendigo surprised Abigail as it flicked its injured leg at her and punctured her leg with the talons on its feet. She yelled while she limped but then had to defend herself as its claws bore down on her. She swatted its claws away, but similar to Owen, its long claws still found their mark across her arm. She grabbed her arm and stumbled back and as the wendigo was about to slash at her again, Owen dug both sets of his claws into its leg and yanked the beast toward him.

It squealed as it looked down to find the source of its pain. Owen kept digging his claws into the wendigo until its claws sliced through Owen. He grabbed his chest and yelled as he fell to the ground. It went to stomp on him, but Owen rolled out of the way and then projected fire toward it when he came to a stop. The wendigo raised its arms to shield itself. As it did, Abigail jumped and sunk her claws into its back. She used the combination of gravity and the loose flesh to allow her to slide her claws down its back until she reached the ground.

As soon as her feet touched the ground, it quickly and forcefully jabbed its claws behind its back. Abigail was impaled by three separate claws into her ribs. She screamed as she slid herself off the claws and quickly fell to the ground. It noticed a sliver of Abigail's flesh on its claw, so it took its long, discolored tongue and licked it off. Owen observed that the tiny amount of Abigail's flesh and blood helped heal a small portion of the wounds on its back.

It went to stab her again with its claws, but Abigail shot flames toward its head. It stopped to shield its face, so she used that opportunity to roll away. She was able to at least get to one knee before it swung its claws down on her. She grabbed the wendigo's arm with both hands but the force behind the attack sent her to the ground. As she slammed into the ground, she lost her grip. The result…the wendigo's claws pierced Abigail's chest near both of her shoulders. Her deep, raspy scream echoed throughout the woods.

Owen's eyes widened as he gasped. He had to act quickly. He stood up, while he kept pressure on his chest, to try to slow the bleeding that poured down him. He also noticed his wounds were beginning to burn, but he couldn't think about that now. Abigail was in danger and the wendigo had its back to him. Owen transitioned deeper and as such, the pain was dulled, but his power and intensity had increased. He found a nearby tree that was close to Abigail and the wendigo, so he climbed it about halfway before he pivoted and leaped from the tree. He roared as he soared toward the beast with his arm raised and his claws extended. His claws glowed from the fire that also tailed off his hand due to his movement through the air. Abigail angled her hands and shot fire into the midsection of the wendigo, which caused it to jerk up and remove its claws from her to shield itself. At that moment, Owen thrust his hand forward as he landed on the wendigo's back.

The wendigo fell forward and used its hands to brace itself, just missing Abigail as they slammed on either side of her head. Owen's hand plunged into the beast's back and stopped when it hit a large, cold object. So cold, that he could feel the frigidness through the flames. He grasped it and poured every ounce of concentration into his hand to send as much, and as intense, fire as he could muster up. The beast let out a high-pitched roar as it pushed itself up and began to try to shake Owen off as it flailed about. He used his free hand to wrap it around the creature and dig his claws into its ribs to keep himself stable. He roared the entire time as he continued his fire stream inside the wendigo. He could feel the ice block around its heart beginning to dwindle.

The beast reached over its shoulder and under its arm to begin to claw and stab at its attacker. Owen grinded his teeth as he could feel the pain from his back being shredded. Then, one of its claws found its way into Owen's ribs. He yelled and almost let go, but he continued to hold onto its heart while he let go with his other hand. He grabbed the claw to prevent it from going any further. Owen was beginning to black out from the pain and exhaustion from the continuous flame he was producing, along with the pain he was experiencing, but his determination never faltered. He felt that the ice was almost gone. He just needed to hold on a little while longer, but with the claw digging inside of him, he wasn't sure if he could.

Just when he was about to fade away, he heard someone yell. The wendigo removed its claw and then Owen heard it grunt and felt it stumble back. He looked over its shoulder and saw Avery standing there with her hammer axe, glaring at the wendigo. With the claw removed and renewed hope, he let out another roar and was able to intensify the flame. The wendigo began to stagger as Owen could see flames coming out of the hole in its back, and now a new hole in its chest from the skin that melted away. Its body was charred and blood and smoke now flowed from its mouth.

Finally, Owen felt the wendigo's heart and when he did, he crushed it while his hand was still on fire. The wendigo squealed in pain until Owen yanked out its mangled, charred heart. The wendigo became silent as it dropped to its knees and then it fell face-first onto the ground while Owen remained on its back. His intense eyes looked up at Avery as he breathed heavily before he got off the creature. Owen let the crumbled heart, which was still on fire, fall to the ground and burn to nothing. He then let out another loud roar and shot flames from his mouth all over the dead wendigo's body and stood over it as it burned.

Avery gently put her arm on his shoulder. Owen's head whipped to her as the intensity still flowed through him. "It's okay Owen, calm down. It's over. We did it. Just calm down and breathe," Avery calmly said.

Owen had to restrain himself from pulling away from Avery and ripping the wendigo's body to shreds. He took a few deep breaths and transitioned down from phase three to two, but then he realized it was a mistake. The pain from all his injuries overcame him as he crumbled to the ground. He could feel all the scratches, cuts, and gouges that the wendigo inflicted on him and they also felt infected. He remembered that the damage from a wendigo could cause this due to how diseased the creature is. However, he had other things to worry about when he turned his head and saw Abigail lying on the ground, motionless.

CHAPTER 26

Owen crawled while Avery ran over to Abigail. He had no choice but to transition deeper to slow the bleeding and to take the edge off the extreme pain he was in. Even then, he could feel the burning pain coming from his chest, back, arms, and especially his side. The pain was bad enough to cause him to have trouble focusing.

"She's alive," Avery yelled.

"If that's what you call it," Abigail sarcastically commented while she grimaced.

"She's burning up," Avery said while her hand was on Abigail's forehead.

"Can you transition any deeper?" Owen inquired.

"A little more. After that, I would be pushing it," Abigail replied.

"Do it. It will help manage the pain until Prisha comes back with something to heal us," Owen suggested. Abigail nodded and went a little further into phase two. Once she did, she was able to at least sit up, but her wounds looked bad, especially the two holes in her shoulders. Her physical appearance favored more of the chimera between the eyes, fangs, claws, voice, and additional fur. However, she was nowhere near Owen's appearance, which was almost unrecognizable because he was deep in phase three. All three of them tore off the bottom part of their shirts to use to help slow the bleeding. One dressing went to Owen's side and the other two went to Abigail's shoulders.

"Where's Aiden?" Owen asked.

"Still back at that rock. He started to struggle with me when I tried to get him to leave so I left him there. Besides, he looked too bad to move anyway," Avery replied.

"We'll have to come back to where he is later so we can heal him. Afterward, he can come here and see that the wendigo is dead and be free of Astrid's mind games," Owen commented.

"I'm surprised we haven't seen Prisha, Bailey, or anyone else. They should have been out by now, even with opposition, they should have made it out," Avery said as she looked around.

"You're right and that makes me worried. I need to investigate," Owen said as he slowly rose to his feet. He could feel the chills coursing through his body as his fever became worse.

"You mean we. I'm going too," Avery said as she quickly stood up.

"No. Stay here with Abigail and help her move to Aiden's location so you can guard them until I come back," Owen directed.

"You're too injured to go in there alone. You could barely stand up just now," Avery commented.

"I'll heal as I go, especially at this level," Owen replied in a raspy voice.

"She's right. You need all the help you can get. Go, I'll be fine. Hailey and Astrid are gone and the wendigo is dead. Heck, no one else knows it is dead so that will keep people away. Also, when it was alive, I'm sure it either ate or scared away the animals so unless I'm in danger of falling leaves, I'll be safe," Abigail remarked.

Owen scoffed and then held her hand. "Fine, but keep your guard up in case anything does go after you. We'll be back as soon as we can." Abigail nodded and the two smiled at each other before he and Avery left for the cabin.

The two jogged through the woods and as they did, Owen wondered what could have happened to cause the other team to be delayed. His worst fear was that Hailey and Astrid returned or that there was a creature loose within the facility. They reached the barrier line, but only Avery crossed while Owen came to a stop.

"Owen, come on. What's wrong?" Avery asked but as she stopped and turned around, her crinkled brow eased as it dawned on her why he stopped.

"I can't cross unless I'm human and I'm not sure if I am strong enough to endure what I will feel once I transition," Owen explained as he fidgeted.

"Let's not chance it. You stay here and I will go check it out," Avery suggested.

"No, I'm not letting you or anybody else go down there alone at this point," Owen said as his eyes drifted to the nearby cabin.

"What do you propose?" Avery inquired.

Owen paused as he went through his options. "I will lean against the barrier and once I transition, I will fall past the line. I'm on a slope so I should clear the line once I fall. If I try anything else then I may collapse before I can pass or hurt myself if I try jumping," Owen replied. He then stood at an angle and leaned against the barrier. It felt weird for him to be leaning without actually leaning on an object.

"I would appreciate it if you could catch me and if I don't clear the line, then pull me away please," Owen added.

"Maybe," Avery jested. Owen grinned and took a few deep breaths to build himself up. "You can do it, Owen," Avery called out as she braced herself to catch him.

Owen took another deep breath and then transitioned to human. The sudden shock from the massive amount of pain that flooded his system made him scream in agony. His vision quickly faded as he toppled over. He then felt Avery shaking him while she was talking, but he couldn't understand what she was saying. Her faint voice grew

363

louder with each passing moment until he finally began to understand what she was saying. "Transition back."

He transitioned and as he did, the pain he felt became more tolerable. Owen laid on the ground while Avery cradled his head. He looked forward and noticed his feet were not too far from the barrier line. As he slowly sat up, he shook his head and then rubbed his face to regain his focus.

"How are you feeling?" Avery asked.

"Like a wendigo used me as a nail sharpener," Owen responded.

"I'm sorry. Do you think you can continue?" Avery inquired.

Owen stood up while he pressed his lips together to contain the additional pain he felt as he moved. "I'll survive. Thank you for not letting me fall," Owen added. He wanted to give her a quick kiss but he already transitioned back to phase three. Now, he had more creature characteristics than human, so he decided to wait.

"I'll always be there to catch you," Avery said and then winked. A few seconds later, she cringed. "Was that too cheesy?"

"So much that this whole area reeks of cheese," Owen teased. Avery laughed and playfully smacked him on his arm; however, she forgot about his injuries…and her strength. Owen winced in pain but laughed.

"Sorry, sorry, sorry," Avery said as she laughed with Owen.

The two then carefully approached the cabin as they checked the surrounding area for any signs of an ambush, but there was nothing. When they reached the cabin, they glanced through the windows and didn't see anyone inside so they cautiously entered. The two of them separated to check the rooms and once again, there was no one there. Not even a trap was built to stop them. They walked to the elevator and entered to begin their descent. They remained quiet as they listened for any signs of life. About three-quarters of the way down, they heard faint pops.

"Is that…gunfire?" Avery asked.

"I believe so and if they haven't made it up by now, that means Astrid's followers are standing near the elevator and blocking it," Owen said as he braced himself for when the doors opened. Avery raised her hammer axe and stood next to Owen. The faint pops became louder by the moment, but as they reached the bottom, they stopped.

"Stay behind me and find cover as quick as you can," Owen directed. He then stood in front of the door and sent waves of flames to his hands. Then, the elevator dinged.

While the doors opened, he stared intently, and as soon as he caught a glimpse of the mercenaries, he ran out of the elevator while shooting flames toward them. As the mercenaries in front of the elevator screamed, Owen stopped and swiftly turned around in a circle to create a wall of fire to help protect them. He heard gunshots and one did graze his leg, but it didn't stop Owen as he growled through the pain and kept spewing fire. He could see Astrid's followers either trying to extinguish the flames on them or running for cover. However, a few did blindly open fire toward the firewall to try to stop him.

At that time, Avery burst from the elevator and hacked a couple of mercenaries down that made it around the firewall before she could survey the area. "Owen, follow me," Avery called out. Owen did and he also used his flames as cover so they could get there safely.

Avery led him to a nearby nook. When they safely arrived, Owen's flames ceased. He took a quick look around and he could immediately see the issue. His friends, including the entire staff, were stuck in the middle between two groups of Astrid's followers. It appeared the staff were ready to go as each of them seemed to be carrying a lot of items. It seemed that Astrid had increased her forces even though most of them were mercenaries.

With the elevator cleared, the staff ran toward it while Bailey, Prisha, and from what Owen could see, only two of Cedric's men,

365

opened fire to allow them a chance to leave. Even then, some staff members were hit and had to be carried, which made things take longer. That, and only so many people could fit on the elevator at once. Owen squinted as he examined what they were up against. It was mainly mercenaries, but he did see a couple of hybrids directing them as well. Avery picked up a semi-automatic rifle from a fallen mercenary and followed Owen as they walked on either side of the fleeing staff members to assist his friends. Then, a pack of mercenaries with mostly melee weapons, led by a hybrid covered in a variety of horns, spikes, and thorns of varying sizes, flanked them.

"Get everyone to safety," Owen called out to Avery before he sent a wave of fire toward the attackers.

Owen raised his lip and lowered his brow before he charged the remaining attackers that weren't engulfed in flames. He smacked the first attacker's sword out of the way and then quickly rotated to his other side and did the same to the other attacker's hatchet. He immediately had to duck to narrowly miss the spiked hand of the hybrid that sailed over his head. With the hybrid's back to him, he sent a sidekick to it that made the hybrid stumble forward and into the first two mercenaries. Owen turned just in time to grab the next mercenary's wrist that held a dagger and thrust his hand back into his chest. As the man convulsed, Owen used him as a human shield while two more mercenaries opened fire and rushed them. When he was close enough, Owen grabbed the now-dead body and pushed his hand all the way through. He then streamed fire from his hand that he pushed through and burned the two unsuspecting mercenaries alive.

He yanked his hand out and as he turned around, he saw a spiked hand coming down on him. He was able to divert the attack using his forearms to deflect it, but the thorns ripped through his skin. Owen grunted and transitioned deeper into phase three. His injuries from the wendigo were not healing as fast as he anticipated and he needed every ounce of strength to fight off his new foes.

Owen kicked the back of the hybrid's knee which made him drop to one knee and as he did, Owen followed up with a slash across his arms. Some of his claws dragged across the horns while the others tore through his flesh. The hybrid grinded his thick, sharp teeth as he glared at Owen with his golden-brown eyes. Owen wasted no time and shot a burst of fire at the hybrid, from his mouth, which caused him to yell and cover his face as he fell and rolled away.

He turned and his eyes widened as the original two mercenaries were both swinging their weapons at Owen. He raised his sluggish arms up to defend himself as he wavered from exhaustion and his wounds. He braced himself because they were too close to counter. Owen then heard a roar that was loud enough to cause the two attackers to stop and turn their heads. They both screamed as Bailey tackled them to the ground. As she collided with them, she sunk her teeth into the neck of one of the mercenaries as they fell. After they landed, she tore out a slab of his neck and spit it at the female mercenary. This caused a large volume of blood to pour out of his neck. As the mercenary was distracted by the bloody pulp that landed on her, Bailey climbed over the dead mercenary and in one motion, slashed her throat with her claws. She held her neck as blood squirted everywhere until her mouth began to gurgle and she fell to the floor.

"Finally, I got your back in battle," Bailey said in a gravelly voice while she stood above the mangled bodies that laid in a pool of blood. Her pale-yellow eyes stared at Owen as she smirked with her blood-stained mouth.

"It's about time," Owen teased.

"We're almost done here. Let's go," Avery called out as another elevator load departed. For the ones that remained, it appeared to be just a few more staff members, Avery, Prisha, Bailey, Owen, and two of Cedric's men…one of whom had the final member over his shoulder. As Bailey and Owen began to head to the elevator, the horned hybrid stood in their path. Owen snarled as flames ignited around his hands and Bailey growled as she extended her claws.

"Hand over the bookbag, and you and your friends may leave, unharmed. If not…" the hybrid said in a deep voice as he casually turned his head and looked over his shoulder. Owen saw more mercenaries with guns drawn at the people near the elevator, as well as Bailey and himself.

Bailey sighed, took off the bookbag that she was wearing, and slowly approached the hybrid. "Is that what I think it is," Owen asked. Bailey nodded. Owen's shoulders dropped as defeat settled in. "It's okay. We will find a way to get it back," Owen added.

Bailey raised the bookbag in front of the hybrid and as she did, all eyes were focused on her. Even some of the mercenaries pointed their guns in her direction. "I guess I'm supposed to take your word that you will allow us to go free," Bailey asked as her brow arched.

"As I see it, you have no other choice," the hybrid said with a smug expression.

Bailey slowly nodded her head. She then turned her head to look at Owen. "It will be okay," Bailey softly said while she had a hint of a smile. Owen's brow knitted to why she said it. She turned back to the hybrid and raised the bag toward him. As he was about to take it, she turned and tossed it to Owen. "Go!" Bailey yelled. Owen grabbed the bookbag just in time to see Bailey turn around and get impaled by multiple spikes when the hybrid punched her in the chest.

"No!" Owen cried out as his eyes teared up, but he immediately had to duck as bullets started to fly by him. He glanced over to Avery and she had secretly got the rest of the people into the elevator. Now, it was just her and Prisha holding a table up as cover from the barrage of bullets. He could see that Avery's mouth was wide open as tears fell.

He quickly put the bookbag on and began to run toward Bailey. As he ran, Owen shot flames around her and the hybrid to clear the mercenaries away from them. Bailey slashed the hybrid's face and then rammed her claws into the hybrid's stomach. He took a few steps back and moaned from the pain but then he charged Bailey.

The hybrid then picked her up and ran with her for a short distance while she clawed his back before he drove her to the floor. As he did, his horns tore into Bailey. When he rolled off her, Owen could see her body was covered in blood from all the puncture wounds. He ran toward her but then was struck in the leg by a bullet. Owen fell to the ground and projected more flames as he dragged himself over to a flipped bench. Once he reached the bench, he began to shoot flames out at the attackers, as well as the hybrid to try to keep him away from Bailey.

"We've got to get out of here! You have the key! Let's go," one of Cedric's men yelled as he stuck his head out and began to lay cover fire for Owen.

"No, I won't abandon her!" Owen hollered as he continued his attack.

Bailey stood up but then fell right back to her knees as two bullets ripped through her leg and shoulder. "Go," Bailey gurgled as blood poured from her mouth, but Owen couldn't make himself do it. He sent a stream of fire from both his hands and his mouth as he limped toward Bailey.

The hybrid grew closer and closer to Bailey as Owen pushed with all his might to reach her. Then, the shooting stopped, as well as Owen's flames as everyone's attention was drawn to the new threat in the room…a werewolf. He didn't know if Bailey planned to transition or not, but he knew he needed to escape.

The werewolf towered over the hybrid as it stood on its hind legs and breathed intensely. The beast was brawny, especially its upper body. Its arms and legs were muscular as well, but leaner and more toned. Its fur covered its entire body and was mainly grey with hints of white fur mixed in. It also had white fur around its snout and eyes. The beast quickly looked around with its wild pale-yellow eyes before it extended its dark, razor-sharp claws and growled. Drool dripped down from the creature's powerful fangs before it slashed the hybrid with enough force that it sent him crashing onto the floor.

Gunfire erupted, but it was all directed at the werewolf so while it was distracted, he hobbled as fast as he could toward the elevator.

Owen could hear the screams from the mercenaries and the werewolf's snarls and growls as it slaughtered everything in its path. He glanced over his shoulder and noticed he caught the werewolf's attention as it grunted and ran toward him, on its hind legs, at an incredible speed. He transitioned deep into phase three and pushed through the pain as he bolted toward the elevator. He then noticed Avery's eyes widen while she pointed behind him. Owen stuck one of his hands out behind his back and did a quick glance and sure enough, the werewolf was almost in striking distance. Owen did a quick burst of fire from his hand that was behind his back while he continued to run. The werewolf slowed down and raised its claws to avoid the fire as the blast grazed it.

"Close it," Owen called out to Avery. She nodded and hit the button. After a moment, the elevator door slowly began to close.

When he was in range, Owen dove through the door and collided with everyone else in the elevator. He swiftly flipped himself around. "Down!" Owen yelled as flames formed around his hands. Everyone dropped to the floor as Owen's flames shot through the opening of the door. He could hear the werewolf snarling and even a few scrapes against the door, but it couldn't make its way in or stop the door from closing due to Owen's flames. Once the door was closed, Owen stopped his fire attack and let his arms drop as the elevator ascended. He could hear a faint howl come from the main level, but then there was silence.

"Here, drink this," Avery said as she put a small vial up to Owen's lips while her other hand raised his head. He gulped the vampire blood down and a few seconds later, he began to feel the pain melt away. By the time the elevator reached the top, Owen was completely healed.

"Thank you," Owen said. He transitioned back to normal and then he stood up and hugged Avery. The door opened and the remaining people, along with their gear, exited the elevator. Owen turned and pulled the emergency lever on the wall next to the elevator. The elevator door slammed closed, followed by a few clangs.

"I can't believe she fully transitioned. I hope she'll be okay," Avery commented as her eyes drifted back to the elevator.

"I hope so too," Owen said as he put his arm around her.

"Do you think she did it on purpose," Avery asked.

"I don't know, but I do hope to be able to ask her about it someday," Owen replied.

"Why did you pull that lever?" Prisha inquired.

"It will keep the elevator at this level and locked. In addition to that, about halfway down the elevator shaft, there is a steel panel that extends out to seal the elevator shaft so that nothing can climb its way up here. It will keep anyone from trying to escape, even the werewolf. We just have to hope that it can kill everyone down there before someone finds a silver weapon," Owen explained.

"The werewolf can operate an elevator?" Prisha asked.

"It's possible if it has enough intelligence to do so. That, or since this kind of werewolf doesn't require a full moon to turn, according to Livia, it could turn back to human and try its luck then," Owen replied.

"Provided it is from a century that had elevators," Avery added.

"Good point," Owen commented.

"I understand. Should we put a sign up or something to warn people not to go down there?" Prisha asked.

"No. The emergency lever is concealed so unless you know where to look, it will keep people out. If they do know what it is for, then it would deter them from going down there since it could be one of many horrible things waiting for them," Owen said before they left the cabin. "Are there enough supplies and food down there in case she transitions back to herself before we return?" Owen asked Avery.

371

"Yes, plenty," Avery responded. This made him feel relieved to hear.

Owen then surveyed the area and it seemed like everyone had made it out. Not only that, but each of them carried supplies. This ranged from their clothes and other personal items to various weapons. Prisha made sure to gather the vampire blood and phoenix tears as well.

Owen opened the backpack and fumbled around its contents until he came across a cedar jewelry box, about six inches long, with a small gold latch on it. He opened it and smiled when he saw the iron key. Upon inspection, he noticed the Roman numeral one was scratched into the handle of the key. He closed the box with the key inside, put it in the backpack, and handed it to Avery.

"Okay. You two start getting everyone situated into the remaining vehicles here while I run over to Abigail and Aiden and give them some vampire blood. I'm also going to torch any remembrance of the wendigo so I may be a bit," Owen directed. Prisha and Avery nodded in agreement and then Prisha handed Owen two vials of vampire blood from the refrigerated bag.

"Make sure anybody else who is injured gets treated too, especially Cedric's people. I thought I noticed one of them was being carried," Owen said as he looked around.

"That person didn't make it," Prisha muttered.

Owen sighed. "Dang it. I'll need to talk to Cedric and express my condolences and gratitude, but not before I tell them first." He then sifted through the crowd until he found the two of them huddled around their fallen friend, distraught. He expressed his sympathies, and appreciation, while he stayed with them for a few minutes. Owen would have stayed longer, but he needed to get to his injured friends.

He rushed deep into the woods and arrived at Abigail's location, who hadn't strayed far from where he left her. Once she received the vial of vampire blood, they ran to Aiden and healed him next. Aiden still needed to see the wendigo so while Abigail and Owen escorted him to its carcass, Owen explained everything that happened in the facility to them. Once they arrived and Aiden laid eyes on the deceased wendigo, he let out a sigh of relief.

Owen and Abigail prepped the area around the wendigo and its feeding area so the trees and brush wouldn't catch on fire. When it was ready, they sprayed fire over the wendigo and its victims. The surrounding area was wet enough and there was more rain that was supposed to come so they felt confident enough to leave the site once the fire died down. When they arrived back at the cabin, Prisha ran and hugged Aiden and now that all the vehicles were full, it was time to head back to Isaac's house.

After the long journey, the fleet of vehicles parked in the open spots in the field behind Isaac's house. The exhausted group entered the house while Owen explained, to Livia, every detail of what happened. While Owen and Livia talked, Avery, Prisha, Abigail, and Aiden helped get everyone as comfortable as possible. People had to share beds and fold-out couches, while others lined the floors with blankets and sleeping bags. Other people used chairs and recliners as makeshift beds. All the supplies were put in the basement for now and as dawn approached, Owen and Avery found a corner in the family room and laid down on a pile of pillows and snuggled with a blanket over them. Between the long night and the joyful, yet relaxing moment he was having with Avery, he soon fell asleep.

People woke up at different times during the day and food was made for everyone, but given out sparingly to make sure everyone had enough food until more could be bought to accommodate everybody. Owen finally woke up around lunchtime.

"How did you sleep?" Avery asked as she snuggled up to him and affectionately smiled.

Owen smiled. "I slept well, but I'll be grateful once I can sleep in a bed without a group of people present. Even better, add not having to worry about what danger we are all facing next. Oh yeah, and not being filthy. Still…I do admire the view," Owen softly said as he winked. The two gave each other a quick peck on the lips before Owen stood up. "I'm going to call Cedric and talk to him," Owen added as he left the room and walked outside.

He first conveyed how terrible he felt for his fallen friend and how appreciative he was of the man who died and all that he did to help. Even though Cedric was aware, because of previous communications with his other friends, he was grateful for Owen's words. He then updated Cedric about the events that happened last night, including the discovery of the iron key. That led to him asking how Selena and Caine were doing. Cedric informed him that she was still a unicorn and Caine spent most of his time in the transition room, watching her from a distance so he wouldn't agitate the unicorn.

Before he ended his call, Owen asked Cedric what he wanted to do about his fallen friend and he requested he be brought back to be buried. Owen relayed that to Cedric's friends and one of them offered to drive the body back while the others remained to continue to help.

As the bathrooms cleared, Owen finally was able to clean himself and get a fresh pair of clothes. He felt refreshed so he searched for Livia. As he searched downstairs, he heard her voice and traced it to Isaac's office. He knocked on the door and Avery let him in. Once he was inside the room, he saw Abigail and Livia as well.

"Who's she on the phone with?" Owen asked.

"Duncan. They have been talking for a long time about that key," Avery responded. Owen and Avery quietly talked while they waited for Livia to be finished. Several minutes later, she hung up the phone.

"Pack your bags because we are headed to the Yukon," Livia announced.

CHAPTER 27

Avery, Abigail, and Owen glanced at each other, with knitted brows, as Livia approached them. "What's in the Yukon you ask? It's one of the original facilities constructed to house the largest of creatures. There are only a handful of these facilities, and they are all located in remote areas around the world. Deserts, rainforests, islands, and so forth," Livia explained.

"And of course, we must go to the one that is in the distant cold corner of Canada and not a secluded island in the Caribbean or heck, even a private beach. Anything is better than the Yukon during this time of the year," Avery complained.

Owen chuckled. "Well, the bright side is at least we aren't going during the peak of the winter season." Avery rolled her eyes. He then turned to Livia. "Is there a way we can just contact that location and they can assist us?"

"Owen, you know what the answer will be. No, we must go there for whatever reason," Avery griped.

Livia scoffed in amusement. "She's right. These locations have been abandoned but never demolished in case there was ever a need for them. I believe Isaac visited the locations once every five years to make sure they were in decent shape and upgraded them as needed."

"An abandoned location could be useful for storing items you truly want to be hidden. Whatever this weapon is, must be something powerful," Abigail commented.

"I hope so. Now, Duncan is making the travel arrangements but it will be us four plus Anders, who will join us in Seattle. He is already in Washington State following up on some leads. After our overnight layover, our next flight into Canada will leave. After that, it will be a short trip in a small plane and then ground transportation to get us the rest of the way. Prisha and Aiden will stay here and look after everyone until we return. With so many civilians here, I figured we needed more than just Cedric's people," Livia explained.

"I always wanted to visit Seattle," Avery commented as she perked up.

"There's your silver lining," Owen remarked to Avery before he turned back to Livia. "No offense, but do you think it's safe that you go? Astrid has already tried to kill you before and between her powers and Hailey's abilities, it will be very dangerous."

"I appreciate your concern but I am tougher than I look," Livia responded and then winked. "Besides, I am planning to use my abilities to break Astrid's control over Hailey."

"You can do that?" Avery asked as her eyes widened.

"Yes. I can turn her mind off the same way I did to Owen back in the Alps and Selena here. Once she is unconscious, I can enter her mind and restore it to its original state." Owen and Avery smiled at the thought of regaining their close friend again.

"Well, I guess there's nothing else to do but pack for another trip," Abigail said.

"Yes, and hopefully when this is over, we can take a real vacation," Avery commented.

Owen left the room and gathered enough stuff to get him to Seattle where he figured they would stay at one of the safe houses. Then, he would gather more supplies for the remainder of the trip. He had to remind Avery of this because, with her excitement, she was packing as if she was going on a long vacation. As it grew closer to the time to leave, Owen made his way through the crowd and checked on everybody before he reached Prisha and Aiden.

"I don't know who I should be more proud of?" Owen said but he stopped when Aiden stepped forward and raised his hand.

"Me. It's me due to my acting job of pretending I was under Astrid's thrall," Aiden blurted out.

"Yeah, you had us all fooled," Prisha sarcastically said before she giggled.

Owen smiled. "What I was going to say was that I don't know who I should be more proud of, the two of you for doing so well on your first assignment, or me for teaching you?" The three of them laughed before Owen continued. "Seriously, the answer to that question would be you two. I can only teach you so much. It's what you do out in the field that really matters. The two of you came so far and I am proud of both of you. Also, the two of you kept me sane while we were stuck with Astrid. That means more to me than you will ever know. Thank you." Owen then gave each of them a hug. Livia joined them afterward and briefed Aiden and Prisha on the new plan.

After hearing the new plan, Prisha gave Owen another hug. "Be careful out there and have a safe journey."

Aiden approached Owen. "She's right. You can't trust anything out there, not even your own eyes. It's remote for a reason." Owen's brow crinkled at Aiden's comment but he then smiled and nodded his head. He presumed Aiden was trying to help with whatever he tried to relay to him.

Later that day, Livia, Avery, Abigail, and Owen left for the airport and didn't arrive in Seattle until close to midnight. As Owen predicted, they drove to a safe house that was on the outskirts of the city. After they arrived and went through the safe house and gathered the items they needed, they quickly got cleaned up and went to bed. It was a smaller condo but they were able to make it work with the sleeping arrangements. After the long flight and the time change, it didn't take long for Owen to fall asleep.

The next morning, the four of them woke up early even though they weren't going to meet up with Anders until later that morning. The four of them, influenced by Avery, decided to spend a couple of hours exploring the city. Avery and Owen had never been to Seattle, or anywhere on the West Coast; whereas Livia hadn't seen the city in over fifty years. For Abigail, it had been about twenty years, so they grabbed their coffees and had fun being tourists. Owen appreciated the break, as well as how Avery finally listened to his advice about enjoying the small moments when you can. Besides, he enjoyed spending time with Avery and they all agreed that a quick, fun outing was preferred over sitting in the condo and doing nothing but dwell on the mission. Later that morning, they met up with Anders outside the airport. Then, they made their way through the airport in time to find an area near the gate to talk while they waited.

"I have good news and I have bad news, which one do you want first?" Anders asked.

Livia sighed. "Let's get it over with…the bad news."

"Hailey and Astrid are not far behind you. It wouldn't surprise me if they fly out today as well," Anders responded.

"Dang it! How?" Avery blurted out.

"Either through informants or they have been just tracking you, knowing that you will lead them to whatever weapon is going to stop Astrid. I'm sure they will want to acquire that weapon first. My sources didn't have all the details," Anders replied.

"Then we need to make sure we get there first. And, the good news?" Owen inquired.

"Astrid has apparently lost her support," Anders replied.

"Seriously?" Abigail asked.

"Yes. From what I have been told, a good portion of her support left once they received their wishes. Another sizable portion includes all the people that our team has killed during this entire mission and that statistic has made her undesirable. No one wants to team up with her or even get paid to work for her. They fear her, and even more…us. Nobody wants to sign up for a death wish," Anders explained.

"Then, it's just her and Hailey," Livia remarked.

"Just. Those two alone are an admirable force," Owen countered.

"True, but our odds are better if it's just them and not them plus an army. Also, if our plan works, we will have Hailey back on our side. We just need to be smart about how we engage them and once we have this weapon, we will have more of an advantage," Livia responded.

"That seems too good to be true, but I hope you're right," Avery commented.

The group chatted more about the travel details and then talked in general until their flight was ready to depart. Livia, Abigail, and Anders sat in the seats to the right of Avery and Owen. It was Owen and Avery's first time flying in first class, so they took advantage of the extra benefits. Owen and Avery chuckled to each other when Anders rolled his eyes at them and Abigail jokingly told them to "pull it together" because of how excited they were. When they weren't taking advantage of the benefits in first class, they rested their eyes and relaxed. Still, they became more alert when the flight attendant came around to offer them drinks and a snack before they had their meal, which they eagerly accepted.

"Look at us in first class with our endless snacks, living the high-society life," Avery mocked.

Owen chuckled. "That we are. Don't tease…you know you are enjoying yourself."

"Um, yeah. If I didn't think my face would shrivel up, I would have endless hot towels on my face and only stop for food," Avery said while she repositioned herself in her seat.

Owen chuckled again. "I bet you would. I can see it."

Avery laughed, but then her face became more neutral. "Owen, promise me something."

"What's that?" Owen asked.

"That you will fight to win…to survive," Avery softly replied.

"I'm confused. Don't I always do that?" Owen asked.

"Yes, but I'm afraid when it comes to Hailey, you won't. You will try your best to stop her, but she will be trying her best to kill you," Avery explained.

"You don't think I will kill her if I must? I would, especially if you or anyone else was in danger," Owen countered.

"Yes, but I don't think you have it in you to have that same mindset if it's just a fight between you two. I'm afraid you will see the old Hailey and not the person she has become. Now, don't get me wrong. I want to save her with every fiber in my body and it would devastate me if she died. I just don't want to lose you because you will see her as a friend, not an enemy. You do what you must to survive. I can't lose you," Avery said as her eyes became glassy.

Owen held her hand. "If I must, I will. I promise you. Besides, I can't die because it seems I need to take you on a beach vacation once this is all done," Owen responded and then smirked.

"That's right," Avery said as a smile appeared on her face before she went back to enjoying her snacks.

While Owen ate, her words haunted his mind. He hoped it didn't come down to it, but if it did, he wondered if he could kill Hailey. Did he have it in him to look her in the eyes and kill her? Not only that but also be able to live with himself afterward. He remembered how horrible he felt when he had to kill Joshua, so he could only imagine how much worse it would be if he had to kill Hailey. Owen mentally prepared himself in case it did come down to it.

After the plane landed. They boarded a small plane that took them the rest of the way into the Yukon Territory. Once they landed, they quickly located a local motel to spend the night so that they could rest before their journey the next day. It was an older motel, but it was clean and had a door that locked so the team was good with it. The air was cold, but not as frigid as he thought it would be. The area had snow on the ground, but only a few inches.

As tired as he was, Owen forced himself to stay awake so he could get adjusted to the time change. Avery, Abigail, and Livia did the same but eventually fell asleep. Anders was already adjusted to the time so he went outside and surveyed the area to make sure they weren't followed.

"The coast is clear," Anders whispered while he quietly closed the door. Avery, who was lying next to Owen, stirred before she settled. Livia and Abigail, who were sleeping on the other bed, didn't budge.

"Good. In that case, I am going to bed. I can barely keep my eyes open," Owen commented.

"Be thankful you weren't here the last few months when there was daylight for most of the day. Even with blackout curtains, it takes time to get used to it. At least you are past that and the daylight hours will continue to decrease over the next month or so as it gets closer to winter. A lot less sun and a lot more snow," Anders commented as he unfolded the sofa couch and then laid down on it.

"That sounds interesting but I bet that extra sunlight gets old quickly," Owen responded. Anders nodded his head in agreement. After a few minutes, Owen finally slid down on the bed and swiftly fell asleep.

They woke up early the following morning and quickly got ready. Anders already secured a large truck, equipped with off-road tires and chains for them when they encounter snow. The bed of the truck was filled with supplies and camping gear, as well as an additional large gasoline tank. The group filed into the truck and studied the map of where the old facility was located. Livia oversaw the map so she sat in the passenger seat while Owen, Abigail, and Avery sat in the back seat. Once they had their bearings, Anders started the truck and they drove off.

Civilization quickly disappeared the further they drove, but the views were beautiful. They drove past a crystal-clear lake and a vast open area filled with tall green trees and grass with yellowish-orange bushes, and the smaller trees had yellow leaves. In the distance, they could see the snowcapped mountains. It was cold outside, but the sun compensated for it.

Owen, who sat in the middle, glanced over to Avery and smiled when he noticed how captivated she was by the views during the peaceful drive. "Is someone enjoying themselves without sand between their toes?"

Avery chuckled. "Yes, I am. The scenery and peacefulness kind of reminds me of the Alps."

"We have a few more hours on this road before we veer off the main road and onto some side road or trail," Livia said as she studied the map closer.

"Ah, the unknown. Always makes things more fun and interesting," Abigail sarcastically commented.

"Don't worry. I'll figure it out, especially once we get there and I can study the terrain. It will make more sense then," Livia responded.

The drive continued as they took advantage of the daylight, only stopping for breaks as needed. As dinner time neared, they finally came across the dirt trail. They drove for a few miles longer to be far enough away from the road so they wouldn't be spotted. Anders pulled off the trail and the group set up the campsite. After they grilled steaks, along with vegetables and potatoes, they sat around the campfire and enjoyed the s'mores that Avery had smuggled onto the truck. Once they were finished, they sat quietly around the campfire and listened to the sounds of the wood crackling and popping within the fire. The same wood that Avery proudly chopped with her hammer axe. The same axe that she almost didn't take because she was afraid it would get lost or stolen in her luggage.

Something caught Owen's eye so he looked into the night sky and smiled. "Everyone, look up."

As they did, their eyes gleamed at the sight of the Northern Lights as the sky was filled with waves of bright green lights. Owen put his arm around Avery as she snuggled into him while they watched the spectacle. Soon, everyone agreed that they needed sleep so they would be refreshed for the next stretch of their journey tomorrow. They decided to sleep in shifts in case Astrid and Hailey tried anything. Anders took the first watch and added a few more logs onto the fire to keep the area warm for everyone, as well as to keep the animals away. The morning quickly arrived as Owen struggled to wake up. Luckily, Livia took the last shift and had a pot of boiling water on the fire that he used for his coffee.

"It was a quiet night for us all. Makes me wonder what Hailey and Astrid are up to," Livia mentioned while she sipped on her coffee.

"I don't know. Hailey has excellent vision when she is in transition. It even surpasses mine, which means she could be watching us now and we wouldn't know it," Owen responded.

"That's creepy," Abigail commented.

"Well, even if she is, that means they have to stay far away from us and they can't act until we do. That means when the time comes, we will have to make the best use of our time before they catch up," Anders said while he finished his cup of coffee.

"We should get moving and travel as far and as fast as we can," Avery suggested. Everyone agreed since it was unknown how close Astrid and Hailey were to them. The group packed and cleared the campsite and extinguished the fire before they loaded the truck and drove away.

Anders couldn't drive as fast as he did on the paved road due to the uneven dirt trail. Not only that, the trail also had random limbs, large potholes, and rocks scattered about it. The closer they got to their destination; the more they wondered what ancient weapon could stop someone like Astrid. It seemed like whatever they tried either didn't harm her or she was already a few steps ahead of them. Even worse, he was sure that she had received more wishes. This would make her even more powerful and dangerous than she was before. Then, to add to it, there was Hailey. His close friend was now Astrid's personal bodyguard and hated him and his friends. Owen hoped Livia could take care of her before things got out of hand.

"Right up here," Livia pointed to a wooded area near where the trail curved.

"There?" Anders reconfirmed while he squinted.

"Yeah. Park over there and we can set up camp and figure out how we will proceed from here," Livia directed. Anders came to a stop just past where the trail curved, so everyone got out and constructed the campsite again. Once they were settled, each of them spread out and surveyed the area, and then reconvened afterward while they ate.

"The trees are dense around this area and I presume there may be some rockier areas near the stream on that map, but after that, it should be a clear shot to the old facility," Owen commented.

"Provided the map is accurate. Nature can change things. That stream may be a river now for all we know," Anders mentioned.

"My guess is the facility is about another two days on foot from here. Especially when you add time to construct and deconstruct a campsite," Livia said while she studied the map.

"If they are tracking us, as soon as they figure out the direction we are headed, Hailey could easily scout ahead and beat us there. Even if they can't get in, they will have time to ambush us when we arrive," Owen said as he leaned forward and rested his elbows on his knees.

"Why do we have to walk?" Avery muttered.

"What do you mean?" Abigail inquired.

"If we can clear a path, then we can drive," Avery suggested.

"By the time we do, we could have walked there," Livia commented.

"Yeah, if we cut down the large thick trees. It will add time and alert them to where we are, but there are plenty of smaller trees around that we can quickly go through and it's not like we have to chop down many. Just enough to get us by," Avery added.

"The smaller trees are around the more uneven terrain. The truck may flip," Anders mentioned.

"Then we make sure that doesn't happen," Owen added. He looked around and saw nothing but blank faces, so he continued. "Livia can drive and Avery can chop down whatever trees she needs to with her trusted hammer axe. Trust me, she won't mind. As for the truck flipping, there are four very strong hybrids that can jump out of the truck and keep it in place while Livia slowly continues. The truck itself has handled the trail relatively easily so it should hold up fine the rest of the way. We can save a day's journey and not be as tired when we reach the old facility. What do you say?"

"It's my original idea so you know I'm in," Avery said and then winked.

"All I have to do is stay in the truck so I'm good," Livia replied while she shrugged.

"Why not? We can give it a try and if it doesn't work, we can walk the rest of the way. The truck is insured anyways in case it doesn't make it back," Anders responded.

"Well, if everyone else is in then I'm not going to be the party pooper. Count me in," Abigail replied.

"Great, it's settled!" Avery exclaimed.

"We should go to bed soon so we can get an early start tomorrow," Livia suggested. The group agreed and shortly went to bed afterward. To be safe, they slept in shifts again.

The group was up shortly before sunrise. The brisk morning air, along with coffee, helped Owen to quickly wake up. With the chance of saving a lot of time, everyone ate fast and cleared the campsite without delay because they wanted to reach the old facility before sundown.

Livia carefully maneuvered the truck over the stumps and debris and drove faster when she could over the less difficult terrain. When they approached more trees, she stopped to allow Avery to chop them down and Anders to move the fallen trees out of the way. With the strength of the cyclops, Avery made short work of the smaller trees. When they came to slopes, especially rocky ones, everyone but Livia got out of the truck, attached ropes around it, and walked alongside the truck as they pulled to keep it from flipping while Livia cautiously drove. With all four of them in transition, the truck was not too heavy. The only difficult part was keeping their footing on the slopes that did have snow on them. Eventually, they came across a clearing.

It was a vast area with nothing but snow and what appeared to be a stream ahead. They drove up to it and sure enough, the stream was a lot bigger than they anticipated. It was almost like a small river, but luckily not as deep and fast-moving. They took a few minutes to search for the best place to cross. They found a shallow spot that had enough rocks so the truck's tires didn't sink into the soft sand of the stream. After they crossed, the group continued their journey over more snow-covered land until they reached a large patch of trees.

Livia stopped the truck and looked at the map. "It should be around here. Maybe it's on the other side of these trees. We can drive along the perimeter to save time as we look."

"Wait," Owen blurted out as he stared at the trees in front of him.

"What do you see?" Livia asked.

"Yeah, what do you see?" Abigail inquired while she leaned forward and squinted her eyes.

Owen scoffed in amusement. "Drive forward and into the patch of trees until you can't go any further."

"Okay, but I doubt we will get far. These trees are large and would take a while to cut down and move," Livia responded as she slowly proceeded. They didn't get too far past the tree line before they had to stop. However, it wasn't because of the trees that they had to stop, but because of a stone wall. Everyone in the car rejoiced.

"How did you know the old facility was in here?" Livia asked.

"Call it a hunch," Owen replied while he smiled as he remembered Aiden's advice.

"I guess this is where we get out," Avery commented.

"Be mindful, the area may not be safe," Anders added. Owen presumed his comment was related to Astrid and Hailey.

The tall stone walls had to be fifty feet tall, yet still under the tree line. The group left their vehicle and followed the wall until they located an iron door. Livia used the key to unlock the door. As she did, Owen could hear multiple clicks until finally, the door popped open. Anders and Owen grabbed the drop ring iron door handle on each door and pulled the double doors open. The doors were so heavy that they both had to transition to be able to open them. Once they were opened, the team proceeded forward to an iron gate, that was already unlocked so they walked through.

"We should close the iron doors and lock it to keep Astrid and Hailey out," Owen suggested but when he looked through the gate, he noticed there were no door handles on the back of the doors. "Well, maybe not. How do you close the doors?"

"Only from the outside. Any gate or door on the inside can be locked and opened as normal, but the iron door that leads inside here can only be locked from the outside. Consider it as a safety measure," Livia explained.

"Safety measure," Avery slowly said as her brow crinkled.

"If a creature ever became loose within here, the doors could be closed and locked from the outside in case the creature had the intelligence to open doors," Livia responded.

The group locked the gate and then carefully walked down a narrow stone tunnel and when they emerged, their eyes widened as they walked into a room the size of a football field. The floor and walls were made of stone, including a handful of small, freestanding, enclosed rooms. These stone enclosures had iron doors and rectangles cut out of the stone for windows, with an iron panel that could slide to close the windows. The high ceiling in the large, main room was made of stone as well. It also had a rope netting that was about ten feet below it, with random metal spikes attached to the ropes.

"I thought we were going to enter a facility and not some empty castle," Abigail commented.

"This design was meant to be part facility and part structure to keep monsters contained," Livia said while she continued to look around.

"Is this where the large creatures went?" Owen asked.

"Yes, or any person who had an unknown creature within them. The space was large enough and strong enough to hold most creatures. The netting above prevented creatures from flying or climbing too high. The rooms you see were to safely observe them. From what Duncan told me, each stone house has an underground tunnel that leads to different areas of the facility itself. That is where the upgrades are typically done unless there is a structural issue that needs to be addressed. The remote location not only keeps people from finding the facility, but it also protects people from the creatures. If a creature did escape, it had a long distance to travel before it reached anybody," Livia explained.

"So, does this place have weapons?" Avery asked.

"Yes, of course. If a monster needed to be killed, they had an arsenal of weapons to choose from," Livia responded.

"That means, one of these houses will lead us to the weapon that can stop Astrid?" Owen inquired.

"In theory, yes," Livia replied.

"Great, we can split up to check the houses quicker," Owen suggested; however, before anyone could respond, a large explosion was heard near the iron gate.

The group turned and watched as Hailey, Astrid, and a third person appeared out of the smoke from the blast. Each one of them had a smug expression while they approached. Owen and his friends formed a line but spread out so they weren't standing too close to each other. They didn't want to make themselves an easy target for Hailey.

"You should really install better locks in this place. You never know what will find its way in here," Astrid said with a devious smile.

"I'll keep that in mind. I see you actually found someone stupid enough to join your failing cause," Livia said as she glared at Astrid.

"Failing, how so?" Astrid inquired.

"The djinn has had enough of you and your abuse. That is why your wishes are becoming harder and more dangerous with each one. Why not wish this weapon away that can stop you? Are you afraid that the djinn will twist it around and make you regret your wish?" Livia provoked. Astrid didn't reply. She simply stood there with a furrowed brow while she stared at Livia. Then, without warning, Livia shot Astrid in the chest. Owen's eyes were wide open when he whipped his head toward Livia before quickly looking back at Astrid. A smile of hope appeared on his face.

"Really, I just bought this shirt. So not cool," Astrid nonchalantly remarked while she rubbed the hole in her shirt. Owen's smile faded away and his hope was replaced with fear when he saw that the bullet didn't even leave a mark on her skin.

"By the sea of confused expressions, I am guessing you are wondering what's up. My good friend Hailey over there let me have a wish. Well, three wishes since it took the other two to fix what the djinn did. I am officially bulletproof so stop ruining my clothes," Astrid explained.

"Perfect," Owen sarcastically commented. "Let me guess. You mind controlled this poor person as well?"

"Who...Fianna? Not at all. She's the only person left brave enough to stand with me. I'm so appreciative of her support that I may give her three wishes all to herself," Astrid responded. Fianna was tall and sleek, with defined cheekbones, blue eyes, tan, and grey pixie-cut hair. Even though her hair was grey, she seemed to be in her late twenties.

"Whatever she promised you, it's not worth dying over. Your so-called leader has gotten people killed from the Alps, to the States, and soon to be here and that's just the ones we know about," Owen commented.

Fianna smirked and then her eyes transitioned to ones similar to Selena's eyes. She then zoomed past Owen as her shoulder rammed into his chest and knocked him to the ground. He shook his head as he winced before he stood up.

"You can't be," Owen muttered.

"Can't be what?" Avery asked.

"What lore comes to mind when I say one of the fastest horses in the world?" Owen inquired.

Avery thought for a moment and then her brow raised. "Odin's horse?"

"Sleiphnir. The eight-legged horse straight from the Norse mythology," Owen added and then looked back to Fianna.

"Correct. Well, at least a descendent of Sleiphnir," Fianna said as she slowly pulled out two curved daggers.

"As you can see, she's quite fast and strong, so unless you want her to reduce you to a pile of minced heroes, I suggest you leave now," Astrid said and then smirked. Even Hailey smiled at her comment.

"Form a tight group," Anders directed. Everyone transitioned before they quickly formed a tight circle. Livia joined the circle, armed with a handgun, while the others raised and extended their claws. Avery, of course, raised her hammer axe as they waited in anticipation of Fianna rushing them.

As they anticipated, Fianna charged them but as soon as she began to run, Owen and Abigail formed a firewall that Fianna ran straight through. Between her speed and the flames, she lost control and crashed hard enough into the iron door in one of the stone enclosures to leave a dent. She shook her head before she slowly stood up. Owen noticed she had some bruises and a cut on her face that was slightly bleeding. She briefly wobbled as she regained her focus.

"Powerful indeed. Did you see what she did to that door? Outstanding," Owen mocked as the rest of his friends played along and chuckled. He provoked her in hopes that she would foolishly attack again without thinking.

Fianna glared at them before she screamed as she charged again. Abigail and Owen put up another firewall but this time she ran circles around it until they couldn't keep up, and that is when she ran through the group. As she did, she sliced Owen and Abigail's hips, which caused them to drop their flames as they winced and held their wounds. She then ran in and out of the group relentlessly as she sliced each member of the group multiple times while they swung wildly. Even Livia's shots were missing her. Fianna was almost a blur at the peak of her speed. Owen and Abigail tried to establish the firewall again, but they were too slow and Fianna was everywhere so they had to stop their current attack before they burned someone other than Fianna.

While Fianna was slowly decimating the group, Owen noticed Astrid walk toward one of the stone enclosures while Hailey approached them with her eyes glowing. Before Owen could warn the others, Hailey stuck out her two hands and screeched as she blanketed the area with lightning bolts from her fingertips. Her attack sent everyone to the ground except for Fianna who was able to escape Hailey's wrath. One of her bolts hit Owen in his shoulder, which he grabbed while he grinded his teeth because of the searing pain he felt. Everyone slowly stood back up while they held the area where Hailey's bolts hit them except for Livia. She sat on the ground while she tried to shake off her injury.

"Stop Astrid," Owen called out to Abigail. She nodded her head before she turned and looked at Astrid while she growled.

"You two give her some cover," Owen directed to Avery and Anders as he motioned to Fianna.

Owen had a purpose behind his orders. Besides him, Abigail was the only one who could attack from a distance to stay away from Astrid's mind control. As for Anders and Avery, they were tough enough and smart enough to handle Fianna as a team. That left Hailey, and the only person from his group who had any chance of defeating her was himself. A thought he dreaded, but he was out of options. He just hoped that he didn't have to kill her.

Abigail charged Astrid with one hand in front of her and one hand behind her, both shooting flames. The front flame caused Astrid to stop before she reached her destination and the fire behind her was to keep Fianna from stopping her. Fianna fidgeted in her spot as she tried to find a way around the flaming blockade but she didn't have time to think because Avery and Anders charged her.

She turned and sped between them and by doing so, knocked them off balance. Then, she raised her daggers and looked at them with a sinister smile. Right before she took off, a gunshot echoed throughout the building at the same time Hailey sent more lightning at Livia. The bolt hit Livia as she fired her weapon and because of it, the bullet meant to kill Fianna hit her in the leg instead. Owen gasped as he saw Livia tumble off and come to a stop while a small amount of smoke drifted off her body. He was worried since she wasn't moving and was lying awkwardly on the ground. He feared the worst but then his attention was redirected back to Fianna when he heard her scream. He noticed that she just tightened her belt around her thigh to act as a tourniquet. Afterward, she grimaced while she limped forward.

Livia's shot didn't go to waste because when Fianna ran toward Avery and Anders, she was still fast, but nowhere near as fast as she was before. This allowed Avery and Anders to be able to now stand their ground as they fought her. Fianna was skilled in using her daggers as she managed to continue to surgically slash away at Anders and Avery. They began to slow down due to the multiple cuts on their bodies but luckily, a well-timed placement of Avery's hammer axe tripped up Fianna. This made her stumble toward Anders who was able to get a couple of heavy slashes in as his claws tore through her upper body. She painfully regained her footing and raised her daggers as her brow lowered.

Before Owen confronted Hailey, he quickly turned his attention to the firefight that was happening on the other side of him. To defend herself from Abigail, Astrid shot fire back at her. The two exchanged blasts of fire while simultaneously dodging their opponent's flames. Abigail made sure to not get too close to Astrid while they fought.

Owen turned around and saw Hailey beginning to raise her electricity-filled hand toward Abigail, so he rushed over to Hailey. She jerked her hand toward him to send her lightening at Owen but it was too late. The bolt shot into the air as he collided with her and the two rolled to a stop. Afterward, they scrambled to their feet.

"I can't believe I ever had feelings for such a piece of nothing like yourself," Hailey said with a furrowed brow while she extended her talons.

"That's not you saying that. It's Astrid. She's in your head. You must fight her," Owen pleaded.

"Oh, it's me. It's the unfiltered me. Astrid told me all about the real you and my so-called friends. She wouldn't lie to me because she knows what's best," Hailey responded and then slashed at Owen.

He jumped backward, but her talons still just barely tore through the skin on his chest.

The chimera's rage fueled Owen enough to attack. She dodged his first attack that missed her right shoulder but his second one connected as his claws slashed across her belly. While she held her stomach, he followed up by punching her in the face. As she stumbled back, Owen sent a short blast of fire at her that slightly burned parts of her body. As she patted the flames on her clothes. Owen raised his claws in the air but he never got a chance to attack because Hailey flew forward and rammed her shoulder into Owen's midsection. She drove him, while still flying, through Avery, Anders, and Fianna and into the ground past them. The impact was hard enough to send the three they flew through onto the ground as well. Owen scurried to his feet while he held his stomach and tried to catch his breath. Meanwhile, Abigail and Astrid were the only ones still fighting, but they were a lot closer to him than before. The others that were on the ground were slowly getting back to their feet.

Hailey had already stood up while the electricity formed around her hands. She drew her hands back and as she was about to electrocute Owen, the lightning disappeared and Hailey stopped moving. Owen paused for a moment before his brow crinkled while he lowered his hands and his body relaxed. His eyes drifted and noticed that Astrid and Abigail were still fighting, but Anders, Avery, and Fianna also stopped fighting and were looking behind him. Owen was confused, so he slowly looked over his shoulder and smiled before he couldn't move anymore. He now realized what the weapon was…something that he would never have guessed but was thrilled to see. The weapon that Selena referred to was Cassandra.

CHAPTER 28

Her eyes fiercely glowed green and her face was filled with intensity as she walked toward them. She wore a black cloak that covered most of her body, with a hood that laid behind her head. "I heard everything but I couldn't see. Which one of them is the leader?" Cassandra asked just as she passed Owen. Once she did, he could feel himself regain control over himself again.

"Astrid, the one that is not in transition that is shooting fire from her hands," Owen replied as his smile grew. She continued without saying anything. "You have no idea how happy I am to see you. How…"

"Not now. We'll catch up later," Cassandra said while she continued to walk forward. Owen's eyes became larger when he noticed she was about to walk past Hailey so he ran up to her and bit her on the arm. He injected enough venom in her to keep her immobilized. When Cassandra walked past her, Hailey became rigid and then fell to the ground.

As she made her way toward Astrid, who was oblivious to what was going on since she was focused on Abigail, she passed Anders. Once he was able to move, he turned and with his back to Cassandra, ran over to Fianna and rammed his claws into her chest. She didn't express any pain, but Owen had a hunch that she felt every bit of it. Sure enough, once Cassandra advanced far enough, Fianna grabbed onto Anders's arm as she hollered in pain. The scream was loud enough to catch the attention of Abigail and Astrid, who both froze as well when they turned to look. Moments after Anders was free, so was Avery. She immediately raised her axe and swung it down, and finished off Fianna by chopping her head off. Blood squirted and spewed from her neck while Anders held her headless body up with one hand. He then ripped her heart out with his other hand and watched her headless, heartless body fall to the ground and splash in its own pool of blood. Anders then crushed her heart in his hand before he tossed it aside.

"Don't get too close to Astrid, she's a psychic and will mess with your mind," Owen called out to Cassandra as she neared Astrid and Abigail.

Cassandra came within ten feet of Astrid before she stopped. "Avery, get Abigail out of there," Owen directed. Avery nodded and ran over to Abigail, being careful to shield her eyes from Cassandra, and picked her up and carried her out of Cassandra's line of sight. As soon as she passed Cassandra, Abigail was able to move again. Owen stood near Hailey in case the venom wore off while the others gathered behind Cassandra.

Owen was impressed by Cassandra's control and power. She immobilized multiple people, from a longer distance, and she didn't show any signs that she was going to lose control. He wasn't sure how she was doing it, but he didn't care. Against Astrid, they needed all the power and luck that they could get.

"I bet you are wondering who I am. My name is Cassandra and if you haven't figured it out already, I am a gorgon. You and your quest for some stupid gem have started a series of events that cost me everything. The love of my life, my best friend, and even my own freedom," Cassandra said. Her voice was laced with hatred, yet sorrow in her voice as Owen could hear her voice crack a couple of times.

Owen's smile slowly vanished when he saw Astrid begin to move. She strained with each step she took as she powered her way toward Cassandra. With each step she took, her foot would stomp hard onto the ground while she leaned forward. Cassandra held her ground while she kept the gorgon's gaze on Astrid, but Owen could see Cassandra's body begin to tremble. The strain on Astrid's face intensified while her muscles tensed, but a smile began to form on her face. Owen feared Astrid would overpower Cassandra. Even worse, gain control of a gorgon.

Cassandra's eyes began to flicker at the same time she put her hands over her ears. "She's screaming inside my mind," she yelled as her face squinched from the pain. Astrid's steps became less labored and her hands ignited.

"She's not going to be able to hold her. We need to take her out now!" Avery exclaimed as she raised her axe.

"No! She'll invade your mind as soon as you get close enough," Owen countered.

"Maybe we don't have to get close. Look at her. She's a sitting duck," Abigail commented as flames appeared around her hands.

"Whatever you do...do it now. If she gets control of Cassandra we're done!" Owen called out. He could feel Hailey struggling so he leaned into her more to keep her in one place. He was afraid to inject her with more venom in fear that too much could kill her.

"No!" Cassandra screamed as her eyes began to glow brighter. While Cassandra screamed, Astrid's smug expression disappeared as the flames left her hands. She began to lose her momentum and eventually, she was not able to move again. Cassandra stopped screaming but her eyes did not dim. "What's the matter, don't have enough energy to continue your progress," Cassandra mocked. "I heard gunshots. Someone fetch me that gun," Cassandra added. Anders ran and retrieved Livia's gun.

"I have the gun," Anders said as he held it out from behind her.

"I can't take my eyes off her so you will have to shoot, but not to kill. I won't blink so you can stand near me. How many bullets are remaining?" Cassandra asked with a hint of a hiss in her voice.

Anders examined the gun. "Three. One in the chamber and two in the clip."

"Good. Fire one in each leg and one in her shoulder...her right shoulder. We can't chance you hitting her heart," Cassandra commanded without emotion.

"My pleasure," Anders replied and then shot Astrid three times, one in each thigh and one in the bone of her right shoulder. Astrid barely moved from the impact of the shots.

"Stop! She's in so much pain. I can hear her screaming," Hailey yelled as she struggled to move. Owen put his foot on her back to keep her from moving too much.

"Good! I hope it hurts because what she is feeling now is just a fraction of how I felt every day since I lost the love of my life. I hope you die in agony," Cassandra scornfully responded.

Owen squinted and he could see a tear rolling down Astrid's face while blood poured from her gunshot wounds. He was conflicted. He already came to terms that if stopping her meant killing her, then so be it. However, he felt uneasy about the torture.

"Okay, that's enough. I know she has done horrible things to all of us, but torture is not the answer. Don't lower yourself to her level. You're better than that," Owen called out.

Cassandra didn't respond. Instead, she let out a loud scream as she leaned toward Astrid. Her hair began to move around back and forth in a snake-like fashion while her skin formed more green scales. Hailey began to struggle more to the point that Owen had to kneel on her back to keep her from moving. He didn't want to inject more venom into her unless he had to.

"No! Astrid! Don't leave me," Hailey cried out over and over as tears poured down her face.

"It'll be okay. We'll find a way to get you back to normal. Don't worry," Owen said to her but Hailey kept crying out to Astrid.

"Owen, I'm sorry." It was only a whisper, but it was loud enough for Owen to quickly look around. It didn't take long for him to realize that the whisper in his mind belonged to Astrid. He looked at her and nodded. "I'm sorry, too," Owen mouthed the words while also saying them in his mind. Right after their exchange, Astrid's skin began to turn grey. Once that started, it didn't take long for her to become solid stone.

Cassandra took a few deep breaths and then transitioned back to human. Except for Hailey crying, everyone else was silent.

Abigail scoffed in amusement. "We did it...we actually did it. We stopped her."

"We won," Avery muttered and then chuckled to herself. She turned and looked at Owen and smiled. He was in shock. The mission was finally over and no more of his friends had to die.

Cassandra marched over to Avery and stuck out her hand. "Hammer axe." Avery's brow knitted while she slowly handed Cassandra her weapon. She took it and held it firmly in her hands as she continued to march toward Astrid. "I am not taking any chances," Cassandra added as she flipped the axe over so that she was wielding the hammer side. "Nobody won today. The only thing that happened here is that someone got what was coming to them," Cassandra added and then lifted the axe above her head.

"Please, don't," Hailey begged.

Cassandra positioned herself behind Astrid so she could see Hailey's face. As the two looked at each other, Cassandra winked before she swung down toward the center of Astrid's back and smashed the statue. Large and small chunks of stone flew in all directions and Astrid's head rolled and came to a stop near Hailey.

"No!" Hailey yelled while she sobbed.

Cassandra strolled over to Astrid's head and let out a scream full of rage as her eyes flared right before she sent the hammer axe down and crushed Astrid's head into dust. Thunder was heard outside the building as a loud screech came from Hailey as her eyes glowed. Then, lightning bolts came striking down through the roof and landed throughout the building, sending large slabs of stone crashing down. Everyone shielded themselves while they looked up to avoid any falling debris as they tried to regain their balance. Hailey screamed as a large electrical flash came from her, sending everyone either to the ground or back a few steps. Hailey, who knew better than to look at Cassandra, turned and focused on the next target in the room...Owen.

Another loud screech came from Hailey as she flew, at chest height, toward Owen. Her shoulder rammed right below his chest as she wrapped her arms around him and sunk her talons into his sides. Her body was electrified, which caused Owen to yell from the pain of being shocked, in addition to her talons jammed into his body. He transitioned to phase three and as he went to counterattack, she rammed him through one of the stone walls of an enclosure. The impact did not slow her down as she plowed Owen through the adjacent stone wall with the same force as the first wall. The enclosure crumbled to the ground as Hailey continued to fly forward. Even while dazed, he felt the pain shooting throughout his body.

Owen finally was able to counter by igniting his hands and sinking his fiery claws into her back. She yelled and then veered off course and smashed through some fallen stones from the ceiling before they rolled to a stop. He grimaced while he held both his sides and carefully got to his knees. He could feel the blood seeping through his fingers while he held his side and he saw random burn marks and burnt fur on his body. He couldn't see his back, but he hoped it didn't look how it felt. Owen shook his head to rid himself of his tunnel vision and dizziness while he looked around and assessed the situation. As he looked, he knew he needed to stay in phase three as long as he could to heal as quickly as possible before Hailey went on the offensive.

He noticed Hailey was bruised and had blood trickling from her temple while blood ran down her back, accompanied by her burnt clothes, feathers, and skin. However, she wasn't as injured as he was and she was in phase two, so he knew he didn't have much time since she was already trying to get up. He then glanced around and saw that they were halfway down the building.

Hailey quickly got to her feet, which made Owen scramble to stand up quicker to defend himself. She shot a small lightning bolt at him the same time Owen shot a small burst of fire at her. They both dodged, but not fully as they both were grazed. That didn't stop them as they continued forward with Hailey taking the first swipe at Owen's head, but he was able to duck under her talons. He followed up with an upward slash that sliced Hailey from her stomach to her chest. She hollered, but it didn't stop her as she was able to counter with a slash across his shoulder and chest. As Owen growled, she extended her talons and lunged her hand toward Owen's face, but he side-stepped her attack and shoved Hailey back.

"Hailey! I know the real you is still in there. You have to hear me. Don't do this. Stop while you can. I don't want to hurt you anymore," Owen pleaded while he took a few steps back.

"Your existence is painful to me," Hailey coldly replied as she sent a fury of slashes at Owen, which he was able to either dodge or deflect. Since it was obvious the venom had left her system due to how far she was in transition, he figured he would try to find a way to bite her again. This time, he would inject more venom to make sure she stayed down longer. However, Hailey was relentless with her attacks, which made his task more difficult. She became more frustrated each time she didn't cause Owen to bleed with one of her attacks.

"Come on Hailey! Remember the good times you had with everybody! It wasn't all bad. There were a lot of good moments…you just have to concentrate hard enough to get past her mind tricks. If not, you will keep killing and hurting your friends," Owen loudly pleaded.

Hailey scowled at Owen before she attacked again. During her barrage of slashes, Owen was able to catch her wrist and hip-toss her to the ground. While he still held her hand, he yanked it toward his mouth so he could sink his fangs into her, but Hailey was able to counter his attack by electrifying her hand. When Owen let go, Hailey tumbled back and that is when Owen decided to go on the offensive. He needed her to be weaker if he had any chance of subduing her.

Hailey stood up and immediately ducked under an overhand swipe of his claws at her. She then swiveled around him and raked her talons across his back. As Owen straightened up, he yelled as the pain radiated throughout his body. He turned around and sent his fist toward Hailey's face, but she deflected his attack and rammed her talons into his stomach. Owen's face crinkled as he yelled from the pain.

"The person I cared for most in this world died moments ago. You, and the rest, are just painful reminders of that," Hailey said through her teeth as she glared at him.

His vision began to fade, but not before he got a hazy look at some of his friends running toward him to help, but they were too far away. His legs became weak but as he was about to collapse, Hailey grabbed his throat to keep him from falling. As he gasped for air, she leaned closer to him.

"After I kill you, I am going to take great pleasure in killing each one of your friends, starting with that treacherous Avery. Maybe then, Astrid will have justice." Hailey let go of her grip and removed her talons from Owen's stomach. He could feel the warm blood rush down his stomach as he collapsed to his knees. Hailey lifted his chin with one talon while she raised her other hand high in the air and stretched her talons out. Then, a sinister smile appeared on her face.

"I'm sorry," Owen faintly said while he breathed heavily.

Hailey scoffed. "For what?"

"For this," Owen replied before he swiftly transitioned deep into phase three. He roared as he smacked her hand away from his face and then reached up and grabbed her shoulder. He yanked her body toward him as he sprung forward and drove his other hand into her chest.

CHAPTER 29

Hailey's eyes opened wide from the shock of Owen's attack as her face strained from the agony she was in. Then, blood spat out of her mouth as she began to cough. Owen stared into her eyes while he snarled at her. Both of their eyes then drifted down to her chest. He could feel his claws around her beating heart. Just before he was about to rip her heart out, Owen's humanity sparked and disrupted the chimera's survival instinct. He transitioned lower within phase three to allow more of himself to shine through so he could think clearer. Their eyes then reconnected.

"I'm sorry…I'm so sorry," Owen said as tears rolled down his face. If he took his hand out, she would die. If he left it in there, she would still die, but slower. Either way, it appeared he was going to have to experience something he didn't want to happen, the death of someone close to him. Even worse…a death caused by him.

Hailey coughed up more blood before she was able to muster up enough strength to speak. "No. Not yet, but soon you will be," Hailey weakly said before her eyes glowed. Then, there was a bright flash and a loud explosion that sent Owen soaring through the air before he landed hard on the floor. He bounced and tumbled for another ten feet before he came to a stop. As he shook his head to regain his senses, he couldn't see much due to the dust but he could hear more of the roof collapsing. Owen then heard a noise that made him gasp as his head whipped around. It was a loud and powerful screech that didn't come from Hailey but from the thunderbird.

The massive creature towered over the roof of what was left of the building, with the rest crumbling to the ground, as it spread its wings and began to move. Its feathers were bluish-black as currents of electricity moved around its body. The wind began to pick up around it while dark clouds formed above it.

"Owen, are you okay?" Abigail asked as she and Anders were the first to arrive. He could see Cassandra running toward them but it was difficult to see anyone else.

"I've been better. What do we do?" Owen inquired

"I don't know but whatever it is, it needs to happen now. The thunderbird will easily be seen on the radar once it gains enough altitude," Anders responded.

Owen had no idea how to stop something of that size. Even if they all turned into their creatures, they couldn't stop it. As they were thinking, they looked up and noticed the thunderbird was staring at them. They held their breath in fear of what it would do, but it did nothing. Instead, it turned its head around and extended its wings as it took a few steps away from the building.

"It must sense we are not evil," Owen commented.

Cassandra finally arrived. "What's the plan? It's too big for me to stop it with my gaze."

"What if you turned into the gorgon?" Owen suggested.

Cassandra's brow furrowed. "Are you insane? I'm not doing that. It would cause more problems and I also don't think I am ready to go back down that road again."

"You're right, sorry. Any other ideas?" Owen asked.

The group paused as they tried to come up with a plan, but then it began to thunder and a few random bolts crashed off in the distance. The thunderbird began to flap its mighty wings, which made the wind pick up to the point they had to hold onto the fallen stones around them.

"Someone can make a wish," Abigail mentioned.

"That's right, I forgot about that," Owen said as his brow raised.

"Make a wish?" Cassandra asked.

"Long story, but we have access to a djinn within Astrid's locket. Hopefully, you didn't destroy it or else there goes our last chance," Owen responded. He turned his head and there was too much dust and dirt being kicked up from the wind to see well. "Avery…" Owen called out into the cloud of dust, but he couldn't finish his sentence as a blast of wind knocked the group over. The noise became greater to the point it sounded like both a hurricane and a tornado were taking place as the thunderbird took flight.

"No!" Owen yelled but that was all he could do. Their world was about to be exposed and he didn't know how to stop it.

Suddenly, the storm ceased and the thunderbird vanished as Hailey fell from the sky. Owen and the rest cheered but it soon ended as they realized Hailey was plummeting out of control. Everyone called out to her and as she was rapidly approaching the ground, she regained her bearing and slowed herself down. She landed about two hundred feet outside the trees that surrounded the building. After they made their way around the rubble and maneuvered through the trees, they sprinted across the clearing toward Hailey. It took a little longer to locate her since she was lying down but as they got closer, Owen could hear her bawling her eyes out. They approached her but stopped within a few feet because they were fearful of how she would react.

Hailey sat up as tears poured from her eyes. "I'm so sorry," Hailey repeated multiple times while she rocked back and forth.

"I guess the full transition erased Astrid's mind control," Abigail commented.

Regardless of their pain, everyone transitioned back to their human state to help calm Hailey down. Owen knelt next to Hailey and put his arm around her. "It's not your fault. You weren't in control," Owen said in a calm tone. At that point, Avery arrived but she needed a moment to catch her breath.

Hailey pushed Owen away, stood up, and began to pace around. "No, no, no. It's my fault. I killed Marcus…I killed Livia. I hurt each one of you on so many levels, especially you Owen. I can't…I can't go on like this! It hurts so much!" Hailey sobbed. She then screamed while she held one hand on her stomach and one hand on her head before she fell to her knees and continued to cry.

"Marcus is dead? Where's Isaac?" Cassandra asked while her eyes were wide open from the revelation.

"He's dead too. Astrid, his daughter, killed him," Avery answered while she stared at Hailey with tears in her eyes.

Owen felt horrible. Hailey was reliving all the heinous acts she committed and all anyone could do was watch and hope she could forgive herself. The group stood around her as she cried to show support, but didn't touch her since she was hysterical and refused to be consoled. He knew that any one of them would be there for her in a heartbeat, but she had to let them first. Avery leaned against Owen as her, and everyone else's eyes watered.

"How did Hailey transition down so quickly? Did someone make a wish?" Cassandra inquired.

"I did," Avery responded as she put her hand on the necklace. "It took me forever to find it between the stones from Astrid and the ceiling, but as soon as I found it, I looked up and saw the thunderbird taking off. I tried to think of something quick and simple that the djinn couldn't twist around too much, so I wished for Hailey to not be in full transition anymore. I'm glad it worked."

"So, you have two more wishes left," Cassandra commented.

"Yes, and I was thinking about using one to help Hailey easily get through this but I'm not sure how to word it yet," Avery replied. Cassandra nodded and rubbed her chin as she began to walk around.

"What are you thinking?" Owen asked.

"I have an idea," Cassandra loudly announced as she stopped and turned around. Owen stared at Cassandra, not because he wanted to, but because he had no choice. Cassandra's eyes were glowing. With her announcement, she tricked the entire group into looking at her so now no one could move.

"My idea is to take the locket and use the wishes to whatever suits me, but not before I kill each of your friends, Owen…right in front of you. Then, I'll trap you somewhere and allow you to relive their deaths over and over until it has consumed you with grief and hatred. Only then, will I kill you…slowly," Cassandra said and then slowly pulled out one of the curved daggers that Fianna had.

"I'm sure if you could talk, you would be asking me why I am doing this. That's a legit question since in your mind, how could you do anything wrong? It's because I promised myself that I would get revenge on everyone involved in the death of my one true love, Ethan. As far as I am concerned, you are the last person alive that was involved in his death. Astrid, Isaac, Klayden, and so many others, including yourself. Yes…you were involved. You had to turn into the chimera instead of finding a different path to take. A path that could have led us all out to safety, besides the one that forced me to use the gorgon's gaze past my limit. All while fully aware that Ethan would have to kill me if I fully transitioned and yet, you still didn't care. I did what I had to, so I could protect people I barely knew, along with the person I loved more than anything in this world. Guess what, the strangers survived while I lost everything," Cassandra loudly added as more scales appeared on her skin.

"I should have died that day, but I didn't. Instead, I lost not only my one true love but also my best friend Kyra. Do you know what it's like…" Cassandra's voice cracked. She paused for a few seconds before she continued. "Do you know what it's like to see the ones you love die by your hands and you have no control over it? Let me paint you a picture. When I transitioned back to human, I was greeted with the following horrors. During the fall, the golem and the gorgon

408

must have been holding on to each other the entire way down, but the golem landed first with the gorgon on top. The impact must have severely hurt the gorgon from the blood I saw but it shattered the golem. Fun fact, when a dead creature reverts to human, the wounds disappear, but body parts don't reattach. So, you can imagine the gruesome sight of seeing Ethan broken up into pieces scattered across the floor. Then, the cherry on top of it all, I found Kyra. Did you know she survived the fall? I didn't think she did but she must have had enough strength to use her flight ability to slow her descent at the end. However, she didn't know about the gorgon until it was too late. The gorgon turned her to stone while she crawled around for help. The look of shock on her face was literally etched in stone."

Cassandra's face hardened while she took a few steps closer to them. A whirlwind of emotions was going through Owen's mind. He wondered if he was truly to blame and if he could have found a different way. On the other hand, he figured Cassandra lost her sanity after what she went through. Either way, he had to push his thoughts aside and put all his concentration into trying to break free if he had any chance of saving himself and his friends.

She was strong, but with her using her gaze on multiple people, he hoped he could use that to his advantage. He tried to transition but he couldn't, so he was already at a disadvantage; therefore, he put all his strength into the one thing that could save him…closing his eyes. He strained with all his might and to his delight, he could feel his eyelids beginning to shut.

"I don't think so, Owen," Cassandra said as her eyes glowed brighter. Any progress he made had now stopped. "You see, Isaac originally had me in the lower levels of the facility because I was too emotional to deal with anything. That, and I was also too afraid of accidentally turning into the gorgon again. Isaac was the only one who knew I was there. He covered everything up to keep my existence a secret. He said it was for my protection and to recover at my own pace, but I knew better. He just wanted to keep his secret weapon. Anyway, he would come down there often and chat with me until he had to go back to the Alps to check on you while you were a statue. We chatted about all sorts of subjects but when he told me about you and your new hybrid self, the small spark I had for revenge ignited into a ball of fury. I killed two people before Isaac was able to knock me out. The next thing I knew, I was in this prison. He told me it was for my own good and that he would come back once the mission was over to help rehabilitate me. So, during my time here, I honed my skills and waited for my time of revenge. In my solitude, I realized nothing was my fault and that you were not the good person I thought you were. It seems good things come to those who wait, and I've waited so long for this moment." Once she finished speaking, an unsettling smile formed on her face.

"Now, the lore says another person cannot make any wishes until the current bearer of the djinn has used all their wishes, or is dead," Cassandra mentioned as she slowly approached Avery and raised the dagger. Owen screamed in his mind while he tried to break free, but he was helpless. Regardless, he continued to try in hopes that Cassandra's hold would weaken or she would slip up.

Cassandra's angle was perfect. If she attacked properly, she could kill Avery and still keep everyone from moving, Owen thought. He continued to internally struggle as sweat formed on his brow. He screamed and begged Cassandra to stop as fear filled every particle within him. Of course, no sound left his lips. Cassandra stood near Avery and drew the blade back and thrust it forward. At that exact moment, everyone stumbled forward, except for Avery.

"No!" Owen yelled as he stumbled forward but his brow knitted when he realized he moved. His head whipped around and that is when he quickly realized why they were able to move. Cassandra had duct tape covering her eyes.

While Cassandra was distracted, Avery grabbed Cassandra's arm and turned her attack back into herself. The blade that was meant for Avery, was now imbedded in Cassandra's chest. A loud crack was heard as Avery twisted the blade inside Cassandra. She screamed as she held onto Avery's arm. Cassandra's scream stopped right before she began to wobble.

"Ethan...I love you," Cassandra whispered as blood trickled out of her mouth. She slowly released her grip on Avery's arm before she toppled over onto the ground and remained there, motionless.

"I'm sorry," Owen said as he lifted his hand and covered her body with fire. It was his way to not only make sure she stayed dead but to also give her some form of a funeral. Especially, if he was the reason, be it his fault or not, that she became vengeful.

"How? You were frozen. How did you make a wish?" Abigail asked Avery. The rest of the group gathered around Avery with interest.

"I didn't," Avery responded. She then smiled and untucked the necklace from under her shirt to show that the locket was missing.

"Wait a second," Owen said and then his eyes widened as he quickly turned around. Sure enough, Livia was walking toward them from the tree line. Owen began to chuckle while others smiled. They approached Livia and they each took a turn giving her a big hug. Especially Hailey, who apologized multiple times for her actions. Of course, Livia understood and accepted her apology, but Hailey kept repeating herself while tears rolled down her face.

Owen lifted Livia's hand to look at her pearl ring. The final pearl was dark grey. "Thank goodness for this ring," Owen commented.

"Yes, but if it follows the same pattern as the other two pearls on my ring, I have one life left before it turns black like the others," Livia commented while she examined her ring.

"So, the next time you die...there's no coming back?" Owen asked.

"That's right," Livia said while she shrugged.

"I'm sorry," Hailey commented while she frowned.

"It's okay. This ring has allowed me to do so much good in this world. Now my life is even more precious than it was before knowing I can't come back anymore, so I need to make the most of it. At least I still won't age," Livia responded while she grinned.

"Anyone else fuzzy about how everything just went down?" Abigail blurted out.

Livia chuckled. "Let me see if I can clear up any confusion. While Avery was searching for the locket, I came back to life, and luckily there was enough commotion going on to drown out her scream when I startled her with my resurrection. After she explained to me what happened while I was out, I informed her about how evil Cassandra had become."

"How did you know?" Anders inquired.

"Because Isaac informed me," Livia replied.

"So, you knew she was here the entire time?" Anders countered as his brow furrowed.

"No, Isaac told me everything but her location since he wanted to make sure she stayed hidden until she was reformed. I didn't even know she was alive until after everyone came back to the States. I figured he placed her on the other side of the world. He just wanted someone other than him to know, so he picked me since I wasn't a resident of the facility," Livia explained. Anders's face eased while he nodded so Livia continued.

"Anyway, once Avery found the locket, we agreed that she would pretend to have it while I made the wishes in secret. The first wish I made was to take Hailey out of transition. Avery knew to tell everyone that it was her who did it and how. I then kept the locket and sent Avery to check on you guys and test Cassandra. She has been imprisoned for a long time so I wasn't sure if she was back to her normal self or not. I hid right behind the tree line and watched and when I saw her use the gorgon's gaze on everyone, I started to think of a wish that the djinn couldn't manipulate. A wish that would also protect everybody since I wasn't sure who she would go after first. When I saw her draw that blade, I wished that if she attacked

412

anybody while using the gorgon's gaze, that duct tape would cover her eyes."

"That is why when she attacked, everyone tumbled forward except me. I trusted that Livia would find the perfect wish to save us so I didn't struggle while I was frozen. I just waited for the opportunity to present itself," Avery added.

"I'm glad you came back to life when you did. Thank you," Owen said as he smiled. He then put his arms around Avery and pulled her in for a long hug.

"You have one wish left. What will you wish for?" Abigail asked.

"I don't know. I was thinking of just making a wish to send us all back to the facility so we don't have to travel all the way back. Once we are there, we could find a way to hide it in the gem mine or something," Livia responded.

"Girl, wish big. This is your chance. Then when you are done, we can all have turns with it before we hide it from the world," Abigail commented. Livia smiled while she stared at the locket.

"You must make a wish. If not, you will have a target on your back until you do. Remember…no one else can make a wish until you are dead or spent your wishes," Avery informed Livia.

"Yeah, but what do I wish for? I'm sure the djinn is already frustrated and annoyed at the abuse of its powers. My wish would have to be crystal clear and foolproof to avoid any backlash that I won't be able to fix. If we passed it along, it would only get worse," Livia responded.

The group paused while they tried to think of a solution. Finally, Owen spoke up. "Set it free."

"What?" Everyone responded at the same time, except for Hailey who stood a few feet back from the group with her arms crossed over her stomach and her head lowered.

"Wish for the djinn to be free of its bonds," Owen added.

"Are you sure about that? It does solve the issue with Livia making her final wish and I doubt the djinn would try to alter it, but then everyone loses a chance at having their wishes granted," Abigail pointed out.

"Do you have any idea how dangerous a free djinn can be?" Anders rhetorically asked.

"They roamed the earth long before humans, and after, before they were captured and used for their wishes. Look, all I know is that I only spent a few months under Astrid's control and I hated it…all the way down to my core. I bet my time with Astrid is only a speck compared to what the djinn had to endure," Owen softly countered. He then looked away as he fought back the memories of the horrible things he had to do and witness while with Astrid.

"I say we do it. Who knows, maybe the djinn will be nice and just leave us alone. Maybe it will grant you a wish for your generosity," Avery commented as she shrugged.

"Or, it will kill us and go about its business," Anders added.

"We all need to be on board with this," Owen mentioned.

"The facility or wherever we hide it would always be under a constant threat and if Livia didn't make her final wish, that threat would extend to her. I'm in," Anders replied.

Abigail huffed. "Gosh, I hate doing the right thing all the time. I'm in."

"You already know I'm in," Avery said while she smiled.

"Me too," Hailey softly spoke without looking up.

"I agree with you, Owen. I just hope you are right," Livia said. She then took a few steps back before she turned around to face the group. She took out the locket and held it in her hand. Then, she took a deep breath and rubbed the locket with her fingers. "I wish the djinn inside this locket was free from its constraints."

CHAPTER 30

The locket flew out of Livia's hand and onto the ground in the center of the group. As soon as it hit the ground, it sprung open and they felt a large breeze pass through them. Afterward, there was silence. Each of them stared at the locket waiting for more and then began to look around at each other while they shrugged.

"Did it work?" Owen asked.

"I don't know," Livia responded.

"If it did, it was very anticlimactic," Abigail commented.

"Oh, I think it worked," Avery remarked as her eyes grew wide while she stared past the group. Each of them followed her eyes until they saw an older gentleman in a black suit. He had his back turned to them and was staring off into the valley.

"Is that the djinn?" Abigail whispered.

"I don't know. I hope so because I really don't feel like fighting anyone else today," Avery quietly commented.

"It must be the djinn," Livia said.

"There is only one way to find out," Anders said and then he began to walk in the man's direction. The rest of the group followed Anders. They came to a stop a handful of feet behind the old man, who never turned around.

"Hello," Avery cautiously said.

The old man scoffed with amusement. "Do you know that is the first non-wish statement that a mortal has said to me in so many millenniums that I lost count?" The voice sounded very familiar to Owen.

"I take it you're the djinn," Anders commented.

"I am," the old man said as he turned around. The entire group gasped while they took a step back.

"Isaac?" Owen asked as his brow knitted.

"Not exactly. I only took this form to make myself more appealing to your eyes. I even added Marcus's suit to my appearance. If you don't favor this mirage, I can always change back to my true form," The djinn stated as its eyes flashed red.

"No, no...Isaac works," Owen quickly responded. He shuddered when he remembered its true form back in the large transition room. Owen's reaction made the djinn grin.

"Admiring the view?" Abigail asked as her eyes shifted over the djinn's shoulder.

"Yes, but of course anything is better than the constant view of the void," the djinn replied.

"So, what happens now? What will you do?" Livia inquired.

"Are you asking because you fear I may bring Armageddon upon this world?" The djinn asked with a straight face.

"Yeah, pretty much," Avery quickly responded before Livia could speak.

The djinn smiled. "I could. Before my imprisonment, making others suffer was one of my delights." Owen tried to remain calm even though he wondered if everyone else's stomach was in their throats after the djinn's comment. "However, I want to explore this world, indulge in its pleasures, and see where it leads. Besides, humans are a peculiar species and as much as a nuisance they can be, their behaviors can be intriguing." The djinn then walked over to Owen. "I heard what you said in regard to my release."

"You did?" Owen asked as his brow knitted.

"Yes, I can hear whenever a wish is being created or discussed. I will admit, I didn't think you and your friends would go through with it. For thousands of years, people made that statement but never fulfilled it. Even for a being of my stature, it was torture," the djinn commented.

"You're welcome," Owen teased.

"My 'thank you' was not killing everyone here," the djinn responded with a deadpan expression.

"We appreciate the 'thank you' then," Owen countered.

The djinn smirked. "I also don't like being in a person's debt so for me to be truly free, I must give you something in exchange."

Abigail was about to speak but the djinn raised his pointer finger in the air. "If you ask me to grant each of you three wishes I will remove your tongue," the djinn said as he gave her a cold stare. Abigail immediately, and tightly, closed her mouth.

"What I will do is grant each of you one wish," the djinn said. Abigail smiled along with the rest of the group. "Of my choosing," the djinn added.

"Of your choosing?" Livia asked.

"Yes. It's the best of both worlds. I won't be in anyone's debt and I will be the one choosing a wish with my own newly acquired free will," the djinn responded.

"How will you know what we want?" Avery asked.

"I'll know," the djinn replied as a devious smile appeared.

"Thank you," Owen respectfully said. The djinn smiled and nodded its head.

Seconds later, the djinn's eyes glowed red, and then suddenly an old scroll, about half a foot long, appeared in everyone's hand. The parchment paper was off-white with twine wrapped around it, with a red wax seal to hold it in place. Owen looked closer and noticed his initials were on the seal.

"Break the seal and read the written words and that wish will come true," the djinn announced and then walked closer to Owen. "My debt has been paid."

"It has been paid. Enjoy your freedom," Owen replied as he smiled.

"Try not to kill anybody...please," Avery blurted out. The djinn looked at her and began to laugh as its body blew away like sand in the wind. Right before the djinn vanished, Owen admired it. Even though it wasn't truly Isaac, it was still good to see and hear from an old friend again.

"Was that laugh a 'ha-ha, funny joke or a ha-ha, I'm going to kill an entire city,' kind of laugh?" Abigail asked as her face cringed. At first, everyone giggled at her comment until the grim reality of how true it may be erased the smiles on everyone's faces.

Owen winced as the pain from where Hailey stabbed him in his stomach was making its presence known. Out of all the injuries he sustained today, that one was by far the worst.

"I'm sorry. I know that doesn't fix anything but I don't know what else to do," Hailey commented and then she started to cry again.

"It's okay. It's not your fault. Besides, there are hopefully some medical supplies in the facility below. We just need to move some rubble around and go find it. In the meantime, we will just stay in transition to help ease the pain," Owen responded and then transitioned deep into phase three.

"I should have asked the djinn to send us back home," Abigail commented while she looked around.

"That would have been a good one," Owen remarked.

"As you wish," the djinn's voice whispered within the slight breeze that passed them. Then, in a blink of an eye, they were back at the cabin at the facility.

Not only were they back, but they were also all healed, clean, not in transition, and wearing new clothes. As Owen rejoiced with his friends, he noticed something in the corner of the cabin. His smile went from ear to ear as he saw Bailey, Selena, Caine, Cedric, Prisha, and Aiden all in the same room. Each of them was confused as to how they got there and why they were holding a scroll.

Owen marched directly over to Bailey and hugged her hard and he didn't care how she felt about hugs. To his good fortune, Bailey hugged him back just as hard besides punching him.

"Next time I tell you to leave…listen," Bailey said while they hugged.

"I'll keep that in mind," Owen replied.

He then walked over to Selena and hugged her. "Thank you. Because of what you did, we were able to stop Astrid."

"I'm just glad it worked," Selena responded.

After everyone hugged and shook hands, Caine cleared his throat while he stood in the dark corner of the room. "This is great and all, but for the ones that did not receive the telegram, will someone please inform us to what is going on?"

"I will give you all the details later, but in short…Astrid is dead and Hailey is back to normal. Also, we freed the djinn and since it didn't want to be in our debt, it granted us…apparently all of us, one wish of its choosing. All you have to do is break the seal and read the scroll and the wish will come true," Owen explained.

"That's great news but is anyone else scared to open their scroll?" Cedric asked.

"The djinn was happy to be free and very determined to not be in our debt, so I doubt there are any tricks within those scrolls. Besides, if it wanted to, it could have killed us all with a snap of its fingers," Livia remarked.

"Who wants to go first?" Prisha asked.

Owen heard a snap as he and everyone else turned to see what caused the sound. It was Abigail who broke the seal on her scroll. "Sorry, I thought we were all just going to bust open our scrolls. Well, the seal is broken, so I might as well continue." She took a deep breath, unraveled her scroll, and read it. "No way," Abigail exclaimed while a large smile appeared on her face. The scroll then crumbled into dust.

"What is it?" Owen asked.

"It said I could eat whatever food I want without any negative consequences," Abigail responded while she bounced in her spot. Owen smiled at her reaction and then noticed something on a chair next to her.

"I believe you have a way to test it out. It may take time, but it's a start," Owen commented and then pointed at the platter and pitcher on a nearby chair.

Abigail picked them up. "They're empty. Is someone going to fill them up for me?"

Owen smiled. "Place them on that table over there and while you are touching them, think of whatever food and drink you would like to have." Abigail's brow arched. "Trust me," Owen added and then winked.

Abigail placed them on the table and then stared at them. Then, a large slice of pizza appeared on the platter while a fizzy dark drink appeared in the pitcher. "Yes!" Abigail exclaimed as she sat down and took a large bite out of the pizza. "It's so good too," She mumbled before she took a sip from the pitcher. "Wow! The root beer is even the correct brand too. How did you know about these?"

"Astrid wished for them and allowed me to use them from time to time," Owen responded as he continued to grin. He was happy for her, yet he also found her excitement over her wish comical as she chomped away, carefree.

"My turn," Avery called out as she opened her scroll. Owen noticed a huge smile appear on Avery's face as she ran outside. The group, minus Caine, followed her.

"Tell me you can fly," Owen said.

Avery slowly floated off the ground. She smiled before she darted into the sky and after a few passes, she landed. "I can fly,"

Avery cheered before she ran over to Owen and hugged him. It warmed his heart to see Avery so happy. They went back inside and continued.

Livia cracked her scroll open and read it and a smile appeared shortly after. She looked at her ring and her eyes immediately began to water. "All three pearls on my ring are solid white again. The djinn reset my ring's powers."

"I guess you have plenty more good deeds to fulfill before it's your time," Owen commented.

"I guess so," Livia said while she beamed.

"Me…me, I want to go next," Aiden responded as he opened his scroll. He then looked all around and found a knife and a small block of wood that the djinn had left. He began to whittle and became excited as it quickly began to take shape. "I am a master whittler!" Aiden exclaimed as he skipped over to an open chair and continued.

"Really?" Prisha commented.

Owen scoffed with amusement. "I'll never understand him."

"Whatever floats your boat," Abigail commented as she started to eat a slice of chocolate cake. Owen did a double take when he realized she had already conjured up something else to eat.

"Prisha, go ahead and open yours next," Owen suggested.

Prisha nodded and opened her scroll and as she did, her brow raised and she quickly reached into her back pocket and pulled out an envelope. She opened it up and smiled as tears rolled down her cheeks.

"Are you okay?" Owen inquired.

"Yes…very. These are tears of joy. I have been wanting to go back to India to visit my family for years but I never had enough money to do so. In this envelope is a round-trip, first-class ticket to India, along with a stack of Indian rupees."

"I want a souvenir," Owen commented.

"Everyone is getting a souvenir," Prisha announced. Owen smiled at how happy she was.

Cedric was the next one to open his scroll and a smile began to grow on his face. He then reached into his back pocket and pulled out an envelope. When he looked inside, he began to chuckle to himself.

"What is it?" Selena asked.

"There's a woman at the club that I have been wanting to ask out for a long time now, but I have been too scared to ask," Cedric responded.

"You, scared...why?" Owen inquired.

"Because she is perfect in every way and I'm scared I'll ruin it," Cedric replied.

"It's not me, or Selena, is it?" Abigail mumbled while she ate.

Cedric laughed. "No, but the scroll did say she likes me as well and then gave me two tickets to a concert that she will love." Cedric continued to smile while he looked at the tickets.

"No reason not to seize the opportunity now. Go for it. You deserve it," Owen said as he patted Cedric on the back.

"Thank you," Cedric replied while he continued to grin as he looked at the tickets.

Owen heard another snap and it was Bailey who opened her scroll next. She smiled and began to take her clothes off. "Whoa...what are you doing?" Owen asked.

"I don't want to ruin my clothes," Bailey replied and once she was down to her bio shorts and bra, she ran outside.

"I got the same question...what are you doing?" Avery asked.

Bailey winked and then fully transitioned. The group all gasped and went back into the cabin, with Owen at the door ready to close it. The werewolf howled and then turned and looked at them. Owen's brow knitted when it began to calmly walk toward them. He walked outside toward the beast.

"Seriously! Get back in here!" Avery loudly whispered.

"It's okay. I just realized she walked within the barrier before she transitioned so I'm safe," Owen replied.

He stood right next to the barrier line, with the werewolf right on the other side of it, staring at him. Even in its calm state, it still breathed somewhat heavily while its fangs showed, but its eyes were not as wild. He then slowly walked past the barrier line as he kept a watchful eye on the werewolf.

"Owen! Are you crazy?" Abigail called out.

Owen didn't respond. Instead, he slowly reached out and petted the werewolf's arm. To his relief, it did not react.

"Bailey, can you understand me?" Owen asked. The werewolf nodded.

"She has full control over the werewolf," Selena commented.

Avery walked out of the cabin and when she was near it, she put her hand on the werewolf and then snapped a selfie. "Not the best angle for me, but I'll take it."

"You really have to stop doing that. That's not the collection you need on your phone," Owen commented.

"Collection…oh yeah, that's right. You remembered me taking a selfie with the chimera," Avery said, followed by a guilty smile.

"Yep," Owen replied as he partially smiled while he slowly shook his head.

"Maybe since Bailey has full control over the werewolf, she can help me get a more flattering selfie with it," Avery commented while she looked at her phone. The werewolf leaned down behind Avery and when its head was right behind hers, it let out a loud growl. Avery jumped and screamed. "Okay, maybe not," Avery added.

Owen chuckled and then leaned toward the werewolf. "Good one."

"Well, she knows I don't like taking selfies so why would it change when I'm a werewolf? If anything, my tolerance is a lot smaller." Owen quickly turned and saw Bailey standing next to him. Her sudden appearance startled them.

"Fair enough," Avery said while she held her chest as she smiled. She took a few deep breaths to calm herself down from the scare.

"So, I take it your wish was that you have full control over your creature," Owen commented.

"Yes, and it was amazing. I remember everything too and the fact that I can transition at will…I'm going to kick some major butt in the future," Bailey said as she smiled while she stood proud. "And now I am going to get dressed because this is awkward," Bailey added before she walked inside.

"Open yours," Selena said to Caine.

"Ladies first," Caine quickly replied.

Selena smiled and rolled her eyes before she opened her scroll. As she read it, a tear ran down her cheek while she smiled. Caine put his hand on her shoulder as she wiped the tear away. "It said I could use my healing ability during a phase one transition," Selena said as she turned to Caine.

He smiled and then looked at the group. "Any volunteers?" Caine asked as his eyes turned red while he exposed his fangs.

Owen extended his arm. "I'll be the guinea pig." Caine smiled and then within a blink of an eye, he had Avery's hammer axe that she left propped against the wall. "Wait a second," Owen said as his eyes widened. Caine sped up to Owen and placed the blade of the axe over his forearm. He smiled while he looked at Owen and swiftly cut the entire length of the top of his forearm. Owen cringed while he grabbed his arm.

"Caine!" Selena exclaimed.

"What? If we are going to test your abilities then it should be something greater than a couple of puncture wounds," Caine responded while he had a devious smile on his face.

"Sorry," Selena said as she approached Owen.

"It's all right. I'm just glad he didn't chop it off," Owen responded.

Selena held his arm and transitioned just enough to change her eyes. She placed her hand on Owen's arm, near his wound, and within moments, the cut was gone. She transitioned back and smiled. "It took no effort to heal you."

"That's amazing," Owen responded while he looked at his arm.

"It's a dream come true. There have been so many people I wanted to heal but I couldn't because the risk of transitioning was too great. That, or I didn't have the strength to hold a phase two transition long enough to heal a person. Now, I won't have that problem…that fear anymore," Selena added.

"Great, she is going to heal every person she sees, right down to the ones with papercuts," Caine sarcastically said.

Selena ignored Caine's remark. "Now, it's your turn."

He lifted his scroll and broke the seal. He read it and after it crumbled to dust, he just stood there staring at the dust on his hands.

"Well?" Selena asked. Caine didn't respond. He walked past everyone until he reached the door. He put his hand on the door and paused before he opened it up and stuck his hand outside. To everyone's surprise, Caine's hand began to smoke. He jerked his hand back inside and shook it around.

"Was that supposed to happen?" Selena inquired.

"Yes," Caine responded while he turned around. His eyes were blood red as he lifted his hand and watched his burn heal.

"Why are you all vamped out? You don't need to be in order to heal," Owen asked.

"I beg to differ," Caine replied. His eyes phased back to human before he winked and walked outside.

"Caine!" Selena yelled as she and the rest rushed outside.

She put her hand over her mouth, while the rest of the group gasped. Caine stood in the sunlight and he was not covered in flames. Everyone was speechless.

His face was pointed toward the sky, with his eyes closed, and his arms were spread out as a smile appeared while he basked in the sunlight. He lowered his arms and took a deep breath before he looked at the group. "I haven't felt the warmth of the sun in centuries. I've almost forgotten how soothing it was," Caine commented.

"Your wish was for sunlight to not harm you?" Selena asked.

"No…it was to be both a human and vampire, but not like a hybrid. My scroll said that except for being ageless, I would only have vampire qualities when my eyes were red. When they are not red, I am human," Caine explained.

"Is it wrong that I'm thinking of all the ways that I can get back at him now," Owen whispered to Cedric.

"Can't be any larger than the list I have in my head," Cedric whispered back. The two then grinned.

"I wonder why he kept the vampire trait of not aging regardless if he is human or not?" Abigail asked as she leaned toward Owen.

"To allow him to be human without fear. If not, he will stay a vampire and only briefly revert to being human from time to time to stay alive longer. Especially, when your friends are hybrids with extended lives," Owen replied as he continued to stare at Caine.

Selena ran to him and gave him a long hug while the rest followed her and congratulated him. Owen didn't know Caine for long, but in the time that he did know him, this was the happiest he ever saw him. As the group dispersed from Caine, Avery approached Owen.

"I thought Caine just wanted to be in the sunlight, like a vampire that isn't hurt by the light. I didn't know he wanted all this. Why would he want any other aspect of being a human?" Avery asked.

"I can think of one reason," Owen commented. He then smiled as he looked in Caine and Selena's direction as they walked toward the cabin while they held hands.

The group jumped when Livia's phone began to ring due to a video call from Duncan, so she answered it. "Hey, I've been trying to reach you for a while now but the call wouldn't go through until now. Can anyone explain why I have a scroll in my hand with my initials on it?"

"Why didn't the djinn send him here with the rest of us?" Bailey inquired.

"So, he could continue to tend to the horses?" Avery responded while she shrugged.

"I'll explain later but Astrid is dead, Hailey is back to normal, and the djinn is free and its gift to us is one free wish each. Just open the scroll. Trust me, it will be fine," Livia explained.

"Okay. I hope you're right," Duncan replied as he situated his phone so he could open the scroll and still see everyone. He then looked up and paused for a moment before he began to chuckle. "It's gone."

"What's gone?" Livia asked.

"Any negative urge that I used to get when I would think about going into town. If I knew I had to go into town, I would have to meditate before going just to last long enough to get what I needed and leave. If not, the urges of drinking, fighting, and partying would surface. Now, those negative thoughts are gone. I may actually get to enjoy myself while in town, in a healthy fashion," Duncan replied.

"Does that mean you enjoy being around people more than horses again?" Owen asked.

"No, I don't think that will ever happen but at least the townspeople are a close second," Duncan responded. Owen laughed at his response. "Well, I would love to sit around and chat but I am headed into town soon. I'll call you later Livia to get all the details," Duncan excitedly added.

"Sounds good. Have fun," Livia said while she smiled. Right after that, the video call ended.

"Good for him. He deserves it and I know he's been wanting to be able to go into town like any other normal person for a long time now. He'll enjoy himself," Bailey commented.

"I guess I'll go next," Anders mentioned and then he read his scroll. As soon as the scroll crumbled and the dust blew away, there was a set of car keys and a note in Anders's hand. Anders scoffed in amusement before he read the note.

"Well?" Owen said as he raised his arms out to either side.

"My dream car that I used to own until some hybrid destroyed it decades ago. Apparently, it's sitting in Isaac's garage back at his house waiting for me," Anders replied as he smiled.

"What kind of car is it?" Avery inquired.

"It's a black 1967 Chevy Impala," Anders responded.

"That's your dream car?" Bailey mocked.

"Hey, that's a classic muscle car that got me through some tough times. Don't speak ill of her," Anders defended.

"No sir, I wouldn't want to offend…her," Bailey teased.

"That's a nice car. Glad you got her back," Owen commented. Anders nodded his head and smiled before he looked back down at his keys.

"Hailey, why don't you go next?" Owen suggested. Hailey didn't respond. She just continued to look at her scroll. "You have been quiet for a while now and have been through so much. Maybe this wish will help you smile again," Owen sincerely said as he put his hand on her shoulder.

"I don't deserve happiness," Hailey muttered.

"Fine, make us happy by seeing something good happen to you," Owen teased.

Hailey grinned. "Okay." She opened the scroll and read it. As the scroll crumbled, Hailey's eyes closed and a bluish-black electrical mass of energy emerged from her entire body. It formed into a sphere, about two feet in diameter, above her head and then slowly drifted upward until it disappeared right before it reached the top of the taller trees.

"Did the thunderbird just leave her body?" Avery asked.

428

"I think so. I know it was such a burden for her, so she will be relieved," Owen responded. He then quickly glanced around to make sure it didn't reappear elsewhere and to his delight, the thunderbird was nowhere to be found.

He then turned to Hailey whose frown disappeared as her eyes opened. "It appears you are not a hybrid anymore. That must be a big relief for you. How do you feel?" Owen softly asked while the others gathered around him.

"I'm sorry, but how do you know my name...and what's a hybrid?" Hailey asked as her brow knitted while her eyes scanned the area.

Owen chuckled. "Very funny. Seriously, how do you feel?"

"Very confused. Who are you?" Hailey asked as she slowly began to panic as her eyes bounced around from person to person. Owen took a step toward her and extended his hand but she backed away. His brow lowered from the weight of confusion.

"You really don't know who I am?" Owen asked.

"I don't know who any of you are! I was here with an older man named Isaac and we were walking up to this cabin. We were going to talk more about him recruiting me into his organization then suddenly, I blinked and he's gone and I'm now surrounded by a bunch of strangers. What's going on?" Hailey nervously inquired while she backpedaled.

"Calm down. We can explain," Avery said. Hailey shook her head, turned around, and went to run away, but Caine was able to swiftly move in front of her by using the shade of the trees as his ally. She screamed and took a step back and that is when Livia came up from behind and placed her hands on Hailey's temples. Hailey quickly became unconscious as she crumbled to the ground.

"What just happened?" Avery asked.

"She didn't recognize any of us," Bailey commented.

Livia laid her hand on Hailey's head for a few moments before she looked up at the group. "I need to do a deep dive into her mind, but at a quick glance, her last memory is of Isaac and her walking up to the cabin. There is nothing else after that," Livia said.

"The djinn took it all away," Owen muttered.

"Took what away?" Abigail asked.

"All the hurt she experienced since she arrived here, including the daily struggle she had with the thunderbird. All the people she lost and hurt...it's all erased. She's not even a hybrid anymore. Her pain must have been strong enough that it was too much to bear, so the djinn gave her a clean slate," Owen commented.

"I'll check her out and see if your guess is valid," Livia said.

"Do you really think she wanted this? To forget everything...like it never happened?" Bailey asked.

"I can't believe we may lose Hailey. Regardless of everything that has happened, she was such a close friend," Avery commented.

"Yes, she was and I don't know if this is what she wanted or not. With how well the other wishes went, it's quite possible. Maybe she just wanted all the hurt to stop and this was the djinn's solution," Owen responded.

"Just remember, a person wishes for something that will make them happy, not to make others happy while they remain sad," Livia added.

"True, but still," Avery said while she frowned.

Owen had mixed emotions over her wish. He was happy that she wasn't in pain anymore but also hurt that she would throw their friendships away so easily. Regardless if he felt her wish was cruel to them, she was happy. She wouldn't remember the constant struggles or the people she lost or killed. He hated to admit it, but it may have been the best wish she could have asked for.

After a short period of silence, Livia turned and spoke to Owen. "You're the last one,"

"With everything that just happened, it can wait. Besides..." Owen paused as he looked at his scroll.

"Besides what?" Livia asked.

"Besides…what if my wish results in me forgetting everyone," Owen softly responded.

"Have you ever wished you could take it all back?" Livia inquired.

"No, never, but what if it did cross my mind for a split second and I forgot? I don't need to open this scroll. I am happy as I am now," Owen replied.

"I've wished for a million dollars before but you don't see a briefcase full of money next to me right now do you? No, because the wishes are coming from a deeper desire. As sad as it is for everyone else, Hailey may have desired this for a long time," Livia commented.

"She's right," Avery added. "As sad as her wish made all of us, for Hailey, it was a wish she wanted. Be happy for her in the same way you were with everyone else today. She would want you to be happy, so open it, please. I'm sure your wish will not only make you happy, but the rest of us as well," Avery said and then gently put her hand on his arm and affectionately smiled.

"I guess you're right…both of you. I wish I could have said goodbye to her first, but at least she will be truly happy again," Owen responded. He then took a deep breath, followed by a long exhale, before he broke the seal.

CHAPTER 31

Owen slowly unraveled the scroll. Afterward, his brow raised, followed by a hint of a smirk. "There is a message at the top of this scroll that says, '*For the one who originally was prepared to lose all his wishes, you now have been granted three.*' Sure enough, there are three wishes listed below the message," Owen said while he examined the scroll.

"I've carved three wooden figurines since my wish," Aiden mentioned as he smiled.

Everyone turned and shared each other's confusion as they looked at him. "Well, that beats my wishes then," Owen sarcastically commented.

"Sorry. This is your time to shine. Go for it. I'll be working on number four," Aiden said as he blissfully went back to work. Owen scoffed in amusement.

"Well, go ahead Mr. Lucky. Read your three wishes," Abigail said and then winked.

Owen smiled and then began to read his scroll. "The first one is that I will have full control over the chimera when I am in full transition."

"I can't wait for you to try that out. It's amazing," Bailey commented.

Owen's smile grew. "I know. That's been one of my biggest fears, especially after the farm incident. Having that weight off my shoulders will be such a relief." He then read the next wish but his brow crinkled. "It says I can interact with anybody through my subconscious, alive or dead, during meditation. How?"

"I haven't seen that happen in ages and it's very rare. Something that takes a strong mind, an expert at meditation, and even magical assistance to accomplish. You can't just conjure up whomever you want to in your mind. What that wish is saying is if your mind felt you needed to talk to let's say, Isaac, you could and it would be as if he was actually there in your mind. Not a memory, but a real conversation based on what your subconscious would think and how he would react. You can even feel things to a point in this state. Like, you can hug Isaac but you wouldn't feel the actual hug, but you would feel comforted. It's truly a gift," Livia explained.

Owen smiled as his mind drifted at the endless possibilities of whom he may see and he became eager to meditate sooner rather than later. After his transformation back in the Alps, he didn't meditate that much anymore because of his control over his mind. Now, the therapeutic aspect of being able to talk to whomever his mind felt would calm his storm was very intriguing.

"You still got one more," Bailey said as she nudged his arm.

Owen shook his head and continued, but his brow knitted again. "It just says, 'A key,' and nothing else." As he read the final wish, the scroll crumbled away and another iron key, with a piece of paper with coordinates on it, appeared where the scroll once was in Owen's hands. He blew off the dust and noticed the key had the number four etched into it.

"Another key," Avery whined.

"Let me see that," Livia asked and then examined it quickly before she handed it back.

"Any idea what this key is for?" Owen inquired.

"When Duncan and I researched the iron keys, we not only found the one in question at the time, but all the others as well. This particular key is to a facility located in Antarctica," Livia replied.

"Seriously! You must be joking! We are going to like...the coldest place on Earth. Why? Owen, did you have some desire to visit that continent or something?" Avery questioned while she felt flustered.

"I doubt it," Livia replied before Owen could answer.

"How do you know? Did you read his mind?" Avery asked.

"Nope, because I was just messing with you. I'm not sure of the exact location offhand, but it's one of the remote islands in the Caribbean," Livia replied before a smile appeared.

"Get out of here!" Avery exclaimed as she smiled and playfully hit Livia on her shoulder.

Owen laughed. "Well, I was thinking of taking you and anyone else that wanted to come to Florida, but that works just as well," Owen commented. Avery's smile could be seen across the globe as she ran and hugged Owen.

"I hope you were serious about the invite," Abigail commented.

Owen chuckled. "Very. After what we went through, everyone is welcome. Now, let's head inside and assess the damage while Livia works on Hailey."

"Aren't you forgetting something?" Bailey mentioned.

Owen's brow lowered until he realized what she was referring to. He nodded and removed his clothes to just his bio shorts. Caine scooped up Hailey, but she was in the sun so it was more of a struggle for him to do so in human form, but he managed to do it. Even more, he did it without showing any frustration. It seemed he had already embraced the human side of himself, which Owen was delighted to see. Once he had Hailey, everyone backed up to the cabin. Owen took it a step further and decided to not go within the barrier line. After Bailey's control over the werewolf, he felt confident that there would not be an incident. Owen took a few quick breaths and then fully transitioned to the chimera. It let out a mighty roar and then all three heads turned and stared at the group.

"I'm not testing to see if Owen is in control," Prisha blurted out while her eyes were wide open. Aiden remained silent while he stepped behind Prisha.

"I'll find out since I am due for some redemption after the farmhouse," Bailey announced as she walked toward the chimera. "Okay Owen, I'm going to pet you and then after that, you can do a couple of my requests to prove you are in control. Sound like a plan?" Bailey asked as she continued her fearless approach to the chimera. Its eyes on all three heads were now focused on Bailey. When she got close enough, she extended her hand to pet the chimera, but the lion's head snapped at her hand. She became startled as she quickly pulled her hand away while she moved back a few feet. "Really, again?" Bailey huffed as she turned to the group.

The chimera came up from behind her and nuzzled Bailey. "Jerk," Bailey remarked while she smiled and petted the lion's head. The group laughed at Owen's prank. "Shoot a quick burst of flames up into the sky," Bailey requested. The chimera backed up and then a short burst of flames shot out of the goat's mouth. "He's a jerk that listens. Works for me," Bailey teased and then walked away.

"Sorry, I couldn't help it," Owen called out after he fully transitioned back. Bailey turned and rolled her eyes which made him laugh. "You're right though, it's an amazing feeling being able to do this. Especially, since now I don't ever have to worry about accidentally hurting or killing one of you or an innocent person," Owen added as a wave of peace swept over him.

Owen got dressed and the entire group entered the cabin, unlocked the elevator, and took it down to the facility itself. It looked like a massacre had occurred between the initial attack and what the werewolf had done. Owen glanced over to Bailey and noticed her jaw had dropped while she examined not only the carnage but also the claw marks left on the walls and trees. Owen knew it was going to take time to clean up and repair everything, as well as remove any of Astrid's changes, but it was something that had to be done.

Selena, Caine, and Livia took Hailey to the medical ward while the rest walked around to see what else needed to be done to the facility. In Owen's mind, he knew on the lower levels the large transition room had to be addressed, in addition to whatever damage was remaining in the entrance to the gem mine. Avery grabbed her phone and notified the others at Isaac's house that the facility was now theirs again. She also gave them a heads up about the work that would have to be done to restore it. To help, Cedric got on his phone to notify some of his associates that their assistance was needed.

Later that day, Owen, and the rest of his friends, minus the ones that originally went to the medical ward, were taking a break and relaxing in one of the less damaged garden areas. "Hey everybody." Owen's eyes grew wide and he held his breath as he turned and looked at Avery. She turned and looked at him and mirrored his reaction. He then looked around and sure enough, it was Hailey.

"Hey. I'm sorry about earlier. I didn't realize Isaac told you about me before my arrival and then to top it off, I freaked out over it. All this, right before I embarrassingly passed out from not eating or drinking as much as I should have today. Any logical person would have known to have done that before going on a hike…and now I am rambling because I am nervous and feel stupid. Sorry!" Hailey said with a nervous smile while she fidgeted.

Owen glanced over Hailey's shoulder to Livia, Caine, and Selena who were behind her. Livia's eyes grew as she nodded for him to play along. Owen's eyes drifted back to Hailey. "It's fine. I wouldn't worry about it. At least your freak-out didn't include slapping us around," Owen light-heartedly replied.

Hailey giggled. "Yeah, that would have been horrible," She paused for a moment while her eyes narrowed. "Have we met before? I feel like I have seen you from somewhere."

Owen slowly shook his head and pressed his lips firmly together, but didn't say anything because he could feel the emotion starting to rise and needed a moment. "Not that I know of. I guess I just have one of those faces."

Hailey shrugged. "Oh well. I guess so. What's your name?"

"Name?" Owen muttered.

"Yes, as in what people call you by," Hailey teased.

Owen paused for a moment before he shook his head. "Oh! Sorry, it's been a long day. My name is Owen."

"Pleased to meet you. My name is Hailey…which you already know. Sorry, long day for me too," Hailey said while she smiled and was flustered. Owen chuckled in response before everyone else introduced themselves to Hailey.

"I wish I could stay longer and get to know everyone better but I must head off to my first assignment. I can't believe I will be assisting in operating a safe house in the Alps," Hailey added while she smiled.

"Oh really," Owen responded and then looked at Livia.

"Yes, she will be helping Duncan on the ranch to allow him time to go into town more often. She can also visit the other safe houses in the area, including Italy, to make sure they are stocked and ready. After that is done, I'm sure we can find other things for her to handle while she is in that area," Livia explained.

"And it works out because my brother died in a hiking accident and his ashes were spread in the Alps so I will get to pay my respects," Hailey added.

"That will be good to be able to pay your respects. You will be able to do that and finally visit Italy. I know that has been on your list for a long time," Owen responded.

"True, but how did you know I wanted to go to Italy?" Hailey asked.

Owen internally panicked once he realized what he had just done. "Um…because isn't Italy on everyone's list?" Owen stuttered while he replied.

"Oh. I know, right? If it isn't on everyone's list then it needs to be added!" Hailey responded. Owen felt relieved that he was able to cover up his mistake.

"Well, I'm sure you will enjoy yourself in the harsh working conditions in Italy and the Alps," Owen teased.

"It will be hard, but I will try," Hailey mocked.

"I'm glad that you are so happy. That smile suits you," Avery commented.

"Thank you. This job is exactly what I needed. It's hard to explain, but I feel like I haven't been happy in a long time. Now, it's like a weight has been lifted and I can allow myself to be happy once more," Hailey responded.

"That's a great thing to hear. Right, Owen and Avery?" Bailey asked as she looked at them with an arched brow while she grinned.

"Yes. Very much so," Owen stuttered but then smiled.

"Very much indeed," Avery added while she smiled. She then took Owen's hand for comfort.

"Since Prisha has a plane to catch and Cedric has plans, I figured the two of you could escort her to Isaac's house and then on to the airport. Hailey has all the itineraries and things she needs for now in her bag, so she is ready to go," Livia suggested.

"Yes, of course," Prisha replied.

"I wish I could tell Isaac bye or at least thank him for letting me stay at his house. It was very generous of him. I am appreciative of not only that but also for him picking me to come to work with him," Hailey mentioned.

"He's a very busy man but I'll let him know what you said," Owen responded before he walked up to Hailey and hugged her. "Have a safe and fun trip and don't forget to enjoy the little moments in life while you are over there. Goodbye."

"I will. Thank you. I hope to see you around sometime," Hailey commented.

Owen smiled and nodded. It was all he could do or else he would have become emotional. He felt sad to see her go, but he took comfort in knowing she was happy, unburdened, and off to enjoy her life. He was also thankful that he was able to give her a proper goodbye.

Hailey turned and was met by a huge hug from Avery. "Wow, everyone is so friendly here…and strong too," Hailey muttered. Owen couldn't help but chuckle to himself. As Hailey and Avery hugged, Bailey came up to them and she put her hand on Hailey's shoulder and smiled. Bailey stood there for a few moments before she and Avery let go.

Owen walked over to Prisha and hugged her and wished her a safe and fun trip before the rest of his friends did. Aiden even gave Prisha a small wooden airplane to take with her. Owen then shook Cedric's hand and wished him good luck on his date. They all huddled together as they watched Hailey, Livia, Prisha, and Cedric walk in the direction of the elevator. Livia walked behind Hailey with her hands near her head in order to alter Hailey's mind so she wouldn't see the images of the battle that took place. Livia stayed with Hailey until they left the cabin.

"I hope she will be okay," Bailey commented once Hailey was on the elevator.

"She will be in good hands with Duncan. Besides, she is free from all her burdens and finally…she is truly happy," Owen responded.

Later that evening, Owen went into his room and prepared to meditate. He wasn't sure what to expect, but he was eager to find out. It didn't take too long for him to slip into a meditative state and find himself on the beach where it all started. This time, it was during the day. The sight was beautiful, but weird because he could hear the waves but he couldn't feel the sand on his feet or the sun on his face.

"You're not going to get all sentimental on me, are you?" Owen turned and saw Joshua standing behind him.

Owen's eyes began to water. "I'll try not to." He walked over to Joshua and the two hugged. Livia was right, he couldn't feel the hug but he did feel comforted by it.

"I'm sorry," Owen muttered.

"For what...killing me or stealing my girl?" Joshua asked as he took a step back with a stern face. Before Owen could reply, Joshua began to talk but a smile formed on his face. "I'm just messing with you. You can't say sorry for things you haven't done. You didn't kill me; you killed that evil vampire that took over my body. As for Avery, you can't steal her from me when I'm dead. Heck, it's not like you two kissed the day after I died or anything like that, so stop feeling guilty. You saved Avery and the rest of your friends from that vampire wearing me as a suit and I wouldn't want Avery with any other man."

"So, I have your blessing then?" Owen teased.

"Once again, I'm dead and this is all in your subconscious but sure...you have my blessing," Joshua replied while he smiled. The two laughed and hugged again. Owen opened his eyes and Joshua was gone. He knew it was all in his mind, but it still felt good to talk to Joshua and get his blessing.

"You know...if the manticore's tail didn't get hit with that tranquilizer dart, I bet it would have beaten the chimera." Owen whipped his head around to see Klayden standing beside him with a crooked grin.

"That's debatable," Owen replied while he smirked. "Why are you here?" Owen asked.

"It's your twisted mind that brought me here besides a boatload of other people that would have made more sense than me," Klayden said while his smile became more devious. "If I had to guess, it would be to tell me that you are sorry that things turned out the way they did. That, and how you wished you could have done things differently to help me. How do I know this? Because you and your annoyingly high morals love a good pity party." Owen couldn't help but chuckle at Klayden's remark. "My response to that is hindsight is twenty-twenty and to stop with the guilt trips that you love to take. I don't see Cassandra walking around here so you were able to do that with her. Just apply that same logic to me and you'll be fine. Also, be thankful you didn't choose the same path as me. Now it's time to focus on what's in front of you out in the real world."

"Will do. Thank you," Owen sincerely responded. With that, Klayden disappeared.

"As much as I can't stand that man, he's right about the guilt trips." Owen looked over his shoulder and he saw Marcus. Owen smiled and as he walked over to him, he heard another voice to his right. "That must have been hard to say," Isaac commented. Owen smiled and was slightly teary-eyed while he gave both Isaac and Marcus a hug.

"I appreciate everything each of you have done for me and I'm sorry that the two of you had to die for this mission to finally be over. I wish I could have done something to prevent it. Even more, I'm so sorry I couldn't save Astrid. I feel like I failed you," Owen said as he wiped his eyes.

"You tried everything you could. However, once she made that wish to not feel anything toward her parents, she became too far gone to understand what true love and friendship were. Deep down, you know that is true. If you didn't, Astrid would be standing here as well. Take solace in the knowledge that even sporadically in her dark times, and definitely soon before she made that wish, her old good-natured personality shined through. Also, you were able to help us reconcile. For that, I can't be mad at you. If anything, I am thankful and I'm sure Astrid is too," Isaac responded. Owen smiled and nodded in return. His smile didn't convey how truly happy, and relieved, he felt after Isaac spoke. His words obliterated the emotional baggage that Owen was carrying related to Isaac and Astrid.

"We are saying the same things that your friends have communicated to you repeatedly. Maybe, you should listen to them more," Marcus suggested.

"I agree. I do need to listen to them more," Owen said and within a blink of an eye, Marcus was gone.

"You know, if your mind can remember all the details of how we look and sound, as well as the scenery around us, you would think it would remember how things would feel to the touch. Maybe, with practice, my theory may come true," Isaac commented and then grinned. Before Owen could reply, Isaac vanished.

Owen looked all around him, but he couldn't see anyone else. He walked toward the shoreline and stuck his hand in the water. The water moved around his hand but he felt nothing. It was even dry when he pulled it out. Owen tried again and for a split second, he could have sworn he felt the coolness of the water on his hand. As he smiled while he looked at his hand, he heard someone clear their throat. He turned his head and saw Amelia, Cassie, and Michael standing behind him.

"You didn't think we would miss this party, did you?" Amelia commented while she smirked.

Owen smiled as his eyes became glassy. "I would have been offended if you didn't show up." He walked up to the three of them and hugged each one of them.

"You know, you still owe me a date. Maybe the next time you meditate you can take me somewhere nice," Amelia playfully said.

Owen chuckled. "Sure, why not."

"He is with Avery now, so he can't go on a date with you," Michael commented.

"I know. It would just be as friends. Besides, this is all in his mind anyway," Amelia countered but then she cringed. "If it's all in your mind then be a gentleman. Don't be gross."

He shook his head as he rolled his eyes. "I'll behave," Owen said before the two of them laughed.

"I'm surprised she isn't asking you to get Caine to go on a date with her," Cassie remarked.

"A hot vampire who is rough around the edges and can now go in the sun and make babies, I'm available any day of the week," Amelia energetically responded. The group then burst into laughter.

"I can't believe my mind brought you three here to talk about this. Don't get me wrong, I am enjoying it. I have missed all of you so much," Owen commented.

"We all miss you too, but don't let your sorrow for us hold you back. Get out there and spend time with your friends and loved ones," Cassie said while she smiled.

"Exactly, especially Avery," Amelia added and then winked.

"Your memories of the loved ones that you have lost are what keeps them always close to you. In a way, they are immortal through you. Remember, we, or anyone, are just a meditation session away," Michael commented.

"Thank you. All of you. I promise I will go live my life with the ones close to me, but trust me when I say I will never forget any of you. However, I'm surprised you didn't make any video game references, Michael," Owen remarked.

"There is no need. You already understand that you are not to blame for my death, or anybody's death during this entire mission. You also know what you need to do once you are done meditating. It's like you have beaten the game. However, if you ever decided to call yourself 'The Chimera,' and suit up to fight crime, I would support you," Michael responded and then winked. Owen chuckled right before the three of them vanished.

Owen stood in the sand and smiled as he looked out into the ocean. He couldn't reminisce too much about the people he just saw, because he heard footsteps on the dock to the right of him. He turned his head and immediately tears rolled down his cheeks. He rushed over to the docks to where his parents and Daniel were standing.

He hugged each of them as hard as he could. "Mom, Dad, Daniel…I have missed you so much and before you disappear, I just wanted to tell you how much I appreciate and love each one of you. I wish you were still alive so we could talk more and spend more time with each other. Hopefully, all of you are proud of the things I have accomplished," Owen said as more tears rolled down his face.

"Man up," Daniel blurted out. Owen scoffed with amusement as he wiped his tears away. "You think it took everything you have done for us to be proud of you?"

"Honey, we were proud of you before we died and never stopped loving or being proud of you," Owen's mom commented.

"Your mother is right. Stop trying to prove yourself and start living your life," Owen's dad added.

"We will always be with you but spend and enjoy the time you have with your new family. As for your girlfriend, she seems nice but also the kind of girl that would level the world to protect you. I like her," Daniel said as he and Owen's parents smiled.

Owen chuckled. "Thank you and you are right. I love you, all of you."

"I love you too," each of them responded at the same time before they disappeared. Owen stood on the dock, motionless and quiet, but his heart was full.

He came out of his meditation and remained on the floor as he thought about everything that just occurred. He smiled and was relieved that his internal demons were slain. He felt free. Owen's main objective, regardless of what his future holds, was to focus on himself and his friends.

Months passed as he and his friends helped restore the facility to its original state. It would have been completed sooner, but they paused for the well-needed holiday breaks. Finally, as spring was almost over, the facility repairs and upgrades were completed. Owen was proud of the work that everyone did and it felt good to see the facility back to its original glory. The staff was ready and excited for things to be back to normal. Anders, and even Cedric, decided to spend more time at the facility to help Livia, along with any new recruits she or they stumbled upon.

Livia took control of the facility and vowed to keep the family environment that Isaac created. Even though she was in charge, she did not reside in Isaac's office. Instead, she created her own office and after they restored Isaac's office to its original state, they placed a rope across his door. This way, people couldn't use his office but could visit it like a memorial. Livia also had an area created within the garden as a memorial for everyone who lost their life during the mission. Their picture was set side-by-side on a smooth, rectangular marble slab, with their name and date of birth and death carved under the picture. It was placed near a pond that had water lilies scattered about it. It was a beautiful sight and Owen made sure to visit Isaac's office, as well as the memorial in the garden, before he left. Of course, he said his farewells to Livia, Cedric, and Anders, but he knew he would be in contact with them frequently so he wasn't too upset about leaving. With everything in place and complete, it was time to venture to the other facility in the Caribbean.

Owen, Avery, Bailey, Abigail, Caine, Selena, Aiden, and Prisha packed up their personal belongings and flew to Florida. After they arrived, they made their way over to the harbor where the pontoon boat that they purchased a while back was docked. Not too long after they arrived, they made their way over to the island. When they reached the island, they were in awe at the crystal-clear blue water and the white sands as the sunlight warmed their bodies. Everyone was excited to be there, but not as much as Avery.

They followed the coordinates to an even more remote area of the island. Hidden among the trees toward the center of the island was a stone hut with an iron door. They unlocked the door and entered the hut and it was no larger than the bedrooms they had back at the facility. It was empty, but they managed to find a hidden trap door on the floor. They took the stairs down to a large area, almost the same size as the garden area, but it was set up differently. All three levels of the facility back in the States were on the same level here. It had some transition rooms, a medical area, a training facility, a stocked pantry, and a supply room with necessities and leisure items. There was one hallway that led to the bedrooms, which both appeared to be a similar setup to the ones back in the States. From what Owen could tell, it must have been visited recently due to the more modern, and less dusty supply items, he found.

What really intrigued everybody was the large transition room. It was similar in size and structure to the one back at the facility, but there wasn't much floor area and it wasn't as tall. The small amount of floor area was also covered in sand. The remainder of the floor area was replaced with a huge, reinforced tank filled with ocean water that was filtered in from outside of the facility. The group quickly came to a consensus that one of the main objectives of this facility was to handle aquatic creatures. The group explored the facility more before they returned to the surface. Once they walked onto the beach, they fanned out to enjoy the view.

Owen and Avery picked up a few seashells while they strolled down the beach. They eventually stopped and stood by the water's edge, allowing the warm water to wash over their feet. The skies were clear and there was a slight breeze that helped tame the heat. Avery leaned over and hugged Owen before they kissed.

"What now, boss?" Avery playfully asked.

"Any suggestions?" Owen asked while he smirked.

"We're legends. I say we deserve a long vacation after everything we accomplished and went through," Avery replied.

"Oh really?" Owen responded.

"Yes, and we didn't achieve that status lightly either. Therefore, we need our rest if we are to be effective in whatever we must do in the future. That, and honestly, we simply deserve it," Avery commented.

"No argument there. I think that we all need a month off to relax and explore the island. Then, we can work on getting this facility fully up and running, but it will require multiple beach breaks to make sure we don't get worn down. Afterward, I guess we will just have to see what happens," Owen said as he smiled.

"You make a good leader," Avery replied and then winked.

"Well, I do try my best," Owen said as he smiled before their lips gently met again.

The two of them had their arms around each other as they looked out into the horizon. Owen turned his head and saw the others enjoying themselves as well. To his left, he noticed that Selena's persistence regarding Caine's skincare finally got the better of him since he seemed to be now covered in sunscreen. He quietly scoffed in amusement at Caine's expense but he also smiled as he watched the two of them enjoy the sun while they walked along the water's edge. To his right, he saw Abigail, Bailey, Prisha, and Aiden splashing around in the water as they laughed. This too, made Owen smile to see how happy they were.

Owen started off his journey on a beach…alone, hurt, and scared. Now, on a different beach, he embarks on a new journey where he is happy, and most importantly, not alone. This time, Owen was surrounded by his girlfriend and his friends. They were all together…as a family.

~ The End ~

Thank you for reading my book! I appreciate your support and I hope you enjoyed it!

You can find me on social media at:
Facebook: Author Brian Marotto
Instagram, Twitter, and TikTok:
@MeBrianNotBrain

If you enjoyed my book and would like to rate it, and even leave a review, I would really appreciate it if you did! Also, recommending my book to others is also very appreciated!

My books can be found at:
https://linktr.ee/AuthorBrianMarotto

DON'T MISS

THE AWAKENING

AND

THE DECEPTION

BOOKS ONE AND TWO IN THE CREATURE WITHIN TRILOGY

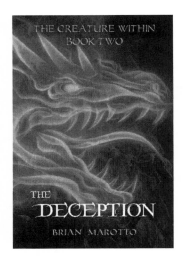

Made in the USA
Columbia, SC
30 April 2025

5de18460-090a-42d7-9c05-0c7cfe644983R01